TERRY and the Pirates

by MILTON CANIFF

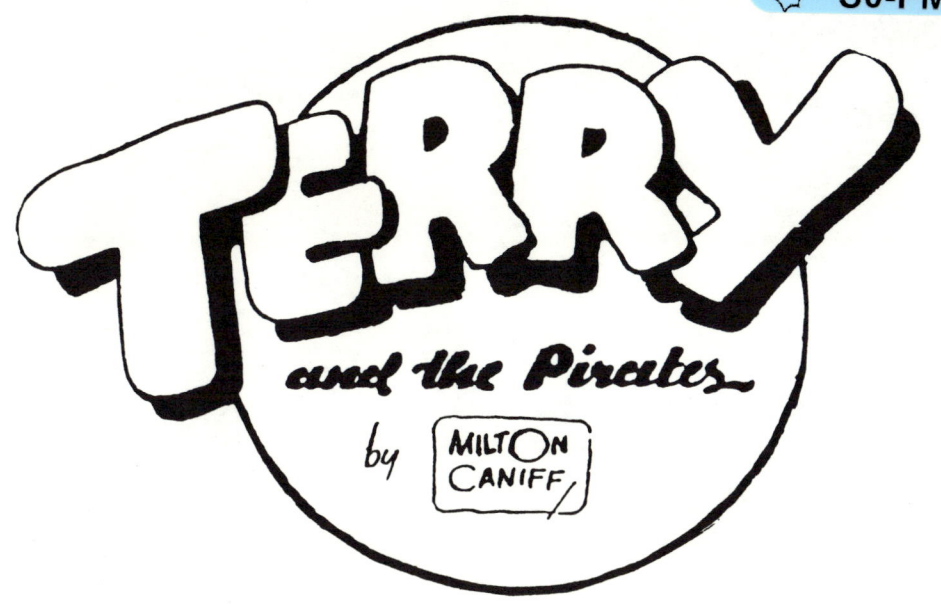

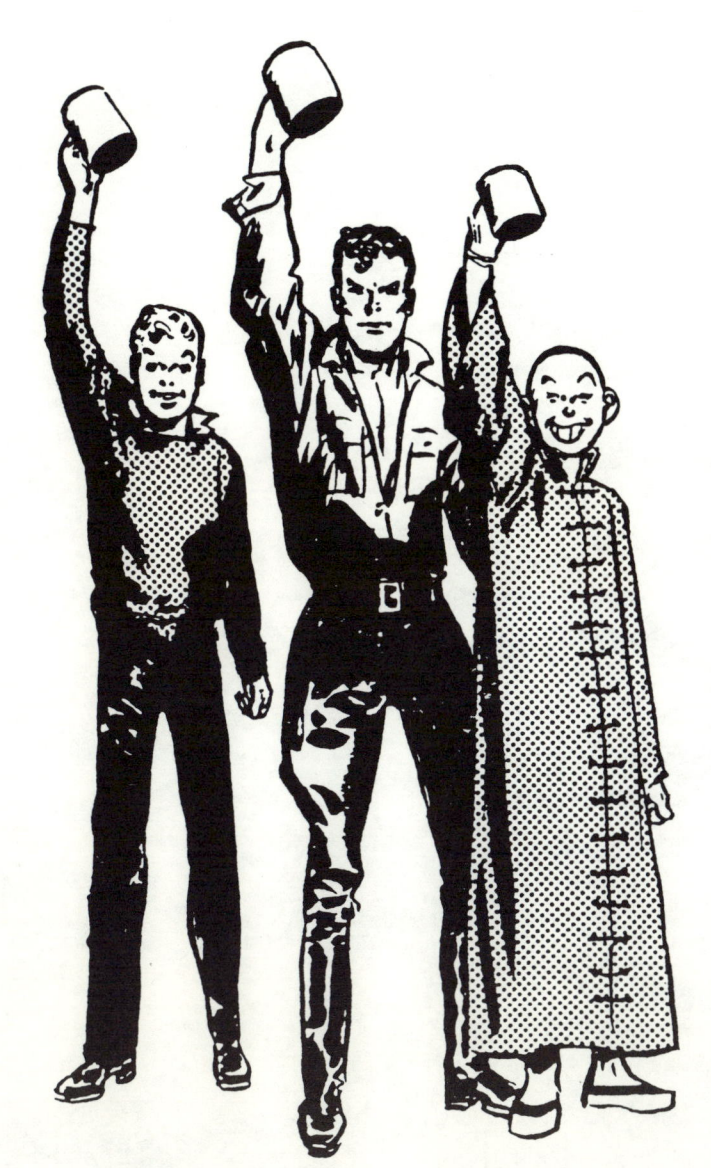

TERRY and the Pirates

by MILTON CANIFF

GETTING SNARED

FLYING BUTTRESS
Classics Library

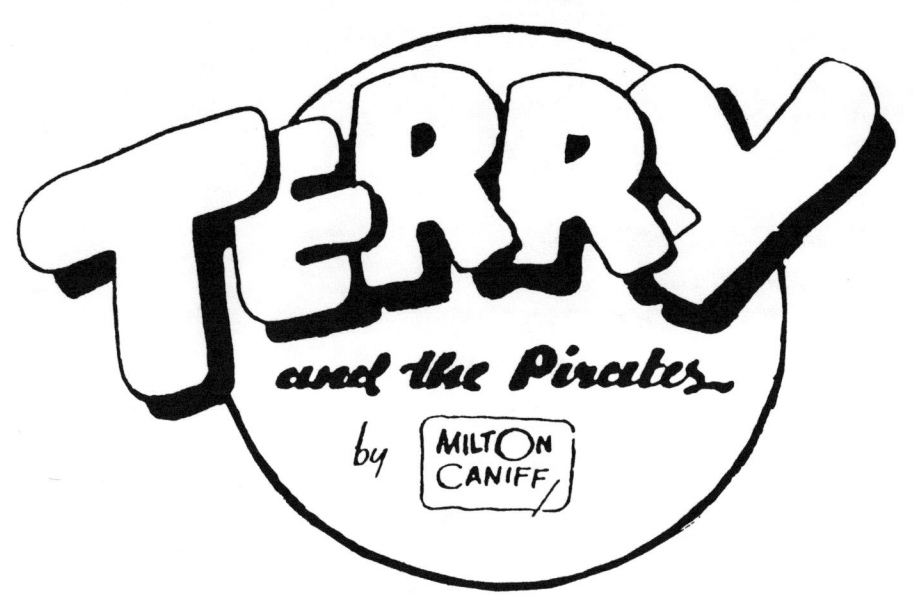

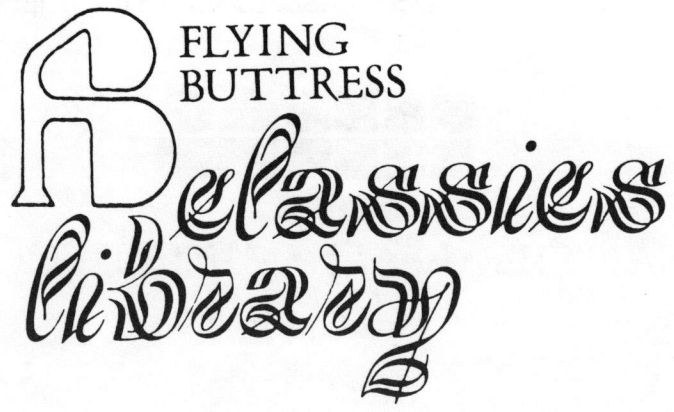

COPYRIGHT 1986 NBM PUBLISHING
COVER DESIGNED AND PAINTED BY RAY FEHRENBACH
ISBN# 0-918348-32-3
LC# 87-090446

Terry & The Pirates is a registered
trademark of Tribune Media Services, Inc.

THE FLYING BUTTRESS CLASSICS LIBRARY is an imprint of:

NANTIER · BEALL · MINOUSTCHINE
Publishing co.
new york

Our Story So Far:

Pat has been kidnapped by the Dragon Lady and sold as a gladiator-slave to Pappy Pyzon, an American born war-lord based in the Chinese mountains (see vol.3 *DRAGON LADY'S REVENGE*). While on a raiding party with Pyzons men, Pat discovers a village filled with only unmarried women. As Pyzon's men are drawn to the village like flies to honey, Pat slips away and is reunited with his pal Terry and their servant Connie who have been searching for him.

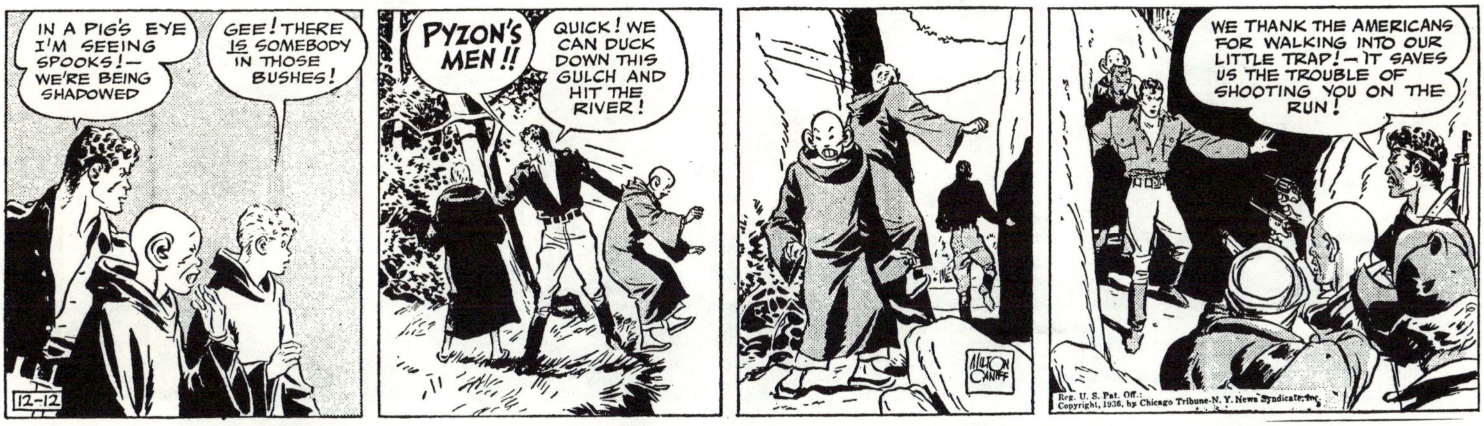

IN A PIG'S EYE I'M SEEING SPOOKS! — WE'RE BEING SHADOWED
GEE! THERE IS SOMEBODY IN THOSE BUSHES!
12-12
PYZON'S MEN!!
QUICK! WE CAN DUCK DOWN THIS GULCH AND HIT THE RIVER!
MILTON CANIFF
WE THANK THE AMERICANS FOR WALKING INTO OUR LITTLE TRAP! — IT SAVES US THE TROUBLE OF SHOOTING YOU ON THE RUN!
Reg. U. S. Pat. Off.: Copyright, 1936, by Chicago Tribune-N. Y. News Syndicate, Inc.

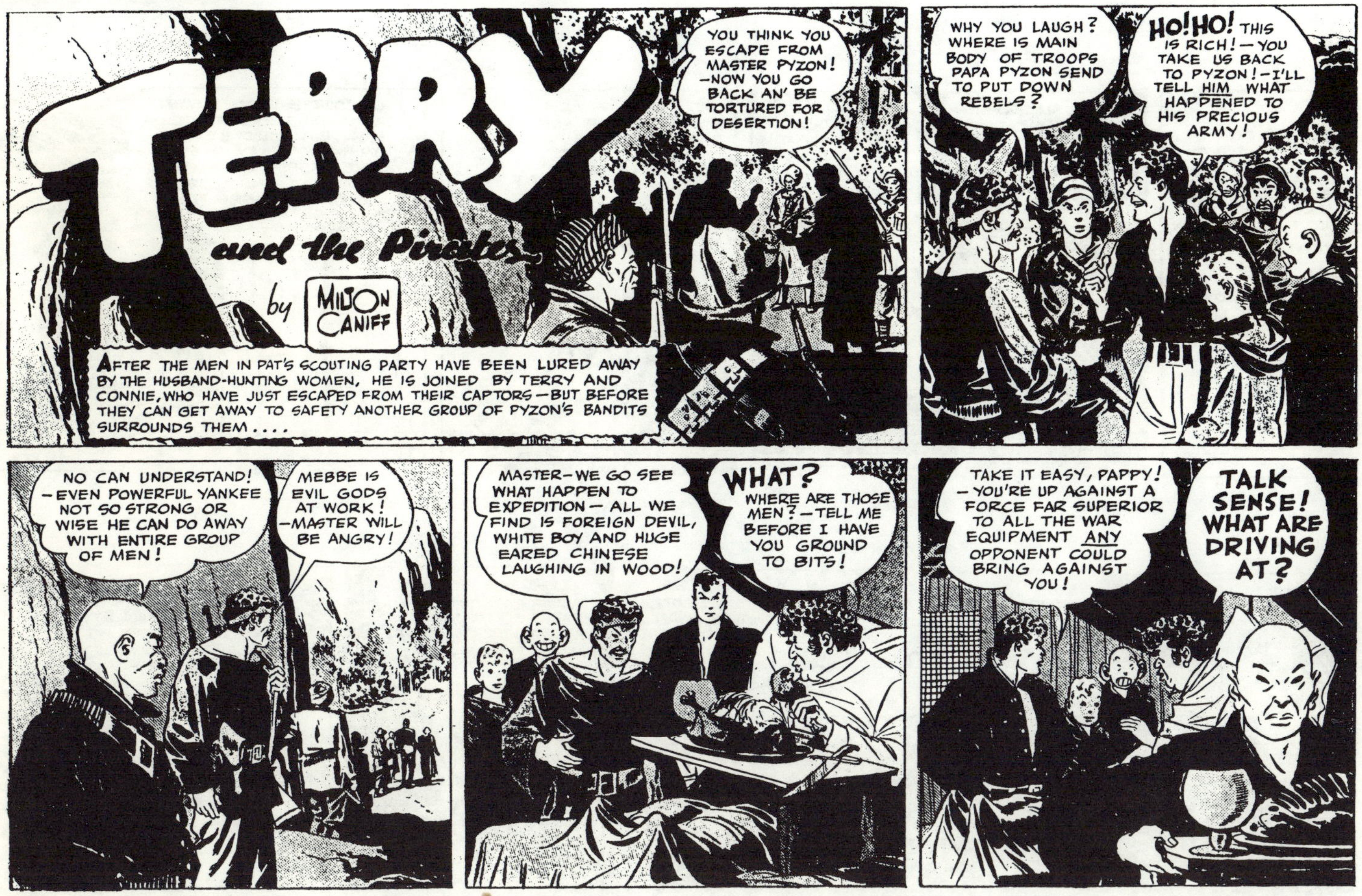

TERRY and the Pirates
by MILTON CANIFF
YOU THINK YOU ESCAPE FROM MASTER PYZON! — NOW YOU GO BACK AN' BE TORTURED FOR DESERTION!
AFTER THE MEN IN PAT'S SCOUTING PARTY HAVE BEEN LURED AWAY BY THE HUSBAND-HUNTING WOMEN, HE IS JOINED BY TERRY AND CONNIE, WHO HAVE JUST ESCAPED FROM THEIR CAPTORS — BUT BEFORE THEY CAN GET AWAY TO SAFETY ANOTHER GROUP OF PYZON'S BANDITS SURROUNDS THEM ....
WHY YOU LAUGH? WHERE IS MAIN BODY OF TROOPS PAPA PYZON SEND TO PUT DOWN REBELS?
HO! HO! THIS IS RICH! — YOU TAKE US BACK TO PYZON! — I'LL TELL HIM WHAT HAPPENED TO HIS PRECIOUS ARMY!
NO CAN UNDERSTAND! — EVEN POWERFUL YANKEE NOT SO STRONG OR WISE HE CAN DO AWAY WITH ENTIRE GROUP OF MEN!
MEBBE IS EVIL GODS AT WORK! — MASTER WILL BE ANGRY!
MASTER — WE GO SEE WHAT HAPPEN TO EXPEDITION — ALL WE FIND IS FOREIGN DEVIL, WHITE BOY AND HUGE EARED CHINESE LAUGHING IN WOOD!
WHAT? WHERE ARE THOSE MEN? — TELL ME BEFORE I HAVE YOU GROUND TO BITS!
TAKE IT EASY, PAPPY! — YOU'RE UP AGAINST A FORCE FAR SUPERIOR TO ALL THE WAR EQUIPMENT ANY OPPONENT COULD BRING AGAINST YOU!
TALK SENSE! WHAT ARE DRIVING AT?

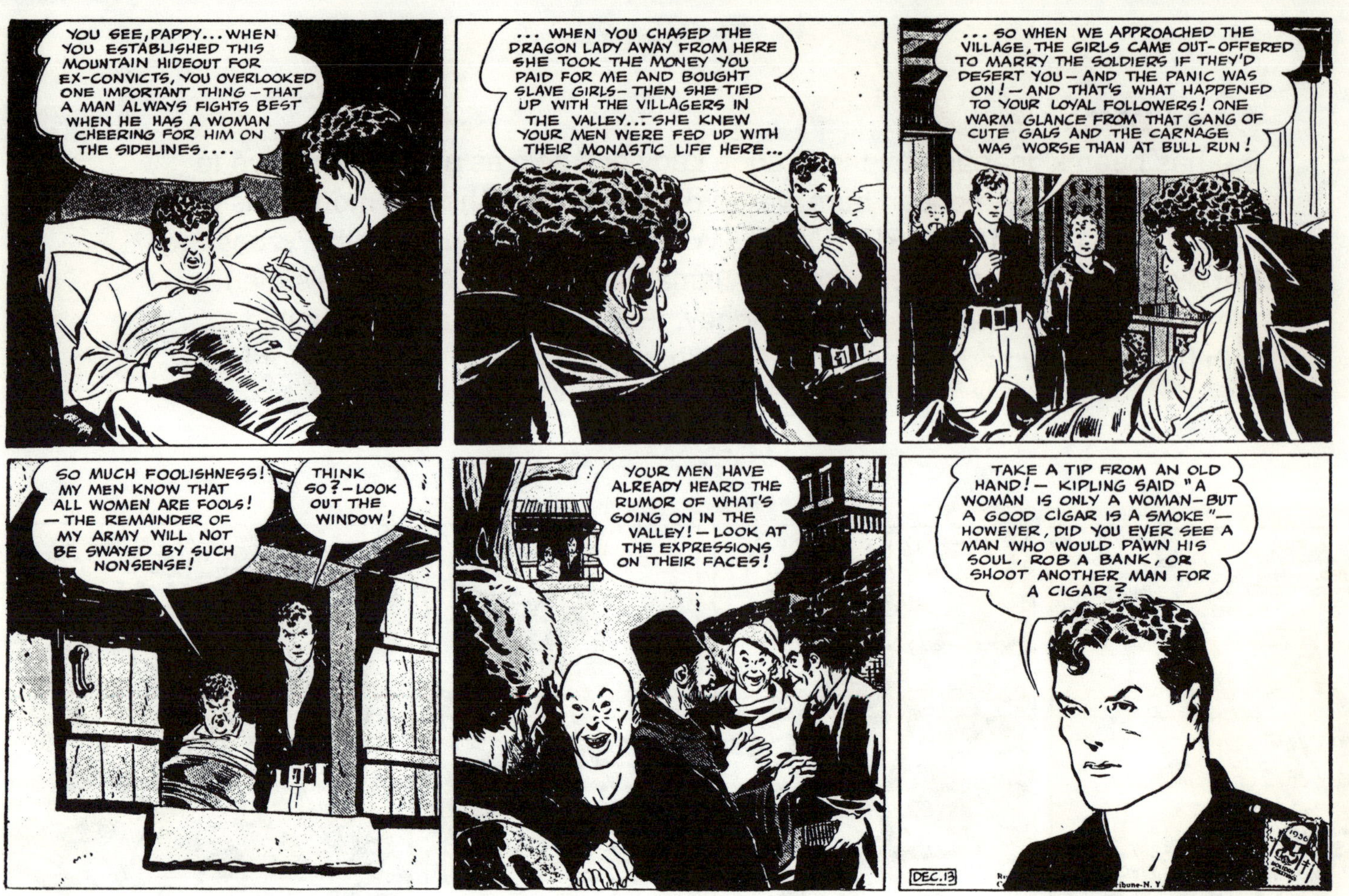
YOU SEE, PAPPY... WHEN YOU ESTABLISHED THIS MOUNTAIN HIDEOUT FOR EX-CONVICTS, YOU OVERLOOKED ONE IMPORTANT THING—THAT A MAN ALWAYS FIGHTS BEST WHEN HE HAS A WOMAN CHEERING FOR HIM ON THE SIDELINES....
... WHEN YOU CHASED THE DRAGON LADY AWAY FROM HERE SHE TOOK THE MONEY YOU PAID FOR ME AND BOUGHT SLAVE GIRLS— THEN SHE TIED UP WITH THE VILLAGERS IN THE VALLEY...—SHE KNEW YOUR MEN WERE FED UP WITH THEIR MONASTIC LIFE HERE...
... SO WHEN WE APPROACHED THE VILLAGE, THE GIRLS CAME OUT—OFFERED TO MARRY THE SOLDIERS IF THEY'D DESERT YOU— AND THE PANIC WAS ON!—AND THAT'S WHAT HAPPENED TO YOUR LOYAL FOLLOWERS! ONE WARM GLANCE FROM THAT GANG OF CUTE GALS AND THE CARNAGE WAS WORSE THAN AT BULL RUN!
SO MUCH FOOLISHNESS! MY MEN KNOW THAT ALL WOMEN ARE FOOLS! —THE REMAINDER OF MY ARMY WILL NOT BE SWAYED BY SUCH NONSENSE!
THINK SO?—LOOK OUT THE WINDOW!
YOUR MEN HAVE ALREADY HEARD THE RUMOR OF WHAT'S GOING ON IN THE VALLEY!—LOOK AT THE EXPRESSIONS ON THEIR FACES!
TAKE A TIP FROM AN OLD HAND!— KIPLING SAID "A WOMAN IS ONLY A WOMAN—BUT A GOOD CIGAR IS A SMOKE"— HOWEVER, DID YOU EVER SEE A MAN WHO WOULD PAWN HIS SOUL, ROB A BANK, OR SHOOT ANOTHER MAN FOR A CIGAR?
DEC. 13

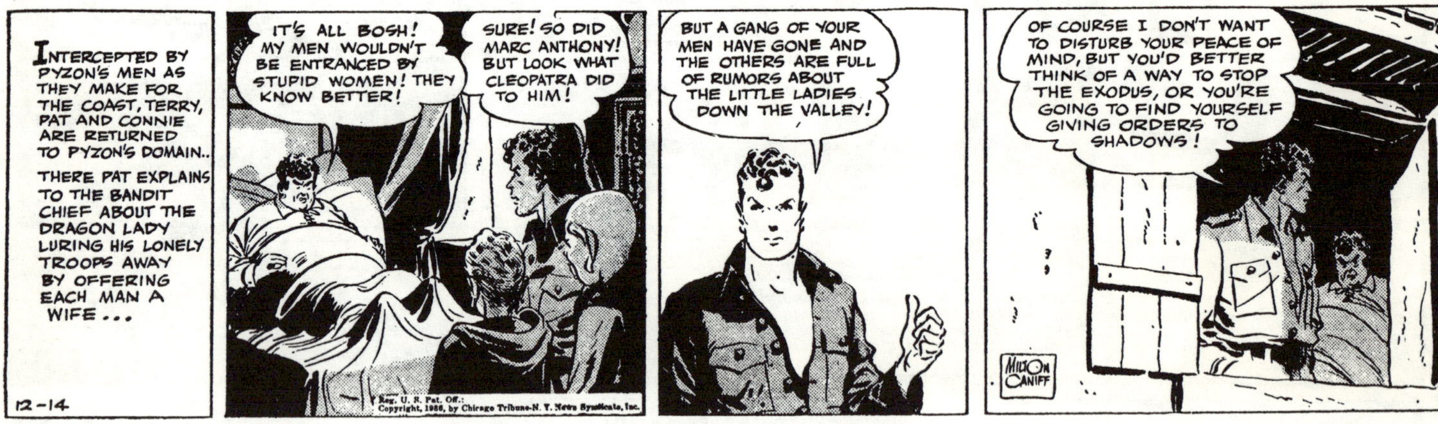
INTERCEPTED BY PYZON'S MEN AS THEY MAKE FOR THE COAST, TERRY, PAT AND CONNIE ARE RETURNED TO PYZON'S DOMAIN.. THERE PAT EXPLAINS TO THE BANDIT CHIEF ABOUT THE DRAGON LADY LURING HIS LONELY TROOPS AWAY BY OFFERING EACH MAN A WIFE...
12-14
IT'S ALL BOSH! MY MEN WOULDN'T BE ENTRANCED BY STUPID WOMEN! THEY KNOW BETTER!
SURE! SO DID MARC ANTHONY! BUT LOOK WHAT CLEOPATRA DID TO HIM!
Reg. U. S. Pat. Off.: Copyright, 1936, by Chicago Tribune-N. Y. News Syndicate, Inc.
BUT A GANG OF YOUR MEN HAVE GONE AND THE OTHERS ARE FULL OF RUMORS ABOUT THE LITTLE LADIES DOWN THE VALLEY!
OF COURSE I DON'T WANT TO DISTURB YOUR PEACE OF MIND, BUT YOU'D BETTER THINK OF A WAY TO STOP THE EXODUS, OR YOU'RE GOING TO FIND YOURSELF GIVING ORDERS TO SHADOWS!
MILTON CANIFF

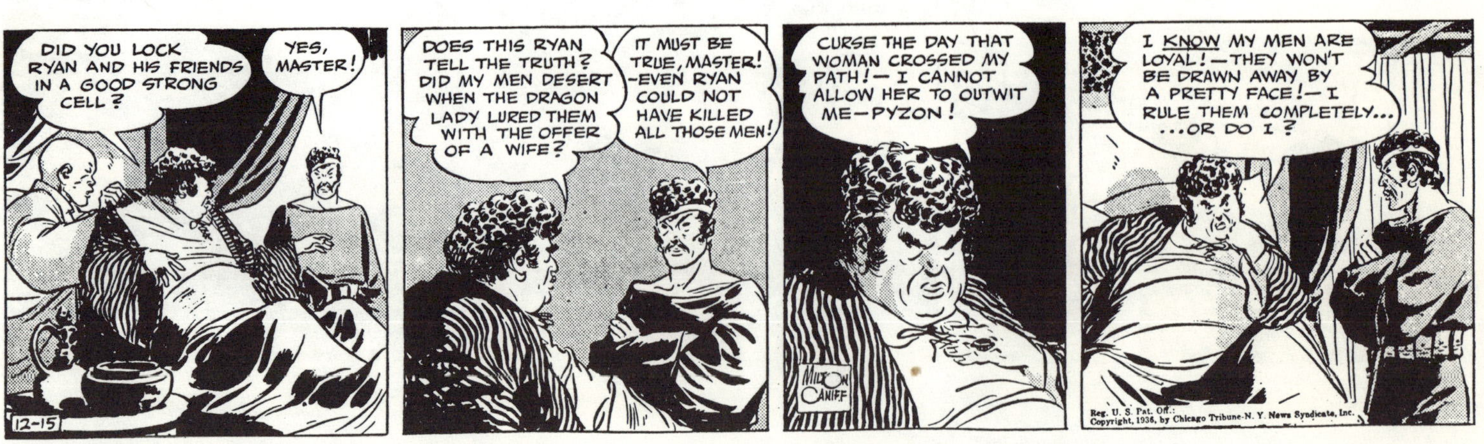
DID YOU LOCK RYAN AND HIS FRIENDS IN A GOOD STRONG CELL?
YES, MASTER!
12-15
DOES THIS RYAN TELL THE TRUTH? DID MY MEN DESERT WHEN THE DRAGON LADY LURED THEM WITH THE OFFER OF A WIFE?
IT MUST BE TRUE, MASTER! —EVEN RYAN COULD NOT HAVE KILLED ALL THOSE MEN!
CURSE THE DAY THAT WOMAN CROSSED MY PATH!— I CANNOT ALLOW HER TO OUTWIT ME—PYZON!
MILTON CANIFF
I KNOW MY MEN ARE LOYAL!—THEY WON'T BE DRAWN AWAY BY A PRETTY FACE!—I RULE THEM COMPLETELY... ...OR DO I?
Reg. U. S. Pat. Off.: Copyright, 1936, by Chicago Tribune-N. Y. News Syndicate, Inc.

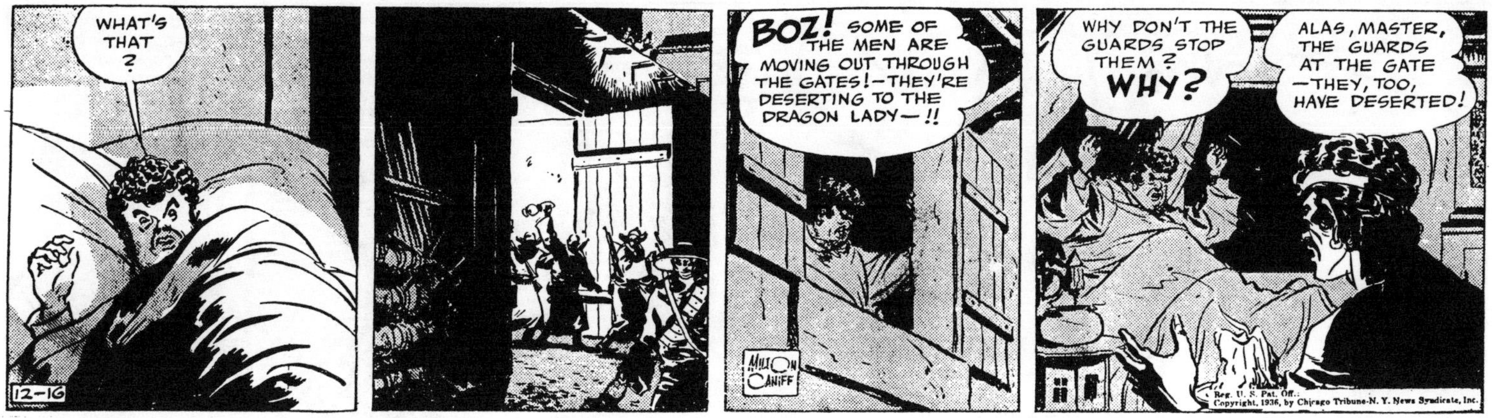
12-16
WHAT'S THAT ?
BOZ! SOME OF THE MEN ARE MOVING OUT THROUGH THE GATES!—THEY'RE DESERTING TO THE DRAGON LADY—!!
MILTON CANIFF
WHY DON'T THE GUARDS STOP THEM ? WHY?
ALAS, MASTER, THE GUARDS AT THE GATE —THEY, TOO, HAVE DESERTED!
Reg. U. S. Pat. Off.: Copyright, 1936, by Chicago Tribune-N. Y. News Syndicate, Inc.

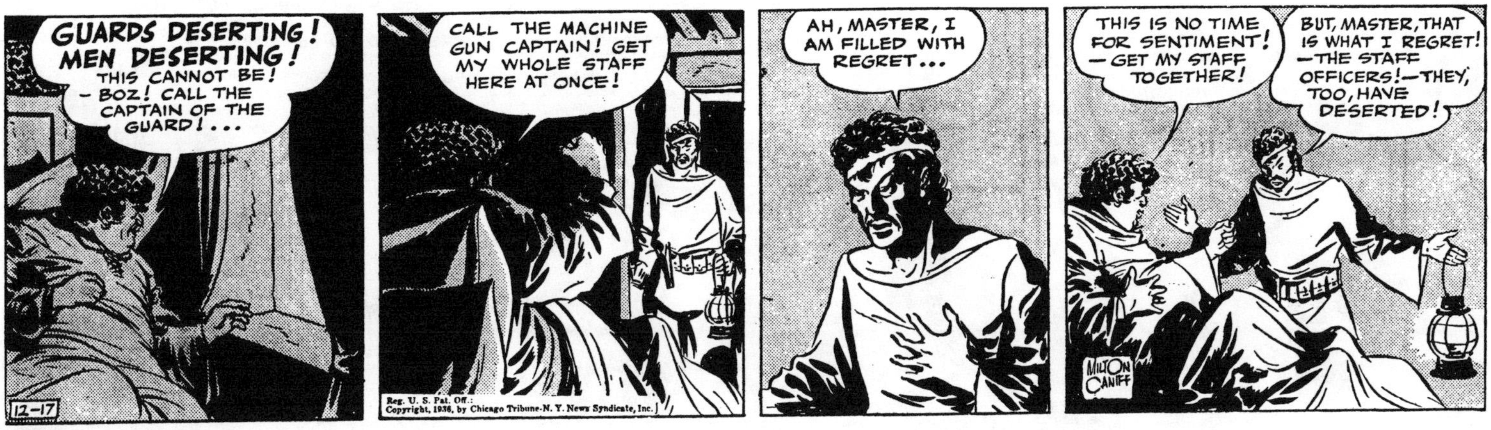
GUARDS DESERTING! MEN DESERTING! THIS CANNOT BE! —BOZ! CALL THE CAPTAIN OF THE GUARD!...
12-17
CALL THE MACHINE GUN CAPTAIN! GET MY WHOLE STAFF HERE AT ONCE!
Reg. U. S. Pat. Off.: Copyright, 1936, by Chicago Tribune-N. Y. News Syndicate, Inc.
AH, MASTER, I AM FILLED WITH REGRET...
THIS IS NO TIME FOR SENTIMENT! —GET MY STAFF TOGETHER!
BUT, MASTER, THAT IS WHAT I REGRET! —THE STAFF OFFICERS!—THEY, TOO, HAVE DESERTED!
MILTON CANIFF

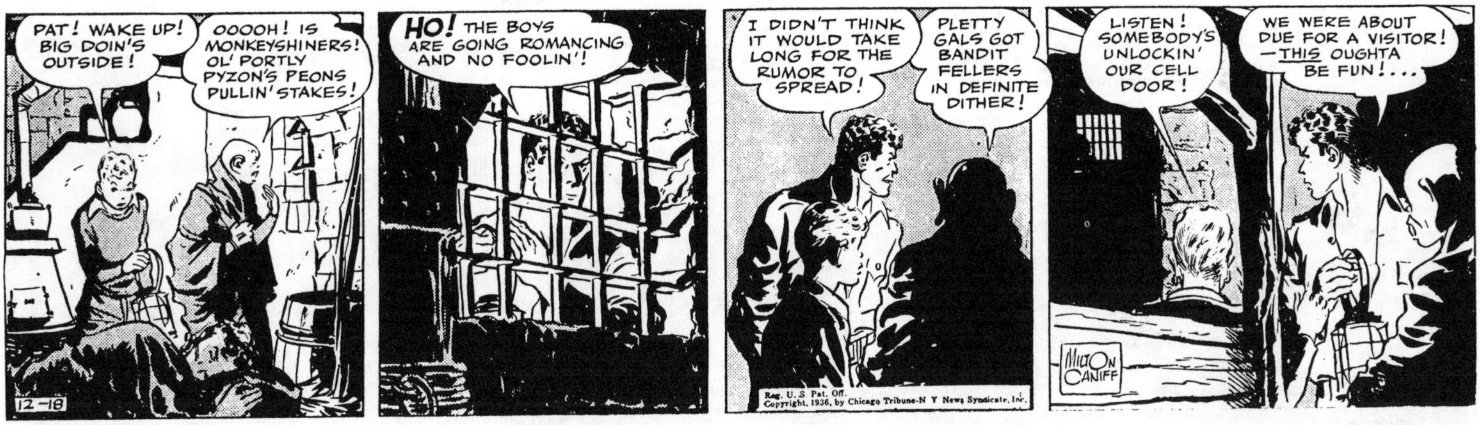
PAT! WAKE UP! BIG DOIN'S OUTSIDE!
OOOOH! IS MONKEYSHINERS! OL' PORTLY PYZON'S PEONS PULLIN' STAKES!
12-18
HO! THE BOYS ARE GOING ROMANCING AND NO FOOLIN'!
I DIDN'T THINK IT WOULD TAKE LONG FOR THE RUMOR TO SPREAD!
PLETTY GALS GOT BANDIT FELLERS IN DEFINITE DITHER!
Reg. U. S. Pat. Off. Copyright, 1936, by Chicago Tribune-N Y News Syndicate, Inc.
LISTEN! SOMEBODY'S UNLOCKIN' OUR CELL DOOR!
WE WERE ABOUT DUE FOR A VISITOR! —THIS OUGHTA BE FUN!...
MILTON CANIFF

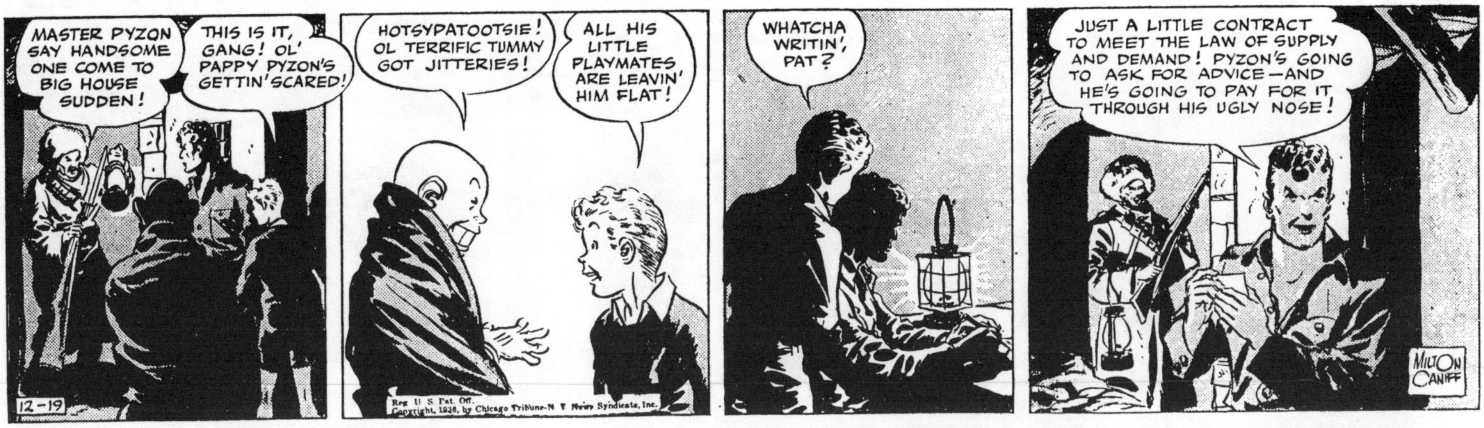
MASTER PYZON SAY HANDSOME ONE COME TO BIG HOUSE SUDDEN!
THIS IS IT, GANG! OL' PAPPY PYZON'S GETTIN' SCARED!
12-19
HOTSYPATOOTSIE! OL TERRIFIC TUMMY GOT JITTERIES!
ALL HIS LITTLE PLAYMATES ARE LEAVIN' HIM FLAT!
Reg U S Pat. Off. Copyright, 1936, by Chicago Tribune-N Y News Syndicate, Inc.
WHATCHA WRITIN', PAT ?
JUST A LITTLE CONTRACT TO MEET THE LAW OF SUPPLY AND DEMAND! PYZON'S GOING TO ASK FOR ADVICE—AND HE'S GOING TO PAY FOR IT THROUGH HIS UGLY NOSE!
MILTON CANIFF

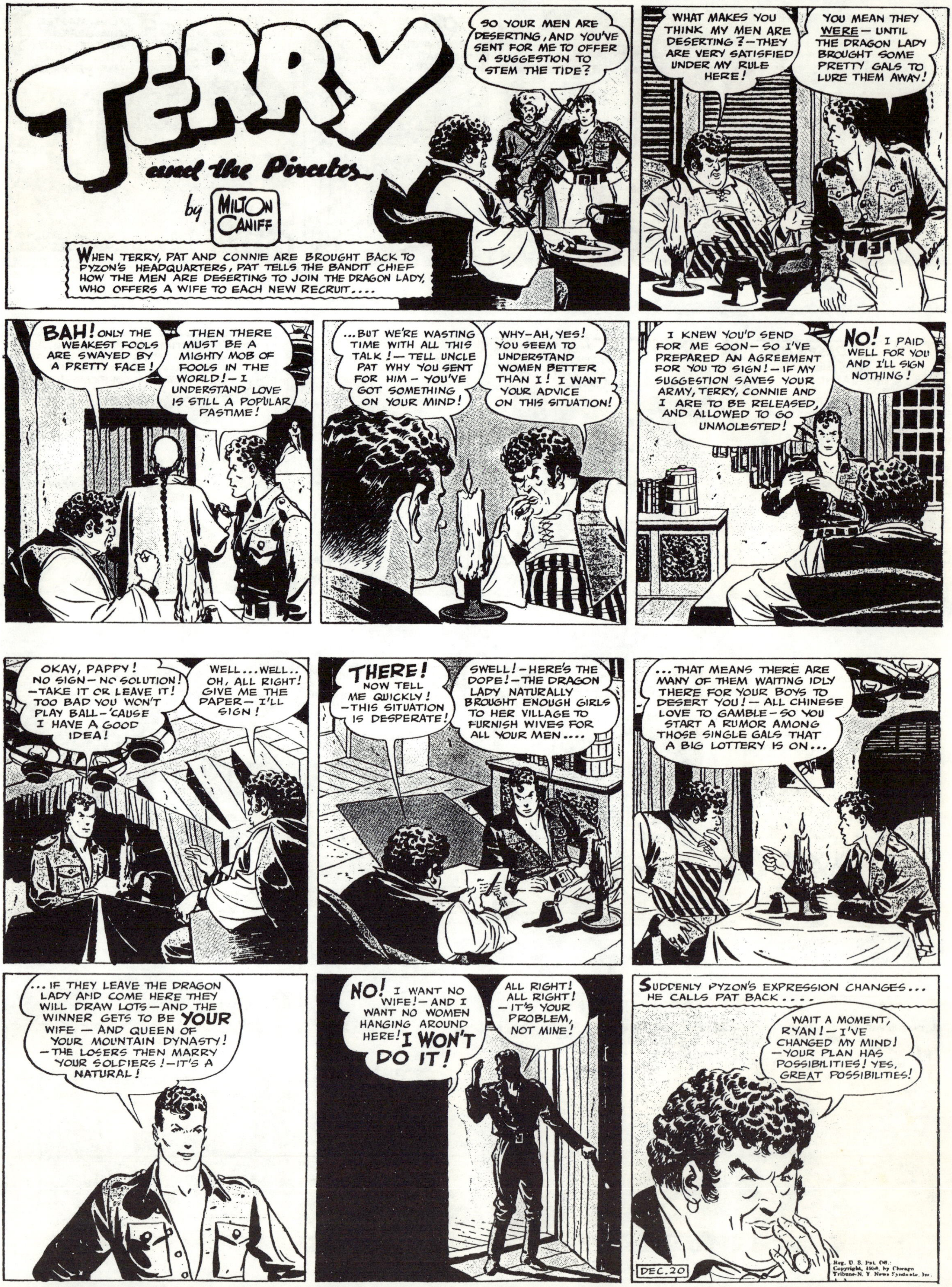
TERRY and the Pirates
by MILTON CANIFF
WHEN TERRY, PAT AND CONNIE ARE BROUGHT BACK TO PYZON'S HEADQUARTERS, PAT TELLS THE BANDIT CHIEF HOW THE MEN ARE DESERTING TO JOIN THE DRAGON LADY, WHO OFFERS A WIFE TO EACH NEW RECRUIT....
SO YOUR MEN ARE DESERTING, AND YOU'VE SENT FOR ME TO OFFER A SUGGESTION TO STEM THE TIDE?
WHAT MAKES YOU THINK MY MEN ARE DESERTING?—THEY ARE VERY SATISFIED UNDER MY RULE HERE!
YOU MEAN THEY WERE—UNTIL THE DRAGON LADY BROUGHT SOME PRETTY GALS TO LURE THEM AWAY!
BAH! ONLY THE WEAKEST FOOLS ARE SWAYED BY A PRETTY FACE!
THEN THERE MUST BE A MIGHTY MOB OF FOOLS IN THE WORLD!—I UNDERSTAND LOVE IS STILL A POPULAR PASTIME!
...BUT WE'RE WASTING TIME WITH ALL THIS TALK!—TELL UNCLE PAT WHY YOU SENT FOR HIM—YOU'VE GOT SOMETHING ON YOUR MIND!
WHY—AH, YES! YOU SEEM TO UNDERSTAND WOMEN BETTER THAN I! I WANT YOUR ADVICE ON THIS SITUATION!
I KNEW YOU'D SEND FOR ME SOON—SO I'VE PREPARED AN AGREEMENT FOR YOU TO SIGN!—IF MY SUGGESTION SAVES YOUR ARMY, TERRY, CONNIE AND I ARE TO BE RELEASED, AND ALLOWED TO GO UNMOLESTED!
NO! I PAID WELL FOR YOU AND I'LL SIGN NOTHING!
OKAY, PAPPY! NO SIGN—NO SOLUTION! —TAKE IT OR LEAVE IT! TOO BAD YOU WON'T PLAY BALL—'CAUSE I HAVE A GOOD IDEA!
WELL...WELL... OH, ALL RIGHT! GIVE ME THE PAPER—I'LL SIGN!
THERE! NOW TELL ME QUICKLY! —THIS SITUATION IS DESPERATE!
SWELL!—HERE'S THE DOPE!—THE DRAGON LADY NATURALLY BROUGHT ENOUGH GIRLS TO HER VILLAGE TO FURNISH WIVES FOR ALL YOUR MEN....
...THAT MEANS THERE ARE MANY OF THEM WAITING IDLY THERE FOR YOUR BOYS TO DESERT YOU!—ALL CHINESE LOVE TO GAMBLE—SO YOU START A RUMOR AMONG THOSE SINGLE GALS THAT A BIG LOTTERY IS ON...
...IF THEY LEAVE THE DRAGON LADY AND COME HERE THEY WILL DRAW LOTS—AND THE WINNER GETS TO BE YOUR WIFE — AND QUEEN OF YOUR MOUNTAIN DYNASTY! —THE LOSERS THEN MARRY YOUR SOLDIERS!—IT'S A NATURAL!
NO! I WANT NO WIFE!—AND I WANT NO WOMEN HANGING AROUND HERE! I WON'T DO IT!
ALL RIGHT! ALL RIGHT! —IT'S YOUR PROBLEM, NOT MINE!
SUDDENLY PYZON'S EXPRESSION CHANGES... HE CALLS PAT BACK....
WAIT A MOMENT, RYAN!—I'VE CHANGED MY MIND! —YOUR PLAN HAS POSSIBILITIES! YES, GREAT POSSIBILITIES!
DEC. 20

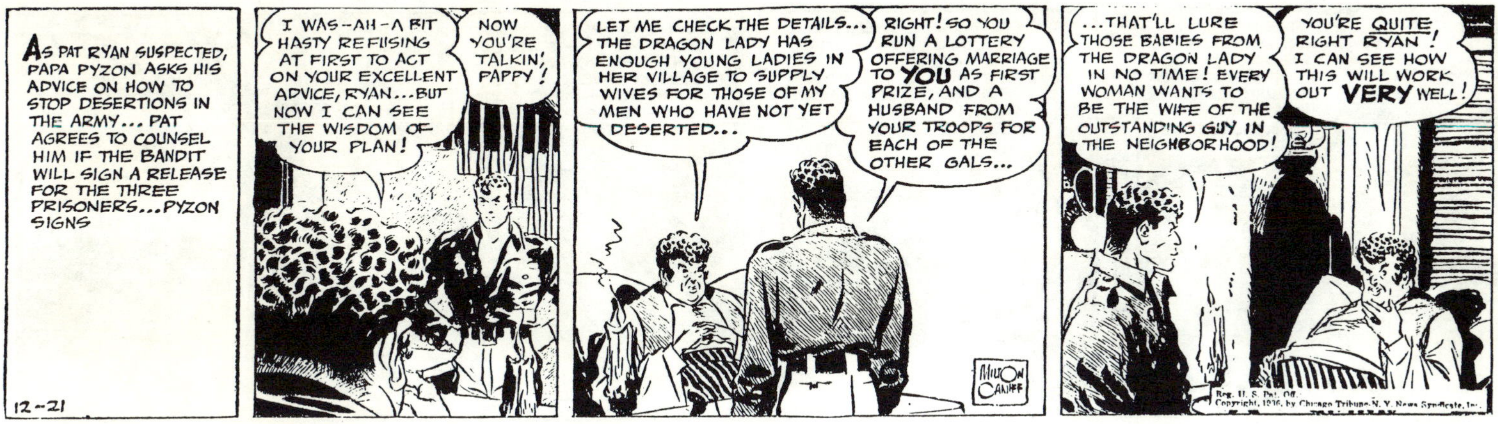
As Pat Ryan suspected, Papa Pyzon asks his advice on how to stop desertions in the army... Pat agrees to counsel him if the bandit will sign a release for the three prisoners... Pyzon signs
12-21
I WAS-AH-A BIT HASTY REFUSING AT FIRST TO ACT ON YOUR EXCELLENT ADVICE, RYAN... BUT NOW I CAN SEE THE WISDOM OF YOUR PLAN!
NOW YOU'RE TALKIN', PAPPY!
LET ME CHECK THE DETAILS... THE DRAGON LADY HAS ENOUGH YOUNG LADIES IN HER VILLAGE TO SUPPLY WIVES FOR THOSE OF MY MEN WHO HAVE NOT YET DESERTED...
RIGHT! SO YOU RUN A LOTTERY OFFERING MARRIAGE TO YOU AS FIRST PRIZE, AND A HUSBAND FROM YOUR TROOPS FOR EACH OF THE OTHER GALS...
MILTON CANIFF
...THAT'LL LURE THOSE BABIES FROM THE DRAGON LADY IN NO TIME! EVERY WOMAN WANTS TO BE THE WIFE OF THE OUTSTANDING GUY IN THE NEIGHBORHOOD!
YOU'RE QUITE RIGHT RYAN! I CAN SEE HOW THIS WILL WORK OUT VERY WELL!

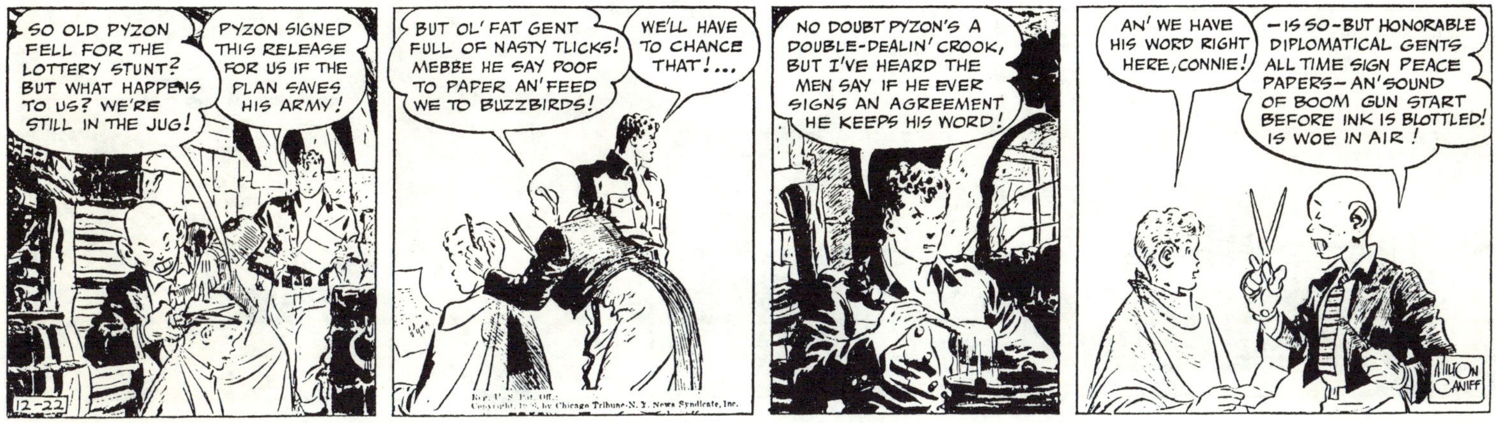
SO OLD PYZON FELL FOR THE LOTTERY STUNT? BUT WHAT HAPPENS TO US? WE'RE STILL IN THE JUG!
PYZON SIGNED THIS RELEASE FOR US IF THE PLAN SAVES HIS ARMY!
12-22
BUT OL' FAT GENT FULL OF NASTY TLICKS! MEBBE HE SAY POOF TO PAPER AN' FEED WE TO BUZZBIRDS!
WE'LL HAVE TO CHANCE THAT!...
NO DOUBT PYZON'S A DOUBLE-DEALIN' CROOK, BUT I'VE HEARD THE MEN SAY IF HE EVER SIGNS AN AGREEMENT HE KEEPS HIS WORD!
AN' WE HAVE HIS WORD RIGHT HERE, CONNIE!
-IS SO-BUT HONORABLE DIPLOMATICAL GENTS ALL TIME SIGN PEACE PAPERS-AN' SOUND OF BOOM GUN START BEFORE INK IS BLOTTLED! IS WOE IN AIR!
MILTON CANIFF

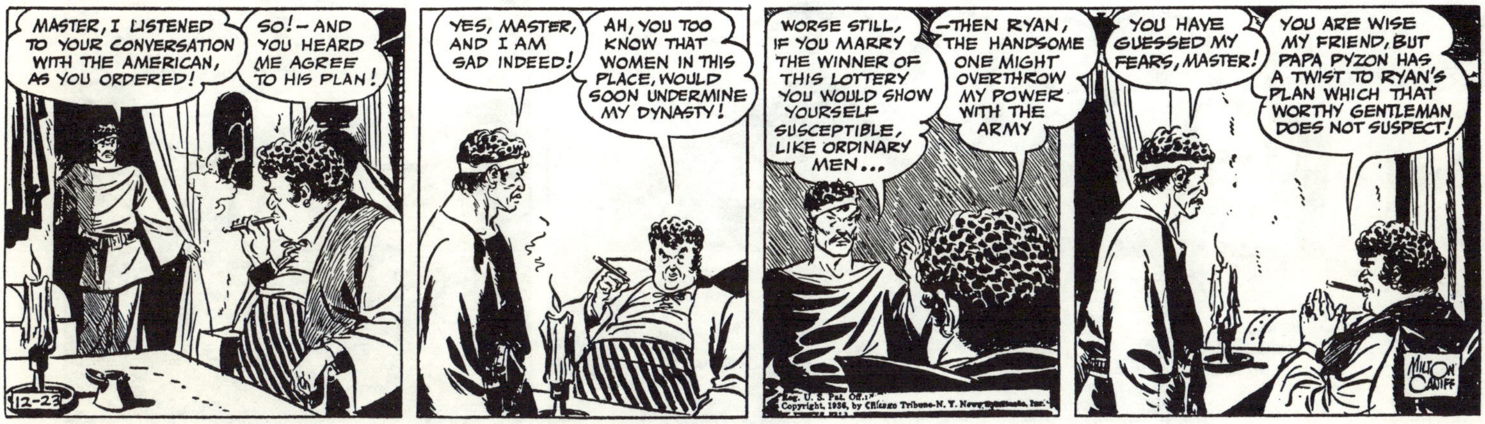
MASTER, I LISTENED TO YOUR CONVERSATION WITH THE AMERICAN, AS YOU ORDERED!
SO!-AND YOU HEARD ME AGREE TO HIS PLAN!
12-23
YES, MASTER, AND I AM SAD INDEED!
AH, YOU TOO KNOW THAT WOMEN IN THIS PLACE, WOULD SOON UNDERMINE MY DYNASTY!
WORSE STILL, IF YOU MARRY THE WINNER OF THIS LOTTERY YOU WOULD SHOW YOURSELF SUSCEPTIBLE, LIKE ORDINARY MEN...
-THEN RYAN, THE HANDSOME ONE MIGHT OVERTHROW MY POWER WITH THE ARMY
YOU HAVE GUESSED MY FEARS, MASTER!
YOU ARE WISE MY FRIEND, BUT PAPA PYZON HAS A TWIST TO RYAN'S PLAN WHICH THAT WORTHY GENTLEMAN DOES NOT SUSPECT!
MILTON CANIFF

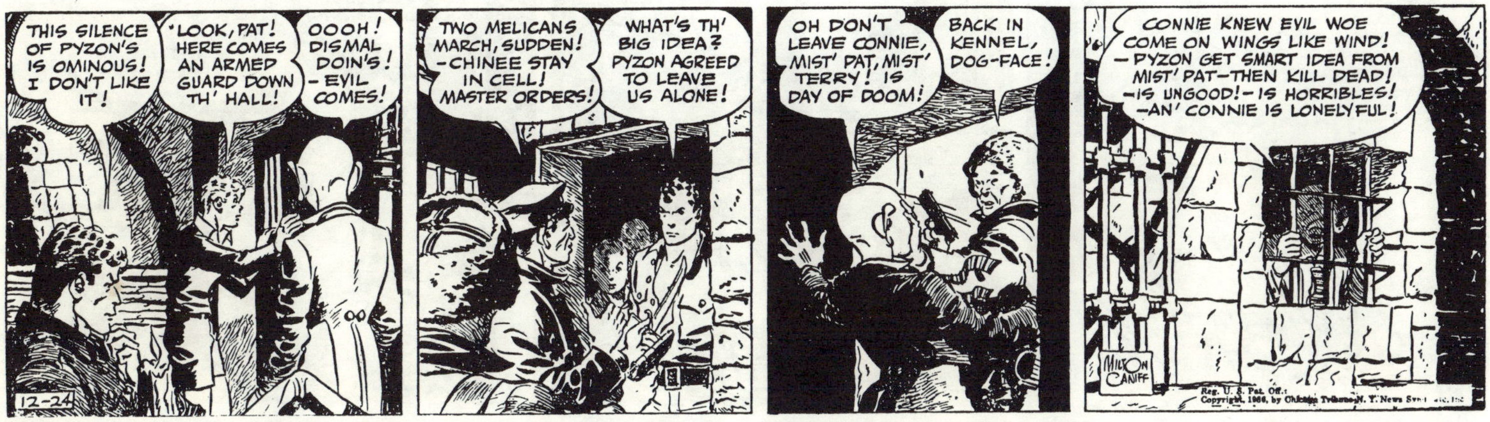
THIS SILENCE OF PYZON'S IS OMINOUS! I DON'T LIKE IT!
LOOK, PAT! HERE COMES AN ARMED GUARD DOWN TH' HALL!
OOOH! DISMAL DOIN'S! -EVIL COMES!
12-24
TWO MELICANS MARCH, SUDDEN! -CHINEE STAY IN CELL! MASTER ORDERS!
WHAT'S TH' BIG IDEA? PYZON AGREED TO LEAVE US ALONE!
OH DON'T LEAVE CONNIE, MIST' PAT, MIST' TERRY! IS DAY OF DOOM!
BACK IN KENNEL, DOG-FACE!
MILTON CANIFF
CONNIE KNEW EVIL WOE COME ON WINGS LIKE WIND! -PYZON GET SMART IDEA FROM MIST' PAT-THEN KILL DEAD! -IS UNGOOD!-IS HORRIBLES! -AN' CONNIE IS LONELYFUL!

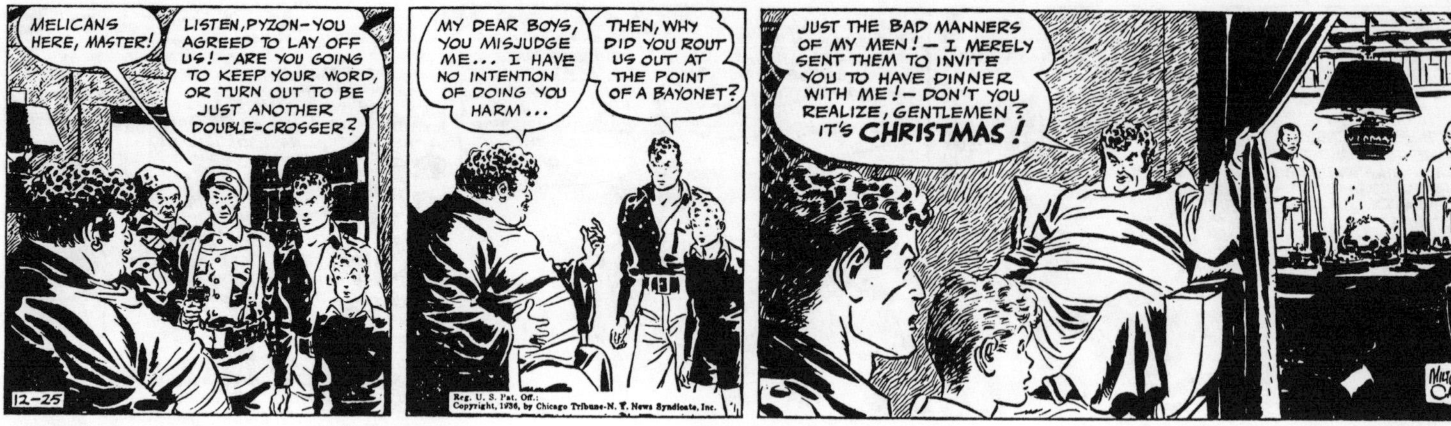
MELICANS HERE, MASTER!
LISTEN, PYZON—YOU AGREED TO LAY OFF US!—ARE YOU GOING TO KEEP YOUR WORD, OR TURN OUT TO BE JUST ANOTHER DOUBLE-CROSSER?
12-25
MY DEAR BOYS, YOU MISJUDGE ME... I HAVE NO INTENTION OF DOING YOU HARM...
THEN, WHY DID YOU ROUT US OUT AT THE POINT OF A BAYONET?
Reg. U. S. Pat. Off.: Copyright, 1936, by Chicago Tribune-N. Y. News Syndicate, Inc.
JUST THE BAD MANNERS OF MY MEN!—I MERELY SENT THEM TO INVITE YOU TO HAVE DINNER WITH ME!—DON'T YOU REALIZE, GENTLEMEN? IT'S CHRISTMAS!
MILTON CANIFF

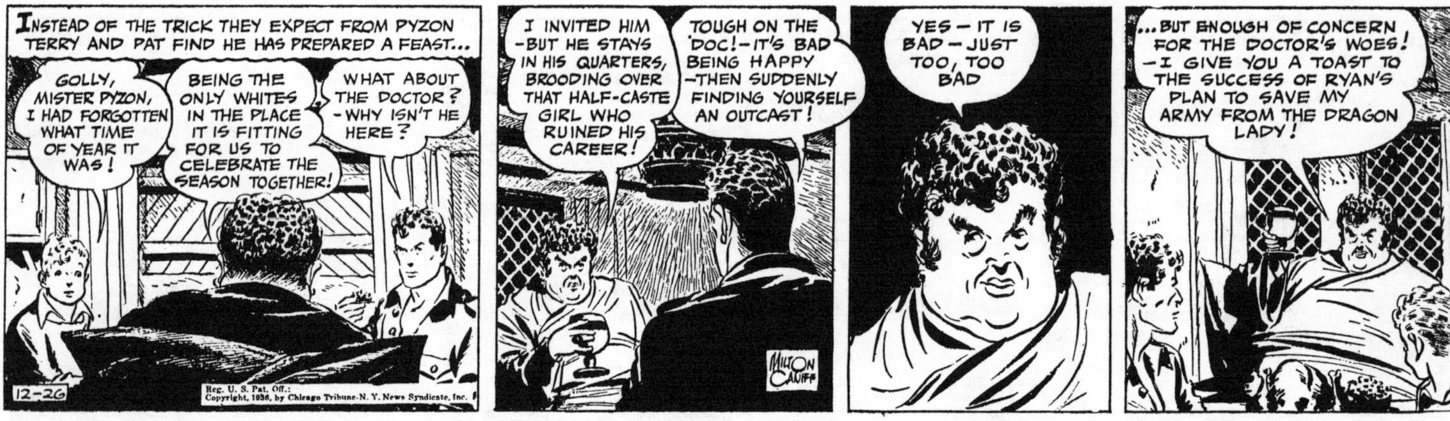
INSTEAD OF THE TRICK THEY EXPECT FROM PYZON TERRY AND PAT FIND HE HAS PREPARED A FEAST...
GOLLY, MISTER PYZON, I HAD FORGOTTEN WHAT TIME OF YEAR IT WAS!
BEING THE ONLY WHITES IN THE PLACE IT IS FITTING FOR US TO CELEBRATE THE SEASON TOGETHER!
WHAT ABOUT THE DOCTOR? -WHY ISN'T HE HERE?
12-26
Reg. U. S. Pat. Off.: Copyright, 1936, by Chicago Tribune-N. Y. News Syndicate, Inc.
I INVITED HIM -BUT HE STAYS IN HIS QUARTERS, BROODING OVER THAT HALF-CASTE GIRL WHO RUINED HIS CAREER!
TOUGH ON THE 'DOC'!—IT'S BAD BEING HAPPY —THEN SUDDENLY FINDING YOURSELF AN OUTCAST!
MILTON CANIFF
YES—IT IS BAD—JUST TOO, TOO BAD
...BUT ENOUGH OF CONCERN FOR THE DOCTOR'S WOES! —I GIVE YOU A TOAST TO THE SUCCESS OF RYAN'S PLAN TO SAVE MY ARMY FROM THE DRAGON LADY!

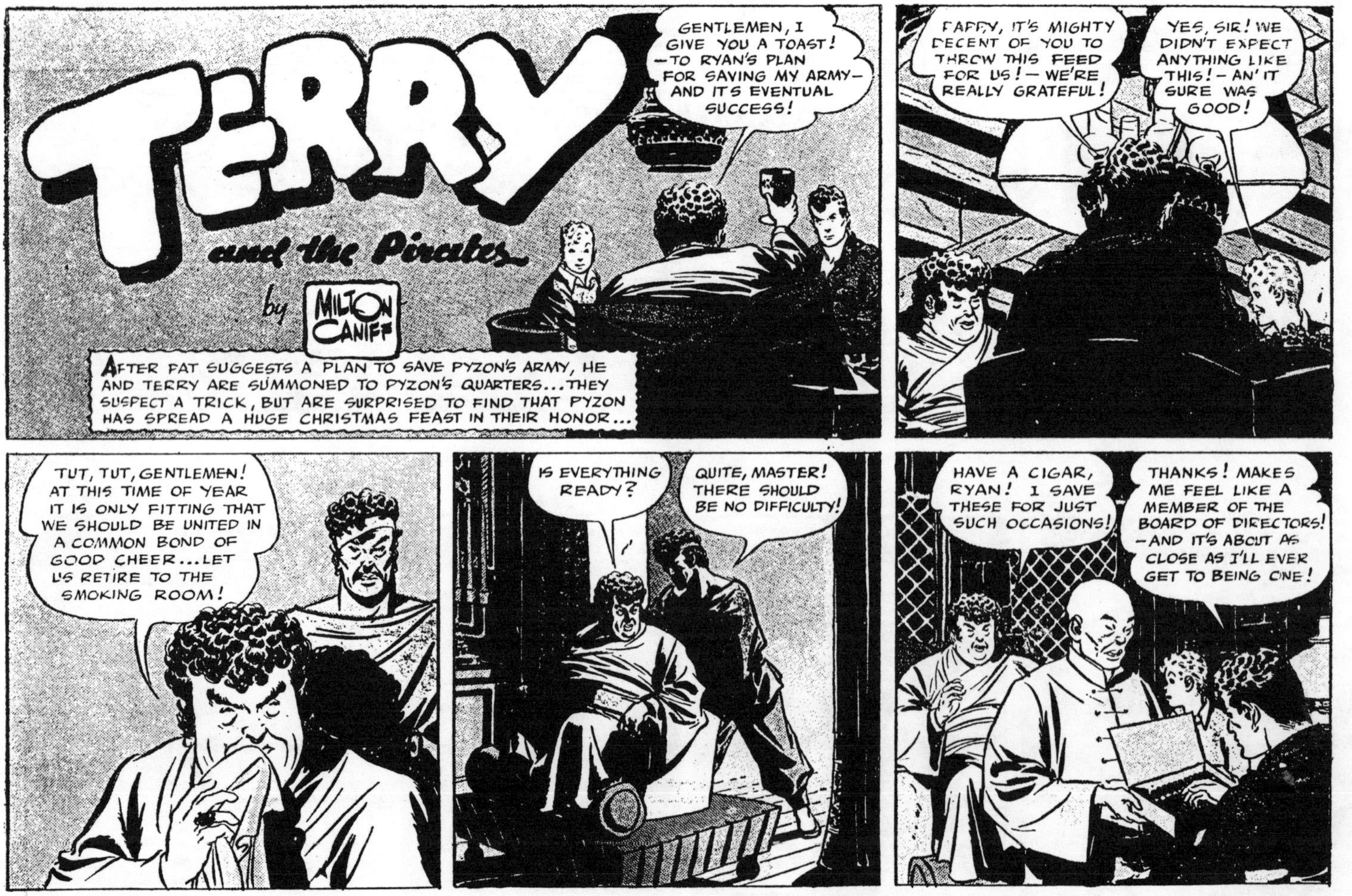
TERRY and the Pirates
by MILTON CANIFF
AFTER PAT SUGGESTS A PLAN TO SAVE PYZON'S ARMY, HE AND TERRY ARE SUMMONED TO PYZON'S QUARTERS... THEY SUSPECT A TRICK, BUT ARE SURPRISED TO FIND THAT PYZON HAS SPREAD A HUGE CHRISTMAS FEAST IN THEIR HONOR...
GENTLEMEN, I GIVE YOU A TOAST! —TO RYAN'S PLAN FOR SAVING MY ARMY— AND ITS EVENTUAL SUCCESS!
FAPPY, IT'S MIGHTY DECENT OF YOU TO THROW THIS FEED FOR US!—WE'RE REALLY GRATEFUL!
YES, SIR! WE DIDN'T EXPECT ANYTHING LIKE THIS!—AN' IT SURE WAS GOOD!
TUT, TUT, GENTLEMEN! AT THIS TIME OF YEAR IT IS ONLY FITTING THAT WE SHOULD BE UNITED IN A COMMON BOND OF GOOD CHEER...LET US RETIRE TO THE SMOKING ROOM!
IS EVERYTHING READY?
QUITE, MASTER! THERE SHOULD BE NO DIFFICULTY!
HAVE A CIGAR, RYAN! I SAVE THESE FOR JUST SUCH OCCASIONS!
THANKS! MAKES ME FEEL LIKE A MEMBER OF THE BOARD OF DIRECTORS! —AND IT'S ABOUT AS CLOSE AS I'LL EVER GET TO BEING ONE!

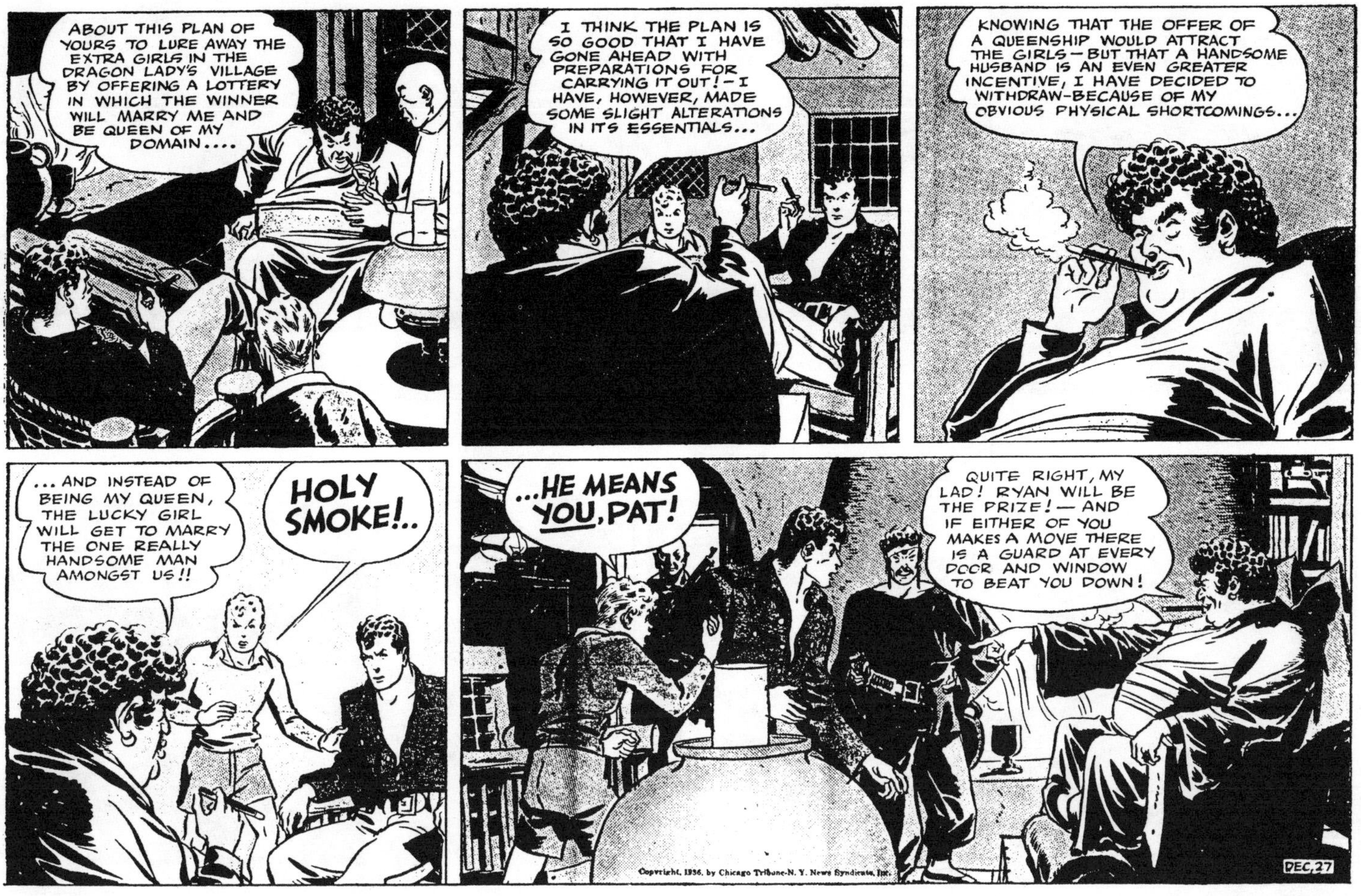
ABOUT THIS PLAN OF YOURS TO LURE AWAY THE EXTRA GIRLS IN THE DRAGON LADY'S VILLAGE BY OFFERING A LOTTERY IN WHICH THE WINNER WILL MARRY ME AND BE QUEEN OF MY DOMAIN....
I THINK THE PLAN IS SO GOOD THAT I HAVE GONE AHEAD WITH PREPARATIONS FOR CARRYING IT OUT!—I HAVE, HOWEVER, MADE SOME SLIGHT ALTERATIONS IN ITS ESSENTIALS...
KNOWING THAT THE OFFER OF A QUEENSHIP WOULD ATTRACT THE GIRLS—BUT THAT A HANDSOME HUSBAND IS AN EVEN GREATER INCENTIVE, I HAVE DECIDED TO WITHDRAW—BECAUSE OF MY OBVIOUS PHYSICAL SHORTCOMINGS...
...AND INSTEAD OF BEING MY QUEEN, THE LUCKY GIRL WILL GET TO MARRY THE ONE REALLY HANDSOME MAN AMONGST US!!
HOLY SMOKE!..
...HE MEANS YOU, PAT!
QUITE RIGHT, MY LAD! RYAN WILL BE THE PRIZE!—AND IF EITHER OF YOU MAKES A MOVE THERE IS A GUARD AT EVERY DOOR AND WINDOW TO BEAT YOU DOWN!
Copyright, 1936, by Chicago Tribune-N. Y. News Syndicate, Inc.
DEC. 27

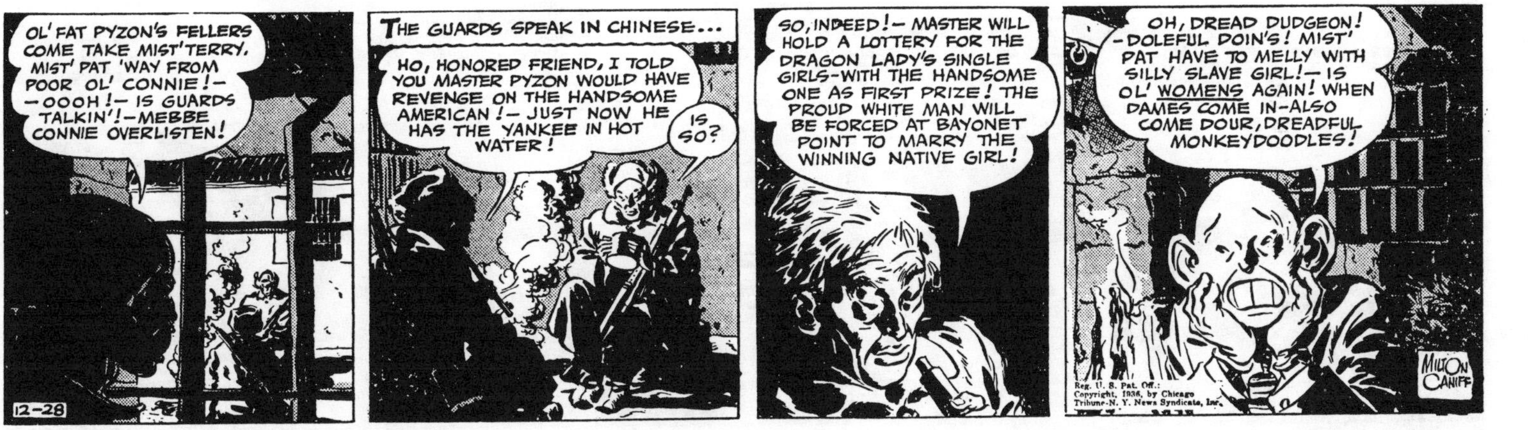
OL' FAT PYZON'S FELLERS COME TAKE MIST' TERRY, MIST' PAT 'WAY FROM POOR OL' CONNIE!—OOOH!—IS GUARDS TALKIN'!—MEBBE CONNIE OVERLISTEN!
12-28
THE GUARDS SPEAK IN CHINESE...
HO, HONORED FRIEND, I TOLD YOU MASTER PYZON WOULD HAVE REVENGE ON THE HANDSOME AMERICAN!—JUST NOW HE HAS THE YANKEE IN HOT WATER!
IS SO?
SO, INDEED!—MASTER WILL HOLD A LOTTERY FOR THE DRAGON LADY'S SINGLE GIRLS—WITH THE HANDSOME ONE AS FIRST PRIZE! THE PROUD WHITE MAN WILL BE FORCED AT BAYONET POINT TO MARRY THE WINNING NATIVE GIRL!
OH, DREAD DUDGEON!—DOLEFUL DOIN'S! MIST' PAT HAVE TO MELLY WITH SILLY SLAVE GIRL!—IS OL' WOMENS AGAIN! WHEN DAMES COME IN—ALSO COME DOUR, DREADFUL MONKEYDOODLES!
Reg. U. S. Pat. Off.: Copyright, 1936, by Chicago Tribune-N. Y. News Syndicate, Inc.
MILTON CANIFF

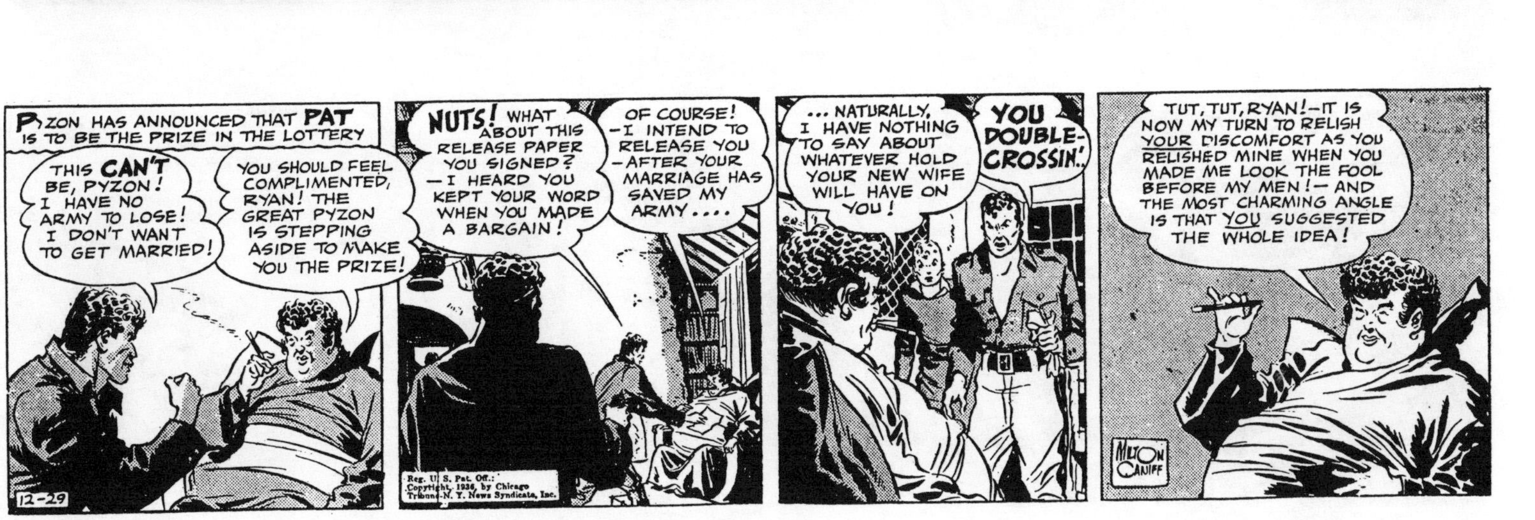
PYZON HAS ANNOUNCED THAT PAT IS TO BE THE PRIZE IN THE LOTTERY
THIS CAN'T BE, PYZON! I HAVE NO ARMY TO LOSE! I DON'T WANT TO GET MARRIED!
YOU SHOULD FEEL COMPLIMENTED, RYAN! THE GREAT PYZON IS STEPPING ASIDE TO MAKE YOU THE PRIZE!
12-29
NUTS! WHAT ABOUT THIS RELEASE PAPER YOU SIGNED?—I HEARD YOU KEPT YOUR WORD WHEN YOU MADE A BARGAIN!
OF COURSE!—I INTEND TO RELEASE YOU—AFTER YOUR MARRIAGE HAS SAVED MY ARMY....
Reg. U. S. Pat. Off.: Copyright, 1936, by Chicago Tribune-N. Y. News Syndicate, Inc.
...NATURALLY, I HAVE NOTHING TO SAY ABOUT WHATEVER HOLD YOUR NEW WIFE WILL HAVE ON YOU!
YOU DOUBLE-CROSSIN'!
TUT, TUT, RYAN!—IT IS NOW MY TURN TO RELISH YOUR DISCOMFORT AS YOU RELISHED MINE WHEN YOU MADE ME LOOK THE FOOL BEFORE MY MEN!—AND THE MOST CHARMING ANGLE IS THAT YOU SUGGESTED THE WHOLE IDEA!
MILTON CANIFF

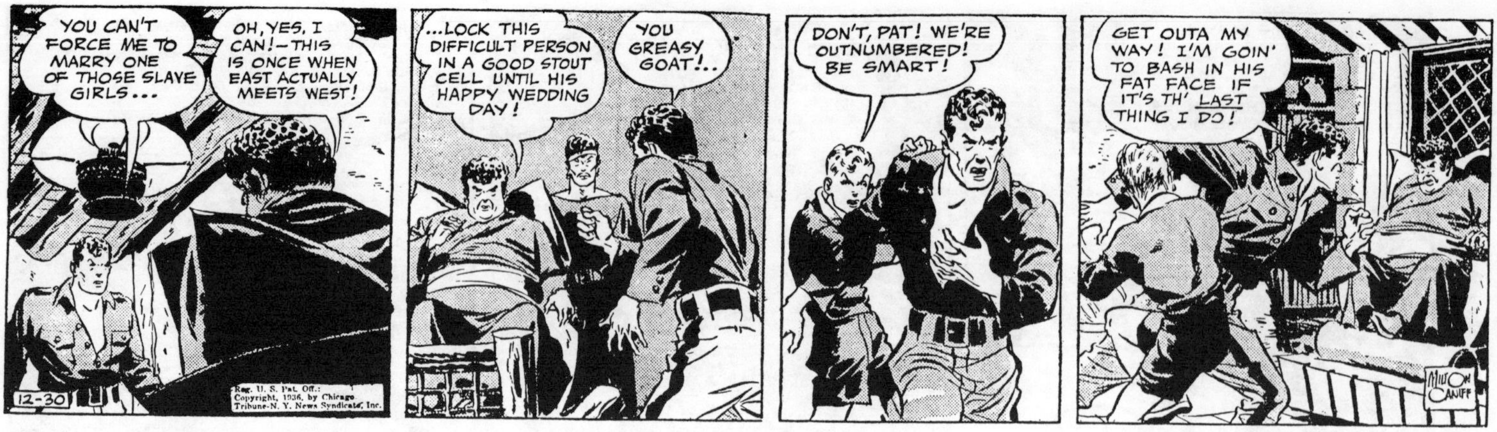
YOU CAN'T FORCE ME TO MARRY ONE OF THOSE SLAVE GIRLS...
OH, YES, I CAN!—THIS IS ONCE WHEN EAST ACTUALLY MEETS WEST!
12-30
Reg. U. S. Pat. Off.: Copyright, 1936, by Chicago Tribune-N. Y. News Syndicate, Inc.
...LOCK THIS DIFFICULT PERSON IN A GOOD STOUT CELL UNTIL HIS HAPPY WEDDING DAY!
YOU GREASY GOAT!..
DON'T, PAT! WE'RE OUTNUMBERED! BE SMART!
GET OUTA MY WAY! I'M GOIN' TO BASH IN HIS FAT FACE IF IT'S TH' LAST THING I DO!
MILTON CANIFF

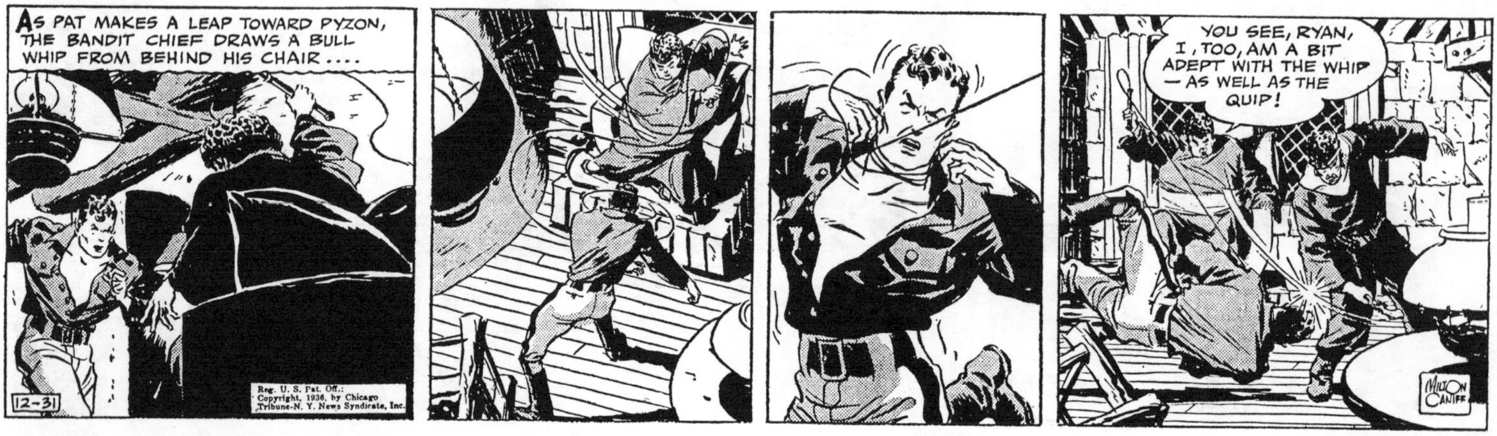
AS PAT MAKES A LEAP TOWARD PYZON, THE BANDIT CHIEF DRAWS A BULL WHIP FROM BEHIND HIS CHAIR....
12-31
Reg. U. S. Pat. Off.: Copyright, 1936, by Chicago Tribune-N. Y. News Syndicate, Inc.
YOU SEE, RYAN, I, TOO, AM A BIT ADEPT WITH THE WHIP —AS WELL AS THE QUIP!
MILTON CANIFF

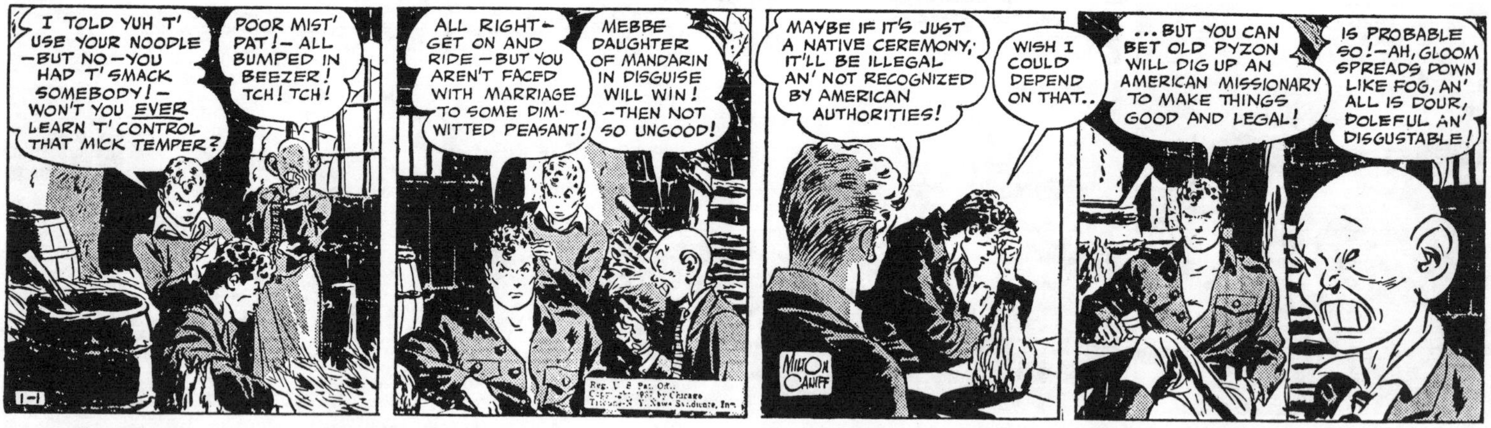
I TOLD YUH T' USE YOUR NOODLE —BUT NO—YOU HAD T' SMACK SOMEBODY!— WON'T YOU EVER LEARN T' CONTROL THAT MICK TEMPER?
POOR MIST' PAT!—ALL BUMPED IN BEEZER! TCH! TCH!
1-1
ALL RIGHT— GET ON AND RIDE—BUT YOU AREN'T FACED WITH MARRIAGE TO SOME DIM-WITTED PEASANT!
MEBBE DAUGHTER OF MANDARIN IN DISGUISE WILL WIN! —THEN NOT SO UNGOOD!
Reg. U. S. Pat. Off.
Tribune-N. Y. News Syndicate, Inc.
MAYBE IF IT'S JUST A NATIVE CEREMONY, IT'LL BE ILLEGAL AN' NOT RECOGNIZED BY AMERICAN AUTHORITIES!
WISH I COULD DEPEND ON THAT..
MILTON CANIFF
...BUT YOU CAN BET OLD PYZON WILL DIG UP AN AMERICAN MISSIONARY TO MAKE THINGS GOOD AND LEGAL!
IS PROBABLE SO!—AH, GLOOM SPREADS DOWN LIKE FOG, AN' ALL IS DOUR, DOLEFUL AN' DISGUSTABLE!

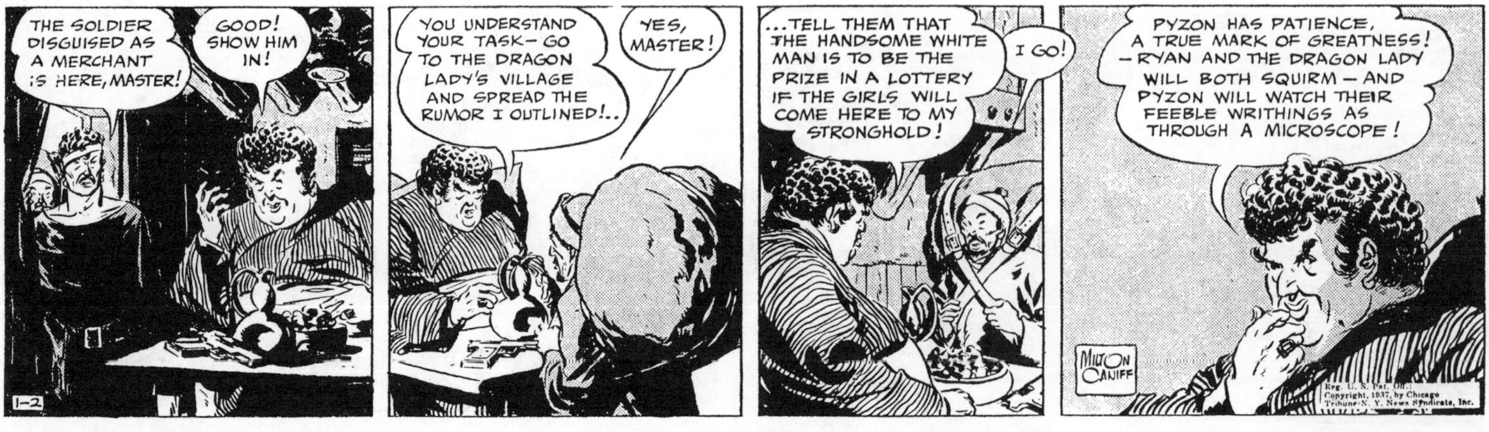
THE SOLDIER DISGUISED AS A MERCHANT IS HERE, MASTER!
GOOD! SHOW HIM IN!
1-2
YOU UNDERSTAND YOUR TASK—GO TO THE DRAGON LADY'S VILLAGE AND SPREAD THE RUMOR I OUTLINED!..
YES, MASTER!
...TELL THEM THAT THE HANDSOME WHITE MAN IS TO BE THE PRIZE IN A LOTTERY IF THE GIRLS WILL COME HERE TO MY STRONGHOLD!
I GO!
MILTON CANIFF
PYZON HAS PATIENCE, A TRUE MARK OF GREATNESS! —RYAN AND THE DRAGON LADY WILL BOTH SQUIRM—AND PYZON WILL WATCH THEIR FEEBLE WRITHINGS AS THROUGH A MICROSCOPE!
Reg. U. S. Pat. Off.: Copyright, 1937, by Chicago Tribune-N. Y. News Syndicate, Inc.

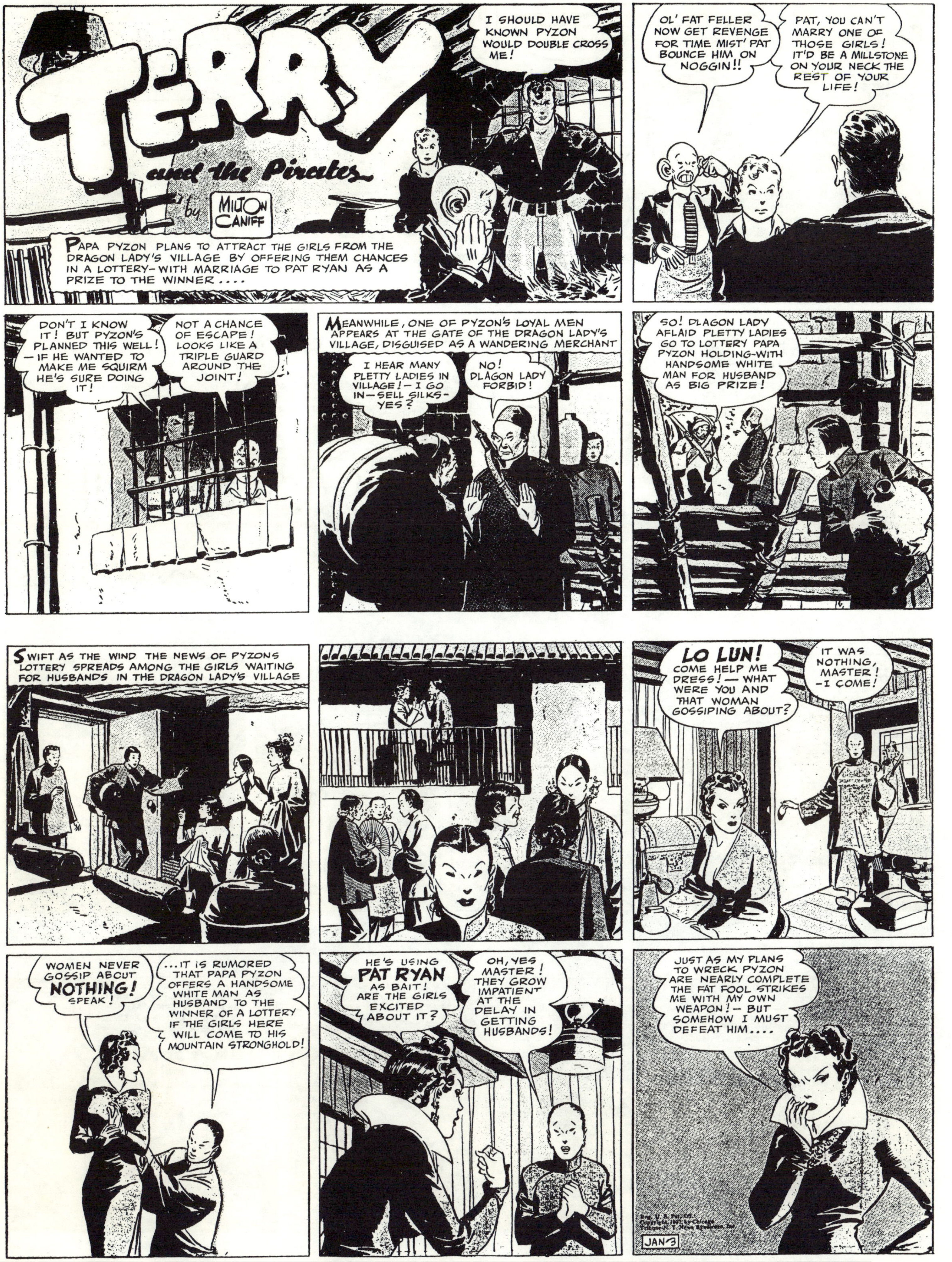
TERRY and the Pirates
by MILTON CANIFF
I SHOULD HAVE KNOWN PYZON WOULD DOUBLE CROSS ME!
PAPA PYZON PLANS TO ATTRACT THE GIRLS FROM THE DRAGON LADY'S VILLAGE BY OFFERING THEM CHANCES IN A LOTTERY—WITH MARRIAGE TO PAT RYAN AS A PRIZE TO THE WINNER....
OL' FAT FELLER NOW GET REVENGE FOR TIME MIST' PAT BOUNCE HIM ON NOGGIN!!
PAT, YOU CAN'T MARRY ONE OF THOSE GIRLS! IT'D BE A MILLSTONE ON YOUR NECK THE REST OF YOUR LIFE!
DON'T I KNOW IT! BUT PYZON'S PLANNED THIS WELL! —IF HE WANTED TO MAKE ME SQUIRM HE'S SURE DOING IT!
NOT A CHANCE OF ESCAPE! LOOKS LIKE A TRIPLE GUARD AROUND THE JOINT!
MEANWHILE, ONE OF PYZON'S LOYAL MEN APPEARS AT THE GATE OF THE DRAGON LADY'S VILLAGE, DISGUISED AS A WANDERING MERCHANT
I HEAR MANY PLETTY LADIES IN VILLAGE!—I GO IN—SELL SILKS—YES?
NO! DLAGON LADY FORBID!
SO! DLAGON LADY AFLAID PLETTY LADIES GO TO LOTTERY PAPA PYZON HOLDING—WITH HANDSOME WHITE MAN FOR HUSBAND AS BIG PRIZE!
SWIFT AS THE WIND THE NEWS OF PYZONS LOTTERY SPREADS AMONG THE GIRLS WAITING FOR HUSBANDS IN THE DRAGON LADY'S VILLAGE
LO LUN! COME HELP ME DRESS!—WHAT WERE YOU AND THAT WOMAN GOSSIPING ABOUT?
IT WAS NOTHING, MASTER! —I COME!
WOMEN NEVER GOSSIP ABOUT NOTHING! SPEAK!
...IT IS RUMORED THAT PAPA PYZON OFFERS A HANDSOME WHITE MAN AS HUSBAND TO THE WINNER OF A LOTTERY IF THE GIRLS HERE WILL COME TO HIS MOUNTAIN STRONGHOLD!
HE'S USING PAT RYAN AS BAIT! ARE THE GIRLS EXCITED ABOUT IT?
OH, YES MASTER! THEY GROW IMPATIENT AT THE DELAY IN GETTING HUSBANDS!
JUST AS MY PLANS TO WRECK PYZON ARE NEARLY COMPLETE THE FAT FOOL STRIKES ME WITH MY OWN WEAPON!—BUT SOMEHOW I MUST DEFEAT HIM....
JAN-3

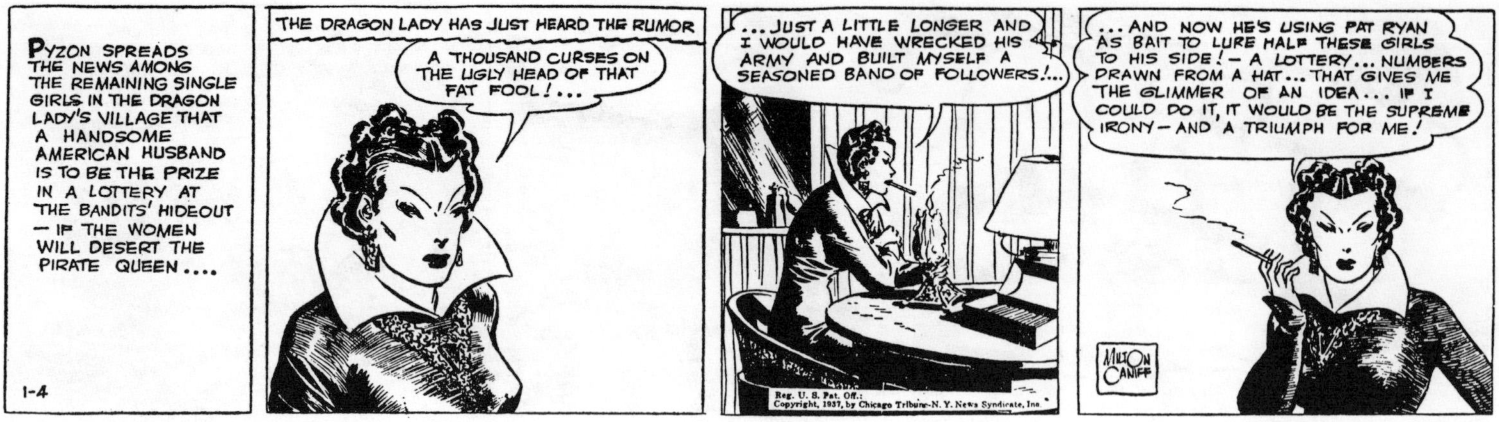
PYZON SPREADS THE NEWS AMONG THE REMAINING SINGLE GIRLS IN THE DRAGON LADY'S VILLAGE THAT A HANDSOME AMERICAN HUSBAND IS TO BE THE PRIZE IN A LOTTERY AT THE BANDITS' HIDEOUT — IF THE WOMEN WILL DESERT THE PIRATE QUEEN....
1-4
THE DRAGON LADY HAS JUST HEARD THE RUMOR
A THOUSAND CURSES ON THE UGLY HEAD OF THAT FAT FOOL!...
...JUST A LITTLE LONGER AND I WOULD HAVE WRECKED HIS ARMY AND BUILT MYSELF A SEASONED BAND OF FOLLOWERS!...
Reg. U. S. Pat. Off.: Copyright, 1937, by Chicago Tribune-N. Y. News Syndicate, Inc.
...AND NOW HE'S USING PAT RYAN AS BAIT TO LURE HALF THESE GIRLS TO HIS SIDE! — A LOTTERY... NUMBERS DRAWN FROM A HAT... THAT GIVES ME THE GLIMMER OF AN IDEA... IF I COULD DO IT, IT WOULD BE THE SUPREME IRONY — AND A TRIUMPH FOR ME!
MILTON CANIFF

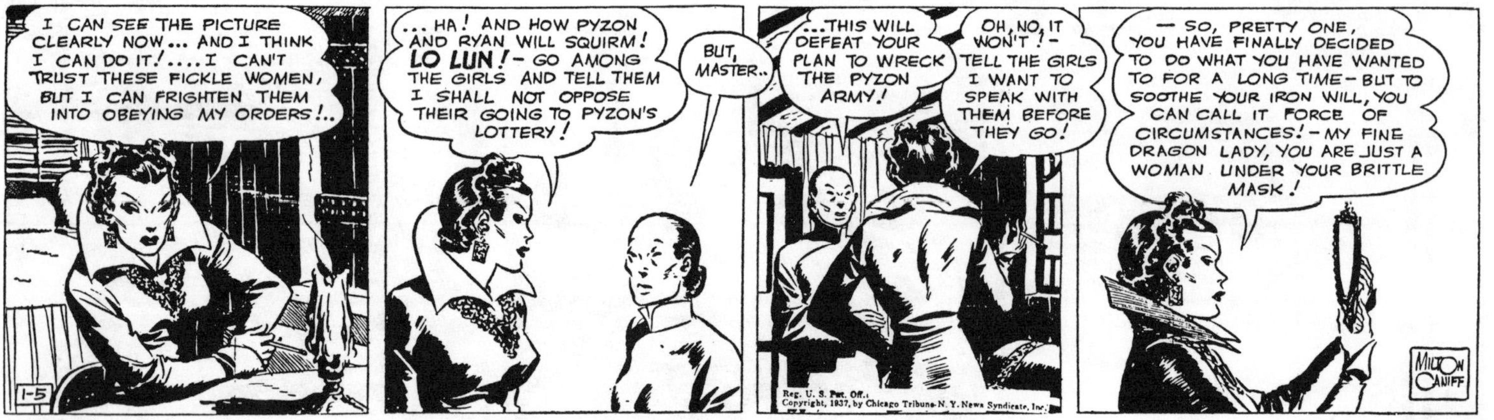
I CAN SEE THE PICTURE CLEARLY NOW... AND I THINK I CAN DO IT!....I CAN'T TRUST THESE FICKLE WOMEN, BUT I CAN FRIGHTEN THEM INTO OBEYING MY ORDERS!..
1-5
...HA! AND HOW PYZON AND RYAN WILL SQUIRM! LO LUN! — GO AMONG THE GIRLS AND TELL THEM I SHALL NOT OPPOSE THEIR GOING TO PYZON'S LOTTERY!
BUT, MASTER..
...THIS WILL DEFEAT YOUR PLAN TO WRECK THE PYZON ARMY!
OH, NO, IT WON'T! — TELL THE GIRLS I WANT TO SPEAK WITH THEM BEFORE THEY GO!
Reg. U. S. Pat. Off.: Copyright, 1937, by Chicago Tribune-N. Y. News Syndicate, Inc.
— SO, PRETTY ONE, YOU HAVE FINALLY DECIDED TO DO WHAT YOU HAVE WANTED TO FOR A LONG TIME — BUT TO SOOTHE YOUR IRON WILL, YOU CAN CALL IT FORCE OF CIRCUMSTANCES! — MY FINE DRAGON LADY, YOU ARE JUST A WOMAN UNDER YOUR BRITTLE MASK!
MILTON CANIFF

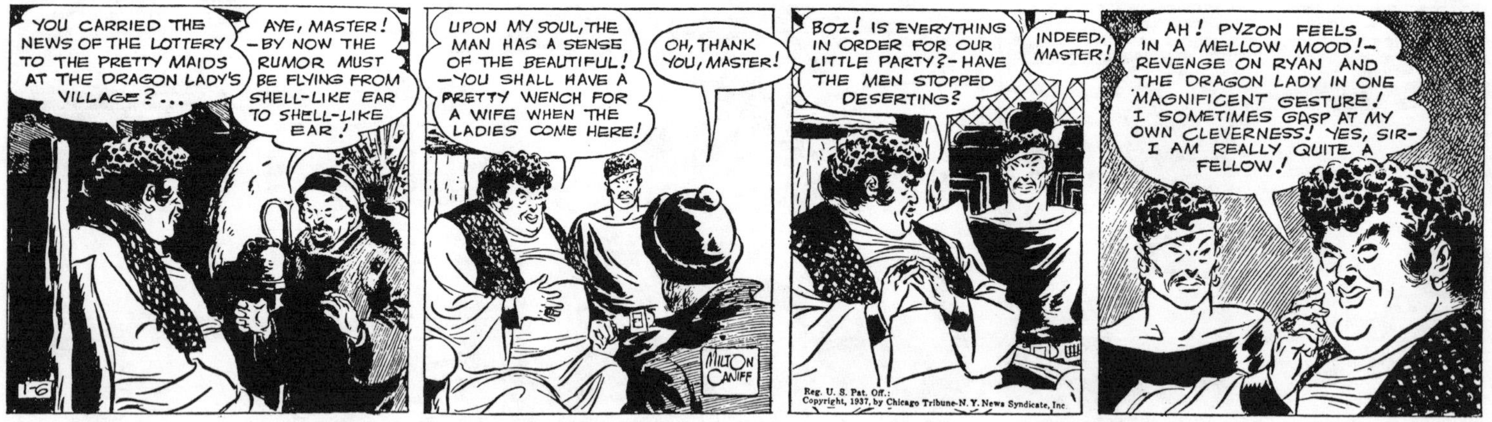
YOU CARRIED THE NEWS OF THE LOTTERY TO THE PRETTY MAIDS AT THE DRAGON LADY'S VILLAGE?...
AYE, MASTER! — BY NOW THE RUMOR MUST BE FLYING FROM SHELL-LIKE EAR TO SHELL-LIKE EAR!
1-6
UPON MY SOUL, THE MAN HAS A SENSE OF THE BEAUTIFUL! — YOU SHALL HAVE A PRETTY WENCH FOR A WIFE WHEN THE LADIES COME HERE!
OH, THANK YOU, MASTER!
MILTON CANIFF
BOZ! IS EVERYTHING IN ORDER FOR OUR LITTLE PARTY? — HAVE THE MEN STOPPED DESERTING?
INDEED, MASTER!
Reg. U. S. Pat. Off.: Copyright, 1937, by Chicago Tribune-N. Y. News Syndicate, Inc.
AH! PYZON FEELS IN A MELLOW MOOD! — REVENGE ON RYAN AND THE DRAGON LADY IN ONE MAGNIFICENT GESTURE! I SOMETIMES GASP AT MY OWN CLEVERNESS! YES, SIR — I AM REALLY QUITE A FELLOW!

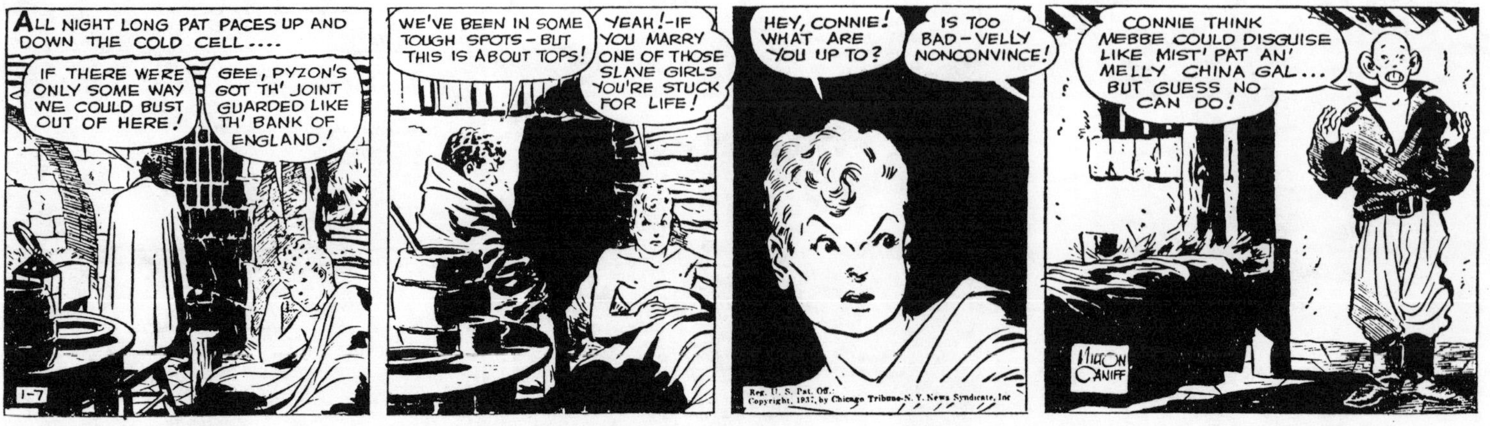
ALL NIGHT LONG PAT PACES UP AND DOWN THE COLD CELL....
IF THERE WERE ONLY SOME WAY WE COULD BUST OUT OF HERE!
GEE, PYZON'S GOT TH' JOINT GUARDED LIKE TH' BANK OF ENGLAND!
1-7
WE'VE BEEN IN SOME TOUGH SPOTS — BUT THIS IS ABOUT TOPS!
YEAH! — IF YOU MARRY ONE OF THOSE SLAVE GIRLS YOU'RE STUCK FOR LIFE!
HEY, CONNIE! WHAT ARE YOU UP TO?
IS TOO BAD — VELLY NONCONVINCE!
Reg. U. S. Pat. Off.: Copyright, 1937, by Chicago Tribune-N. Y. News Syndicate, Inc.
CONNIE THINK MEBBE COULD DISGUISE LIKE MIST' PAT AN' MELLY CHINA GAL... BUT GUESS NO CAN DO!
MILTON CANIFF

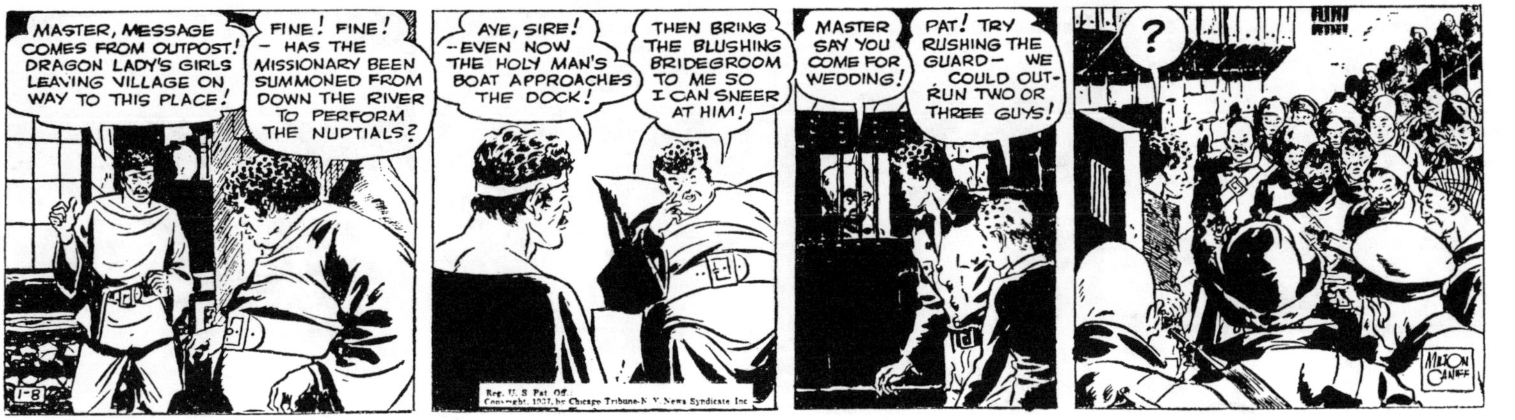
MASTER, MESSAGE COMES FROM OUTPOST! DRAGON LADY'S GIRLS LEAVING VILLAGE ON WAY TO THIS PLACE!
FINE! FINE! — HAS THE MISSIONARY BEEN SUMMONED FROM DOWN THE RIVER TO PERFORM THE NUPTIALS?
1-8
AYE, SIRE! —EVEN NOW THE HOLY MAN'S BOAT APPROACHES THE DOCK!
THEN BRING THE BLUSHING BRIDEGROOM TO ME SO I CAN SNEER AT HIM!
Reg. U. S. Pat. Off. Copyright, 1937, by Chicago Tribune-N. Y. News Syndicate Inc.
MASTER SAY YOU COME FOR WEDDING!
PAT! TRY RUSHING THE GUARD— WE COULD OUT-RUN TWO OR THREE GUYS!
?
MILTON CANIFF

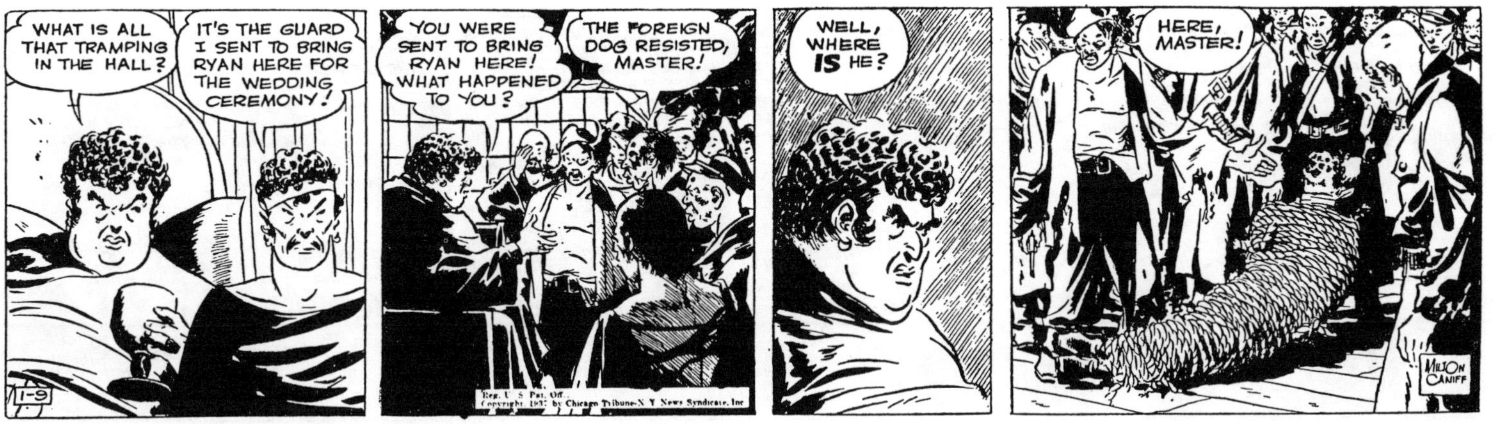
WHAT IS ALL THAT TRAMPING IN THE HALL?
IT'S THE GUARD I SENT TO BRING RYAN HERE FOR THE WEDDING CEREMONY!
1-9
YOU WERE SENT TO BRING RYAN HERE! WHAT HAPPENED TO YOU?
THE FOREIGN DOG RESISTED, MASTER!
Reg. U. S. Pat. Off. Copyright, 1937, by Chicago Tribune-N. Y. News Syndicate, Inc.
WELL, WHERE IS HE?
HERE, MASTER!
MILTON CANIFF

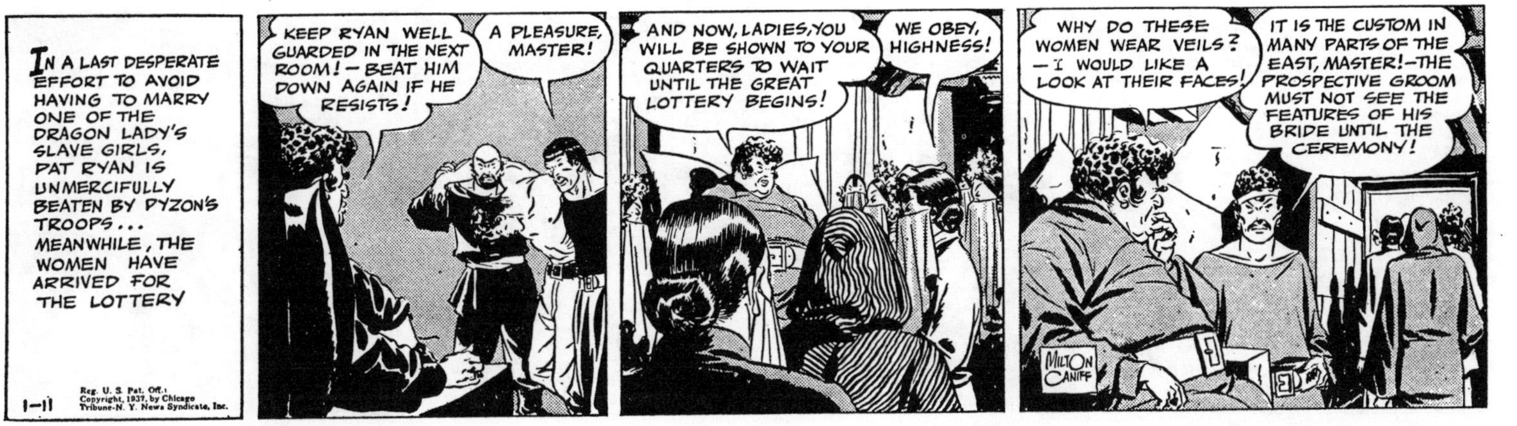
IN A LAST DESPERATE EFFORT TO AVOID HAVING TO MARRY ONE OF THE DRAGON LADY'S SLAVE GIRLS, PAT RYAN IS UNMERCIFULLY BEATEN BY PYZON'S TROOPS ... MEANWHILE, THE WOMEN HAVE ARRIVED FOR THE LOTTERY
1-11
Reg. U. S. Pat. Off.: Copyright, 1937, by Chicago Tribune-N. Y. News Syndicate, Inc.
KEEP RYAN WELL GUARDED IN THE NEXT ROOM! — BEAT HIM DOWN AGAIN IF HE RESISTS!
A PLEASURE, MASTER!
AND NOW, LADIES, YOU WILL BE SHOWN TO YOUR QUARTERS TO WAIT UNTIL THE GREAT LOTTERY BEGINS!
WE OBEY, HIGHNESS!
WHY DO THESE WOMEN WEAR VEILS? — I WOULD LIKE A LOOK AT THEIR FACES!
IT IS THE CUSTOM IN MANY PARTS OF THE EAST, MASTER! —THE PROSPECTIVE GROOM MUST NOT SEE THE FEATURES OF HIS BRIDE UNTIL THE CEREMONY!
MILTON CANIFF

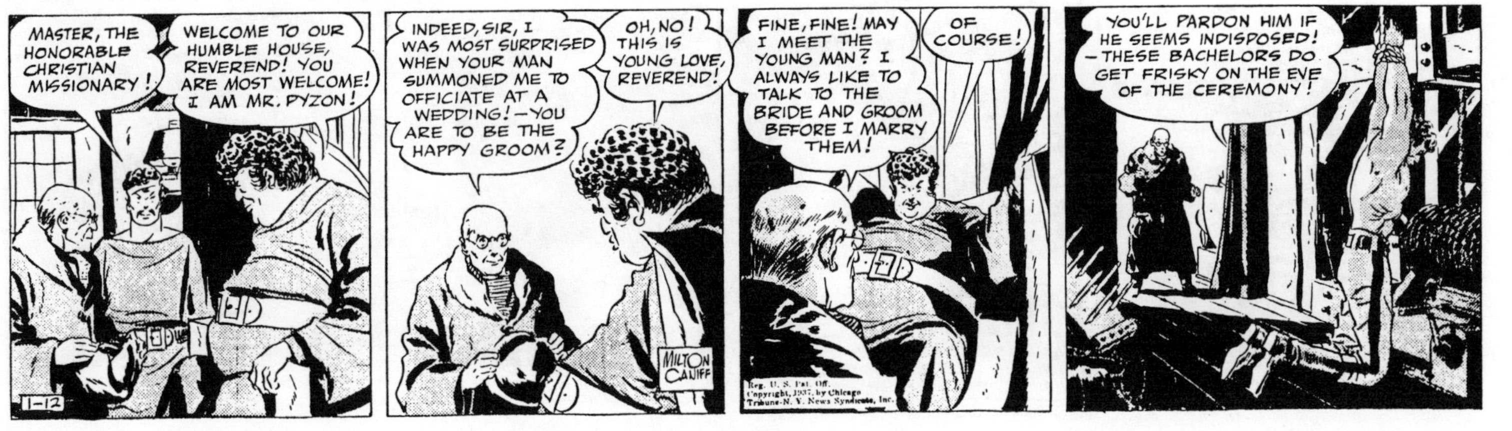
MASTER, THE HONORABLE CHRISTIAN MISSIONARY!
WELCOME TO OUR HUMBLE HOUSE, REVEREND! YOU ARE MOST WELCOME! I AM MR. PYZON!
1-12
INDEED, SIR, I WAS MOST SURPRISED WHEN YOUR MAN SUMMONED ME TO OFFICIATE AT A WEDDING! —YOU ARE TO BE THE HAPPY GROOM?
OH, NO! THIS IS YOUNG LOVE, REVEREND!
MILTON CANIFF
FINE, FINE! MAY I MEET THE YOUNG MAN? I ALWAYS LIKE TO TALK TO THE BRIDE AND GROOM BEFORE I MARRY THEM!
OF COURSE!
Reg. U. S. Pat. Off. Copyright, 1937, by Chicago Tribune-N. Y. News Syndicate, Inc.
YOU'LL PARDON HIM IF HE SEEMS INDISPOSED! — THESE BACHELORS DO GET FRISKY ON THE EVE OF THE CEREMONY!

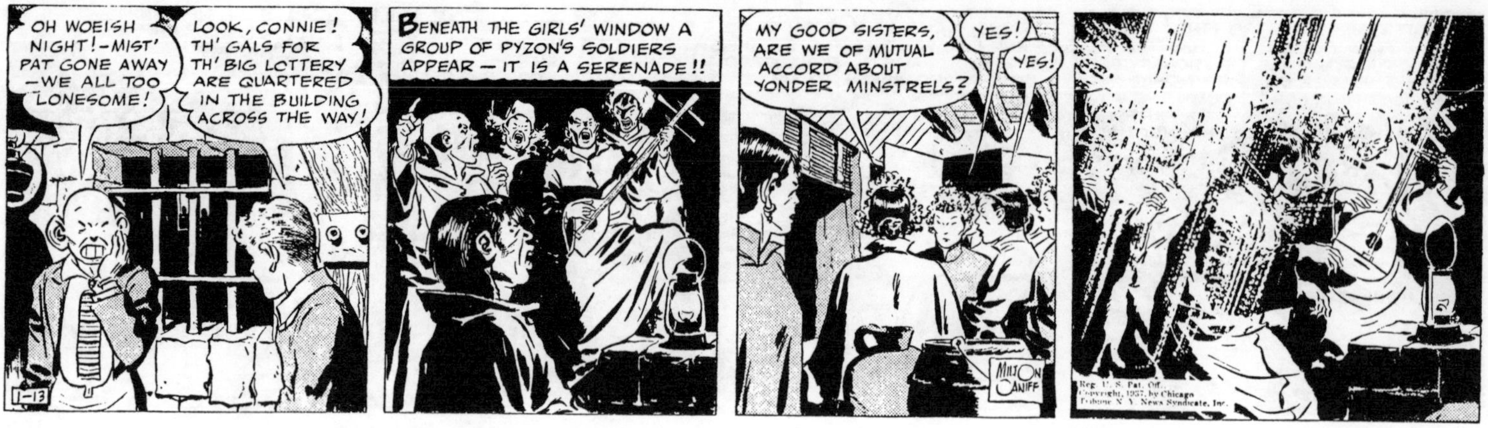
OH WOEISH NIGHT! – MIST' PAT GONE AWAY – WE ALL TOO LONESOME!
LOOK, CONNIE! TH' GALS FOR TH' BIG LOTTERY ARE QUARTERED IN THE BUILDING ACROSS THE WAY!
1-13
BENEATH THE GIRLS' WINDOW A GROUP OF PYZON'S SOLDIERS APPEAR – IT IS A SERENADE!!
MY GOOD SISTERS, ARE WE OF MUTUAL ACCORD ABOUT YONDER MINSTRELS?
YES!
YES!
MILTON CANIFF
Reg. U. S. Pat. Off.; Copyright, 1937, by Chicago Tribune N. Y. News Syndicate, Inc.

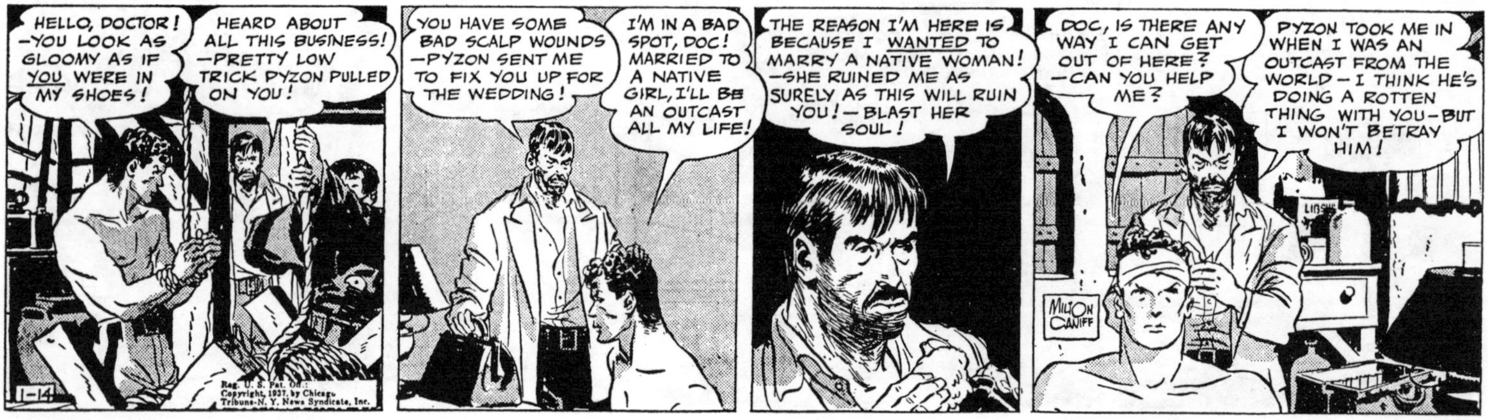
HELLO, DOCTOR! – YOU LOOK AS GLOOMY AS IF YOU WERE IN MY SHOES!
HEARD ABOUT ALL THIS BUSINESS! – PRETTY LOW TRICK PYZON PULLED ON YOU!
1-14
Reg. U. S. Pat. Off.; Copyright, 1937, by Chicago Tribune-N. Y. News Syndicate, Inc.
YOU HAVE SOME BAD SCALP WOUNDS – PYZON SENT ME TO FIX YOU UP FOR THE WEDDING!
I'M IN A BAD SPOT, DOC! MARRIED TO A NATIVE GIRL, I'LL BE AN OUTCAST ALL MY LIFE!
THE REASON I'M HERE IS BECAUSE I WANTED TO MARRY A NATIVE WOMAN! – SHE RUINED ME AS SURELY AS THIS WILL RUIN YOU! – BLAST HER SOUL!
DOC, IS THERE ANY WAY I CAN GET OUT OF HERE? – CAN YOU HELP ME?
PYZON TOOK ME IN WHEN I WAS AN OUTCAST FROM THE WORLD – I THINK HE'S DOING A ROTTEN THING WITH YOU – BUT I WON'T BETRAY HIM!
MILTON CANIFF

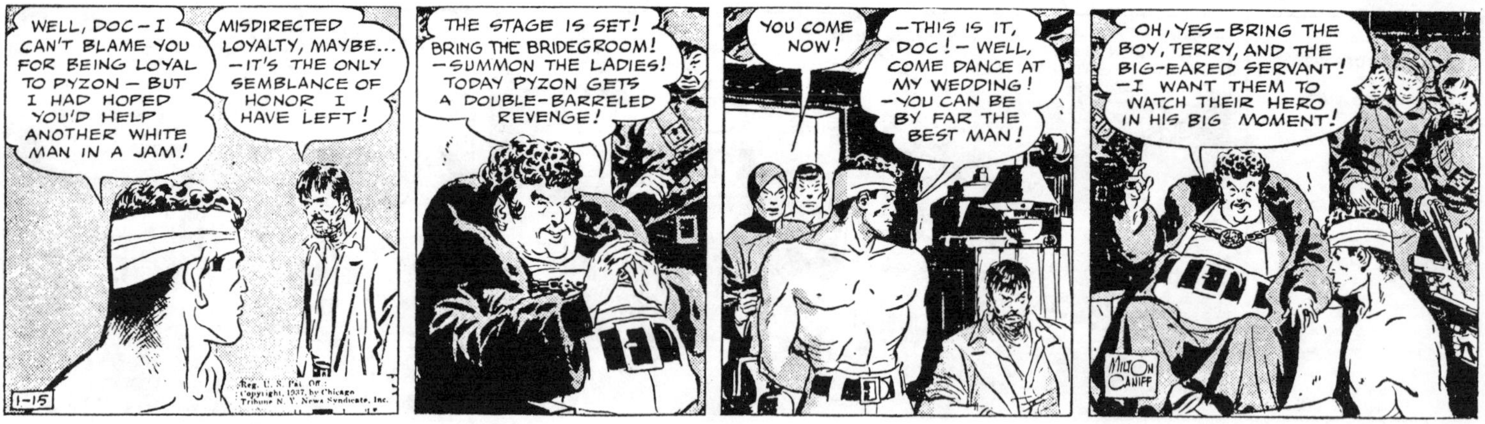
WELL, DOC – I CAN'T BLAME YOU FOR BEING LOYAL TO PYZON – BUT I HAD HOPED YOU'D HELP ANOTHER WHITE MAN IN A JAM!
MISDIRECTED LOYALTY, MAYBE... – IT'S THE ONLY SEMBLANCE OF HONOR I HAVE LEFT!
1-15
Reg. U. S. Pat. Off.; Copyright, 1937, by Chicago Tribune-N. Y. News Syndicate, Inc.
THE STAGE IS SET! BRING THE BRIDEGROOM! – SUMMON THE LADIES! TODAY PYZON GETS A DOUBLE-BARRELED REVENGE!
YOU COME NOW!
– THIS IS IT, DOC! – WELL, COME DANCE AT MY WEDDING! – YOU CAN BE BY FAR THE BEST MAN!
OH, YES – BRING THE BOY, TERRY, AND THE BIG-EARED SERVANT! – I WANT THEM TO WATCH THEIR HERO IN HIS BIG MOMENT!
MILTON CANIFF

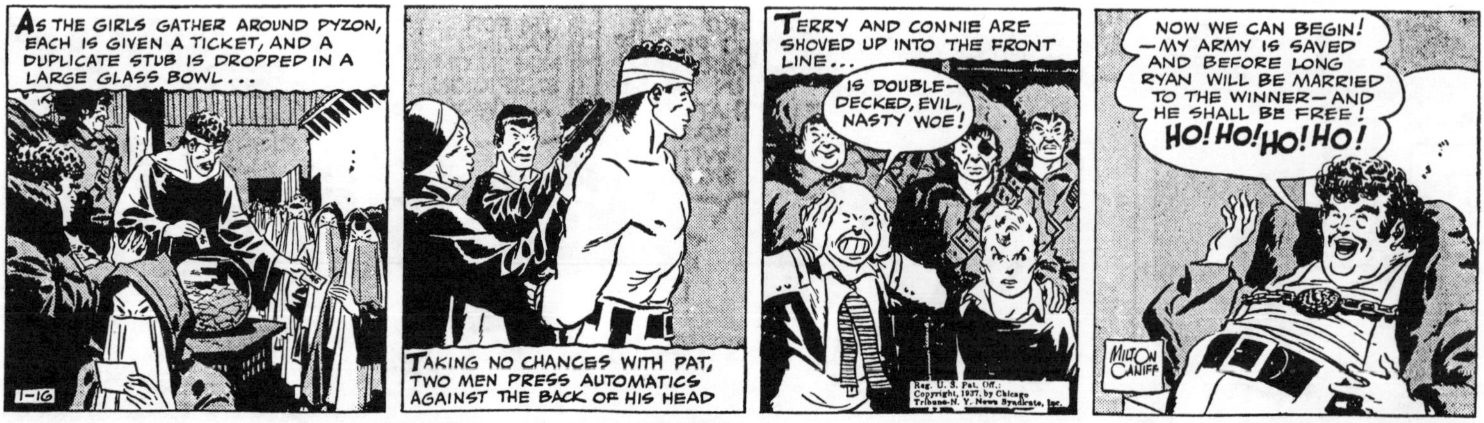
AS THE GIRLS GATHER AROUND PYZON, EACH IS GIVEN A TICKET, AND A DUPLICATE STUB IS DROPPED IN A LARGE GLASS BOWL...
1-16
TAKING NO CHANCES WITH PAT, TWO MEN PRESS AUTOMATICS AGAINST THE BACK OF HIS HEAD
TERRY AND CONNIE ARE SHOVED UP INTO THE FRONT LINE...
IS DOUBLE-DECKED, EVIL, NASTY WOE!
Reg. U. S. Pat. Off.; Copyright, 1937, by Chicago Tribune-N. Y. News Syndicate, Inc.
NOW WE CAN BEGIN! – MY ARMY IS SAVED AND BEFORE LONG RYAN WILL BE MARRIED TO THE WINNER – AND HE SHALL BE FREE!
HO! HO! HO! HO!
MILTON CANIFF

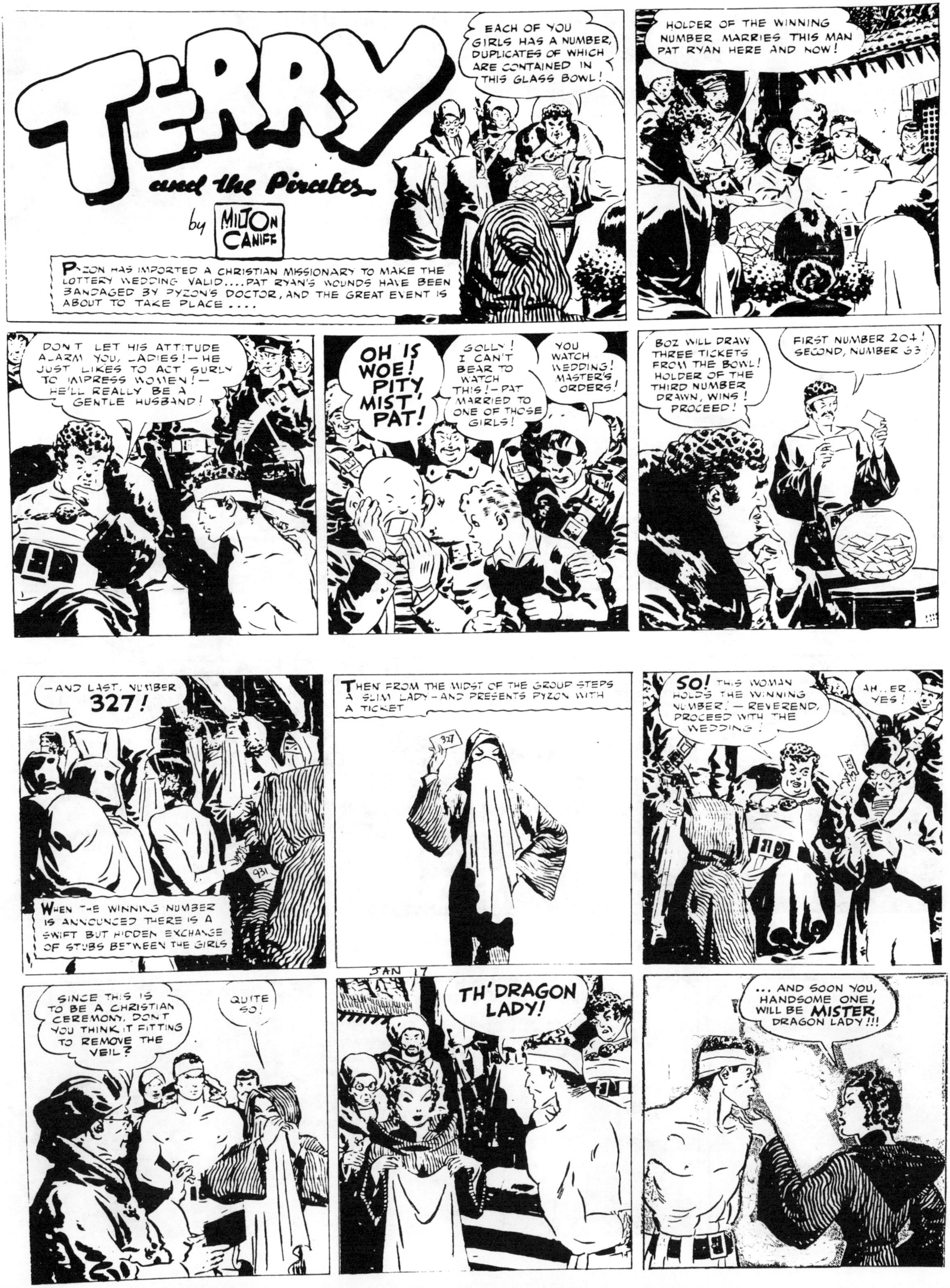

TERRY and the Pirates
by MILTON CANIFF
PYZON HAS IMPORTED A CHRISTIAN MISSIONARY TO MAKE THE LOTTERY WEDDING VALID.... PAT RYAN'S WOUNDS HAVE BEEN BANDAGED BY PYZON'S DOCTOR, AND THE GREAT EVENT IS ABOUT TO TAKE PLACE....
EACH OF YOU GIRLS HAS A NUMBER, DUPLICATES OF WHICH ARE CONTAINED IN THIS GLASS BOWL!
HOLDER OF THE WINNING NUMBER MARRIES THIS MAN PAT RYAN HERE AND NOW!
DON'T LET HIS ATTITUDE ALARM YOU, LADIES! — HE JUST LIKES TO ACT SURLY TO IMPRESS WOMEN! — HE'LL REALLY BE A GENTLE HUSBAND!
OH IS WOE! PITY MIST' PAT!
GOLLY! I CAN'T BEAR TO WATCH THIS! — PAT MARRIED TO ONE OF THOSE GIRLS!
YOU WATCH WEDDING! MASTER'S ORDERS!
BOZ WILL DRAW THREE TICKETS FROM THE BOWL! HOLDER OF THE THIRD NUMBER DRAWN, WINS! PROCEED!
FIRST NUMBER 204! SECOND, NUMBER 63!
— AND LAST, NUMBER 327!
931
WHEN THE WINNING NUMBER IS ANNOUNCED THERE IS A SWIFT BUT HIDDEN EXCHANGE OF STUBS BETWEEN THE GIRLS
THEN FROM THE MIDST OF THE GROUP STEPS A SLIM LADY — AND PRESENTS PYZON WITH A TICKET
327
SO! THIS WOMAN HOLDS THE WINNING NUMBER! — REVEREND, PROCEED WITH THE WEDDING!
AH...ER... YES!
JAN 17
SINCE THIS IS TO BE A CHRISTIAN CEREMONY, DON'T YOU THINK IT FITTING TO REMOVE THE VEIL?
QUITE SO!
TH' DRAGON LADY!
... AND SOON YOU, HANDSOME ONE, WILL BE MISTER DRAGON LADY!!!

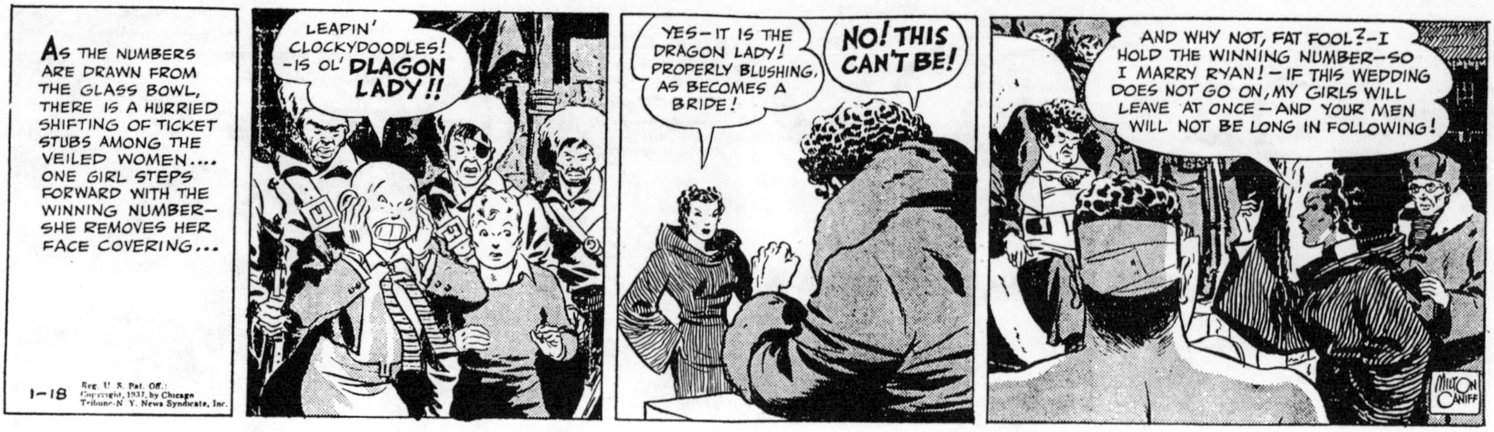
AS THE NUMBERS ARE DRAWN FROM THE GLASS BOWL, THERE IS A HURRIED SHIFTING OF TICKET STUBS AMONG THE VEILED WOMEN.... ONE GIRL STEPS FORWARD WITH THE WINNING NUMBER— SHE REMOVES HER FACE COVERING...
1-18
Reg. U. S. Pat. Off.: Copyright, 1937, by Chicago Tribune-N. Y. News Syndicate, Inc.
LEAPIN' CLOCKYDOODLES! —IS OL' DLAGON LADY!!
YES—IT IS THE DRAGON LADY! PROPERLY BLUSHING, AS BECOMES A BRIDE!
NO! THIS CAN'T BE!
AND WHY NOT, FAT FOOL?—I HOLD THE WINNING NUMBER—SO I MARRY RYAN!—IF THIS WEDDING DOES NOT GO ON, MY GIRLS WILL LEAVE AT ONCE—AND YOUR MEN WILL NOT BE LONG IN FOLLOWING!
MILTON CANIFF

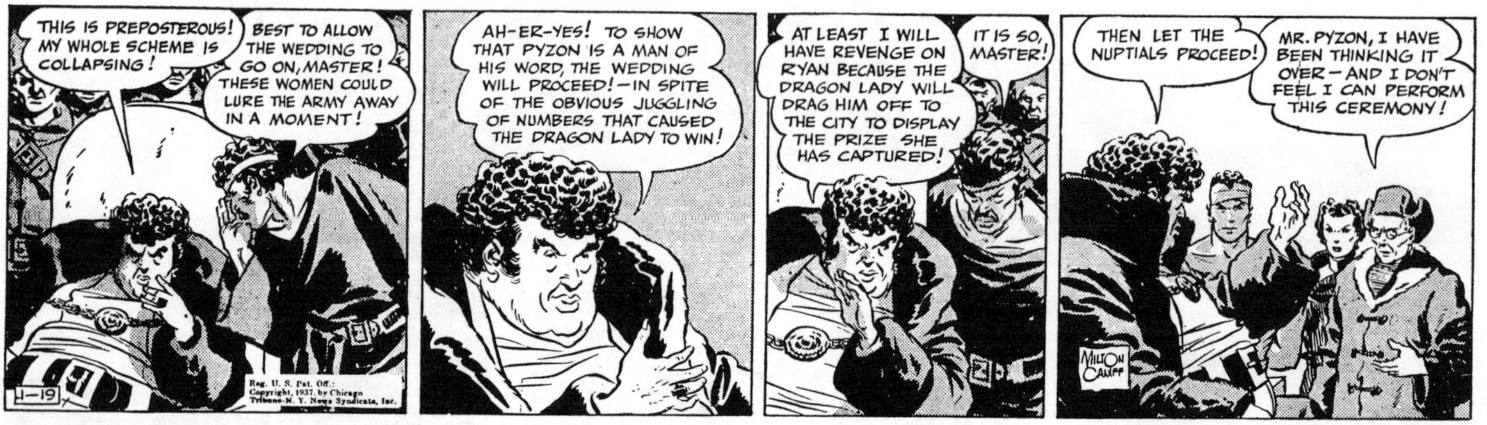
THIS IS PREPOSTEROUS! MY WHOLE SCHEME IS COLLAPSING!
BEST TO ALLOW THE WEDDING TO GO ON, MASTER! THESE WOMEN COULD LURE THE ARMY AWAY IN A MOMENT!
1-19
Reg. U. S. Pat. Off.: Copyright, 1937, by Chicago Tribune-N. Y. News Syndicate, Inc.
AH-ER-YES! TO SHOW THAT PYZON IS A MAN OF HIS WORD, THE WEDDING WILL PROCEED!—IN SPITE OF THE OBVIOUS JUGGLING OF NUMBERS THAT CAUSED THE DRAGON LADY TO WIN!
AT LEAST I WILL HAVE REVENGE ON RYAN BECAUSE THE DRAGON LADY WILL DRAG HIM OFF TO THE CITY TO DISPLAY THE PRIZE SHE HAS CAPTURED!
IT IS SO, MASTER!
THEN LET THE NUPTIALS PROCEED!
MR. PYZON, I HAVE BEEN THINKING IT OVER—AND I DON'T FEEL I CAN PERFORM THIS CEREMONY!
MILTON CANIFF

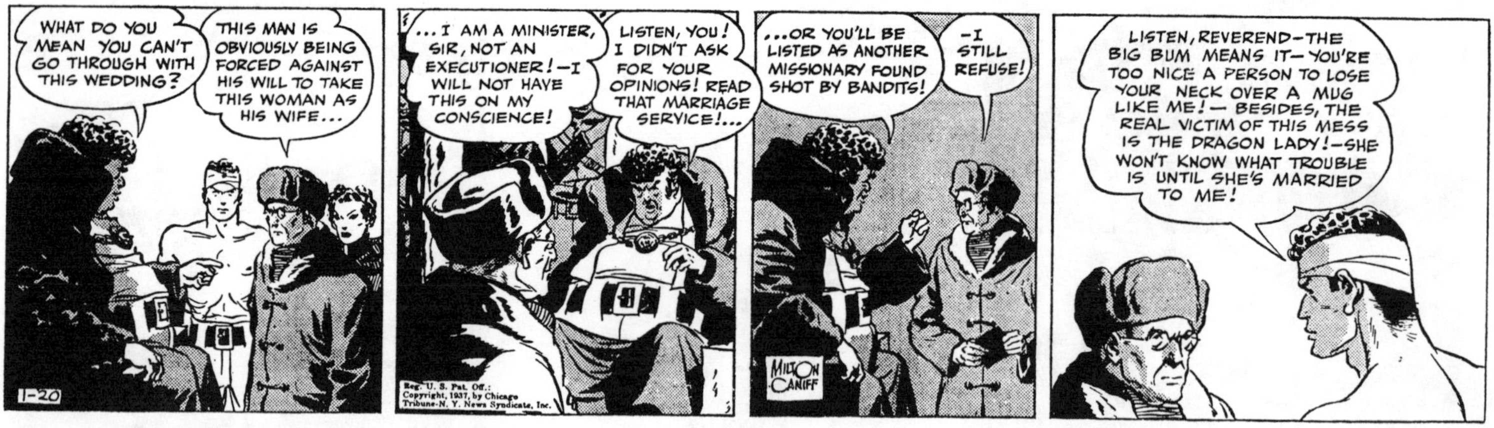
WHAT DO YOU MEAN YOU CAN'T GO THROUGH WITH THIS WEDDING?
THIS MAN IS OBVIOUSLY BEING FORCED AGAINST HIS WILL TO TAKE THIS WOMAN AS HIS WIFE...
1-20
...I AM A MINISTER, SIR, NOT AN EXECUTIONER!—I WILL NOT HAVE THIS ON MY CONSCIENCE!
LISTEN, YOU! I DIDN'T ASK FOR YOUR OPINIONS! READ THAT MARRIAGE SERVICE!...
Reg. U. S. Pat. Off.: Copyright, 1937, by Chicago Tribune-N. Y. News Syndicate, Inc.
...OR YOU'LL BE LISTED AS ANOTHER MISSIONARY FOUND SHOT BY BANDITS!
—I STILL REFUSE!
MILTON CANIFF
LISTEN, REVEREND—THE BIG BUM MEANS IT—YOU'RE TOO NICE A PERSON TO LOSE YOUR NECK OVER A MUG LIKE ME!—BESIDES, THE REAL VICTIM OF THIS MESS IS THE DRAGON LADY!—SHE WON'T KNOW WHAT TROUBLE IS UNTIL SHE'S MARRIED TO ME!

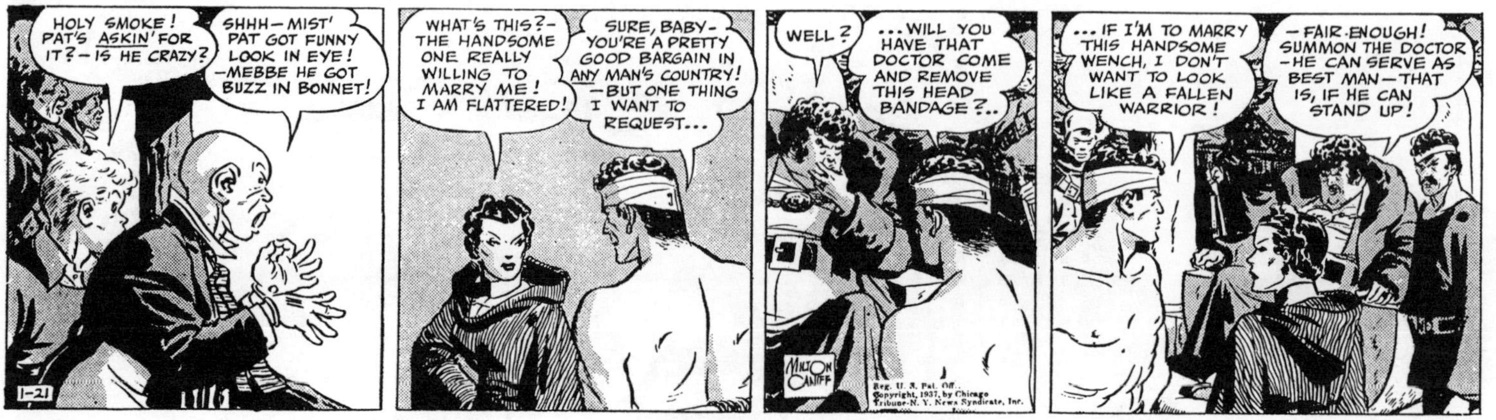
HOLY SMOKE! PAT'S ASKIN' FOR IT?—IS HE CRAZY?
SHHH—MIST' PAT GOT FUNNY LOOK IN EYE! —MEBBE HE GOT BUZZ IN BONNET!
1-21
WHAT'S THIS?— THE HANDSOME ONE REALLY WILLING TO MARRY ME! I AM FLATTERED!
SURE, BABY— YOU'RE A PRETTY GOOD BARGAIN IN ANY MAN'S COUNTRY! —BUT ONE THING I WANT TO REQUEST...
WELL?
...WILL YOU HAVE THAT DOCTOR COME AND REMOVE THIS HEAD BANDAGE?..
MILTON CANIFF
Reg. U. S. Pat. Off.: Copyright, 1937, by Chicago Tribune-N. Y. News Syndicate, Inc.
...IF I'M TO MARRY THIS HANDSOME WENCH, I DON'T WANT TO LOOK LIKE A FALLEN WARRIOR!
—FAIR ENOUGH! SUMMON THE DOCTOR —HE CAN SERVE AS BEST MAN—THAT IS, IF HE CAN STAND UP!

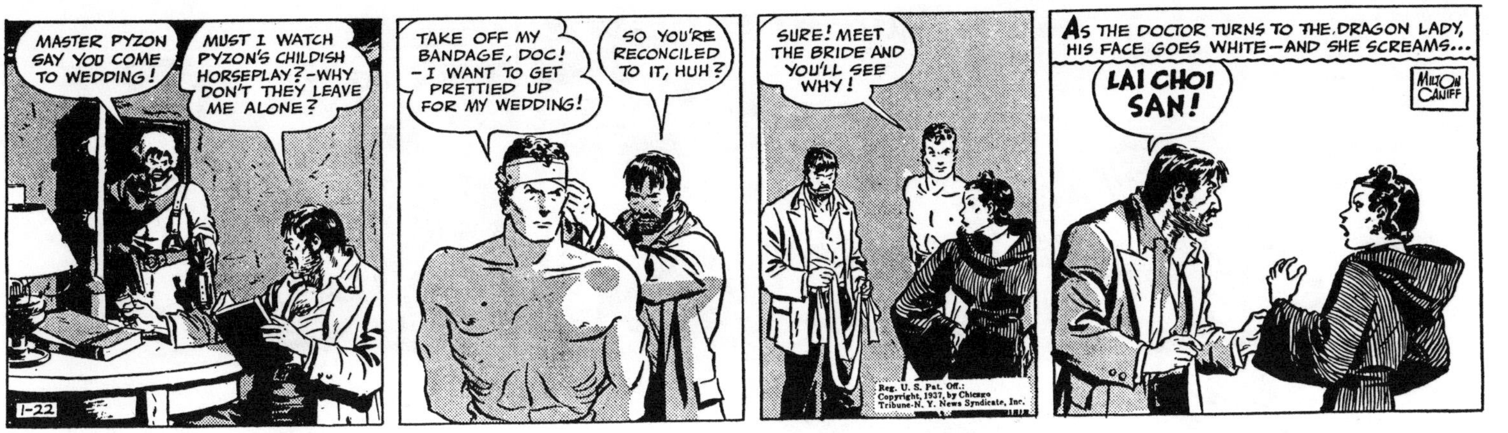
MASTER PYZON SAY YOU COME TO WEDDING!
MUST I WATCH PYZON'S CHILDISH HORSEPLAY? —WHY DON'T THEY LEAVE ME ALONE?
1-22
TAKE OFF MY BANDAGE, DOC! —I WANT TO GET PRETTIED UP FOR MY WEDDING!
SO YOU'RE RECONCILED TO IT, HUH?
SURE! MEET THE BRIDE AND YOU'LL SEE WHY!
Reg. U. S. Pat. Off.: Copyright, 1937, by Chicago Tribune-N. Y. News Syndicate, Inc.
AS THE DOCTOR TURNS TO THE DRAGON LADY, HIS FACE GOES WHITE—AND SHE SCREAMS...
LAI CHOI SAN!
MILTON CANIFF

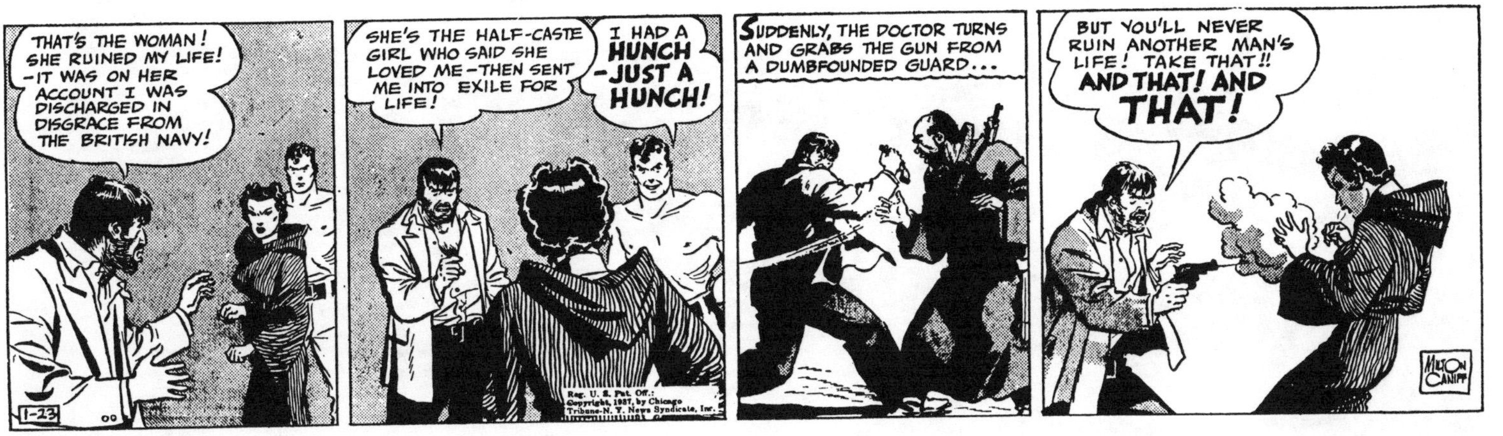
THAT'S THE WOMAN! SHE RUINED MY LIFE! —IT WAS ON HER ACCOUNT I WAS DISCHARGED IN DISGRACE FROM THE BRITISH NAVY!
1-23
SHE'S THE HALF-CASTE GIRL WHO SAID SHE LOVED ME—THEN SENT ME INTO EXILE FOR LIFE!
I HAD A HUNCH —JUST A HUNCH!
Reg. U. S. Pat. Off.: Copyright, 1937, by Chicago Tribune-N. Y. News Syndicate, Inc.
SUDDENLY, THE DOCTOR TURNS AND GRABS THE GUN FROM A DUMBFOUNDED GUARD...
BUT YOU'LL NEVER RUIN ANOTHER MAN'S LIFE! TAKE THAT!! AND THAT! AND THAT!
MILTON CANIFF

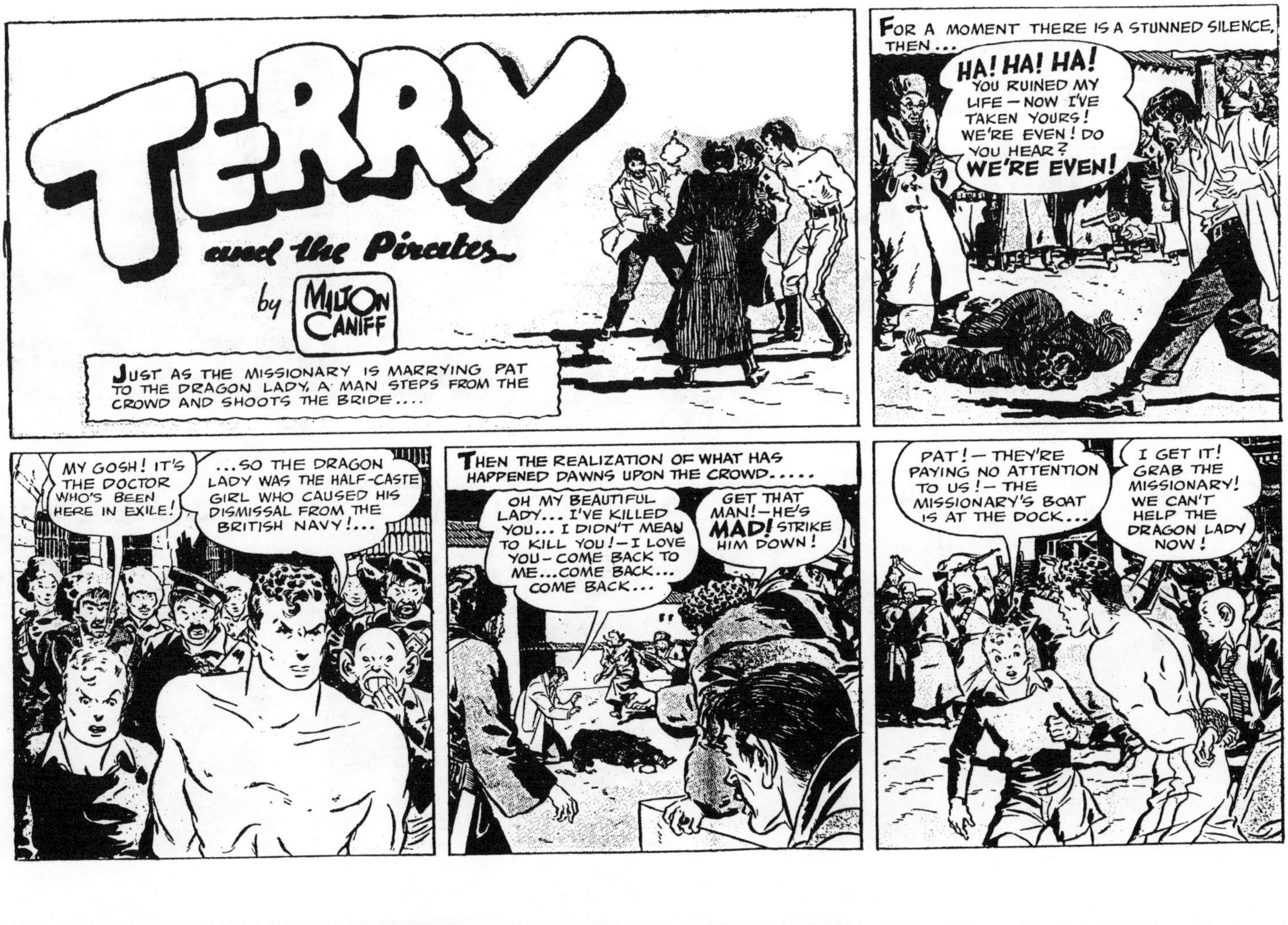
TERRY and the Pirates
by MILTON CANIFF
JUST AS THE MISSIONARY IS MARRYING PAT TO THE DRAGON LADY, A MAN STEPS FROM THE CROWD AND SHOOTS THE BRIDE....
FOR A MOMENT THERE IS A STUNNED SILENCE, THEN...
HA! HA! HA! YOU RUINED MY LIFE—NOW I'VE TAKEN YOURS! WE'RE EVEN! DO YOU HEAR? WE'RE EVEN!
MY GOSH! IT'S THE DOCTOR WHO'S BEEN HERE IN EXILE!
...SO THE DRAGON LADY WAS THE HALF-CASTE GIRL WHO CAUSED HIS DISMISSAL FROM THE BRITISH NAVY!...
THEN THE REALIZATION OF WHAT HAS HAPPENED DAWNS UPON THE CROWD.....
OH MY BEAUTIFUL LADY... I'VE KILLED YOU... I DIDN'T MEAN TO KILL YOU! —I LOVE YOU—COME BACK TO ME...COME BACK... COME BACK...
GET THAT MAN! —HE'S MAD! STRIKE HIM DOWN!
PAT! —THEY'RE PAYING NO ATTENTION TO US! —THE MISSIONARY'S BOAT IS AT THE DOCK...
I GET IT! GRAB THE MISSIONARY! WE CAN'T HELP THE DRAGON LADY NOW!

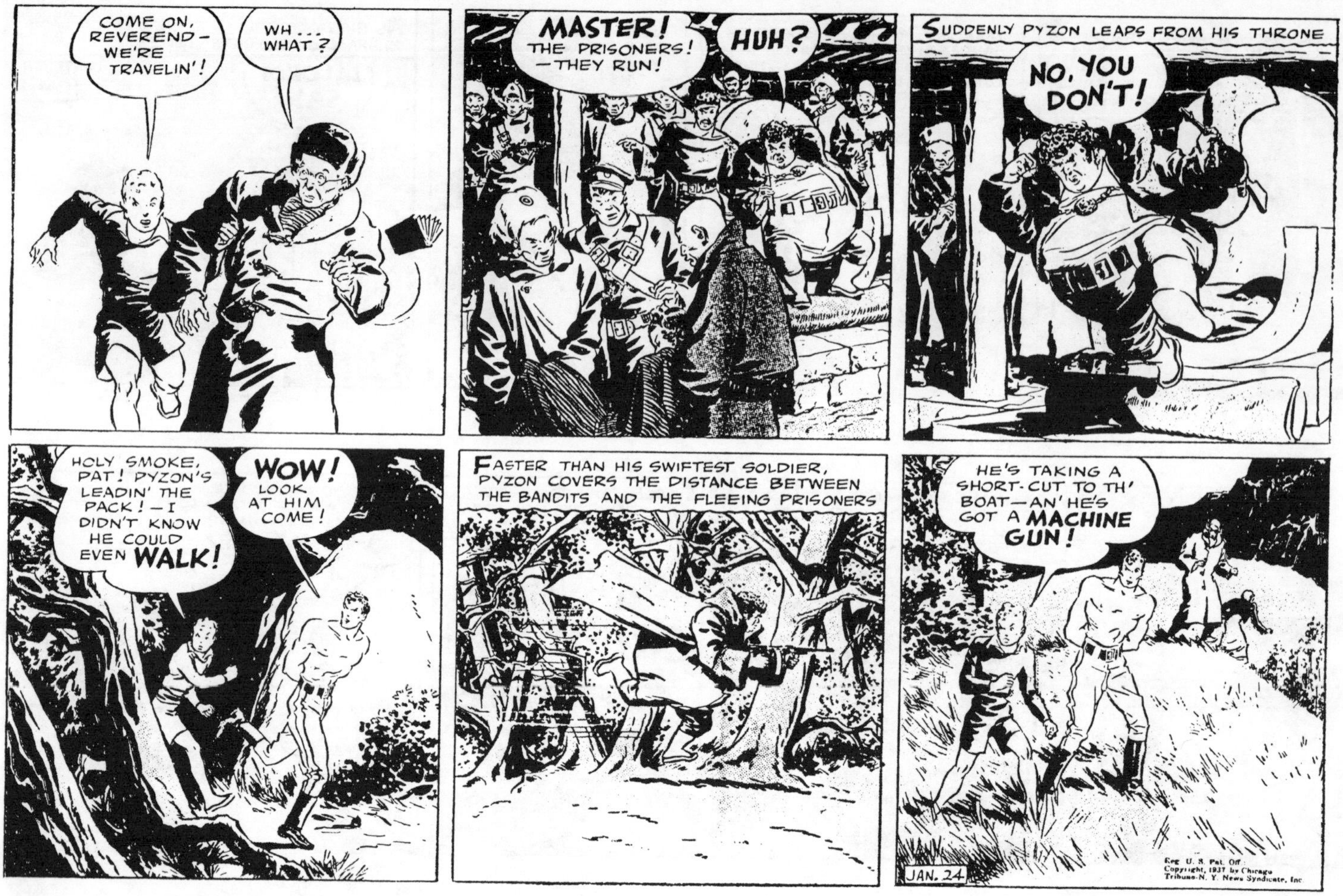
COME ON, REVEREND — WE'RE TRAVELIN'!
WH... WHAT?
MASTER! THE PRISONERS! —THEY RUN!
HUH?
SUDDENLY PYZON LEAPS FROM HIS THRONE
NO, YOU DON'T!
HOLY SMOKE, PAT! PYZON'S LEADIN' THE PACK! — I DIDN'T KNOW HE COULD EVEN WALK!
WOW! LOOK AT HIM COME!
FASTER THAN HIS SWIFTEST SOLDIER, PYZON COVERS THE DISTANCE BETWEEN THE BANDITS AND THE FLEEING PRISONERS
HE'S TAKING A SHORT-CUT TO TH' BOAT—AN' HE'S GOT A MACHINE GUN!
JAN. 24
Reg. U. S. Pat. Off.: Copyright, 1937, by Chicago Tribune-N. Y. News Syndicate, Inc.

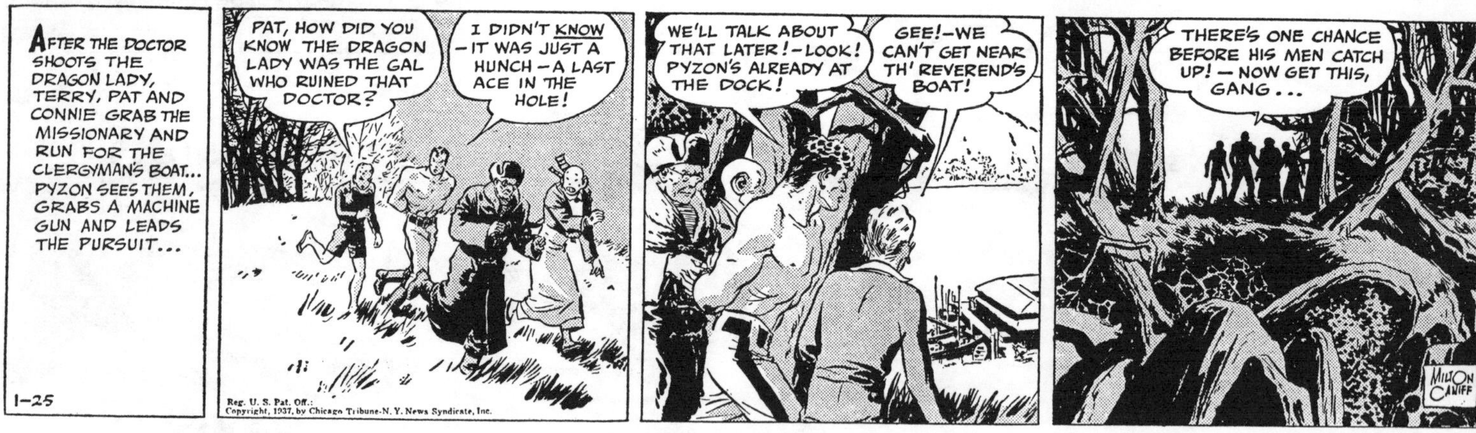
AFTER THE DOCTOR SHOOTS THE DRAGON LADY, TERRY, PAT AND CONNIE GRAB THE MISSIONARY AND RUN FOR THE CLERGYMAN'S BOAT... PYZON SEES THEM, GRABS A MACHINE GUN AND LEADS THE PURSUIT...
1-25
PAT, HOW DID YOU KNOW THE DRAGON LADY WAS THE GAL WHO RUINED THAT DOCTOR?
I DIDN'T KNOW —IT WAS JUST A HUNCH — A LAST ACE IN THE HOLE!
Reg. U. S. Pat. Off.: Copyright, 1937, by Chicago Tribune-N. Y. News Syndicate, Inc.
WE'LL TALK ABOUT THAT LATER! — LOOK! PYZON'S ALREADY AT THE DOCK!
GEE! — WE CAN'T GET NEAR TH' REVEREND'S BOAT!
THERE'S ONE CHANCE BEFORE HIS MEN CATCH UP! — NOW GET THIS, GANG...
MILTON CANIFF

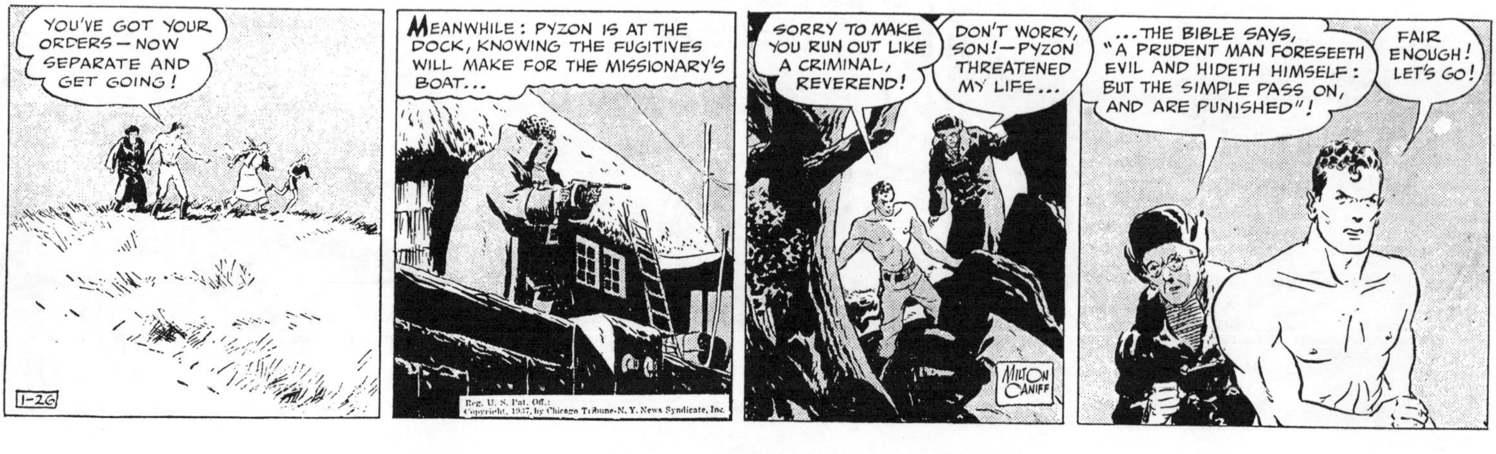
YOU'VE GOT YOUR ORDERS — NOW SEPARATE AND GET GOING!
1-26
MEANWHILE: PYZON IS AT THE DOCK, KNOWING THE FUGITIVES WILL MAKE FOR THE MISSIONARY'S BOAT...
Reg. U. S. Pat. Off.: Copyright, 1937, by Chicago Tribune-N. Y. News Syndicate, Inc.
SORRY TO MAKE YOU RUN OUT LIKE A CRIMINAL, REVEREND!
DON'T WORRY, SON! — PYZON THREATENED MY LIFE...
MILTON CANIFF
... THE BIBLE SAYS, "A PRUDENT MAN FORESEETH EVIL AND HIDETH HIMSELF: BUT THE SIMPLE PASS ON, AND ARE PUNISHED"!
FAIR ENOUGH! LET'S GO!

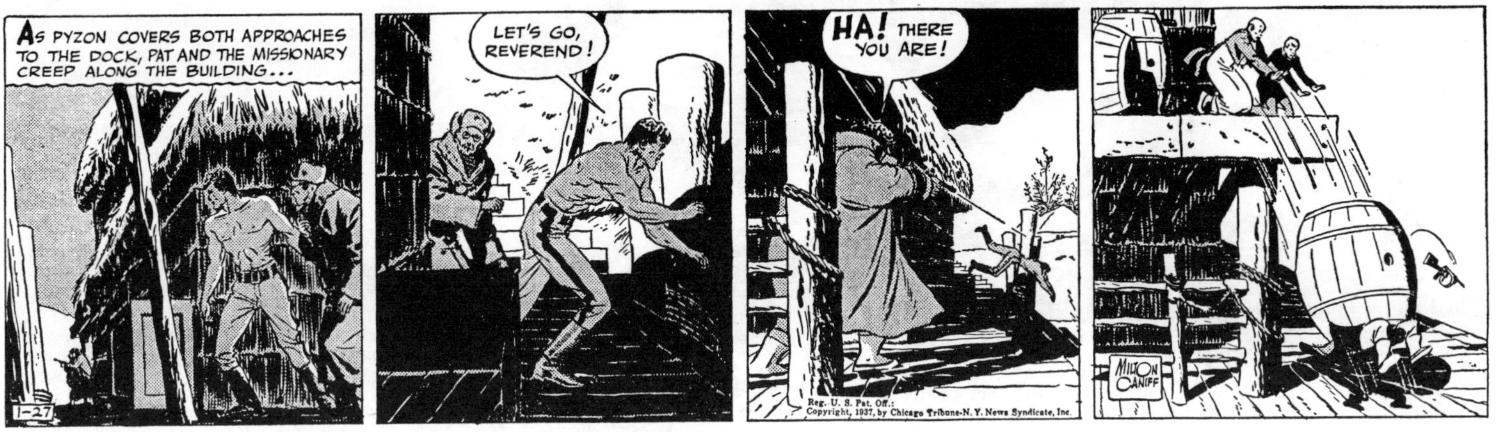

As Pyzon covers both approaches to the dock, Pat and the missionary creep along the building...
1-27
LET'S GO, REVEREND!
HA! THERE YOU ARE!
Reg. U. S. Pat. Off.: Copyright, 1937, by Chicago Tribune-N. Y. News Syndicate, Inc.
MILTON CANIFF

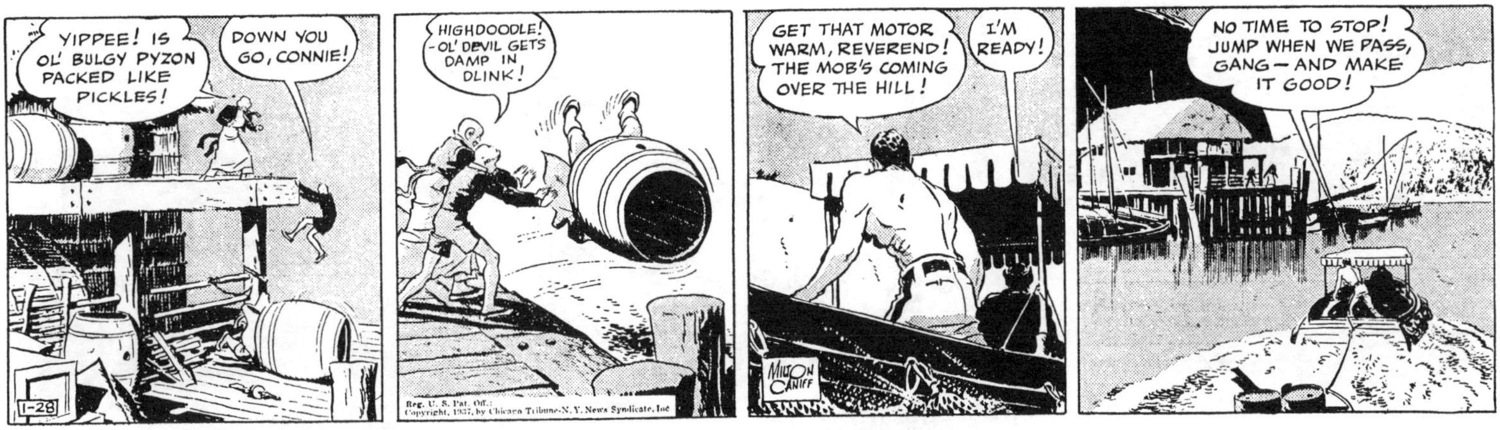

YIPPEE! IS OL' BULGY PYZON PACKED LIKE PICKLES!
DOWN YOU GO, CONNIE!
1-28
HIGHDOODLE! -OL' DEVIL GETS DAMP IN DLINK!
Reg. U. S. Pat. Off.: Copyright, 1937, by Chicago Tribune-N. Y. News Syndicate, Inc.
GET THAT MOTOR WARM, REVEREND! THE MOB'S COMING OVER THE HILL!
I'M READY!
MILTON CANIFF
NO TIME TO STOP! JUMP WHEN WE PASS, GANG — AND MAKE IT GOOD!

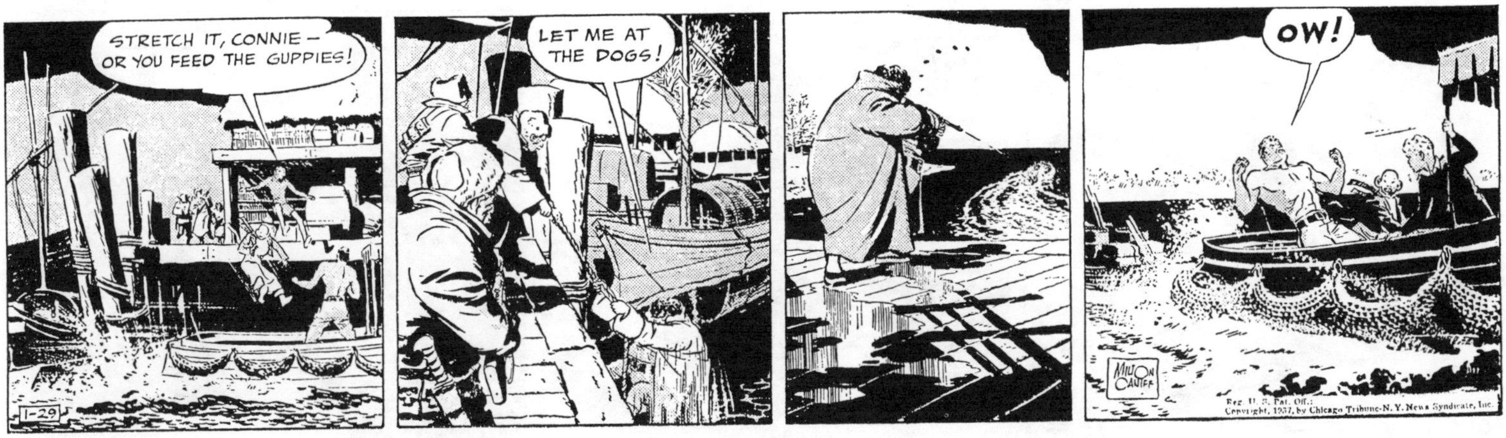

STRETCH IT, CONNIE — OR YOU FEED THE GUPPIES!
1-29
LET ME AT THE DOGS!
OW!
MILTON CANIFF
Reg. U. S. Pat. Off.: Copyright, 1937, by Chicago Tribune-N. Y. News Syndicate, Inc.

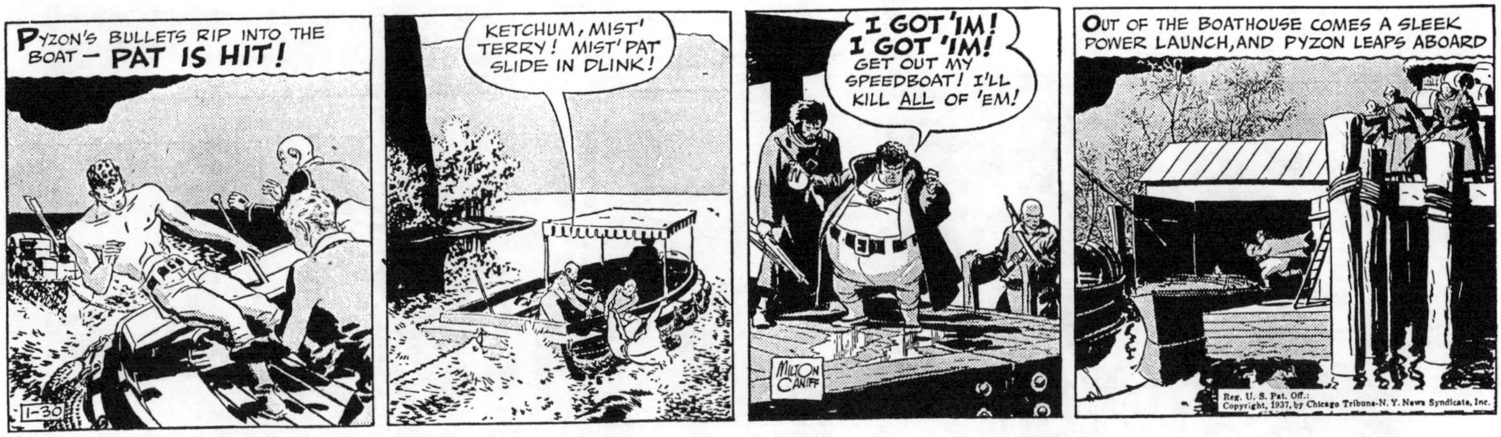

Pyzon's bullets rip into the boat — PAT IS HIT!
1-30
KETCHUM, MIST' TERRY! MIST' PAT SLIDE IN DLINK!
I GOT 'IM! I GOT 'IM! GET OUT MY SPEEDBOAT! I'LL KILL ALL OF 'EM!
MILTON CANIFF
Out of the boathouse comes a sleek power launch, and Pyzon leaps aboard
Reg. U. S. Pat. Off.: Copyright, 1937, by Chicago Tribune-N. Y. News Syndicate, Inc.

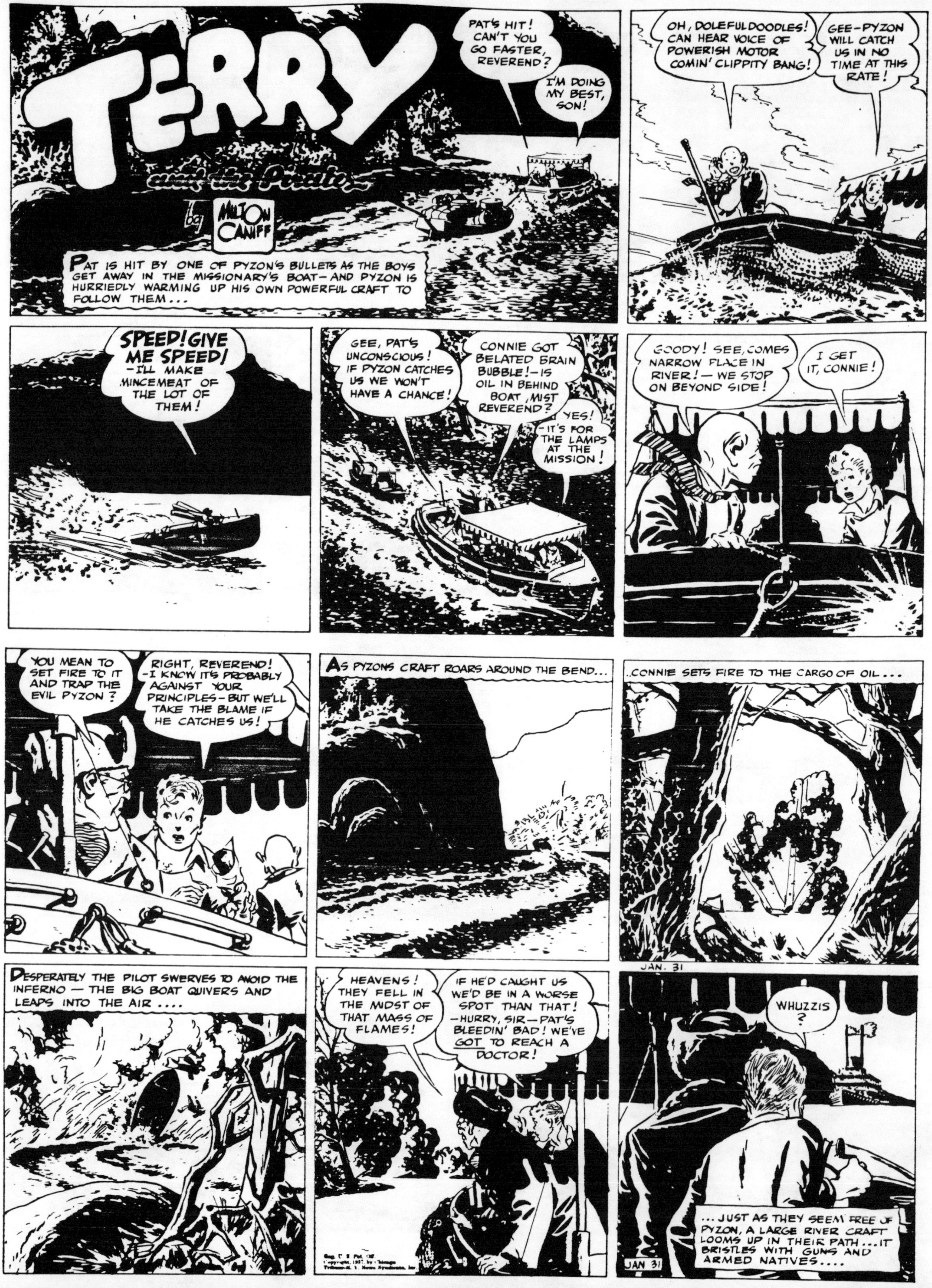
TERRY and the Pirates
by MILTON CANIFF
PAT'S HIT! CAN'T YOU GO FASTER, REVEREND?
I'M DOING MY BEST, SON!
PAT IS HIT BY ONE OF PYZON'S BULLETS AS THE BOYS GET AWAY IN THE MISSIONARY'S BOAT—AND PYZON IS HURRIEDLY WARMING UP HIS OWN POWERFUL CRAFT TO FOLLOW THEM...
OH, DOLEFULDOODLES! CAN HEAR VOICE OF POWERISH MOTOR COMIN' CLIPPITY BANG!
GEE—PYZON WILL CATCH US IN NO TIME AT THIS RATE!
SPEED! GIVE ME SPEED! —I'LL MAKE MINCEMEAT OF THE LOT OF THEM!
GEE, PAT'S UNCONSCIOUS! IF PYZON CATCHES US WE WON'T HAVE A CHANCE!
CONNIE GOT BELATED BRAIN BUBBLE!—IS OIL IN BEHIND BOAT, MIST REVEREND?
YES! —IT'S FOR THE LAMPS AT THE MISSION!
GOODY! SEE, COMES NARROW PLACE IN RIVER!—WE STOP ON BEYOND SIDE!
I GET IT, CONNIE!
YOU MEAN TO SET FIRE TO IT AND TRAP THE EVIL PYZON?
RIGHT, REVEREND! —I KNOW IT'S PROBABLY AGAINST YOUR PRINCIPLES—BUT WE'LL TAKE THE BLAME IF HE CATCHES US!
AS PYZON'S CRAFT ROARS AROUND THE BEND...
..CONNIE SETS FIRE TO THE CARGO OF OIL...
DESPERATELY THE PILOT SWERVES TO AVOID THE INFERNO — THE BIG BOAT QUIVERS AND LEAPS INTO THE AIR....
HEAVENS! THEY FELL IN THE MIDST OF THAT MASS OF FLAMES!
IF HE'D CAUGHT US WE'D BE IN A WORSE SPOT THAN THAT! —HURRY, SIR—PAT'S BLEEDIN' BAD! WE'VE GOT TO REACH A DOCTOR!
JAN. 31
WHUZZIS?
...JUST AS THEY SEEM FREE OF PYZON, A LARGE RIVER CRAFT LOOMS UP IN THEIR PATH...IT BRISTLES WITH GUNS AND ARMED NATIVES....
JAN 31

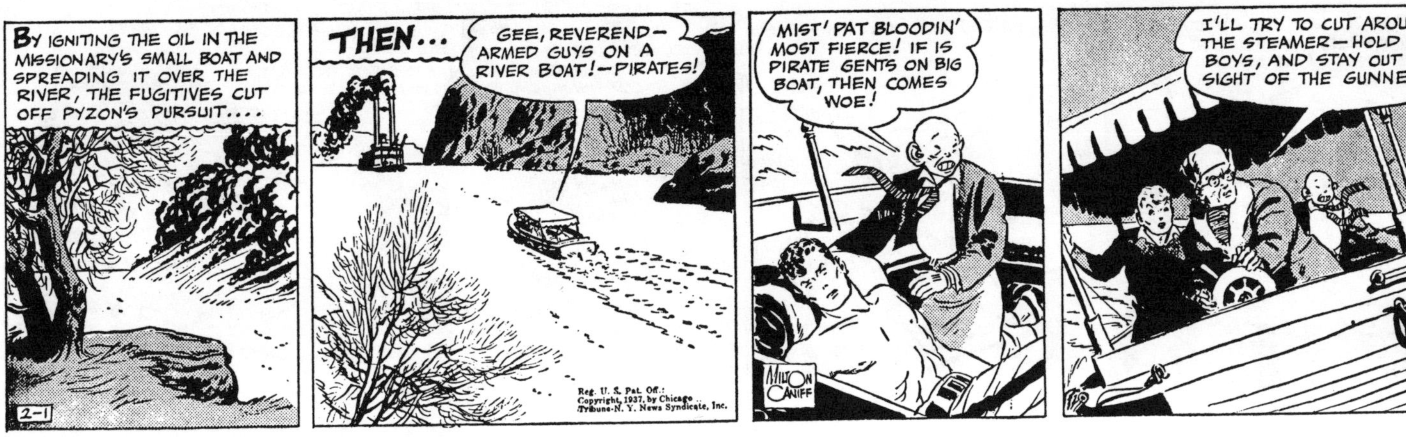
By igniting the oil in the missionary's small boat and spreading it over the river, the fugitives cut off Pyzon's pursuit....
2-1
Then...
Gee, Reverend—armed guys on a river boat!—Pirates!
Reg. U. S. Pat. Off.: Copyright, 1937, by Chicago Tribune-N. Y. News Syndicate, Inc.
Mist' Pat bloodin' most fierce! If is pirate gents on big boat, then comes woe!
Milton Caniff
I'll try to cut around the steamer—hold on, boys, and stay out of sight of the gunners!

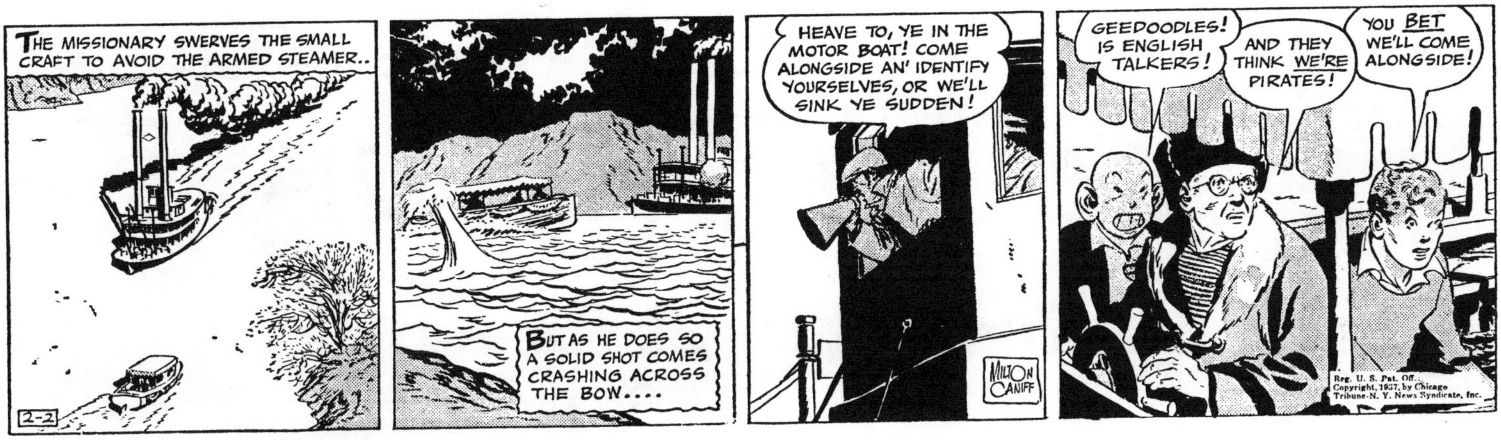
The missionary swerves the small craft to avoid the armed steamer..
2-2
But as he does so a solid shot comes crashing across the bow....
Heave to, ye in the motor boat! Come alongside an' identify yourselves, or we'll sink ye sudden!
Milton Caniff
Geedoodles! Is English talkers!
And they think we're pirates!
You bet we'll come alongside!
Reg. U. S. Pat. Off., Copyright, 1937, by Chicago Tribune-N. Y. News Syndicate, Inc.

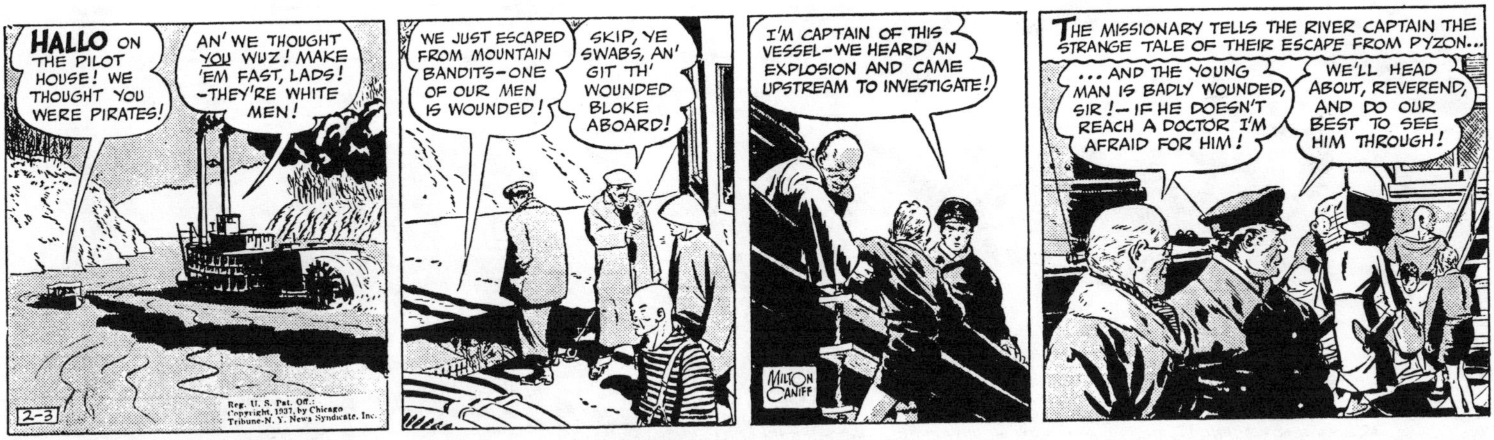
Hallo on the pilot house! We thought you were pirates!
An' we thought you wuz! Make 'em fast, lads! —They're white men!
2-3
Reg. U. S. Pat. Off.: Copyright, 1937, by Chicago Tribune-N. Y. News Syndicate, Inc.
We just escaped from mountain bandits—one of our men is wounded!
Skip, ye swabs, an' git th' wounded bloke aboard!
I'm captain of this vessel—we heard an explosion and came upstream to investigate!
Milton Caniff
The missionary tells the river captain the strange tale of their escape from Pyzon...
...And the young man is badly wounded, sir!—If he doesn't reach a doctor I'm afraid for him!
We'll head about, Reverend, and do our best to see him through!

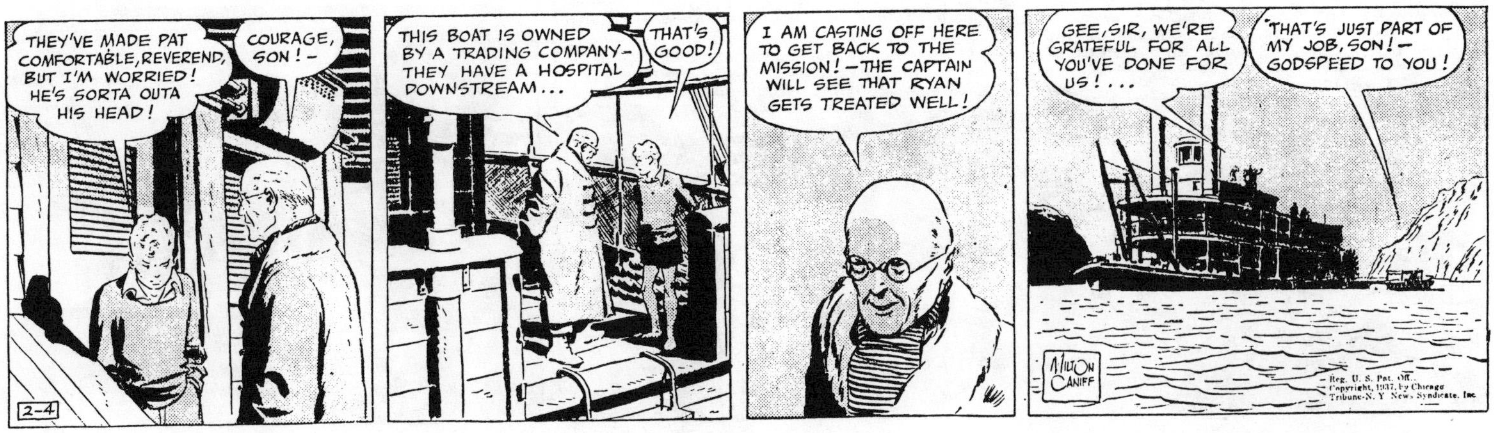
They've made Pat comfortable, Reverend, but I'm worried! He's sorta outa his head!
Courage, son!—
2-4
This boat is owned by a trading company—they have a hospital downstream...
That's good!
I am casting off here to get back to the mission!—The captain will see that Ryan gets treated well!
Gee, sir, we're grateful for all you've done for us!...
That's just part of my job, son!—Godspeed to you!
Milton Caniff
Reg. U. S. Pat. Off., Copyright, 1937, by Chicago Tribune-N. Y. News Syndicate, Inc.

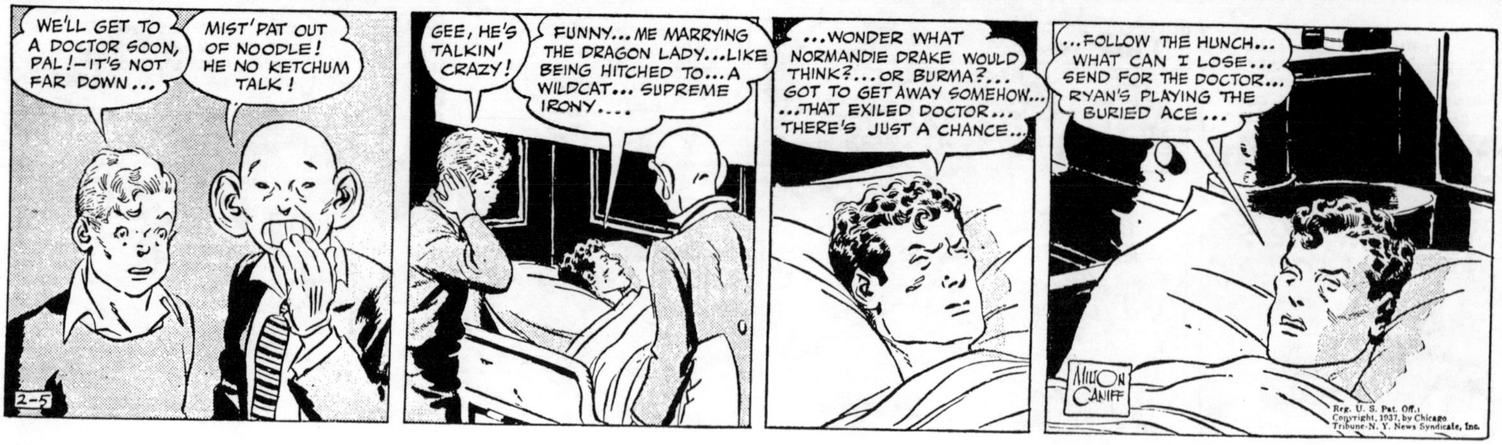
WE'LL GET TO A DOCTOR SOON, PAL! —IT'S NOT FAR DOWN...
MIST' PAT OUT OF NOODLE! HE NO KETCHUM TALK!
2-5
GEE, HE'S TALKIN' CRAZY!
FUNNY... ME MARRYING THE DRAGON LADY... LIKE BEING HITCHED TO... A WILDCAT... SUPREME IRONY....
...WONDER WHAT NORMANDIE DRAKE WOULD THINK?... OR BURMA?... GOT TO GET AWAY SOMEHOW... ...THAT EXILED DOCTOR... THERE'S JUST A CHANCE...
...FOLLOW THE HUNCH... WHAT CAN I LOSE... SEND FOR THE DOCTOR... RYAN'S PLAYING THE BURIED ACE...
MILTON CANIFF
Reg. U. S. Pat. Off.: Copyright, 1937, by Chicago Tribune-N. Y. News Syndicate, Inc.

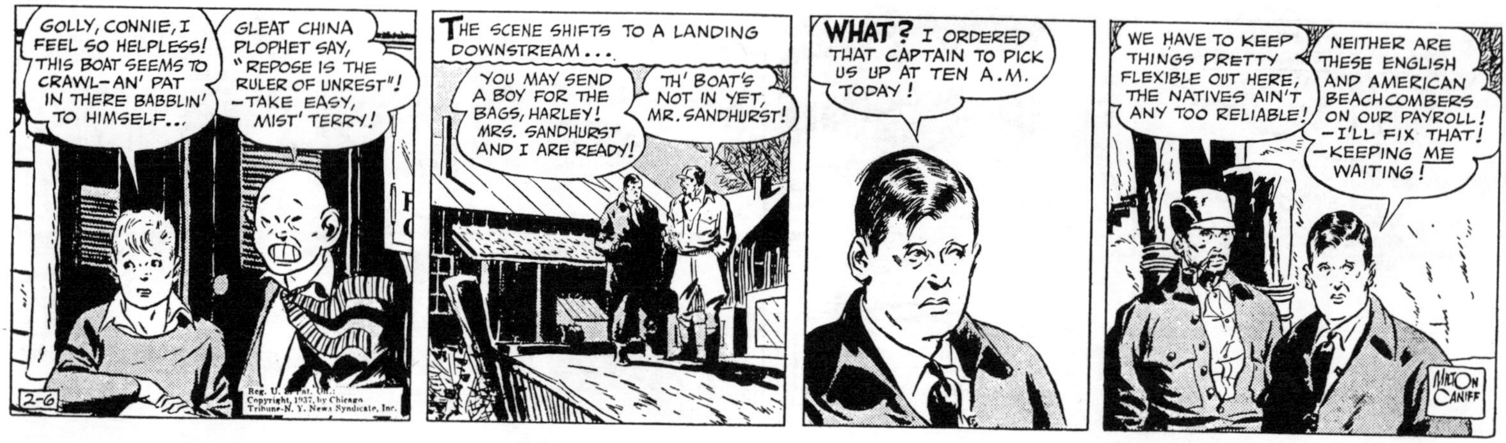
GOLLY, CONNIE, I FEEL SO HELPLESS! THIS BOAT SEEMS TO CRAWL—AN' PAT IN THERE BABBLIN' TO HIMSELF...
GLEAT CHINA PLOPHET SAY, "REPOSE IS THE RULER OF UNREST"! —TAKE EASY, MIST' TERRY!
2-6
Reg. U. S. Pat. Off.: Copyright, 1937, by Chicago Tribune-N. Y. News Syndicate, Inc.
THE SCENE SHIFTS TO A LANDING DOWNSTREAM...
YOU MAY SEND A BOY FOR THE BAGS, HARLEY! MRS. SANDHURST AND I ARE READY!
TH' BOAT'S NOT IN YET, MR. SANDHURST!
WHAT? I ORDERED THAT CAPTAIN TO PICK US UP AT TEN A.M. TODAY!
WE HAVE TO KEEP THINGS PRETTY FLEXIBLE OUT HERE, THE NATIVES AIN'T ANY TOO RELIABLE!
NEITHER ARE THESE ENGLISH AND AMERICAN BEACHCOMBERS ON OUR PAYROLL! —I'LL FIX THAT! —KEEPING ME WAITING!
MILTON CANIFF

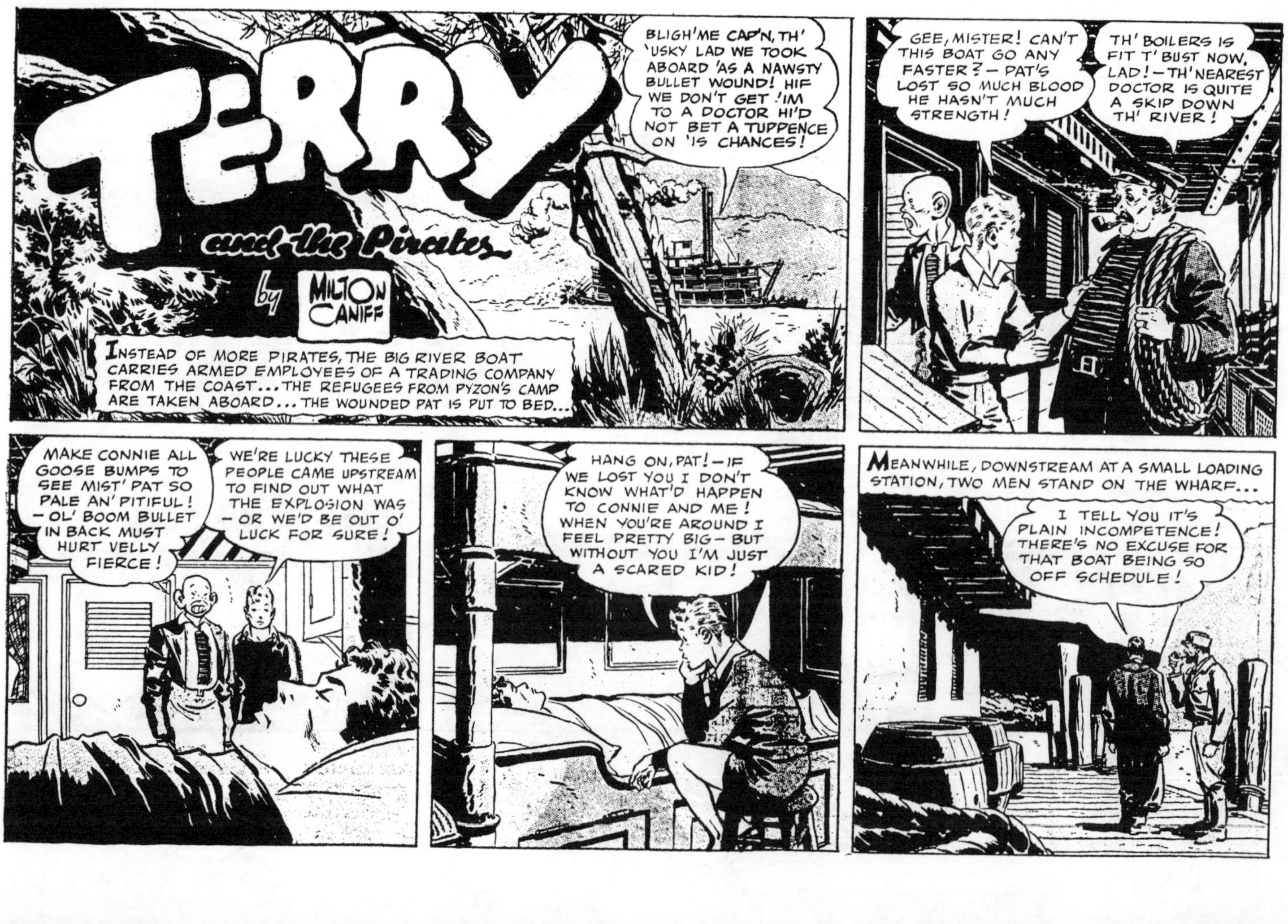
TERRY and the Pirates
by MILTON CANIFF
BLIGH'ME CAP'N, TH' 'USKY LAD WE TOOK ABOARD 'AS A NAWSTY BULLET WOUND! HIF WE DON'T GET 'IM TO A DOCTOR HI'D NOT BET A TUPPENCE ON 'IS CHANCES!
INSTEAD OF MORE PIRATES, THE BIG RIVER BOAT CARRIES ARMED EMPLOYEES OF A TRADING COMPANY FROM THE COAST... THE REFUGEES FROM PYZON'S CAMP ARE TAKEN ABOARD... THE WOUNDED PAT IS PUT TO BED...
GEE, MISTER! CAN'T THIS BOAT GO ANY FASTER? —PAT'S LOST SO MUCH BLOOD HE HASN'T MUCH STRENGTH!
TH' BOILERS IS FIT T' BUST NOW, LAD! —TH' NEAREST DOCTOR IS QUITE A SKIP DOWN TH' RIVER!
MAKE CONNIE ALL GOOSE BUMPS TO SEE MIST' PAT SO PALE AN' PITIFUL! —OL' BOOM BULLET IN BACK MUST HURT VELLY FIERCE!
WE'RE LUCKY THESE PEOPLE CAME UPSTREAM TO FIND OUT WHAT THE EXPLOSION WAS —OR WE'D BE OUT O' LUCK FOR SURE!
HANG ON, PAT! —IF WE LOST YOU I DON'T KNOW WHAT'D HAPPEN TO CONNIE AND ME! WHEN YOU'RE AROUND I FEEL PRETTY BIG— BUT WITHOUT YOU I'M JUST A SCARED KID!
MEANWHILE, DOWNSTREAM AT A SMALL LOADING STATION, TWO MEN STAND ON THE WHARF...
I TELL YOU IT'S PLAIN INCOMPETENCE! THERE'S NO EXCUSE FOR THAT BOAT BEING SO OFF SCHEDULE!

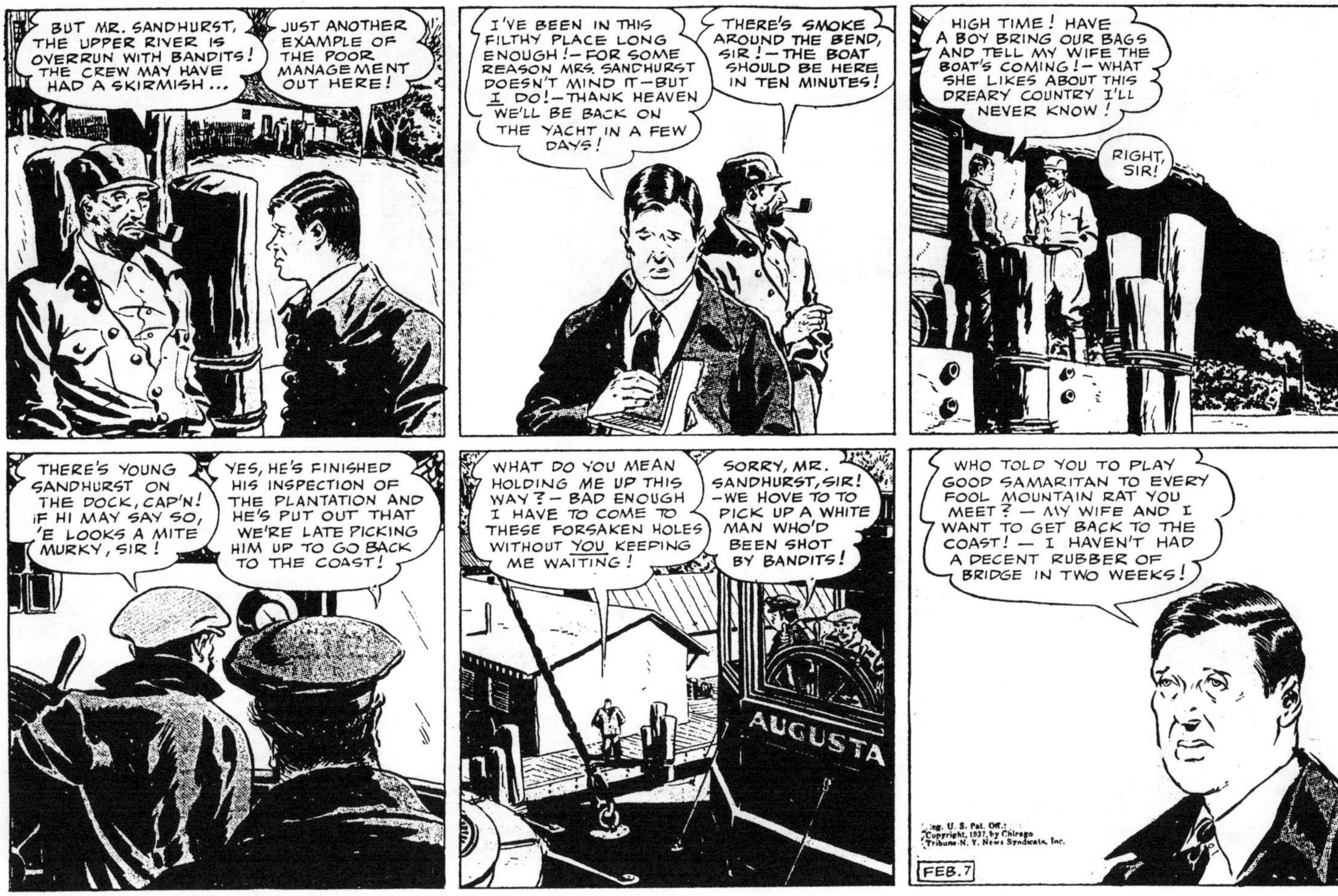

BUT MR. SANDHURST, THE UPPER RIVER IS OVERRUN WITH BANDITS! THE CREW MAY HAVE HAD A SKIRMISH...
JUST ANOTHER EXAMPLE OF THE POOR MANAGEMENT OUT HERE!
I'VE BEEN IN THIS FILTHY PLACE LONG ENOUGH!—FOR SOME REASON MRS. SANDHURST DOESN'T MIND IT—BUT I DO!—THANK HEAVEN WE'LL BE BACK ON THE YACHT IN A FEW DAYS!
THERE'S SMOKE AROUND THE BEND, SIR!—THE BOAT SHOULD BE HERE IN TEN MINUTES!
HIGH TIME! HAVE A BOY BRING OUR BAGS AND TELL MY WIFE THE BOAT'S COMING!—WHAT SHE LIKES ABOUT THIS DREARY COUNTRY I'LL NEVER KNOW!
RIGHT, SIR!
THERE'S YOUNG SANDHURST ON THE DOCK, CAP'N! IF HI MAY SAY SO, 'E LOOKS A MITE MURKY, SIR!
YES, HE'S FINISHED HIS INSPECTION OF THE PLANTATION AND HE'S PUT OUT THAT WE'RE LATE PICKING HIM UP TO GO BACK TO THE COAST!
WHAT DO YOU MEAN HOLDING ME UP THIS WAY?—BAD ENOUGH I HAVE TO COME TO THESE FORSAKEN HOLES WITHOUT YOU KEEPING ME WAITING!
SORRY, MR. SANDHURST, SIR!—WE HOVE TO TO PICK UP A WHITE MAN WHO'D BEEN SHOT BY BANDITS!
AUGUSTA
WHO TOLD YOU TO PLAY GOOD SAMARITAN TO EVERY FOOL MOUNTAIN RAT YOU MEET?—MY WIFE AND I WANT TO GET BACK TO THE COAST!—I HAVEN'T HAD A DECENT RUBBER OF BRIDGE IN TWO WEEKS!
Reg. U. S. Pat. Off.: Copyright, 1937, by Chicago Tribune-N. Y. News Syndicate, Inc.
FEB. 7

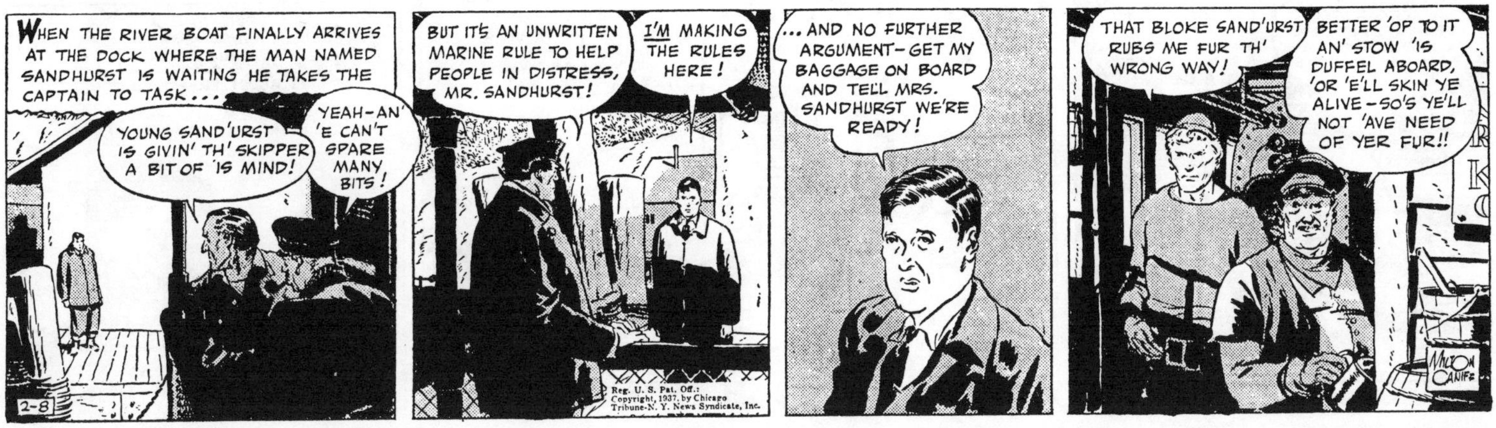

WHEN THE RIVER BOAT FINALLY ARRIVES AT THE DOCK WHERE THE MAN NAMED SANDHURST IS WAITING HE TAKES THE CAPTAIN TO TASK...
YOUNG SAND'URST IS GIVIN' TH' SKIPPER A BIT OF 'IS MIND!
YEAH—AN' 'E CAN'T SPARE MANY BITS!
2-8
BUT IT'S AN UNWRITTEN MARINE RULE TO HELP PEOPLE IN DISTRESS, MR. SANDHURST!
I'M MAKING THE RULES HERE!
Reg. U. S. Pat. Off.: Copyright, 1937, by Chicago Tribune-N. Y. News Syndicate, Inc.
...AND NO FURTHER ARGUMENT—GET MY BAGGAGE ON BOARD AND TELL MRS. SANDHURST WE'RE READY!
THAT BLOKE SAND'URST RUBS ME FUR TH' WRONG WAY!
BETTER 'OP TO IT AN' STOW 'IS DUFFEL ABOARD, 'OR 'E'LL SKIN YE ALIVE—SO'S YE'LL NOT 'AVE NEED OF YER FUR!!
MILTON CANIFF

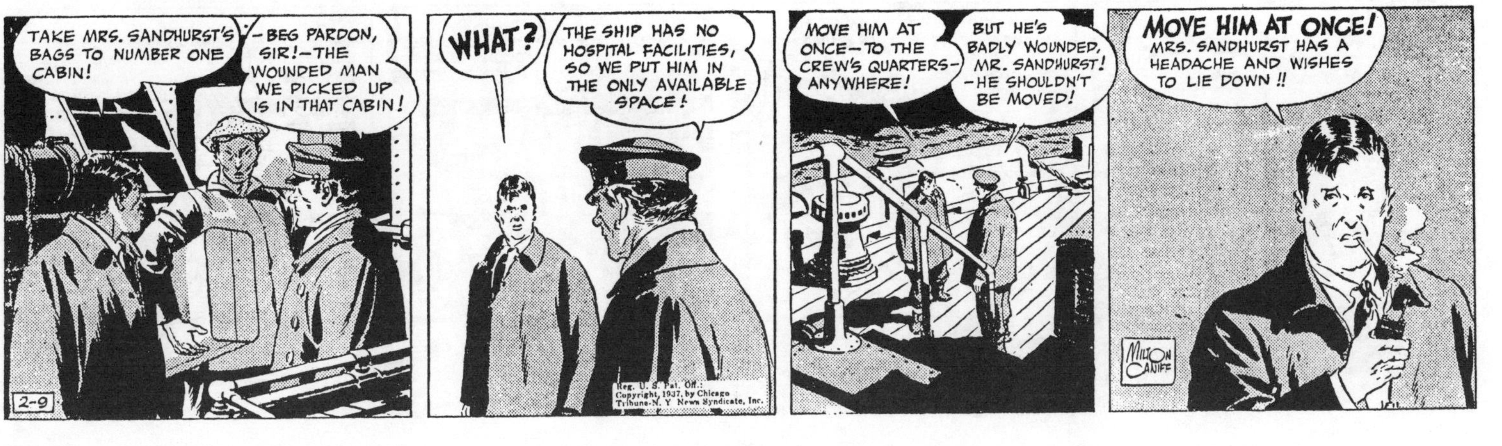

TAKE MRS. SANDHURST'S BAGS TO NUMBER ONE CABIN!
—BEG PARDON, SIR!—THE WOUNDED MAN WE PICKED UP IS IN THAT CABIN!
2-9
WHAT?
THE SHIP HAS NO HOSPITAL FACILITIES, SO WE PUT HIM IN THE ONLY AVAILABLE SPACE!
Reg. U. S. Pat. Off.: Copyright, 1937, by Chicago Tribune-N. Y. News Syndicate, Inc.
MOVE HIM AT ONCE—TO THE CREW'S QUARTERS—ANYWHERE!
BUT HE'S BADLY WOUNDED, MR. SANDHURST!—HE SHOULDN'T BE MOVED!
MILTON CANIFF
MOVE HIM AT ONCE! MRS. SANDHURST HAS A HEADACHE AND WISHES TO LIE DOWN!!

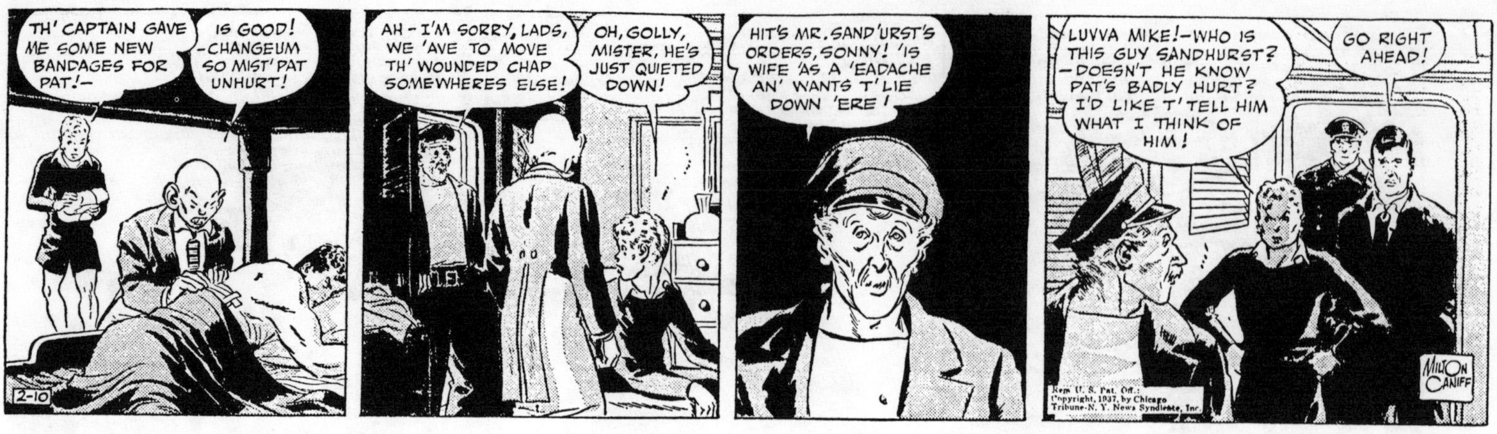
TH' CAPTAIN GAVE ME SOME NEW BANDAGES FOR PAT!—
IS GOOD! —CHANGEUM SO MIST' PAT UNHURT!
2-10
AH – I'M SORRY, LADS, WE 'AVE TO MOVE TH' WOUNDED CHAP SOMEWHERES ELSE!
OH, GOLLY, MISTER, HE'S JUST QUIETED DOWN!
HIT'S MR. SAND'URST'S ORDERS, SONNY! 'IS WIFE 'AS A 'EADACHE AN' WANTS T' LIE DOWN 'ERE!
LUVVA MIKE!—WHO IS THIS GUY SANDHURST? —DOESN'T HE KNOW PAT'S BADLY HURT? I'D LIKE T' TELL HIM WHAT I THINK OF HIM!
GO RIGHT AHEAD!
Reg. U. S. Pat. Off.: Copyright, 1937, by Chicago Tribune-N. Y. News Syndicate, Inc.
MILTON CANIFF

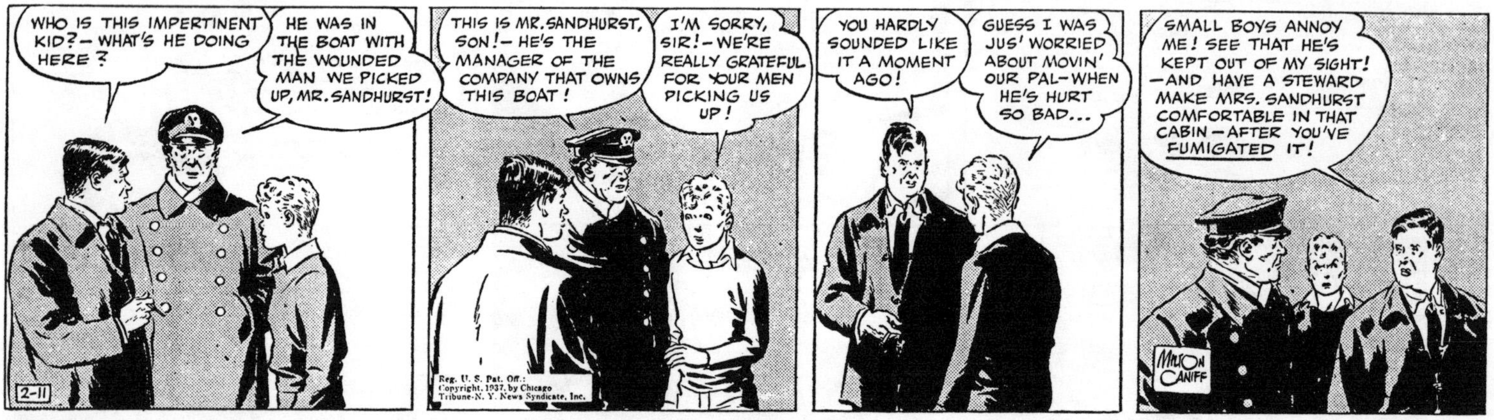
WHO IS THIS IMPERTINENT KID?— WHAT'S HE DOING HERE?
HE WAS IN THE BOAT WITH THE WOUNDED MAN WE PICKED UP, MR. SANDHURST!
2-11
THIS IS MR. SANDHURST, SON!— HE'S THE MANAGER OF THE COMPANY THAT OWNS THIS BOAT!
I'M SORRY, SIR!—WE'RE REALLY GRATEFUL FOR YOUR MEN PICKING US UP!
Reg. U. S. Pat. Off.: Copyright, 1937, by Chicago Tribune-N. Y. News Syndicate, Inc.
YOU HARDLY SOUNDED LIKE IT A MOMENT AGO!
GUESS I WAS JUS' WORRIED ABOUT MOVIN' OUR PAL—WHEN HE'S HURT SO BAD...
SMALL BOYS ANNOY ME! SEE THAT HE'S KEPT OUT OF MY SIGHT! —AND HAVE A STEWARD MAKE MRS. SANDHURST COMFORTABLE IN THAT CABIN—AFTER YOU'VE FUMIGATED IT!
MILTON CANIFF

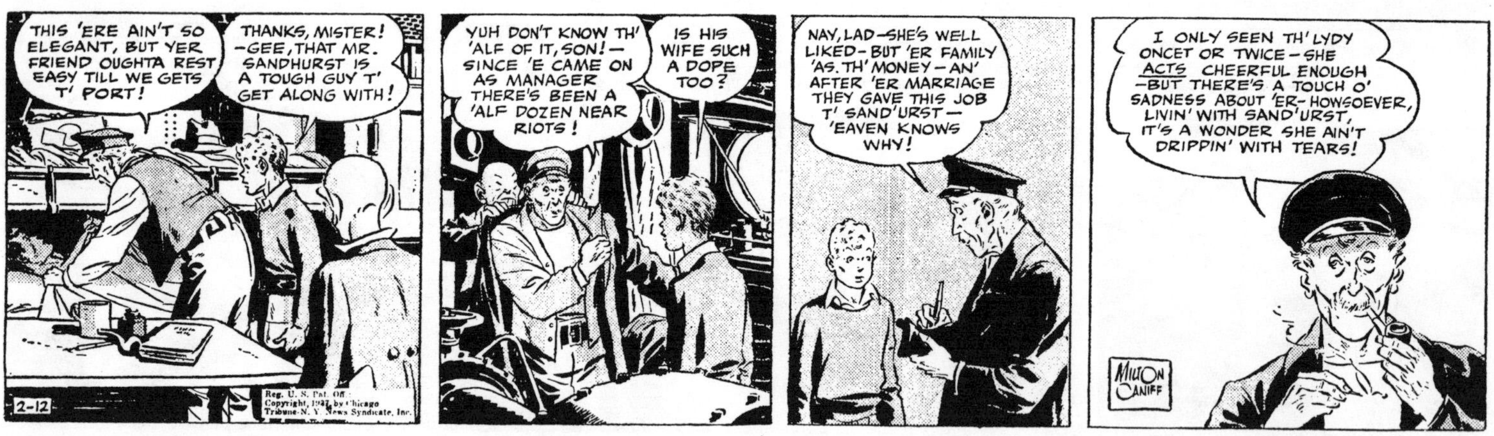
THIS 'ERE AIN'T SO ELEGANT, BUT YER FRIEND OUGHTA REST EASY TILL WE GETS T' PORT!
THANKS, MISTER! —GEE, THAT MR. SANDHURST IS A TOUGH GUY T' GET ALONG WITH!
2-12
Reg. U. S. Pat. Off.: Copyright, 1937, by Chicago Tribune-N. Y. News Syndicate, Inc.
YUH DON'T KNOW TH' 'ALF OF IT, SON!— SINCE 'E CAME ON AS MANAGER THERE'S BEEN A 'ALF DOZEN NEAR RIOTS!
IS HIS WIFE SUCH A DOPE TOO?
NAY, LAD—SHE'S WELL LIKED—BUT 'ER FAMILY 'AS TH' MONEY—AN' AFTER 'ER MARRIAGE THEY GAVE THIS JOB T' SAND'URST— 'EAVEN KNOWS WHY!
I ONLY SEEN TH' LYDY ONCET OR TWICE—SHE ACTS CHEERFUL ENOUGH —BUT THERE'S A TOUCH O' SADNESS ABOUT 'ER—HOWSOEVER, LIVIN' WITH SAND'URST, IT'S A WONDER SHE AIN'T DRIPPIN' WITH TEARS!
MILTON CANIFF

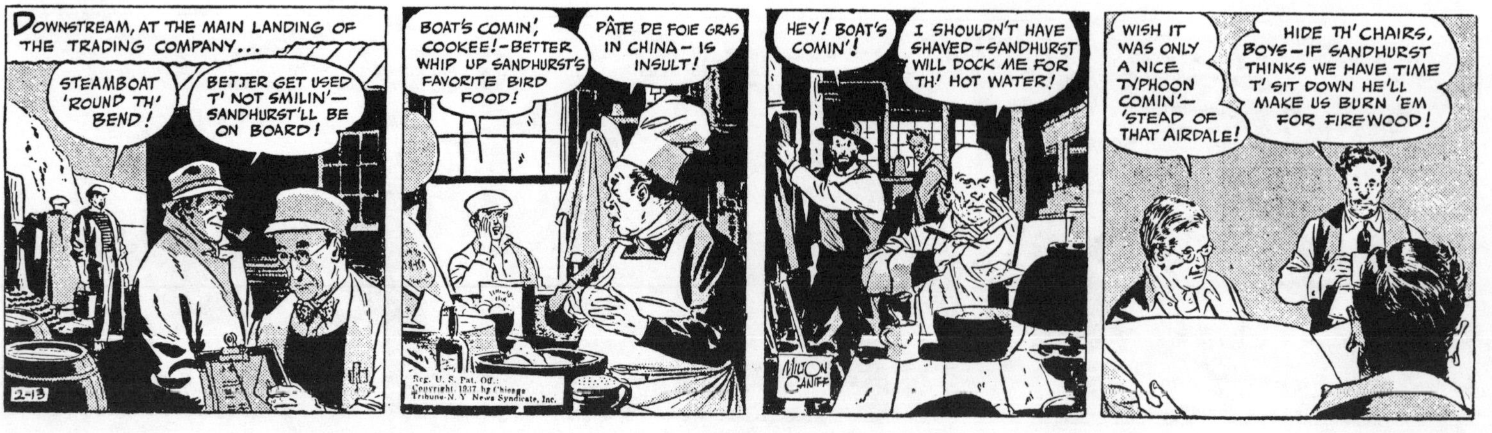
DOWNSTREAM, AT THE MAIN LANDING OF THE TRADING COMPANY...
STEAMBOAT 'ROUND TH' BEND!
BETTER GET USED T' NOT SMILIN'— SANDHURST'LL BE ON BOARD!
2-13
BOAT'S COMIN', COOKEE!—BETTER WHIP UP SANDHURST'S FAVORITE BIRD FOOD!
PÂTE DE FOIE GRAS IN CHINA—IS INSULT!
Reg. U. S. Pat. Off.: Copyright, 1937 by Chicago Tribune-N. Y. News Syndicate, Inc.
HEY! BOAT'S COMIN'!
I SHOULDN'T HAVE SHAVED—SANDHURST WILL DOCK ME FOR TH' HOT WATER!
MILTON CANIFF
WISH IT WAS ONLY A NICE TYPHOON COMIN'— 'STEAD OF THAT AIRDALE!
HIDE TH' CHAIRS, BOYS—IF SANDHURST THINKS WE HAVE TIME T' SIT DOWN HE'LL MAKE US BURN 'EM FOR FIREWOOD!

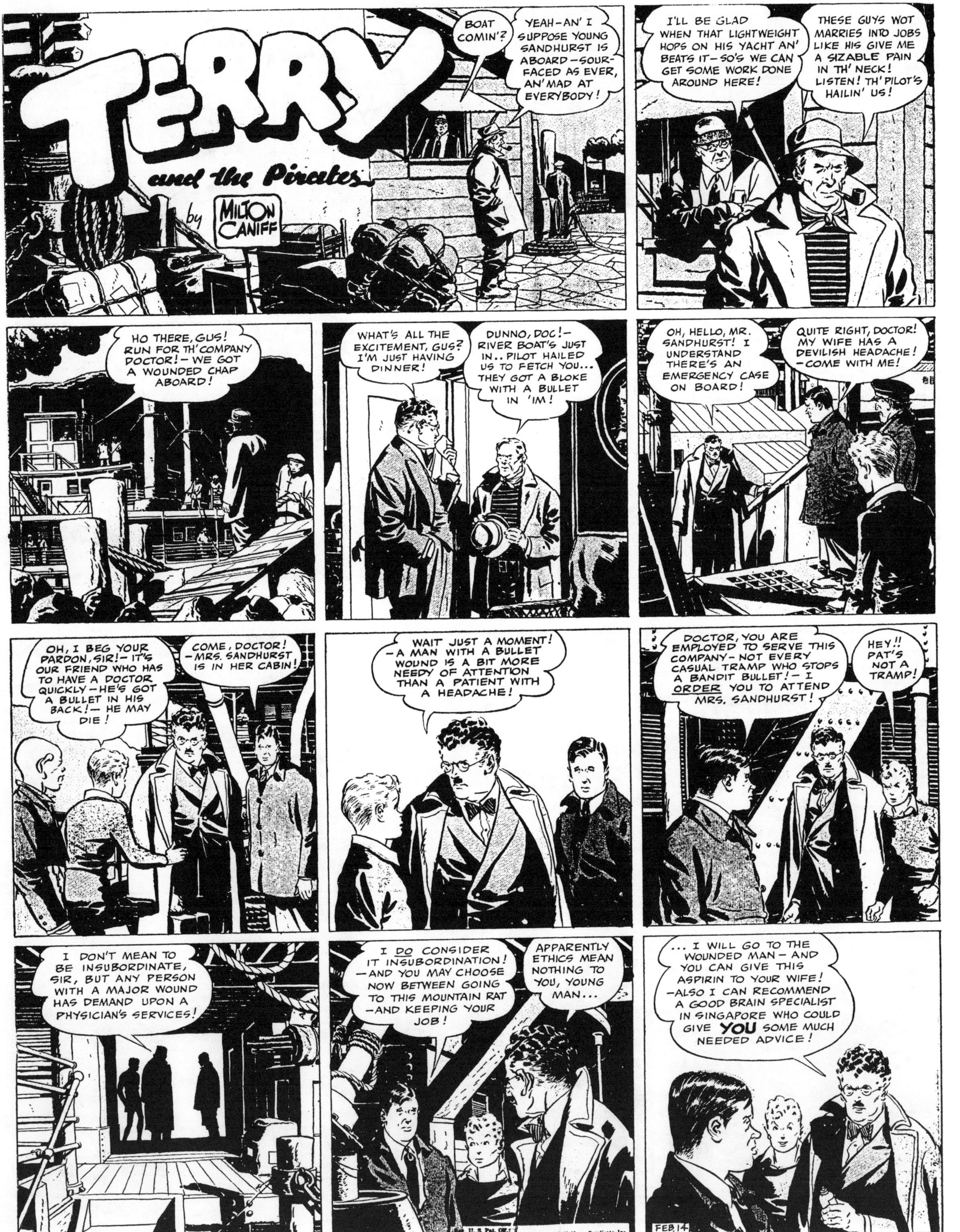
Terry and the Pirates
by Milton Caniff
BOAT COMIN'?
YEAH-AN' I SUPPOSE YOUNG SANDHURST IS ABOARD-SOUR-FACED AS EVER, AN' MAD AT EVERYBODY!
I'LL BE GLAD WHEN THAT LIGHTWEIGHT HOPS ON HIS YACHT AN' BEATS IT-SO'S WE CAN GET SOME WORK DONE AROUND HERE!
THESE GUYS WOT MARRIES INTO JOBS LIKE HIS GIVE ME A SIZABLE PAIN IN TH' NECK! LISTEN! TH' PILOT'S HAILIN' US!
HO THERE, GUS! RUN FOR TH' COMPANY DOCTOR!-WE GOT A WOUNDED CHAP ABOARD!
WHAT'S ALL THE EXCITEMENT, GUS? I'M JUST HAVING DINNER!
DUNNO, DOC!-RIVER BOAT'S JUST IN.. PILOT HAILED US TO FETCH YOU... THEY GOT A BLOKE WITH A BULLET IN 'IM!
OH, HELLO, MR. SANDHURST! I UNDERSTAND THERE'S AN EMERGENCY CASE ON BOARD!
QUITE RIGHT, DOCTOR! MY WIFE HAS A DEVILISH HEADACHE! -COME WITH ME!
OH, I BEG YOUR PARDON, SIR!-IT'S OUR FRIEND WHO HAS TO HAVE A DOCTOR QUICKLY-HE'S GOT A BULLET IN HIS BACK!-HE MAY DIE!
COME, DOCTOR! -MRS. SANDHURST IS IN HER CABIN!
WAIT JUST A MOMENT! -A MAN WITH A BULLET WOUND IS A BIT MORE NEEDY OF ATTENTION THAN A PATIENT WITH A HEADACHE!
DOCTOR, YOU ARE EMPLOYED TO SERVE THIS COMPANY-NOT EVERY CASUAL TRAMP WHO STOPS A BANDIT BULLET!-I ORDER YOU TO ATTEND MRS. SANDHURST!
HEY!! PAT'S NOT A TRAMP!
I DON'T MEAN TO BE INSUBORDINATE, SIR, BUT ANY PERSON WITH A MAJOR WOUND HAS DEMAND UPON A PHYSICIAN'S SERVICES!
I DO CONSIDER IT INSUBORDINATION! -AND YOU MAY CHOOSE NOW BETWEEN GOING TO THIS MOUNTAIN RAT -AND KEEPING YOUR JOB!
APPARENTLY ETHICS MEAN NOTHING TO YOU, YOUNG MAN...
... I WILL GO TO THE WOUNDED MAN-AND YOU CAN GIVE THIS ASPIRIN TO YOUR WIFE! -ALSO I CAN RECOMMEND A GOOD BRAIN SPECIALIST IN SINGAPORE WHO COULD GIVE YOU SOME MUCH NEEDED ADVICE!
Reg. U. S. Pat. Off.:
Copyright 1937 by Chicago Tribune-N. Y. News Syndicate, Inc.
FEB. 14

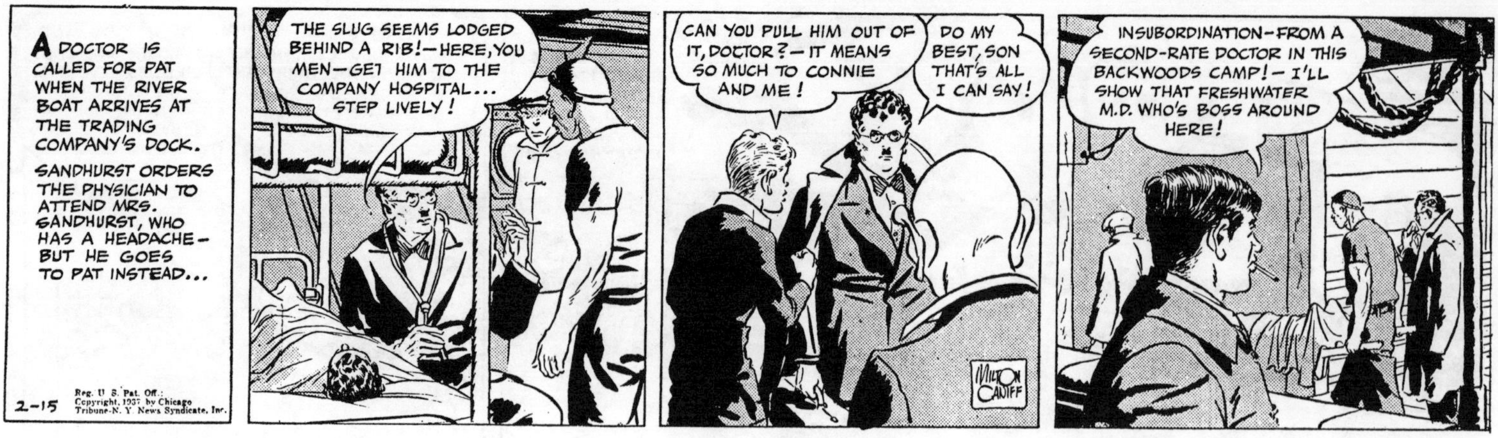
A DOCTOR IS CALLED FOR PAT WHEN THE RIVER BOAT ARRIVES AT THE TRADING COMPANY'S DOCK.
SANDHURST ORDERS THE PHYSICIAN TO ATTEND MRS. SANDHURST, WHO HAS A HEADACHE- BUT HE GOES TO PAT INSTEAD...
2-15
Reg. U. S. Pat. Off.: Copyright, 1937, by Chicago Tribune-N. Y. News Syndicate, Inc.
THE SLUG SEEMS LODGED BEHIND A RIB! — HERE, YOU MEN — GET HIM TO THE COMPANY HOSPITAL... STEP LIVELY!
CAN YOU PULL HIM OUT OF IT, DOCTOR? — IT MEANS SO MUCH TO CONNIE AND ME!
DO MY BEST, SON THAT'S ALL I CAN SAY!
MILTON CANIFF
INSUBORDINATION — FROM A SECOND-RATE DOCTOR IN THIS BACKWOODS CAMP! — I'LL SHOW THAT FRESHWATER M.D. WHO'S BOSS AROUND HERE!

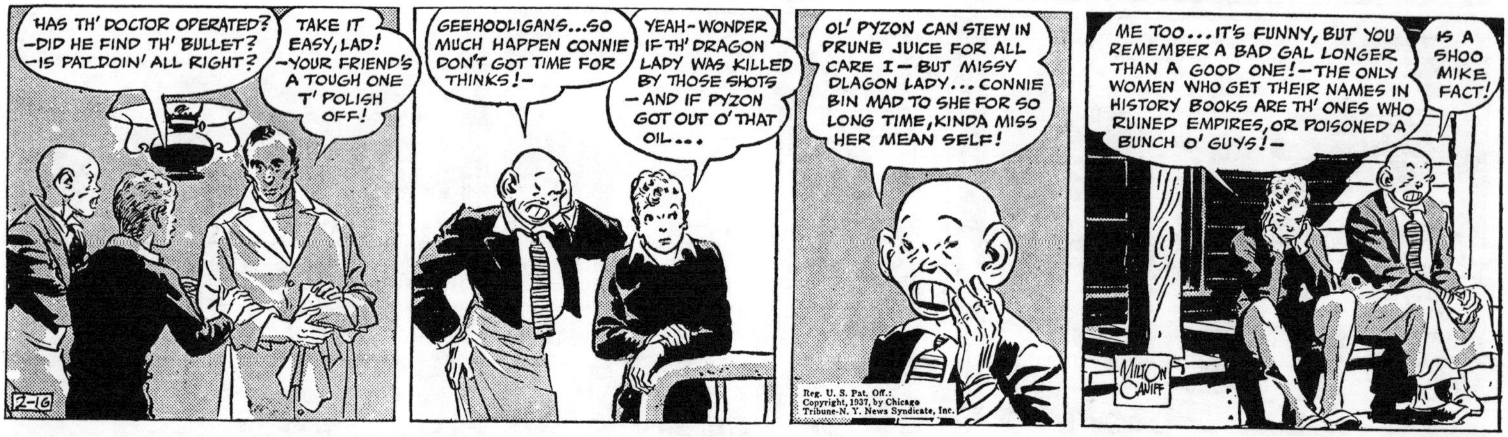
HAS TH' DOCTOR OPERATED? — DID HE FIND TH' BULLET? — IS PAT DOIN' ALL RIGHT?
TAKE IT EASY, LAD! — YOUR FRIEND'S A TOUGH ONE T' POLISH OFF!
2-16
GEEHOOLIGANS... SO MUCH HAPPEN CONNIE DON'T GOT TIME FOR THINKS! —
YEAH — WONDER IF TH' DRAGON LADY WAS KILLED BY THOSE SHOTS — AND IF PYZON GOT OUT O' THAT OIL...
OL' PYZON CAN STEW IN PRUNE JUICE FOR ALL CARE I — BUT MISSY DLAGON LADY... CONNIE BIN MAD TO SHE FOR SO LONG TIME, KINDA MISS HER MEAN SELF!
Reg. U. S. Pat. Off.: Copyright, 1937, by Chicago Tribune-N. Y. News Syndicate, Inc.
ME TOO... IT'S FUNNY, BUT YOU REMEMBER A BAD GAL LONGER THAN A GOOD ONE! — THE ONLY WOMEN WHO GET THEIR NAMES IN HISTORY BOOKS ARE TH' ONES WHO RUINED EMPIRES, OR POISONED A BUNCH O' GUYS! —
IS A SHOO MIKE FACT!
MILTON CANIFF

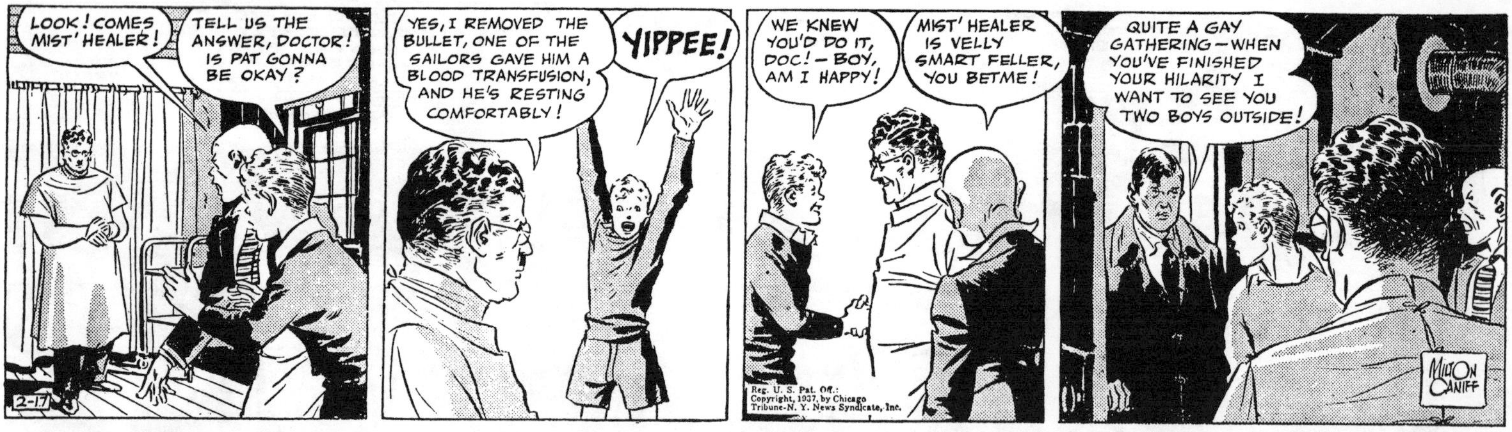
LOOK! COMES MIST' HEALER!
TELL US THE ANSWER, DOCTOR! IS PAT GONNA BE OKAY?
2-17
YES, I REMOVED THE BULLET, ONE OF THE SAILORS GAVE HIM A BLOOD TRANSFUSION, AND HE'S RESTING COMFORTABLY!
YIPPEE!
WE KNEW YOU'D DO IT, DOC! — BOY, AM I HAPPY!
MIST' HEALER IS VELLY SMART FELLER, YOU BETME!
Reg. U. S. Pat. Off.: Copyright, 1937, by Chicago Tribune-N. Y. News Syndicate, Inc.
QUITE A GAY GATHERING — WHEN YOU'VE FINISHED YOUR HILARITY I WANT TO SEE YOU TWO BOYS OUTSIDE!
MILTON CANIFF

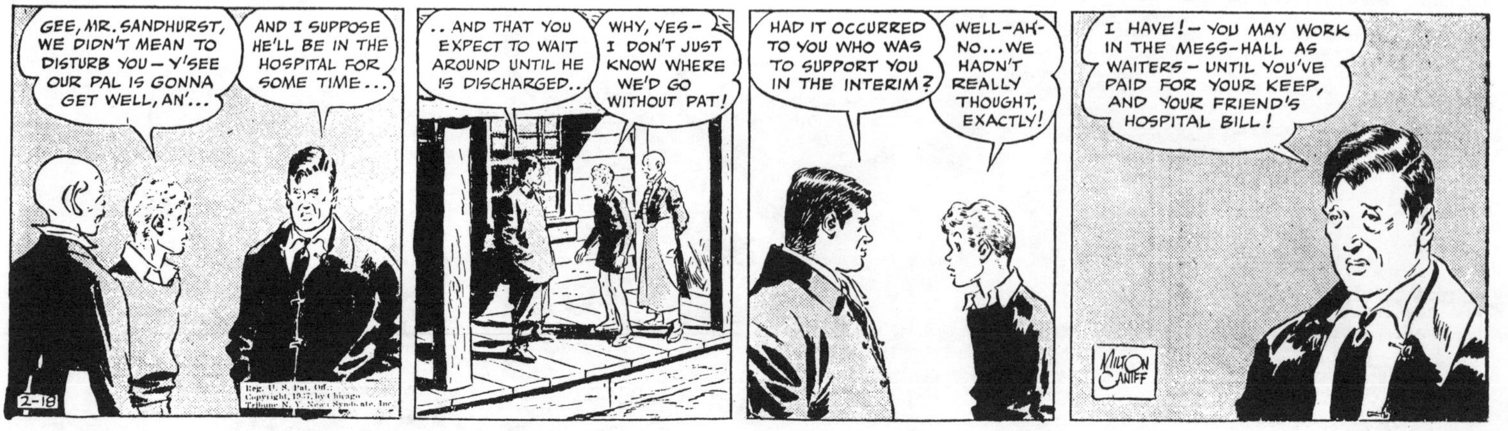
GEE, MR. SANDHURST, WE DIDN'T MEAN TO DISTURB YOU — Y'SEE OUR PAL IS GONNA GET WELL, AN'...
AND I SUPPOSE HE'LL BE IN THE HOSPITAL FOR SOME TIME...
2-18
.. AND THAT YOU EXPECT TO WAIT AROUND UNTIL HE IS DISCHARGED..
WHY, YES — I DON'T JUST KNOW WHERE WE'D GO WITHOUT PAT!
Reg. U. S. Pat. Off.: Copyright, 1937, by Chicago Tribune-N. Y. News Syndicate, Inc.
HAD IT OCCURRED TO YOU WHO WAS TO SUPPORT YOU IN THE INTERIM?
WELL — AH — NO... WE HADN'T REALLY THOUGHT, EXACTLY!
MILTON CANIFF
I HAVE! — YOU MAY WORK IN THE MESS-HALL AS WAITERS — UNTIL YOU'VE PAID FOR YOUR KEEP, AND YOUR FRIEND'S HOSPITAL BILL!

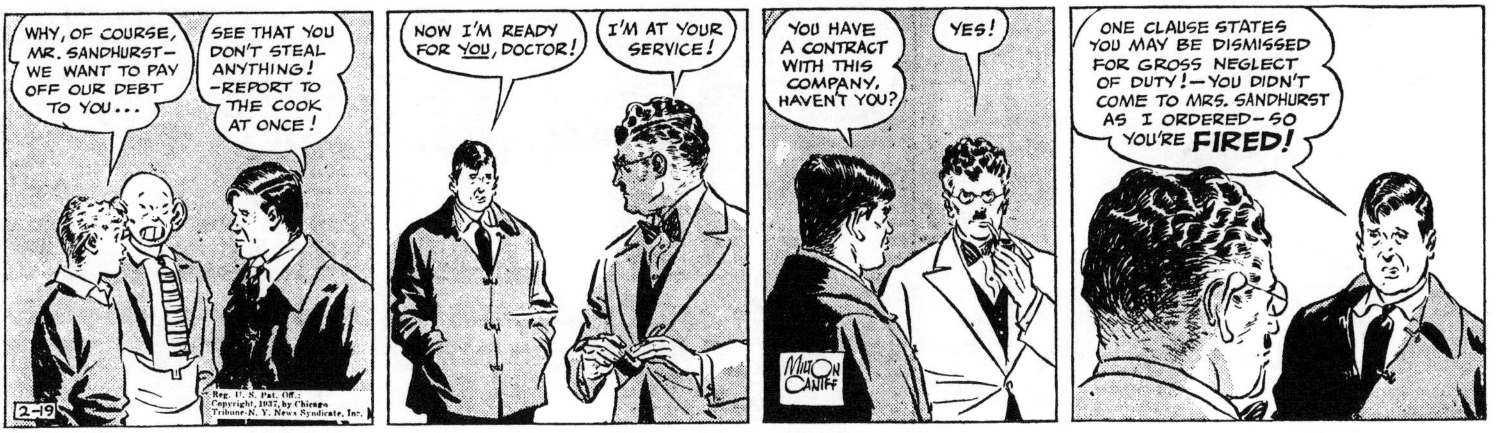
WHY, OF COURSE, MR. SANDHURST– WE WANT TO PAY OFF OUR DEBT TO YOU...
SEE THAT YOU DON'T STEAL ANYTHING! –REPORT TO THE COOK AT ONCE!
2-19
Reg. U. S. Pat. Off.: Copyright, 1937, by Chicago Tribune-N. Y. News Syndicate, Inc.
NOW I'M READY FOR YOU, DOCTOR!
I'M AT YOUR SERVICE!
YOU HAVE A CONTRACT WITH THIS COMPANY, HAVEN'T YOU?
YES!
MILTON CANIFF
ONE CLAUSE STATES YOU MAY BE DISMISSED FOR GROSS NEGLECT OF DUTY!—YOU DIDN'T COME TO MRS. SANDHURST AS I ORDERED–SO YOU'RE FIRED!

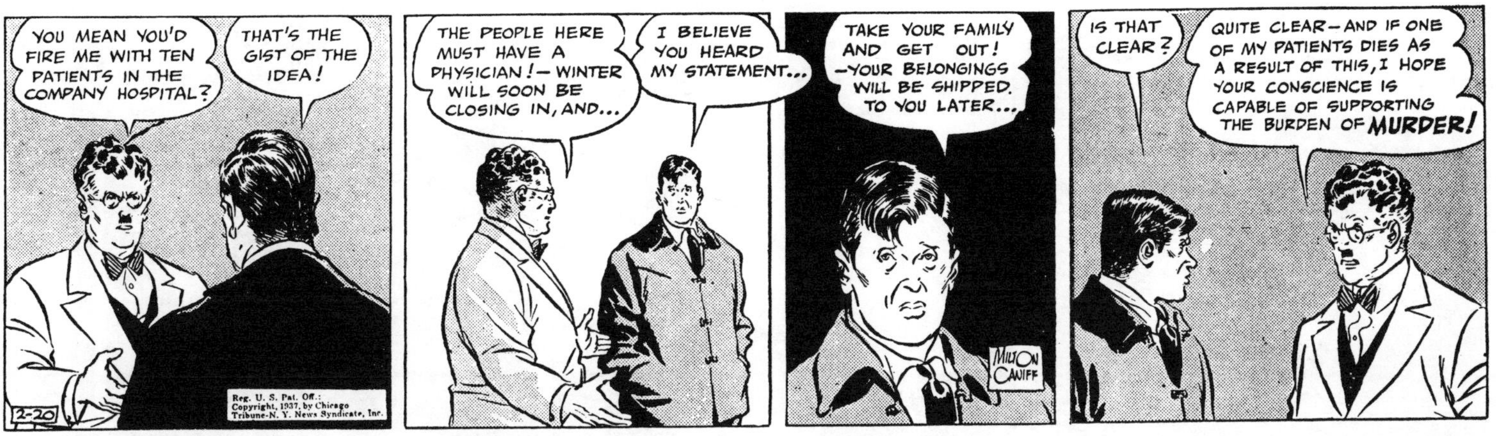
YOU MEAN YOU'D FIRE ME WITH TEN PATIENTS IN THE COMPANY HOSPITAL?
THAT'S THE GIST OF THE IDEA!
2-20
Reg. U. S. Pat. Off.: Copyright, 1937, by Chicago Tribune-N. Y. News Syndicate, Inc.
THE PEOPLE HERE MUST HAVE A PHYSICIAN!—WINTER WILL SOON BE CLOSING IN, AND...
I BELIEVE YOU HEARD MY STATEMENT...
TAKE YOUR FAMILY AND GET OUT! –YOUR BELONGINGS WILL BE SHIPPED TO YOU LATER...
MILTON CANIFF
IS THAT CLEAR?
QUITE CLEAR—AND IF ONE OF MY PATIENTS DIES AS A RESULT OF THIS, I HOPE YOUR CONSCIENCE IS CAPABLE OF SUPPORTING THE BURDEN OF MURDER!

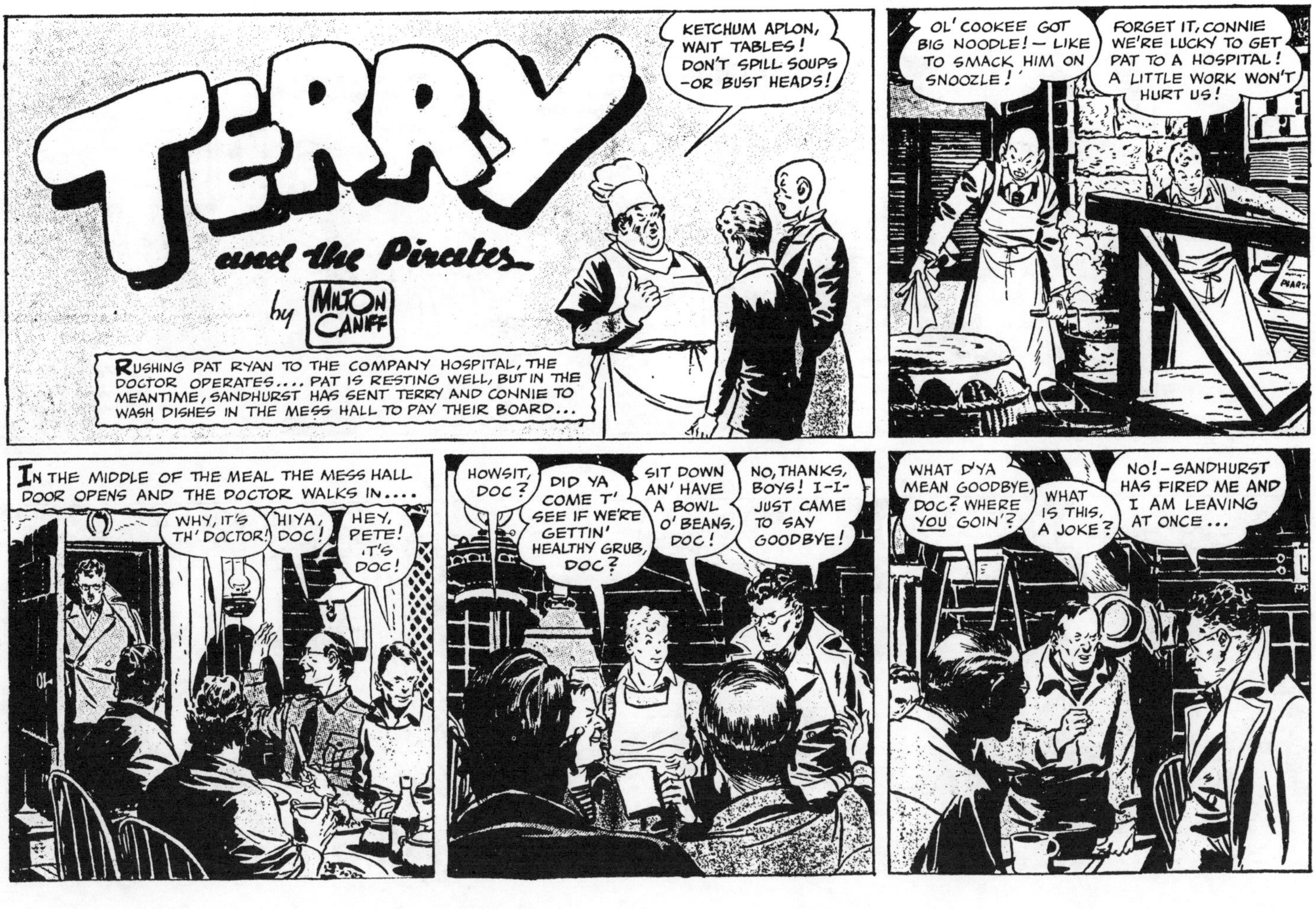
TERRY and the Pirates by MILTON CANIFF
KETCHUM APLON, WAIT TABLES! DON'T SPILL SOUPS –OR BUST HEADS!
RUSHING PAT RYAN TO THE COMPANY HOSPITAL, THE DOCTOR OPERATES.... PAT IS RESTING WELL, BUT IN THE MEANTIME, SANDHURST HAS SENT TERRY AND CONNIE TO WASH DISHES IN THE MESS HALL TO PAY THEIR BOARD...
OL' COOKEE GOT BIG NOODLE!—LIKE TO SMACK HIM ON SNOOZLE!
FORGET IT, CONNIE WE'RE LUCKY TO GET PAT TO A HOSPITAL! A LITTLE WORK WON'T HURT US!
IN THE MIDDLE OF THE MEAL THE MESS HALL DOOR OPENS AND THE DOCTOR WALKS IN....
WHY, IT'S TH' DOCTOR!
HIYA, DOC!
HEY, PETE! IT'S DOC!
HOWSIT, DOC?
DID YA COME T' SEE IF WE'RE GETTIN' HEALTHY GRUB, DOC?
SIT DOWN AN' HAVE A BOWL O' BEANS, DOC!
NO, THANKS, BOYS! I-I-JUST CAME TO SAY GOODBYE!
WHAT D'YA MEAN GOODBYE, DOC? WHERE YOU GOIN'?
WHAT IS THIS, A JOKE?
NO!—SANDHURST HAS FIRED ME AND I AM LEAVING AT ONCE...

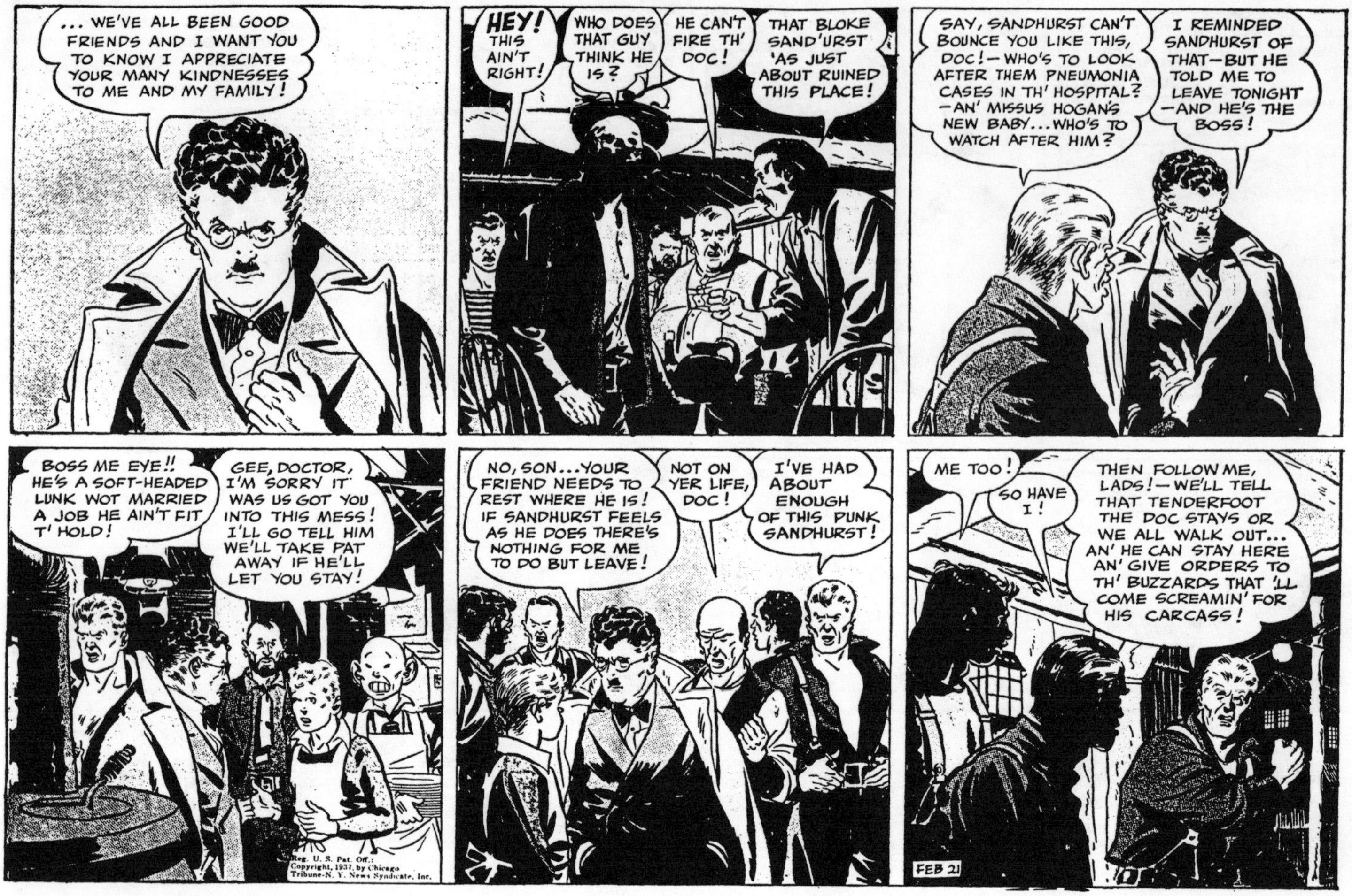
... WE'VE ALL BEEN GOOD FRIENDS AND I WANT YOU TO KNOW I APPRECIATE YOUR MANY KINDNESSES TO ME AND MY FAMILY!
HEY! THIS AIN'T RIGHT!
WHO DOES THAT GUY THINK HE IS?
HE CAN'T FIRE TH' DOC!
THAT BLOKE SAND'URST 'AS JUST ABOUT RUINED THIS PLACE!
SAY, SANDHURST CAN'T BOUNCE YOU LIKE THIS, DOC!—WHO'S TO LOOK AFTER THEM PNEUMONIA CASES IN TH' HOSPITAL? —AN' MISSUS HOGAN'S NEW BABY... WHO'S TO WATCH AFTER HIM?
I REMINDED SANDHURST OF THAT—BUT HE TOLD ME TO LEAVE TONIGHT —AND HE'S THE BOSS!
BOSS ME EYE!! HE'S A SOFT-HEADED LUNK WOT MARRIED A JOB HE AIN'T FIT T' HOLD!
GEE, DOCTOR, I'M SORRY IT WAS US GOT YOU INTO THIS MESS! I'LL GO TELL HIM WE'LL TAKE PAT AWAY IF HE'LL LET YOU STAY!
Reg. U. S. Pat. Off.: Copyright, 1937, by Chicago Tribune-N. Y. News Syndicate, Inc.
NO, SON... YOUR FRIEND NEEDS TO REST WHERE HE IS! IF SANDHURST FEELS AS HE DOES THERE'S NOTHING FOR ME TO DO BUT LEAVE!
NOT ON YER LIFE, DOC!
I'VE HAD ABOUT ENOUGH OF THIS PUNK SANDHURST!
FEB 21
ME TOO!
SO HAVE I!
THEN FOLLOW ME, LADS!—WE'LL TELL THAT TENDERFOOT THE DOC STAYS OR WE ALL WALK OUT... AN' HE CAN STAY HERE AN' GIVE ORDERS TO TH' BUZZARDS THAT 'LL COME SCREAMIN' FOR HIS CARCASS!

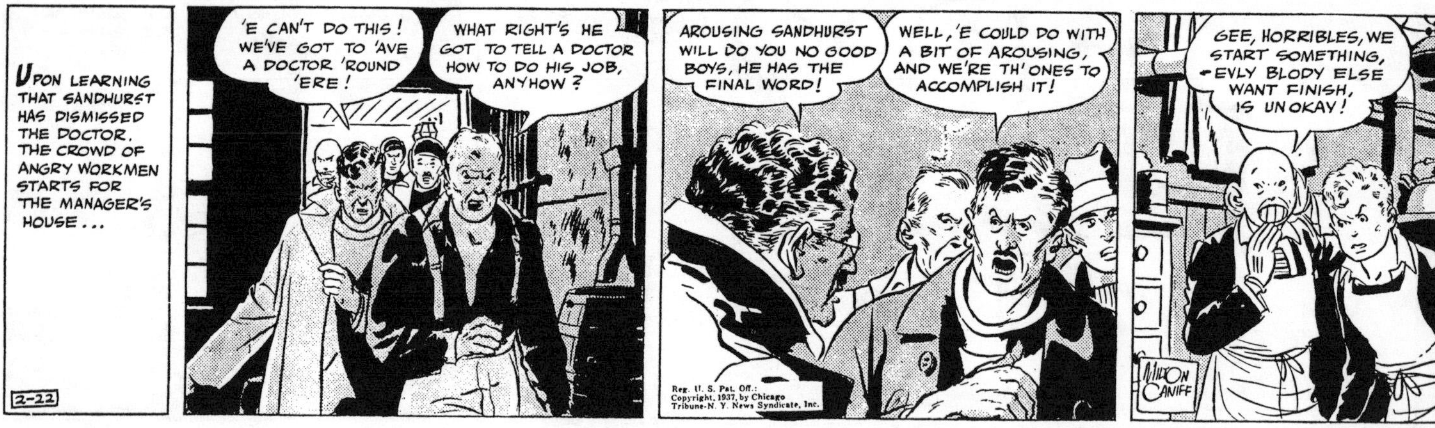
UPON LEARNING THAT SANDHURST HAS DISMISSED THE DOCTOR. THE CROWD OF ANGRY WORKMEN STARTS FOR THE MANAGER'S HOUSE...
2-22
'E CAN'T DO THIS! WE'VE GOT TO 'AVE A DOCTOR 'ROUND 'ERE!
WHAT RIGHT'S HE GOT TO TELL A DOCTOR HOW TO DO HIS JOB, ANYHOW?
AROUSING SANDHURST WILL DO YOU NO GOOD BOYS, HE HAS THE FINAL WORD!
WELL, 'E COULD DO WITH A BIT OF AROUSING, AND WE'RE TH' ONES TO ACCOMPLISH IT!
Reg. U. S. Pat. Off.: Copyright, 1937, by Chicago Tribune-N. Y. News Syndicate, Inc.
GEE, HORRIBLES, WE START SOMETHING, EVLY BLODY ELSE WANT FINISH, IS UNOKAY!
MILTON CANIFF

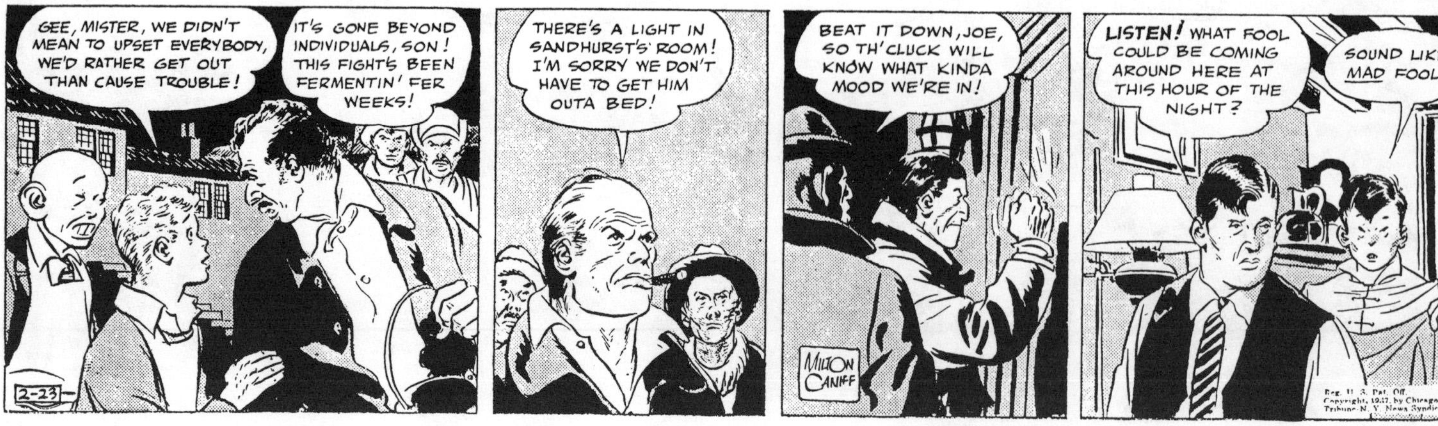
GEE, MISTER, WE DIDN'T MEAN TO UPSET EVERYBODY, WE'D RATHER GET OUT THAN CAUSE TROUBLE!
IT'S GONE BEYOND INDIVIDUALS, SON! THIS FIGHT'S BEEN FERMENTIN' FER WEEKS!
2-23
THERE'S A LIGHT IN SANDHURST'S ROOM! I'M SORRY WE DON'T HAVE TO GET HIM OUTA BED!
BEAT IT DOWN, JOE, SO TH' CLUCK WILL KNOW WHAT KINDA MOOD WE'RE IN!
MILTON CANIFF
LISTEN! WHAT FOOL COULD BE COMING AROUND HERE AT THIS HOUR OF THE NIGHT?
SOUND LIKE MAD FOOL!
Reg. U. S. Pat. Off. Copyright, 1937, by Chicago Tribune-N. Y. News Syndicate, Inc.

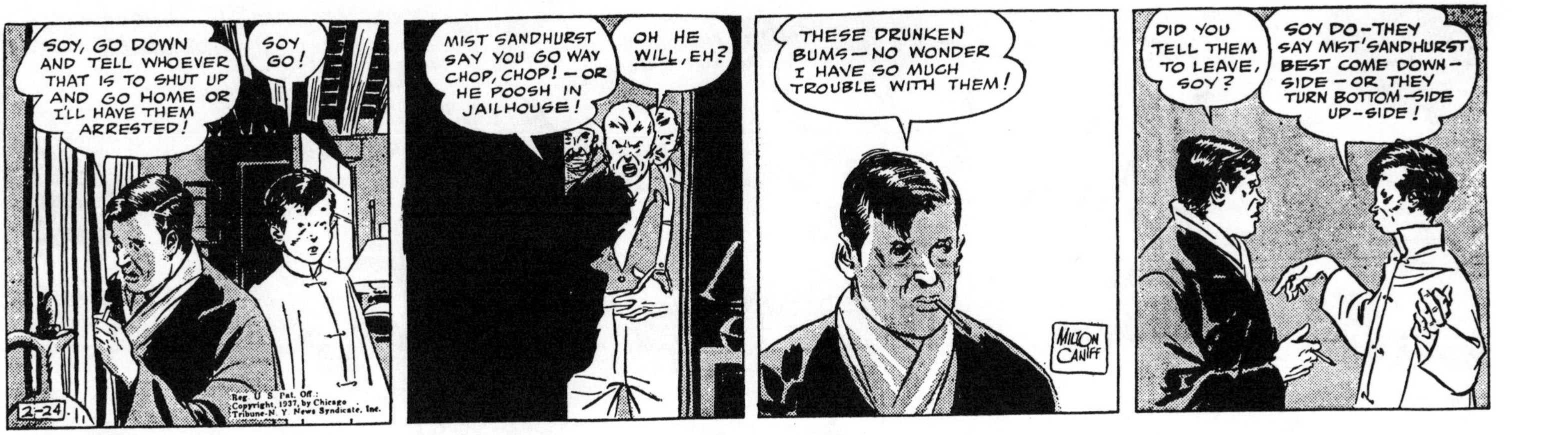
SOY, GO DOWN AND TELL WHOEVER THAT IS TO SHUT UP AND GO HOME OR I'LL HAVE THEM ARRESTED!
SOY GO!
2-24
Reg U S Pat Off: Copyright, 1937, by Chicago Tribune-N Y News Syndicate, Inc.
MIST SANDHURST SAY YOU GO WAY CHOP, CHOP! – OR HE POOSH IN JAILHOUSE!
OH HE WILL, EH?
THESE DRUNKEN BUMS – NO WONDER I HAVE SO MUCH TROUBLE WITH THEM!
MILTON CANIFF
DID YOU TELL THEM TO LEAVE, SOY?
SOY DO – THEY SAY MIST' SANDHURST BEST COME DOWN-SIDE – OR THEY TURN BOTTOM-SIDE UP-SIDE!

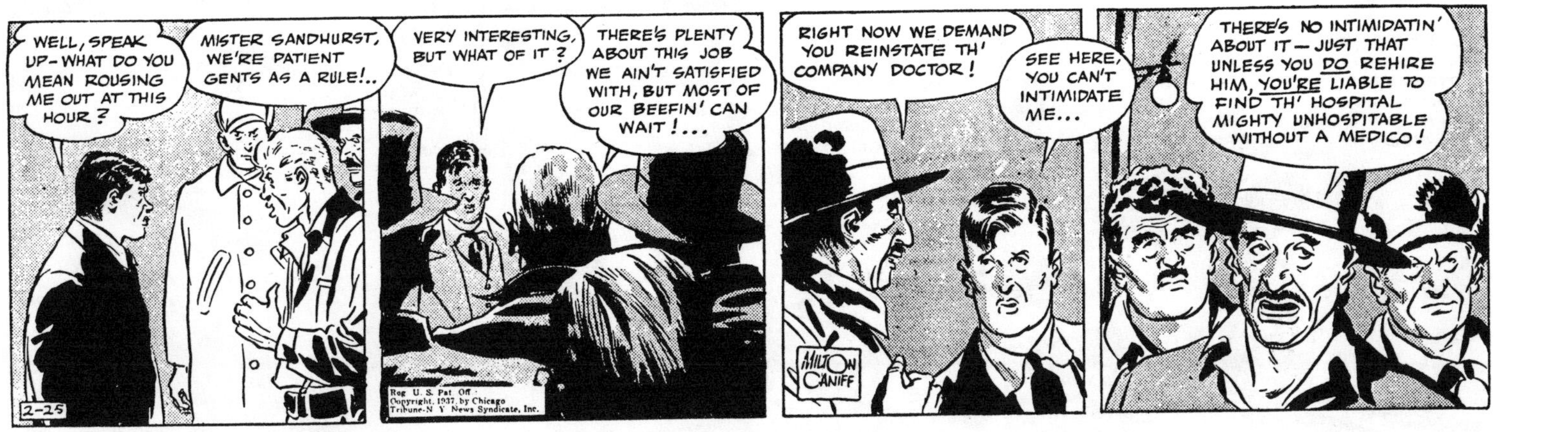
WELL, SPEAK UP – WHAT DO YOU MEAN ROUSING ME OUT AT THIS HOUR?
MISTER SANDHURST, WE'RE PATIENT GENTS AS A RULE!..
2-25
VERY INTERESTING, BUT WHAT OF IT?
THERE'S PLENTY ABOUT THIS JOB WE AIN'T SATISFIED WITH, BUT MOST OF OUR BEEFIN' CAN WAIT!...
Reg U. S. Pat. Off.: Copyright, 1937, by Chicago Tribune-N Y News Syndicate, Inc.
RIGHT NOW WE DEMAND YOU REINSTATE TH' COMPANY DOCTOR!
SEE HERE, YOU CAN'T INTIMIDATE ME...
MILTON CANIFF
THERE'S NO INTIMIDATIN' ABOUT IT – JUST THAT UNLESS YOU DO REHIRE HIM, YOU'RE LIABLE TO FIND TH' HOSPITAL MIGHTY UNHOSPITABLE WITHOUT A MEDICO!

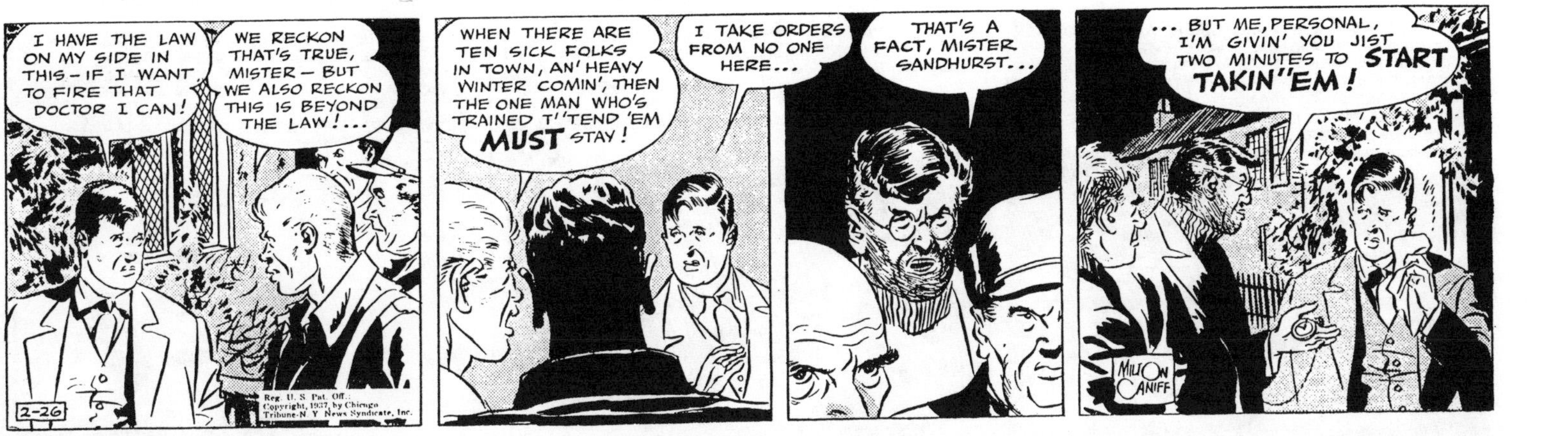
I HAVE THE LAW ON MY SIDE IN THIS – IF I WANT TO FIRE THAT DOCTOR I CAN!
WE RECKON THAT'S TRUE, MISTER – BUT WE ALSO RECKON THIS IS BEYOND THE LAW!...
2-26
Reg. U. S. Pat. Off.: Copyright, 1937, by Chicago Tribune-N Y News Syndicate, Inc.
WHEN THERE ARE TEN SICK FOLKS IN TOWN, AN' HEAVY WINTER COMIN', THEN THE ONE MAN WHO'S TRAINED T' 'TEND 'EM MUST STAY!
I TAKE ORDERS FROM NO ONE HERE...
THAT'S A FACT, MISTER SANDHURST...
... BUT ME, PERSONAL, I'M GIVIN' YOU JIST TWO MINUTES TO START TAKIN' 'EM!
MILTON CANIFF

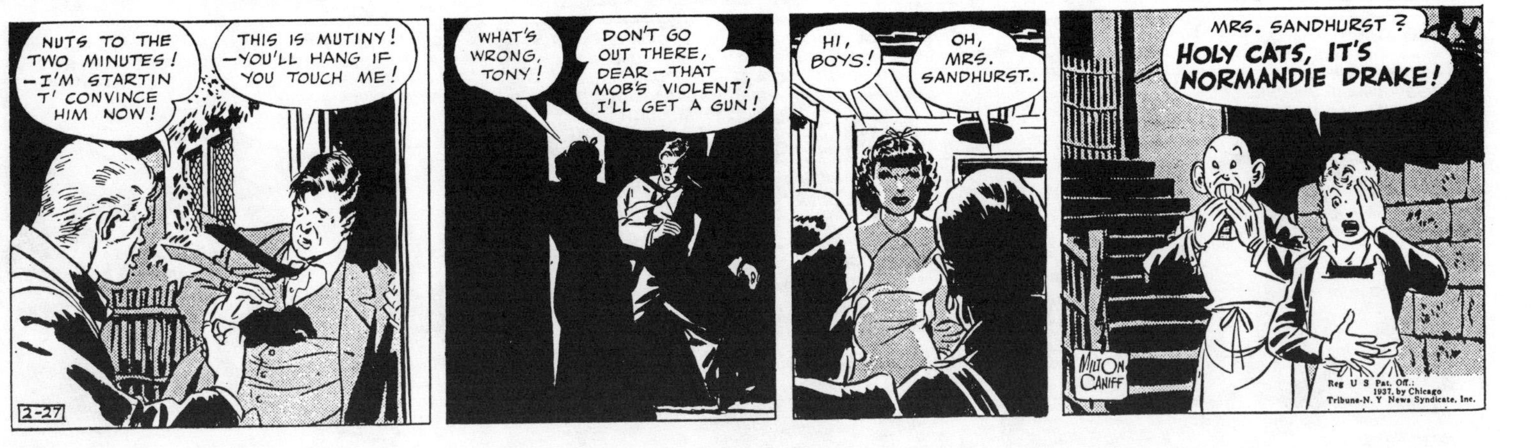
NUTS TO THE TWO MINUTES! – I'M STARTIN T' CONVINCE HIM NOW!
THIS IS MUTINY! – YOU'LL HANG IF YOU TOUCH ME!
2-27
WHAT'S WRONG, TONY!
DON'T GO OUT THERE, DEAR – THAT MOB'S VIOLENT! I'LL GET A GUN!
HI, BOYS!
OH, MRS. SANDHURST..
MRS. SANDHURST?
HOLY CATS, IT'S NORMANDIE DRAKE!
MILTON CANIFF
Reg U S Pat. Off.: 1937, by Chicago Tribune-N Y News Syndicate, Inc.

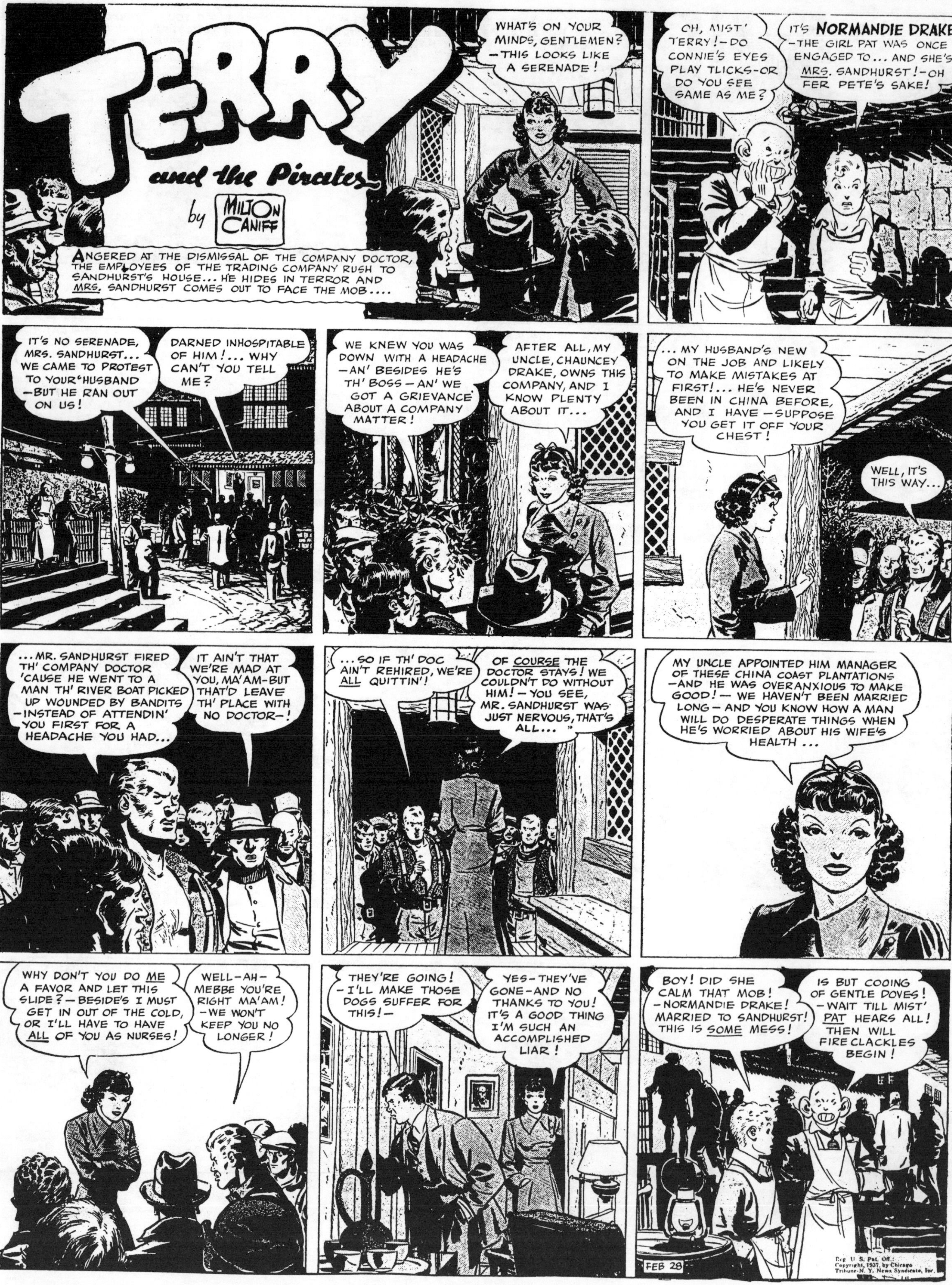
TERRY and the Pirates
by MILTON CANIFF
ANGERED AT THE DISMISSAL OF THE COMPANY DOCTOR, THE EMPLOYEES OF THE TRADING COMPANY RUSH TO SANDHURST'S HOUSE... HE HIDES IN TERROR AND MRS. SANDHURST COMES OUT TO FACE THE MOB....
WHAT'S ON YOUR MINDS, GENTLEMEN? —THIS LOOKS LIKE A SERENADE!
OH, MIST' TERRY!—DO CONNIE'S EYES PLAY TLICKS—OR DO YOU SEE SAME AS ME?
IT'S NORMANDIE DRAKE! —THE GIRL PAT WAS ONCE ENGAGED TO... AND SHE'S MRS. SANDHURST!—OH FER PETE'S SAKE!
IT'S NO SERENADE, MRS. SANDHURST... WE CAME TO PROTEST TO YOUR HUSBAND —BUT HE RAN OUT ON US!
DARNED INHOSPITABLE OF HIM!... WHY CAN'T YOU TELL ME?
WE KNEW YOU WAS DOWN WITH A HEADACHE —AN' BESIDES HE'S TH' BOSS—AN' WE GOT A GRIEVANCE ABOUT A COMPANY MATTER!
AFTER ALL, MY UNCLE, CHAUNCEY DRAKE, OWNS THIS COMPANY, AND I KNOW PLENTY ABOUT IT...
... MY HUSBAND'S NEW ON THE JOB AND LIKELY TO MAKE MISTAKES AT FIRST!... HE'S NEVER BEEN IN CHINA BEFORE, AND I HAVE—SUPPOSE YOU GET IT OFF YOUR CHEST!
WELL, IT'S THIS WAY...
...MR. SANDHURST FIRED TH' COMPANY DOCTOR 'CAUSE HE WENT TO A MAN TH' RIVER BOAT PICKED UP WOUNDED BY BANDITS —INSTEAD OF ATTENDIN' YOU FIRST FOR A HEADACHE YOU HAD...
IT AIN'T THAT WE'RE MAD AT YOU, MA'AM—BUT THAT'D LEAVE TH' PLACE WITH NO DOCTOR—!
...SO IF TH' DOC AIN'T REHIRED, WE'RE ALL QUITTIN'!
OF COURSE THE DOCTOR STAYS! WE COULDN'T DO WITHOUT HIM!—YOU SEE, MR. SANDHURST WAS JUST NERVOUS, THAT'S ALL...
MY UNCLE APPOINTED HIM MANAGER OF THESE CHINA COAST PLANTATIONS —AND HE WAS OVERANXIOUS TO MAKE GOOD!—WE HAVEN'T BEEN MARRIED LONG—AND YOU KNOW HOW A MAN WILL DO DESPERATE THINGS WHEN HE'S WORRIED ABOUT HIS WIFE'S HEALTH...
WHY DON'T YOU DO ME A FAVOR AND LET THIS SLIDE?—BESIDE'S I MUST GET IN OUT OF THE COLD, OR I'LL HAVE TO HAVE ALL OF YOU AS NURSES!
WELL—AH— MEBBE YOU'RE RIGHT MA'AM! —WE WON'T KEEP YOU NO LONGER!
THEY'RE GOING! —I'LL MAKE THOSE DOGS SUFFER FOR THIS!—
YES—THEY'VE GONE—AND NO THANKS TO YOU! IT'S A GOOD THING I'M SUCH AN ACCOMPLISHED LIAR!
FEB 28
BOY! DID SHE CALM THAT MOB! —NORMANDIE DRAKE! MARRIED TO SANDHURST! THIS IS SOME MESS!
IS BUT COOING OF GENTLE DOVES! —WAIT TILL MIST' PAT HEARS ALL! THEN WILL FIRECLACKLES BEGIN!
Reg. U. S. Pat. Off.: Copyright, 1937, by Chicago Tribune-N. Y. News Syndicate, Inc.

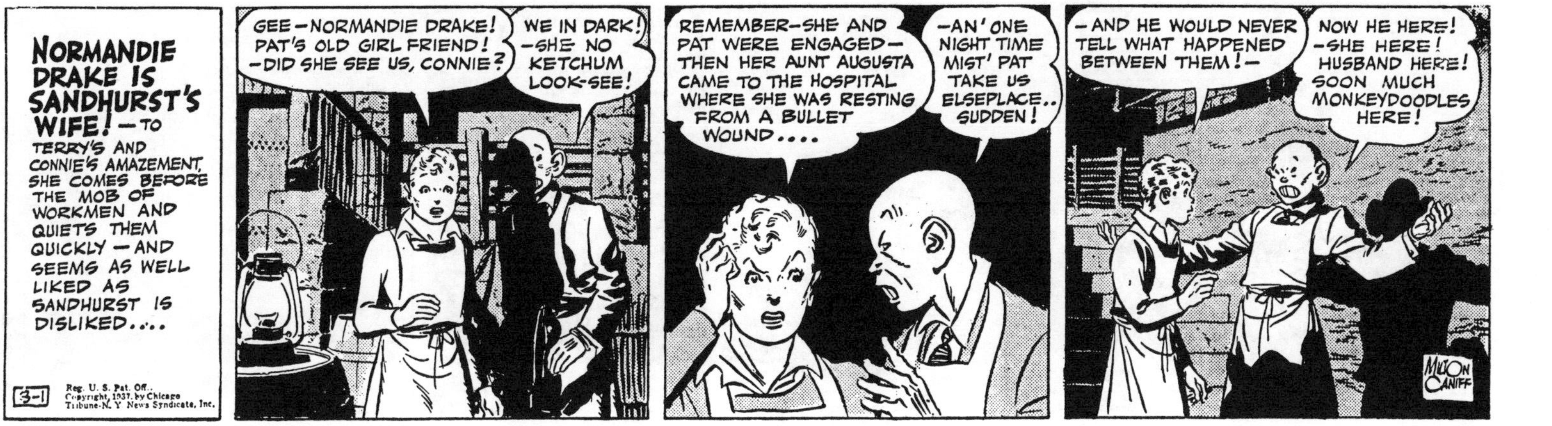
NORMANDIE DRAKE IS SANDHURST'S WIFE! —TO TERRY'S AND CONNIE'S AMAZEMENT, SHE COMES BEFORE THE MOB OF WORKMEN AND QUIETS THEM QUICKLY —AND SEEMS AS WELL LIKED AS SANDHURST IS DISLIKED....
3-1
Reg. U. S. Pat. Off.: Copyright, 1937, by Chicago Tribune-N. Y. News Syndicate, Inc.
GEE—NORMANDIE DRAKE! PAT'S OLD GIRL FRIEND! —DID SHE SEE US, CONNIE?
WE IN DARK! —SHE NO KETCHUM LOOK-SEE!
REMEMBER—SHE AND PAT WERE ENGAGED—THEN HER AUNT AUGUSTA CAME TO THE HOSPITAL WHERE SHE WAS RESTING FROM A BULLET WOUND....
—AN' ONE NIGHT TIME MIST' PAT TAKE US ELSEPLACE.. SUDDEN!
—AND HE WOULD NEVER TELL WHAT HAPPENED BETWEEN THEM!—
NOW HE HERE! —SHE HERE! HUSBAND HERE! SOON MUCH MONKEYDOODLES HERE!
MILTON CANIFF

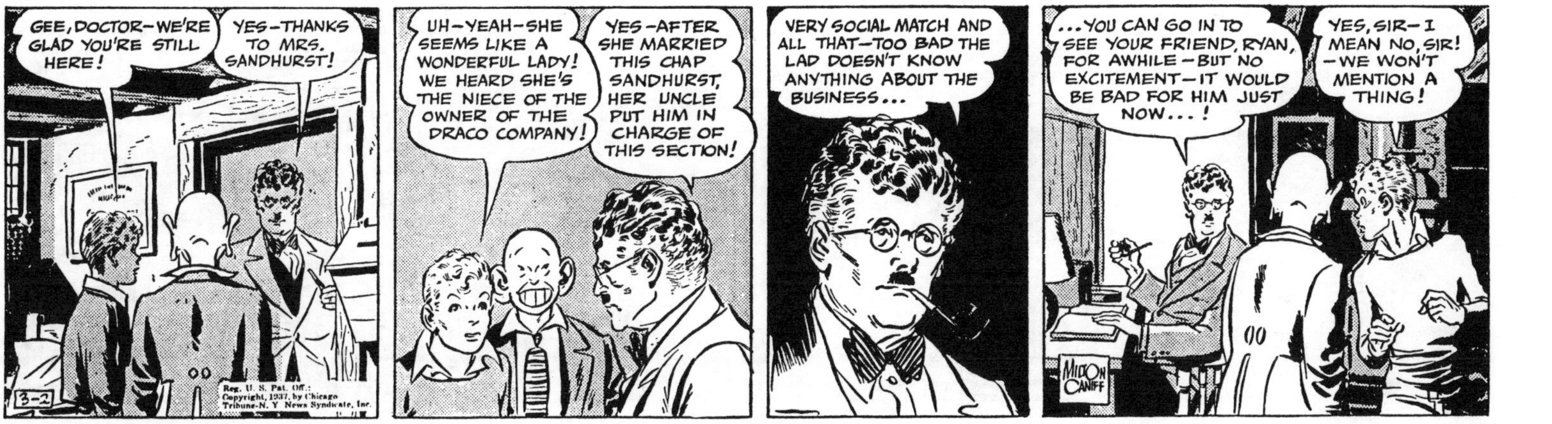
GEE, DOCTOR—WE'RE GLAD YOU'RE STILL HERE!
YES—THANKS TO MRS. SANDHURST!
3-2
Reg. U. S. Pat. Off.: Copyright, 1937, by Chicago Tribune-N. Y. News Syndicate, Inc.
UH—YEAH—SHE SEEMS LIKE A WONDERFUL LADY! WE HEARD SHE'S THE NIECE OF THE OWNER OF THE DRACO COMPANY!
YES—AFTER SHE MARRIED THIS CHAP SANDHURST, HER UNCLE PUT HIM IN CHARGE OF THIS SECTION!
VERY SOCIAL MATCH AND ALL THAT—TOO BAD THE LAD DOESN'T KNOW ANYTHING ABOUT THE BUSINESS...
...YOU CAN GO IN TO SEE YOUR FRIEND, RYAN, FOR AWHILE—BUT NO EXCITEMENT—IT WOULD BE BAD FOR HIM JUST NOW...!
YES, SIR—I MEAN NO, SIR! —WE WON'T MENTION A THING!
MILTON CANIFF

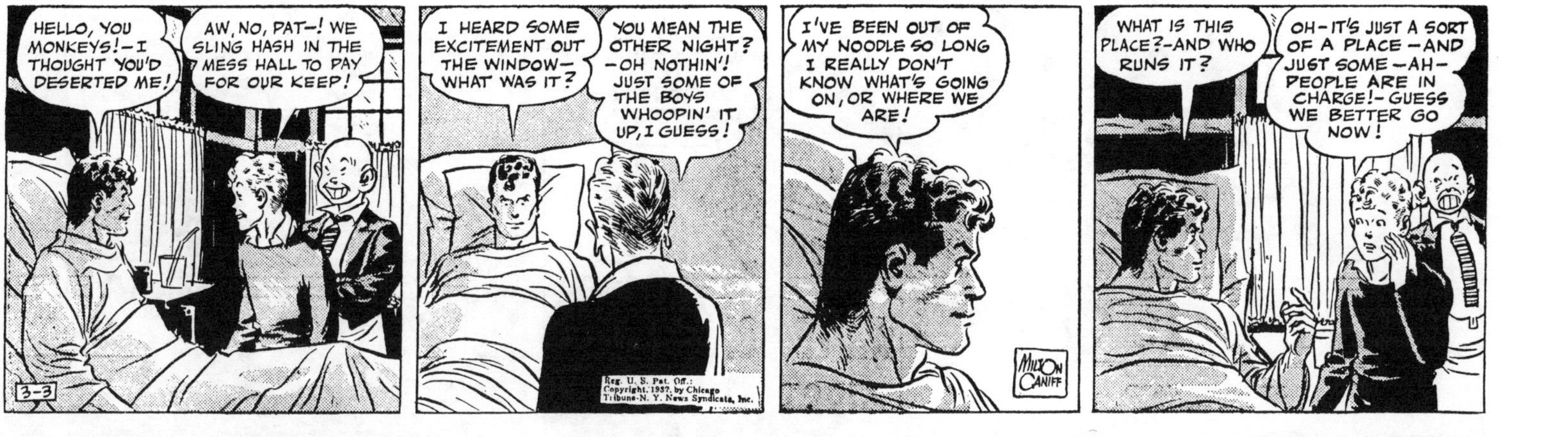
HELLO, YOU MONKEYS! —I THOUGHT YOU'D DESERTED ME!
AW, NO, PAT—! WE SLING HASH IN THE MESS HALL TO PAY FOR OUR KEEP!
3-3
I HEARD SOME EXCITEMENT OUT THE WINDOW—WHAT WAS IT?
YOU MEAN THE OTHER NIGHT? —OH NOTHIN'! JUST SOME OF THE BOYS WHOOPIN' IT UP, I GUESS!
Reg. U. S. Pat. Off.: Copyright, 1937, by Chicago Tribune-N. Y. News Syndicate, Inc.
I'VE BEEN OUT OF MY NOODLE SO LONG I REALLY DON'T KNOW WHAT'S GOING ON, OR WHERE WE ARE!
MILTON CANIFF
WHAT IS THIS PLACE?—AND WHO RUNS IT?
OH—IT'S JUST A SORT OF A PLACE —AND JUST SOME —AH— PEOPLE ARE IN CHARGE!—GUESS WE BETTER GO NOW!

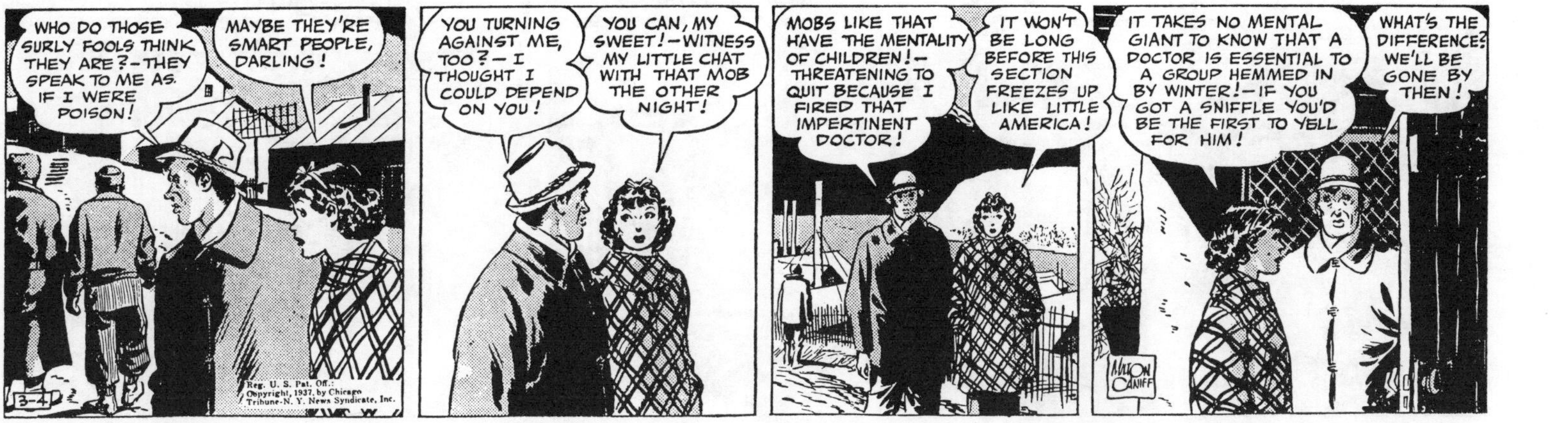
WHO DO THOSE SURLY FOOLS THINK THEY ARE?—THEY SPEAK TO ME AS IF I WERE POISON!
MAYBE THEY'RE SMART PEOPLE, DARLING!
3-4
Reg. U. S. Pat. Off.: Copyright, 1937, by Chicago Tribune-N. Y. News Syndicate, Inc.
YOU TURNING AGAINST ME, TOO?—I THOUGHT I COULD DEPEND ON YOU!
YOU CAN, MY SWEET!—WITNESS MY LITTLE CHAT WITH THAT MOB THE OTHER NIGHT!
MOBS LIKE THAT HAVE THE MENTALITY OF CHILDREN!—THREATENING TO QUIT BECAUSE I FIRED THAT IMPERTINENT DOCTOR!
IT WON'T BE LONG BEFORE THIS SECTION FREEZES UP LIKE LITTLE AMERICA!
IT TAKES NO MENTAL GIANT TO KNOW THAT A DOCTOR IS ESSENTIAL TO A GROUP HEMMED IN BY WINTER!—IF YOU GOT A SNIFFLE YOU'D BE THE FIRST TO YELL FOR HIM!
WHAT'S THE DIFFERENCE? WE'LL BE GONE BY THEN!
MILTON CANIFF

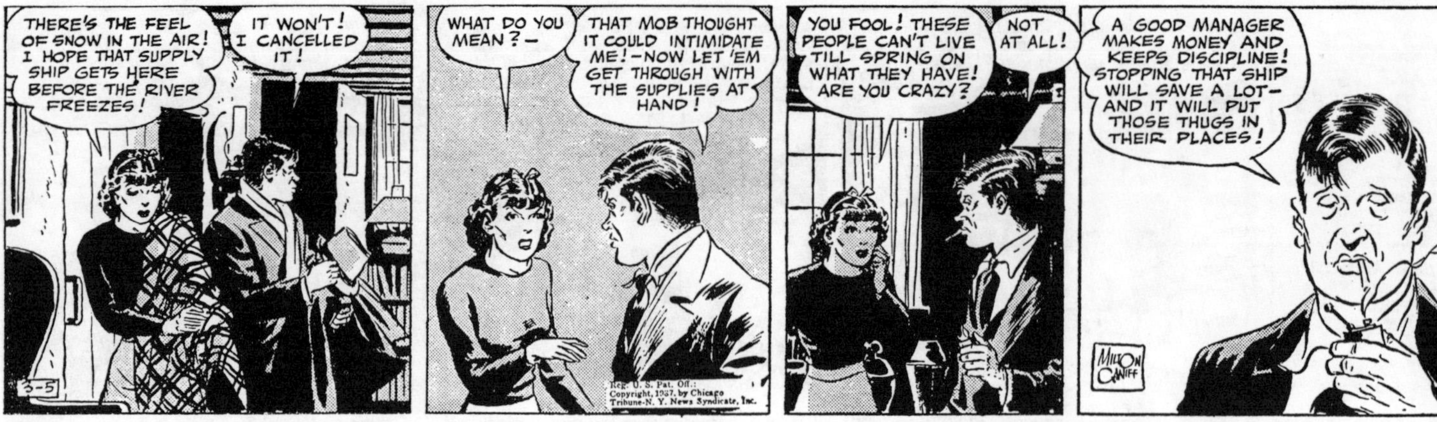
THERE'S THE FEEL OF SNOW IN THE AIR! I HOPE THAT SUPPLY SHIP GETS HERE BEFORE THE RIVER FREEZES!
IT WON'T! I CANCELLED IT!
3-5
WHAT DO YOU MEAN?—
THAT MOB THOUGHT IT COULD INTIMIDATE ME!—NOW LET 'EM GET THROUGH WITH THE SUPPLIES AT HAND!
Reg. U. S. Pat. Off.: Copyright, 1937, by Chicago Tribune-N. Y. News Syndicate, Inc.
YOU FOOL! THESE PEOPLE CAN'T LIVE TILL SPRING ON WHAT THEY HAVE! ARE YOU CRAZY?
NOT AT ALL!
A GOOD MANAGER MAKES MONEY AND KEEPS DISCIPLINE! STOPPING THAT SHIP WILL SAVE A LOT—AND IT WILL PUT THOSE THUGS IN THEIR PLACES!
MILTON CANIFF

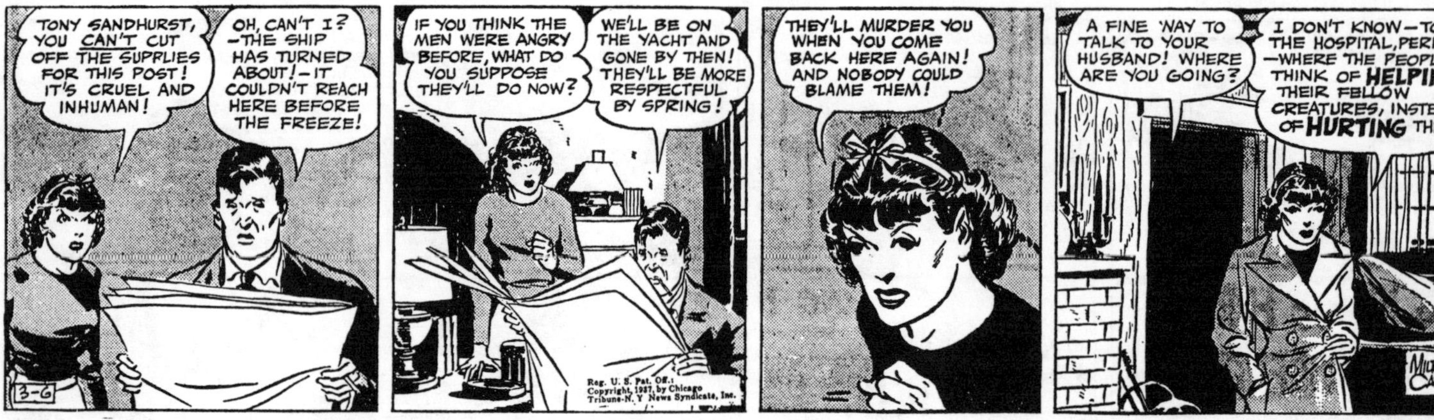
TONY SANDHURST, YOU CAN'T CUT OFF THE SUPPLIES FOR THIS POST! IT'S CRUEL AND INHUMAN!
OH, CAN'T I? —THE SHIP HAS TURNED ABOUT!—IT COULDN'T REACH HERE BEFORE THE FREEZE!
3-6
IF YOU THINK THE MEN WERE ANGRY BEFORE, WHAT DO YOU SUPPOSE THEY'LL DO NOW?
WE'LL BE ON THE YACHT AND GONE BY THEN! THEY'LL BE MORE RESPECTFUL BY SPRING!
Reg. U. S. Pat. Off.: Copyright, 1937, by Chicago Tribune-N. Y. News Syndicate, Inc.
THEY'LL MURDER YOU WHEN YOU COME BACK HERE AGAIN! AND NOBODY COULD BLAME THEM!
A FINE WAY TO TALK TO YOUR HUSBAND! WHERE ARE YOU GOING?
I DON'T KNOW—TO THE HOSPITAL, PERHAPS! —WHERE THE PEOPLE THINK OF HELPING THEIR FELLOW CREATURES, INSTEAD OF HURTING THEM!
MILTON CANIFF

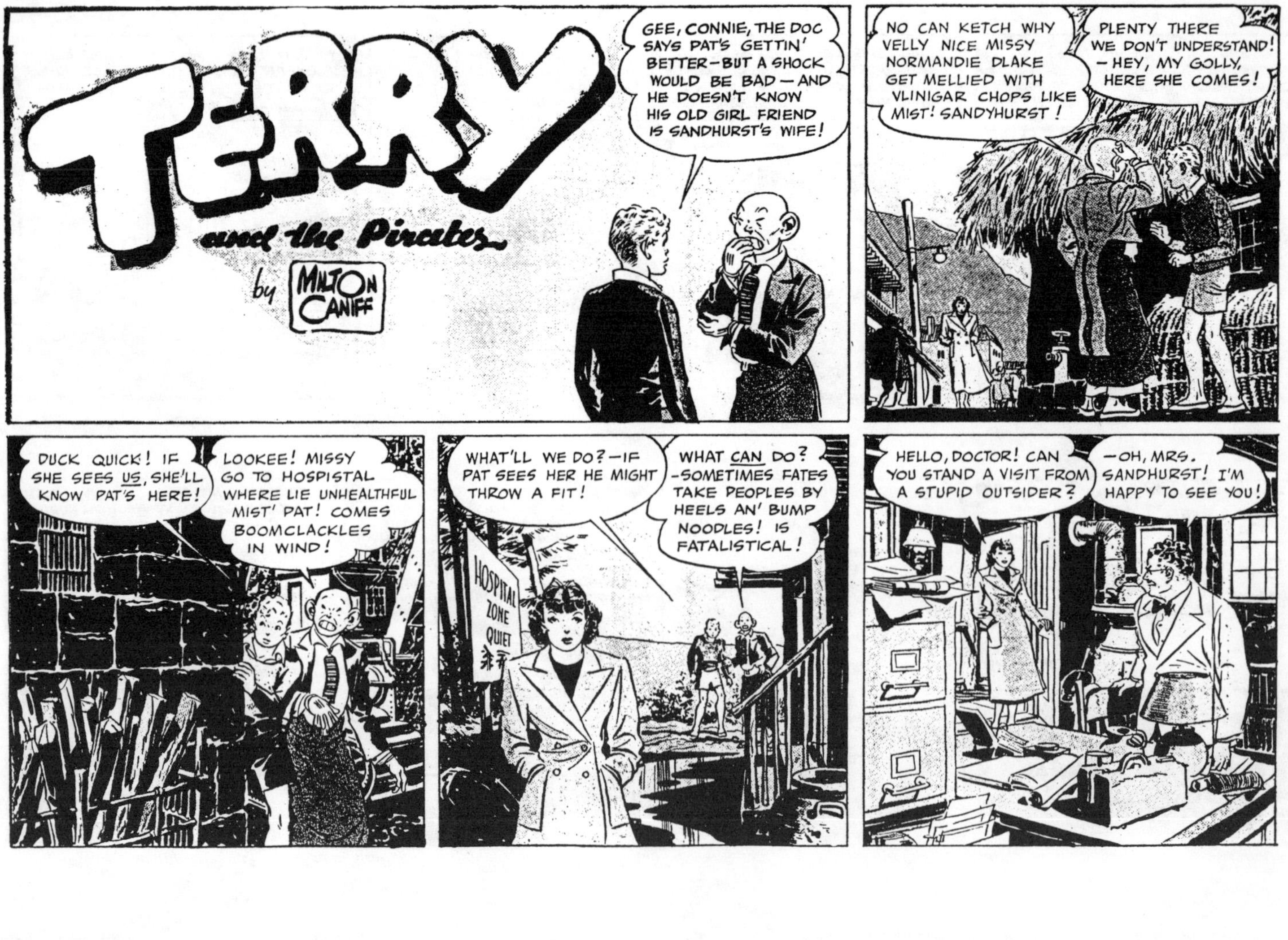
TERRY
and the Pirates
by MILTON CANIFF
GEE, CONNIE, THE DOC SAYS PAT'S GETTIN' BETTER—BUT A SHOCK WOULD BE BAD—AND HE DOESN'T KNOW HIS OLD GIRL FRIEND IS SANDHURST'S WIFE!
NO CAN KETCH WHY VELLY NICE MISSY NORMANDIE DLAKE GET MELLIED WITH VLINIGAR CHOPS LIKE MIST' SANDYHURST!
PLENTY THERE WE DON'T UNDERSTAND! —HEY, MY GOLLY, HERE SHE COMES!
DUCK QUICK! IF SHE SEES US, SHE'LL KNOW PAT'S HERE!
LOOKEE! MISSY GO TO HOSPISTAL WHERE LIE UNHEALTHFUL MIST' PAT! COMES BOOMCLACKLES IN WIND!
WHAT'LL WE DO?—IF PAT SEES HER HE MIGHT THROW A FIT!
WHAT CAN DO? —SOMETIMES FATES TAKE PEOPLES BY HEELS AN' BUMP NOODLES! IS FATALISTICAL!
HOSPITAL ZONE QUIET
HELLO, DOCTOR! CAN YOU STAND A VISIT FROM A STUPID OUTSIDER?
—OH, MRS. SANDHURST! I'M HAPPY TO SEE YOU!

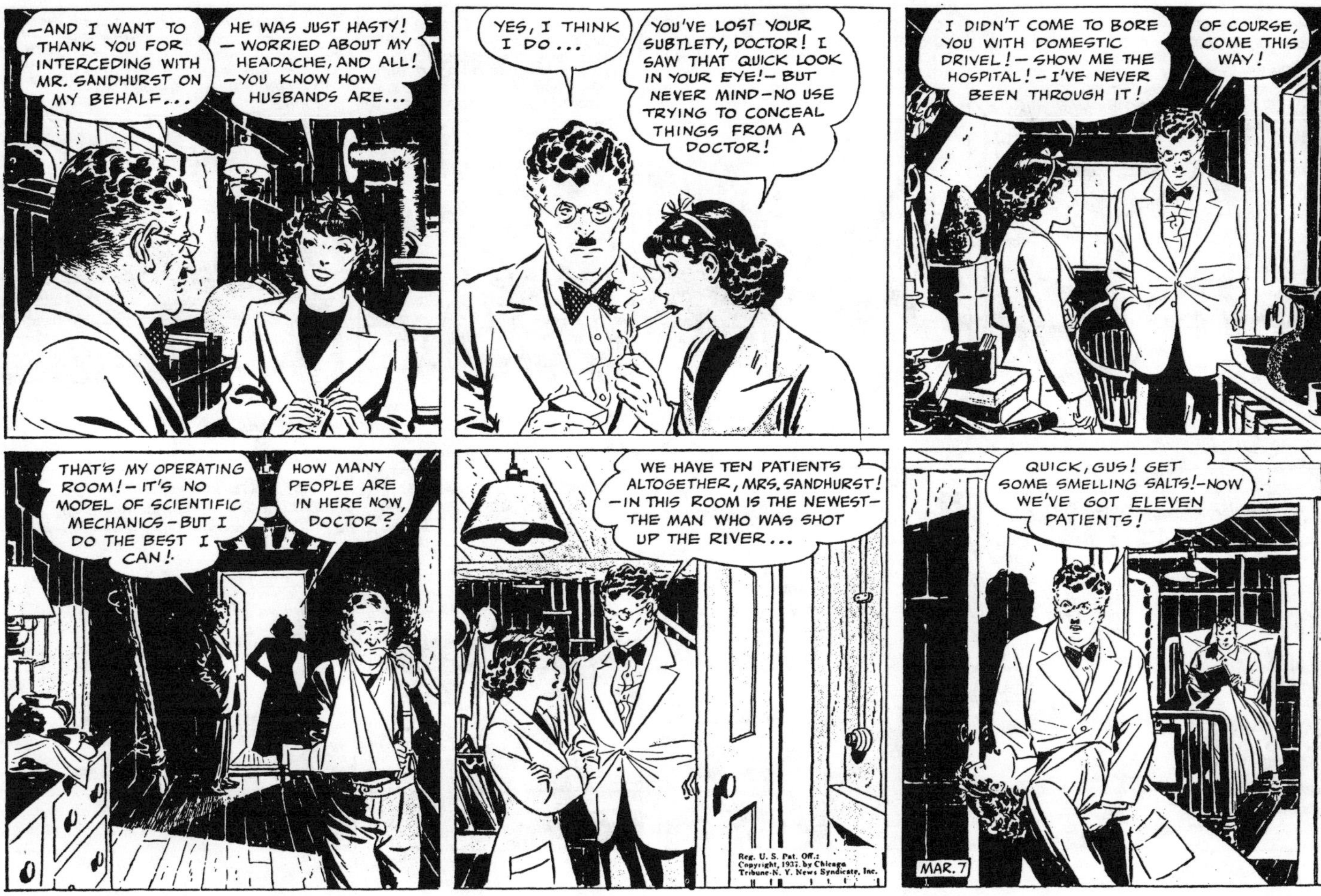
—AND I WANT TO THANK YOU FOR INTERCEDING WITH MR. SANDHURST ON MY BEHALF...
HE WAS JUST HASTY! —WORRIED ABOUT MY HEADACHE, AND ALL! —YOU KNOW HOW HUSBANDS ARE...
YES, I THINK I DO...
YOU'VE LOST YOUR SUBTLETY, DOCTOR! I SAW THAT QUICK LOOK IN YOUR EYE!—BUT NEVER MIND—NO USE TRYING TO CONCEAL THINGS FROM A DOCTOR!
I DIDN'T COME TO BORE YOU WITH DOMESTIC DRIVEL!—SHOW ME THE HOSPITAL!—I'VE NEVER BEEN THROUGH IT!
OF COURSE, COME THIS WAY!
THAT'S MY OPERATING ROOM!—IT'S NO MODEL OF SCIENTIFIC MECHANICS—BUT I DO THE BEST I CAN!
HOW MANY PEOPLE ARE IN HERE NOW, DOCTOR?
WE HAVE TEN PATIENTS ALTOGETHER, MRS. SANDHURST! —IN THIS ROOM IS THE NEWEST—THE MAN WHO WAS SHOT UP THE RIVER...
Reg. U. S. Pat. Off.: Copyright, 1937, by Chicago Tribune-N. Y. News Syndicate, Inc.
QUICK, GUS! GET SOME SMELLING SALTS!—NOW WE'VE GOT ELEVEN PATIENTS!
MAR. 7

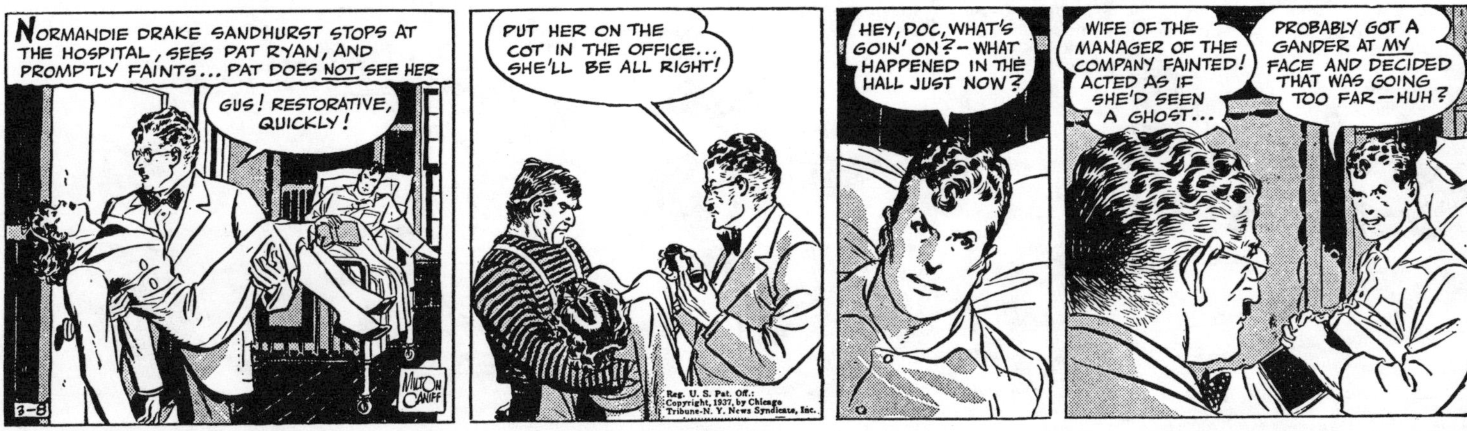
NORMANDIE DRAKE SANDHURST STOPS AT THE HOSPITAL, SEES PAT RYAN, AND PROMPTLY FAINTS... PAT DOES NOT SEE HER
GUS! RESTORATIVE, QUICKLY!
MILTON CANIFF
3-8
PUT HER ON THE COT IN THE OFFICE... SHE'LL BE ALL RIGHT!
Reg. U. S. Pat. Off.: Copyright, 1937, by Chicago Tribune-N. Y. News Syndicate, Inc.
HEY, DOC, WHAT'S GOIN' ON?—WHAT HAPPENED IN THE HALL JUST NOW?
WIFE OF THE MANAGER OF THE COMPANY FAINTED! ACTED AS IF SHE'D SEEN A GHOST...
PROBABLY GOT A GANDER AT MY FACE AND DECIDED THAT WAS GOING TOO FAR—HUH?

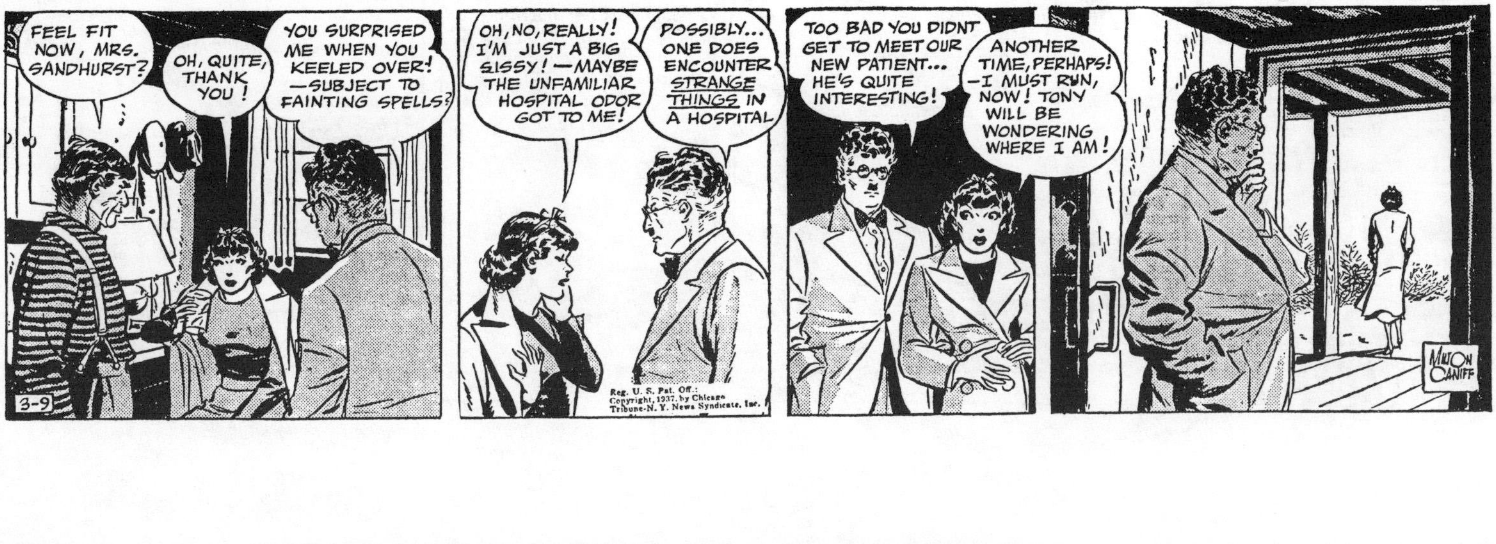
FEEL FIT NOW, MRS. SANDHURST?
OH, QUITE, THANK YOU!
YOU SURPRISED ME WHEN YOU KEELED OVER! —SUBJECT TO FAINTING SPELLS?
3-9
OH, NO, REALLY! I'M JUST A BIG SISSY!—MAYBE THE UNFAMILIAR HOSPITAL ODOR GOT TO ME!
POSSIBLY... ONE DOES ENCOUNTER STRANGE THINGS IN A HOSPITAL
Reg. U. S. Pat. Off.: Copyright, 1937, by Chicago Tribune-N. Y. News Syndicate, Inc.
TOO BAD YOU DIDNT GET TO MEET OUR NEW PATIENT... HE'S QUITE INTERESTING!
ANOTHER TIME, PERHAPS! —I MUST RUN, NOW! TONY WILL BE WONDERING WHERE I AM!
MILTON CANIFF

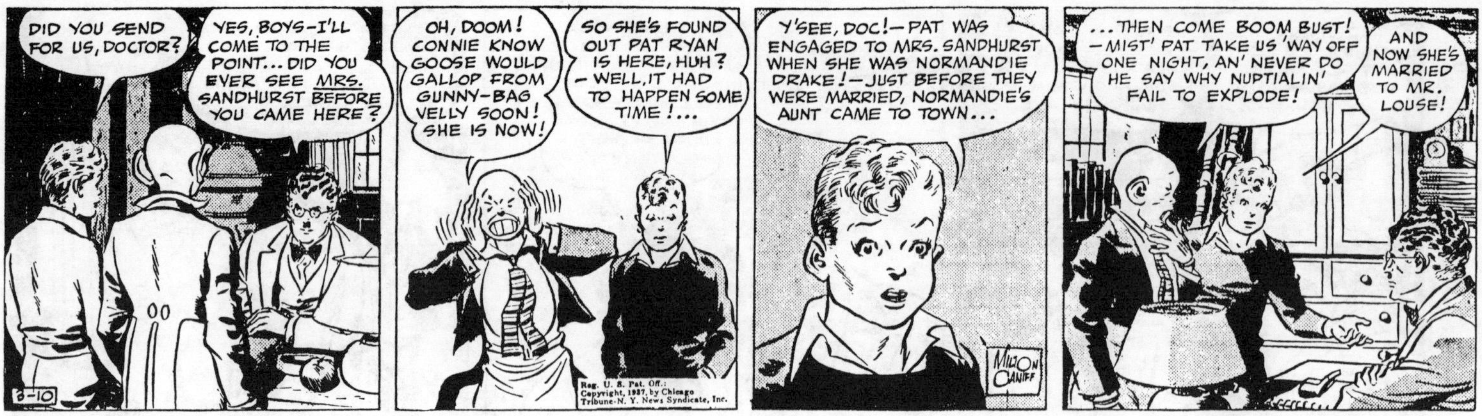
DID YOU SEND FOR US, DOCTOR?
YES, BOYS–I'LL COME TO THE POINT... DID YOU EVER SEE MRS. SANDHURST BEFORE YOU CAME HERE?
3-10
OH, DOOM! CONNIE KNOW GOOSE WOULD GALLOP FROM GUNNY-BAG VELLY SOON! SHE IS NOW!
SO SHE'S FOUND OUT PAT RYAN IS HERE, HUH? –WELL, IT HAD TO HAPPEN SOME TIME!...
Reg. U. S. Pat. Off.: Copyright, 1937, by Chicago Tribune-N. Y. News Syndicate, Inc.
Y'SEE, DOC!–PAT WAS ENGAGED TO MRS. SANDHURST WHEN SHE WAS NORMANDIE DRAKE!–JUST BEFORE THEY WERE MARRIED, NORMANDIE'S AUNT CAME TO TOWN...
MILTON CANIFF
...THEN COME BOOM BUST! –MIST' PAT TAKE US 'WAY OFF ONE NIGHT, AN' NEVER DO HE SAY WHY NUPTIALIN' FAIL TO EXPLODE!
AND NOW SHE'S MARRIED TO MR. LOUSE!

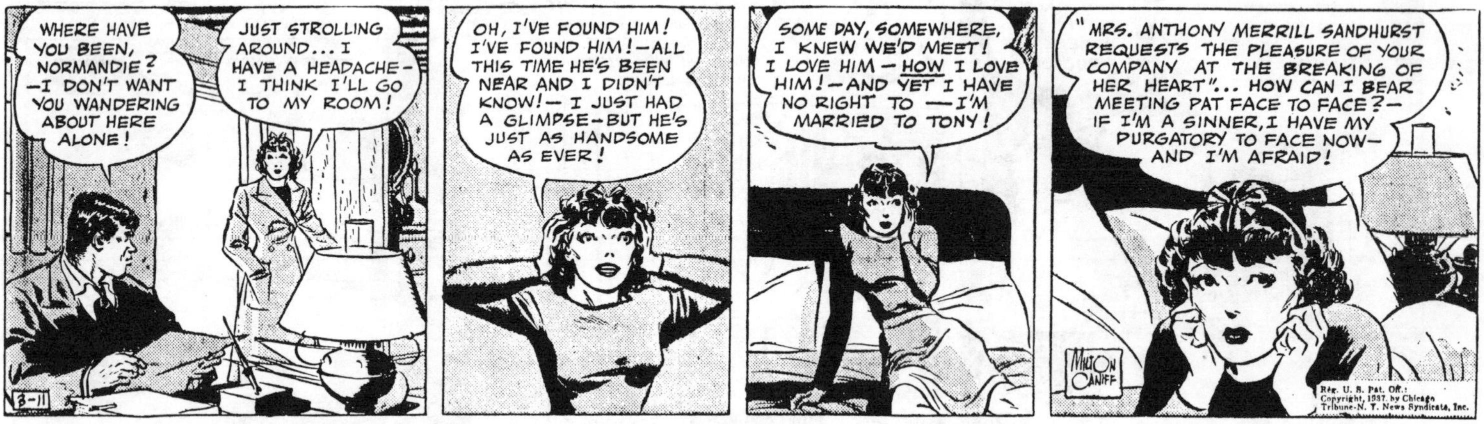
WHERE HAVE YOU BEEN, NORMANDIE? –I DON'T WANT YOU WANDERING ABOUT HERE ALONE!
JUST STROLLING AROUND... I HAVE A HEADACHE– I THINK I'LL GO TO MY ROOM!
3-11
OH, I'VE FOUND HIM! I'VE FOUND HIM!–ALL THIS TIME HE'S BEEN NEAR AND I DIDN'T KNOW!–I JUST HAD A GLIMPSE–BUT HE'S JUST AS HANDSOME AS EVER!
SOME DAY, SOMEWHERE, I KNEW WE'D MEET! I LOVE HIM–HOW I LOVE HIM!–AND YET I HAVE NO RIGHT TO –I'M MARRIED TO TONY!
"MRS. ANTHONY MERRILL SANDHURST REQUESTS THE PLEASURE OF YOUR COMPANY AT THE BREAKING OF HER HEART"... HOW CAN I BEAR MEETING PAT FACE TO FACE?– IF I'M A SINNER, I HAVE MY PURGATORY TO FACE NOW– AND I'M AFRAID!
MILTON CANIFF
Reg. U. S. Pat. Off.: Copyright, 1937, by Chicago Tribune-N. Y. News Syndicate, Inc.

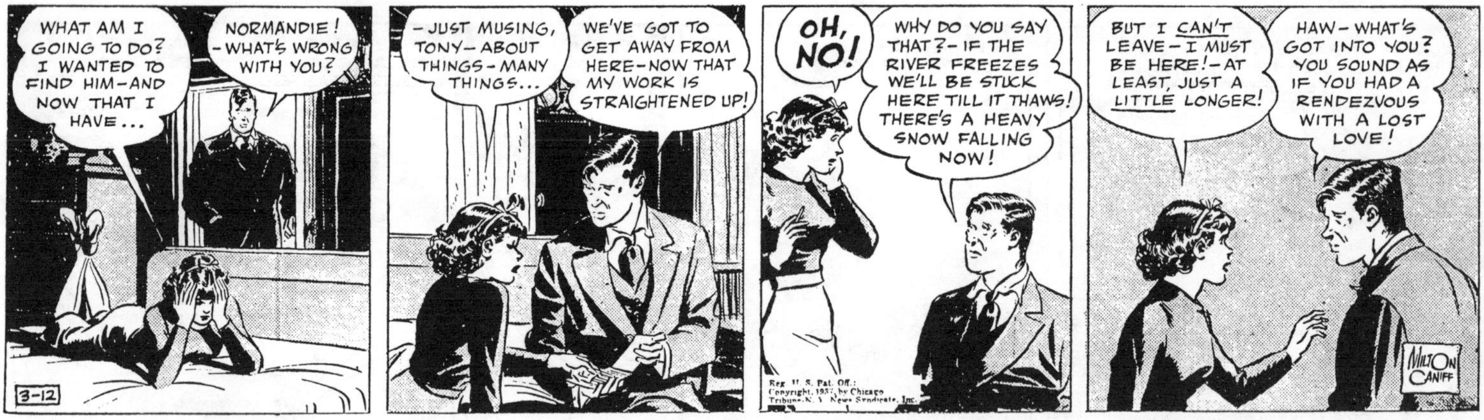
WHAT AM I GOING TO DO? I WANTED TO FIND HIM–AND NOW THAT I HAVE...
NORMANDIE! –WHAT'S WRONG WITH YOU?
3-12
–JUST MUSING, TONY–ABOUT THINGS–MANY THINGS...
WE'VE GOT TO GET AWAY FROM HERE–NOW THAT MY WORK IS STRAIGHTENED UP!
OH, NO!
WHY DO YOU SAY THAT?–IF THE RIVER FREEZES WE'LL BE STUCK HERE TILL IT THAWS! THERE'S A HEAVY SNOW FALLING NOW!
Reg. U. S. Pat. Off.: Copyright, 1937, by Chicago Tribune-N. Y. News Syndicate, Inc.
BUT I CAN'T LEAVE–I MUST BE HERE!–AT LEAST, JUST A LITTLE LONGER!
HAW–WHAT'S GOT INTO YOU? YOU SOUND AS IF YOU HAD A RENDEZVOUS WITH A LOST LOVE!
MILTON CANIFF

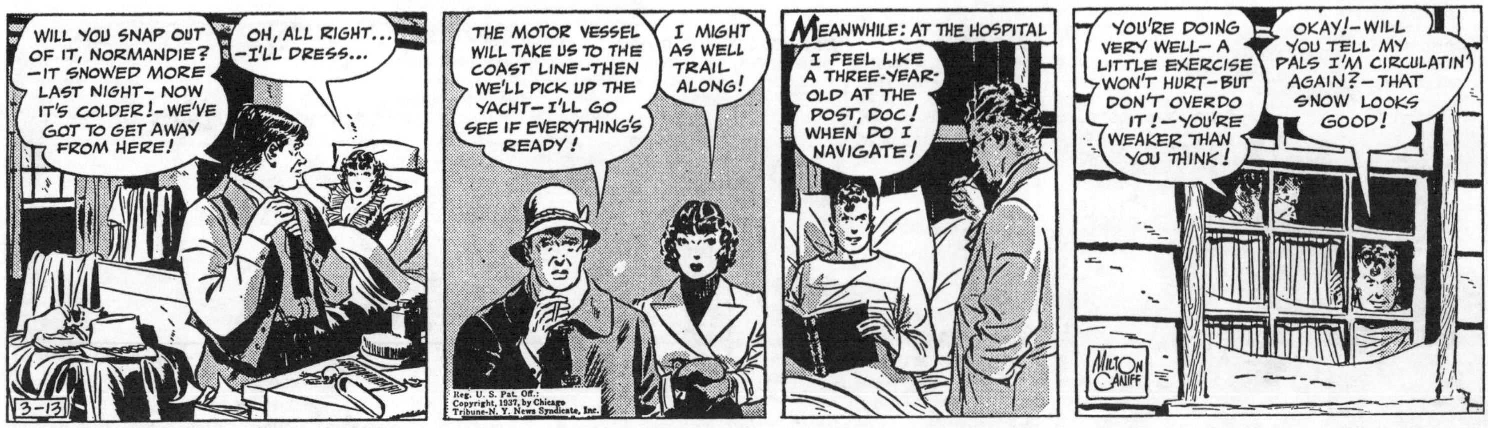
WILL YOU SNAP OUT OF IT, NORMANDIE? –IT SNOWED MORE LAST NIGHT–NOW IT'S COLDER!–WE'VE GOT TO GET AWAY FROM HERE!
OH, ALL RIGHT... –I'LL DRESS...
3-13
THE MOTOR VESSEL WILL TAKE US TO THE COAST LINE–THEN WE'LL PICK UP THE YACHT–I'LL GO SEE IF EVERYTHING'S READY!
I MIGHT AS WELL TRAIL ALONG!
Reg. U. S. Pat. Off.: Copyright, 1937, by Chicago Tribune-N. Y. News Syndicate, Inc.
MEANWHILE: AT THE HOSPITAL
I FEEL LIKE A THREE-YEAR-OLD AT THE POST, DOC! WHEN DO I NAVIGATE!
YOU'RE DOING VERY WELL–A LITTLE EXERCISE WON'T HURT–BUT DON'T OVERDO IT!–YOU'RE WEAKER THAN YOU THINK!
OKAY!–WILL YOU TELL MY PALS I'M CIRCULATIN' AGAIN?–THAT SNOW LOOKS GOOD!
MILTON CANIFF

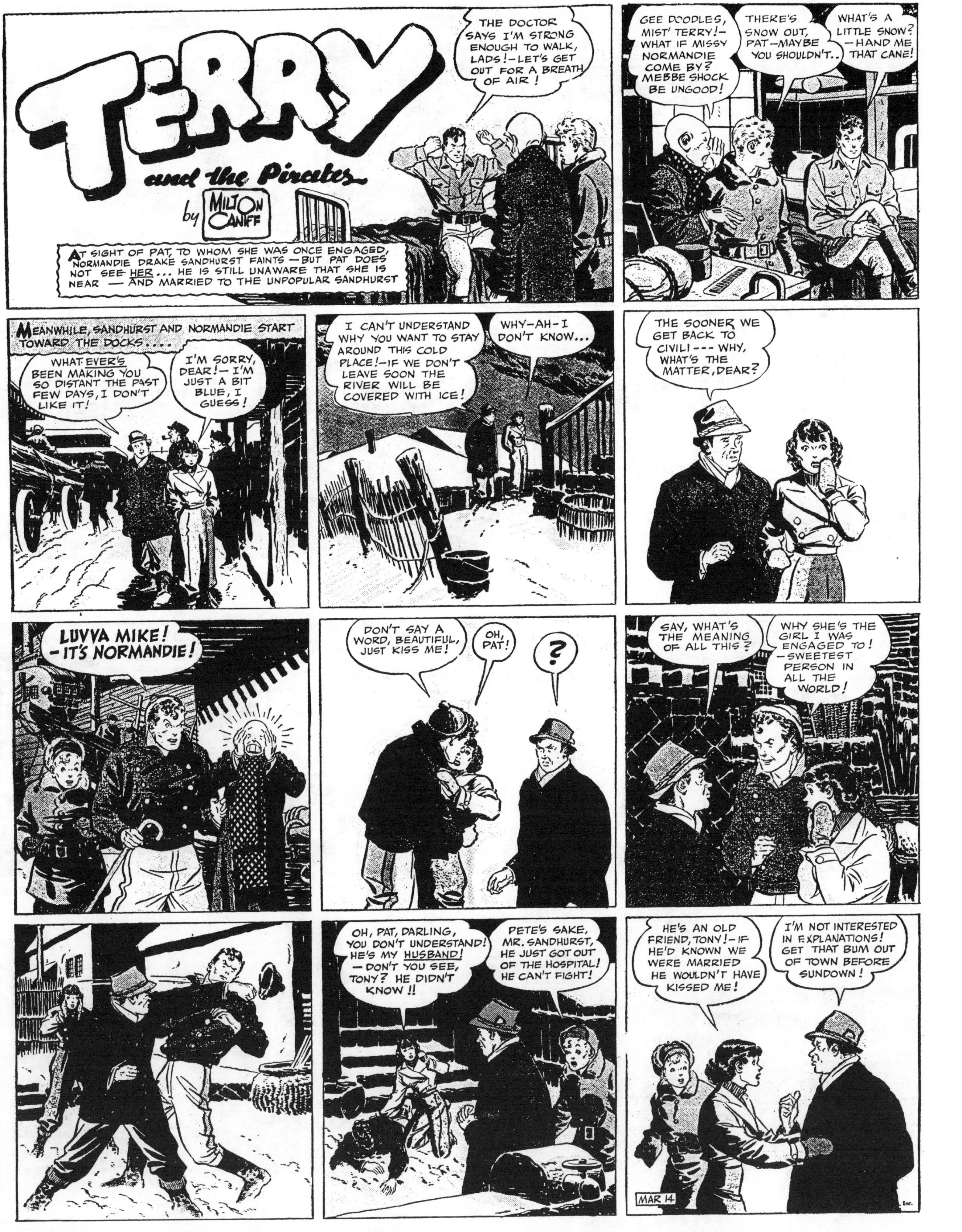
TERRY and the Pirates
by MILTON CANIFF
THE DOCTOR SAYS I'M STRONG ENOUGH TO WALK, LADS! – LET'S GET OUT FOR A BREATH OF AIR!
AT SIGHT OF PAT, TO WHOM SHE WAS ONCE ENGAGED, NORMANDIE DRAKE SANDHURST FAINTS – BUT PAT DOES NOT SEE HER... HE IS STILL UNAWARE THAT SHE IS NEAR — AND MARRIED TO THE UNPOPULAR SANDHURST
GEE DOODLES, MIST' TERRY! – WHAT IF MISSY NORMANDIE COME BY? MEBBE SHOCK BE UNGOOD!
THERE'S SNOW OUT, PAT – MAYBE YOU SHOULDN'T..
WHAT'S A LITTLE SNOW? – HAND ME THAT CANE!
MEANWHILE, SANDHURST AND NORMANDIE START TOWARD THE DOCKS....
WHAT EVER'S BEEN MAKING YOU SO DISTANT THE PAST FEW DAYS, I DON'T LIKE IT!
I'M SORRY, DEAR! – I'M JUST A BIT BLUE, I GUESS!
I CAN'T UNDERSTAND WHY YOU WANT TO STAY AROUND THIS COLD PLACE! – IF WE DON'T LEAVE SOON THE RIVER WILL BE COVERED WITH ICE!
WHY – AH – I DON'T KNOW...
THE SOONER WE GET BACK TO CIVILI--- WHY, WHAT'S THE MATTER, DEAR?
LUVVA MIKE! – IT'S NORMANDIE!
DON'T SAY A WORD, BEAUTIFUL, JUST KISS ME!
OH, PAT!
?
SAY, WHAT'S THE MEANING OF ALL THIS?
WHY SHE'S THE GIRL I WAS ENGAGED TO! – SWEETEST PERSON IN ALL THE WORLD!
OH, PAT, DARLING, YOU DON'T UNDERSTAND! HE'S MY HUSBAND! – DON'T YOU SEE, TONY? HE DIDN'T KNOW!!
PETE'S SAKE, MR. SANDHURST, HE JUST GOT OUT OF THE HOSPITAL! HE CAN'T FIGHT!
HE'S AN OLD FRIEND, TONY! – IF HE'D KNOWN WE WERE MARRIED HE WOULDN'T HAVE KISSED ME!
I'M NOT INTERESTED IN EXPLANATIONS! GET THAT BUM OUT OF TOWN BEFORE SUNDOWN!
MAR 14

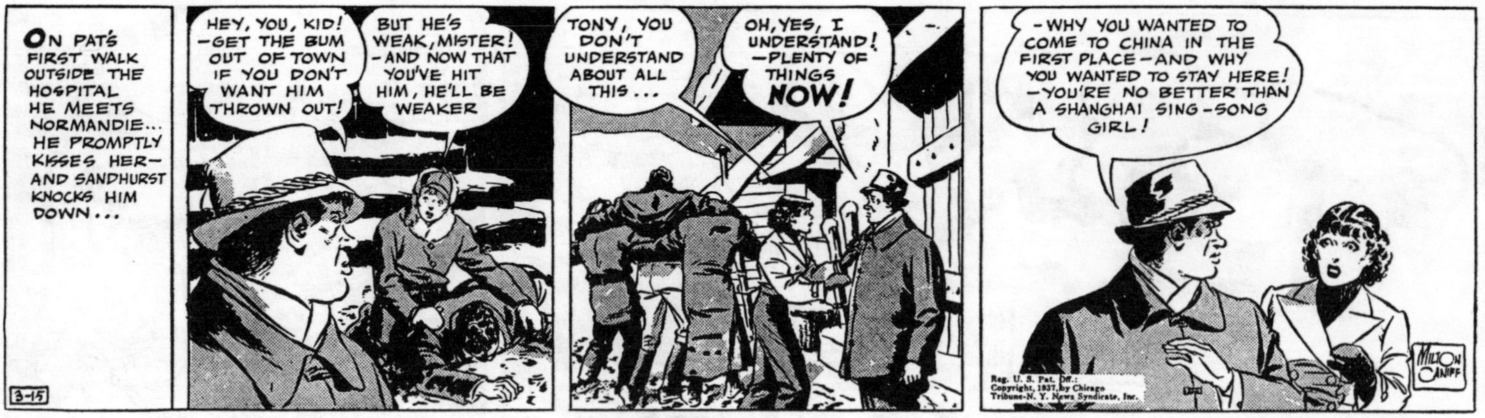
ON PAT'S FIRST WALK OUTSIDE THE HOSPITAL HE MEETS NORMANDIE... HE PROMPTLY KISSES HER— AND SANDHURST KNOCKS HIM DOWN...
3-15
HEY, YOU, KID! —GET THE BUM OUT OF TOWN IF YOU DON'T WANT HIM THROWN OUT!
BUT HE'S WEAK, MISTER! —AND NOW THAT YOU'VE HIT HIM, HE'LL BE WEAKER
TONY, YOU DON'T UNDERSTAND ABOUT ALL THIS...
OH, YES, I UNDERSTAND! —PLENTY OF THINGS NOW!
—WHY YOU WANTED TO COME TO CHINA IN THE FIRST PLACE—AND WHY YOU WANTED TO STAY HERE! —YOU'RE NO BETTER THAN A SHANGHAI SING-SONG GIRL!
Reg. U. S. Pat. Off.: Copyright, 1937, by Chicago Tribune-N. Y. News Syndicate, Inc.
MILTON CANIFF

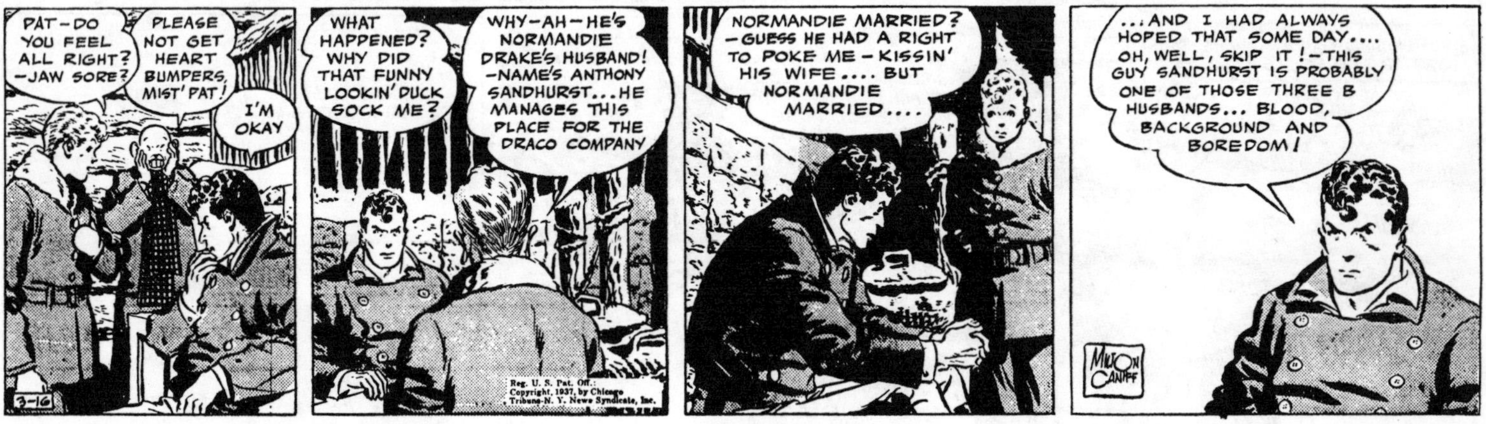
PAT—DO YOU FEEL ALL RIGHT? —JAW SORE?
PLEASE NOT GET HEART BUMPERS, MIST' PAT!
I'M OKAY
3-16
WHAT HAPPENED? WHY DID THAT FUNNY LOOKIN' DUCK SOCK ME?
WHY—AH—HE'S NORMANDIE DRAKE'S HUSBAND! —NAME'S ANTHONY SANDHURST...HE MANAGES THIS PLACE FOR THE DRACO COMPANY
Reg. U. S. Pat. Off.: Copyright, 1937, by Chicago Tribune-N. Y. News Syndicate, Inc.
NORMANDIE MARRIED? —GUESS HE HAD A RIGHT TO POKE ME—KISSIN' HIS WIFE.... BUT NORMANDIE MARRIED....
...AND I HAD ALWAYS HOPED THAT SOME DAY.... OH, WELL, SKIP IT!—THIS GUY SANDHURST IS PROBABLY ONE OF THOSE THREE B HUSBANDS... BLOOD, BACKGROUND AND BOREDOM!
MILTON CANIFF

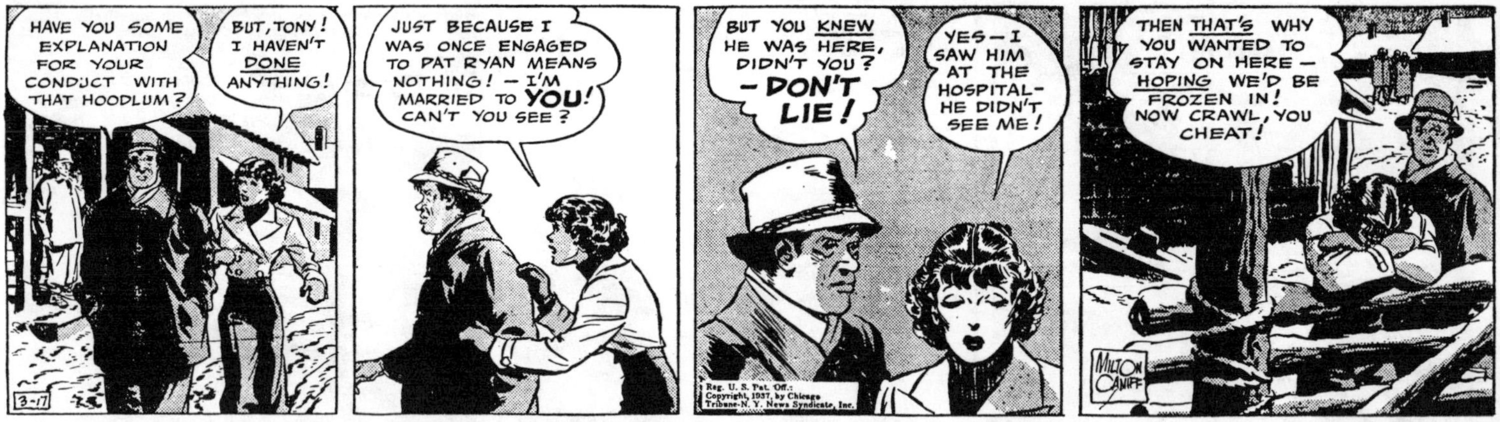
HAVE YOU SOME EXPLANATION FOR YOUR CONDUCT WITH THAT HOODLUM?
BUT, TONY! I HAVEN'T DONE ANYTHING!
3-17
JUST BECAUSE I WAS ONCE ENGAGED TO PAT RYAN MEANS NOTHING! —I'M MARRIED TO YOU! CAN'T YOU SEE?
BUT YOU KNEW HE WAS HERE, DIDN'T YOU? —DON'T LIE!
YES—I SAW HIM AT THE HOSPITAL— HE DIDN'T SEE ME!
Reg. U. S. Pat. Off.: Copyright, 1937, by Chicago Tribune-N. Y. News Syndicate, Inc.
THEN THAT'S WHY YOU WANTED TO STAY ON HERE— HOPING WE'D BE FROZEN IN! NOW CRAWL, YOU CHEAT!
MILTON CANIFF

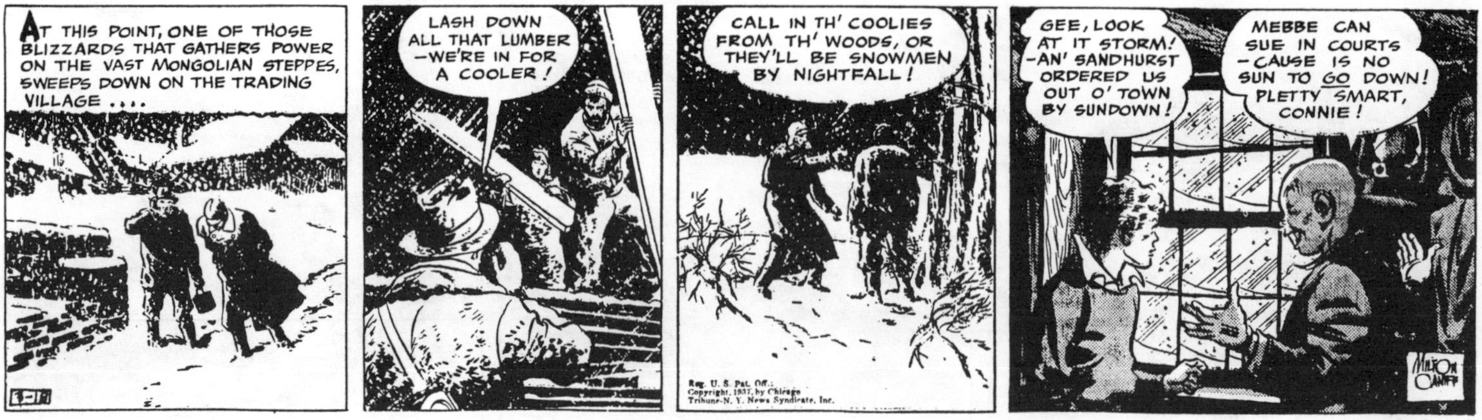
AT THIS POINT, ONE OF THOSE BLIZZARDS THAT GATHERS POWER ON THE VAST MONGOLIAN STEPPES, SWEEPS DOWN ON THE TRADING VILLAGE....
LASH DOWN ALL THAT LUMBER —WE'RE IN FOR A COOLER!
CALL IN TH' COOLIES FROM TH' WOODS, OR THEY'LL BE SNOWMEN BY NIGHTFALL!
Reg. U. S. Pat. Off.: Copyright, 1937, by Chicago Tribune-N. Y. News Syndicate, Inc.
GEE, LOOK AT IT STORM! —AN' SANDHURST ORDERED US OUT O' TOWN BY SUNDOWN!
MEBBE CAN SUE IN COURTS —CAUSE IS NO SUN TO GO DOWN! PLETTY SMART, CONNIE!
MILTON CANIFF

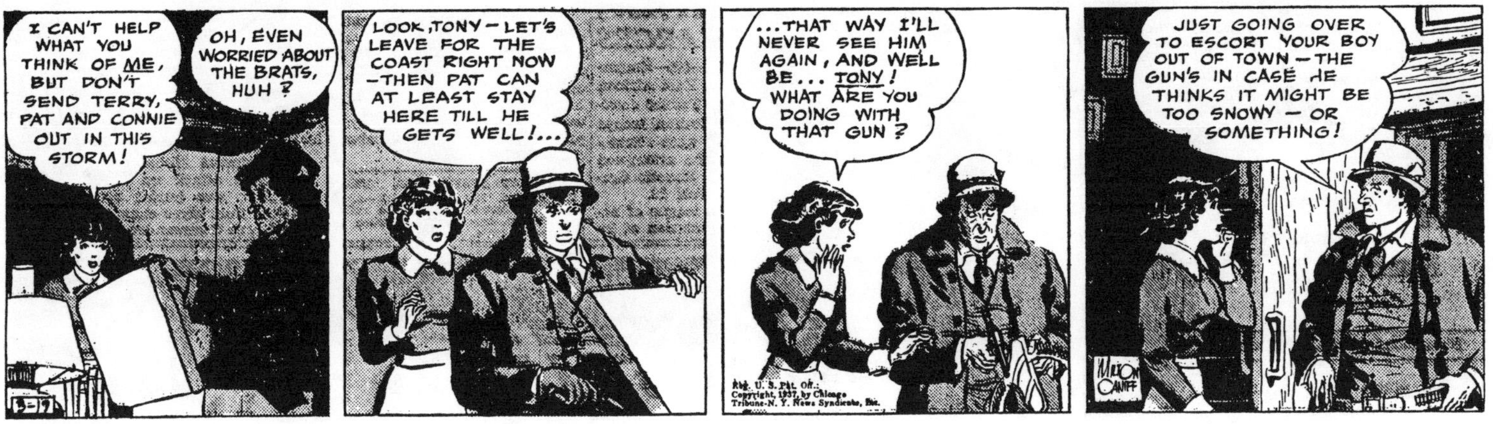
3-19
I CAN'T HELP WHAT YOU THINK OF ME, BUT DON'T SEND TERRY, PAT AND CONNIE OUT IN THIS STORM!
OH, EVEN WORRIED ABOUT THE BRATS, HUH?
LOOK, TONY – LET'S LEAVE FOR THE COAST RIGHT NOW – THEN PAT CAN AT LEAST STAY HERE TILL HE GETS WELL!...
...THAT WAY I'LL NEVER SEE HIM AGAIN, AND WE'LL BE... TONY! WHAT ARE YOU DOING WITH THAT GUN?
Reg. U. S. Pat. Off.: Copyright, 1937, by Chicago Tribune-N. Y. News Syndicate, Inc.
JUST GOING OVER TO ESCORT YOUR BOY OUT OF TOWN – THE GUN'S IN CASE HE THINKS IT MIGHT BE TOO SNOWY – OR SOMETHING!
MILTON CANIFF

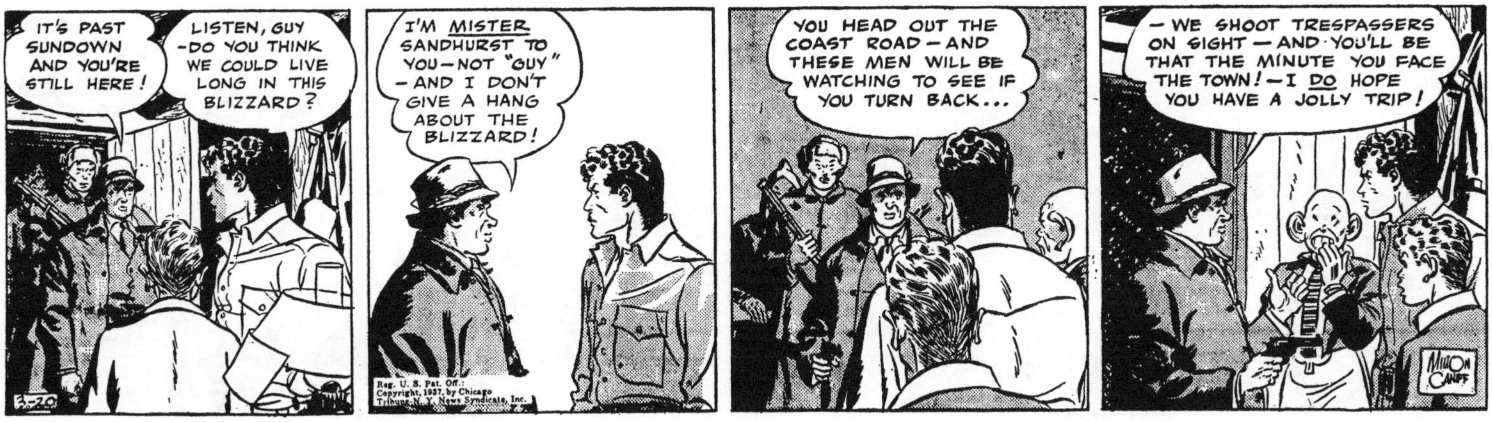
3-20
IT'S PAST SUNDOWN AND YOU'RE STILL HERE!
LISTEN, GUY – DO YOU THINK WE COULD LIVE LONG IN THIS BLIZZARD?
I'M MISTER SANDHURST TO YOU – NOT "GUY" – AND I DON'T GIVE A HANG ABOUT THE BLIZZARD!
Reg. U. S. Pat. Off.: Copyright, 1937, by Chicago Tribune-N. Y. News Syndicate, Inc.
YOU HEAD OUT THE COAST ROAD – AND THESE MEN WILL BE WATCHING TO SEE IF YOU TURN BACK...
– WE SHOOT TRESPASSERS ON SIGHT – AND YOU'LL BE THAT THE MINUTE YOU FACE THE TOWN! – I DO HOPE YOU HAVE A JOLLY TRIP!
MILTON CANIFF

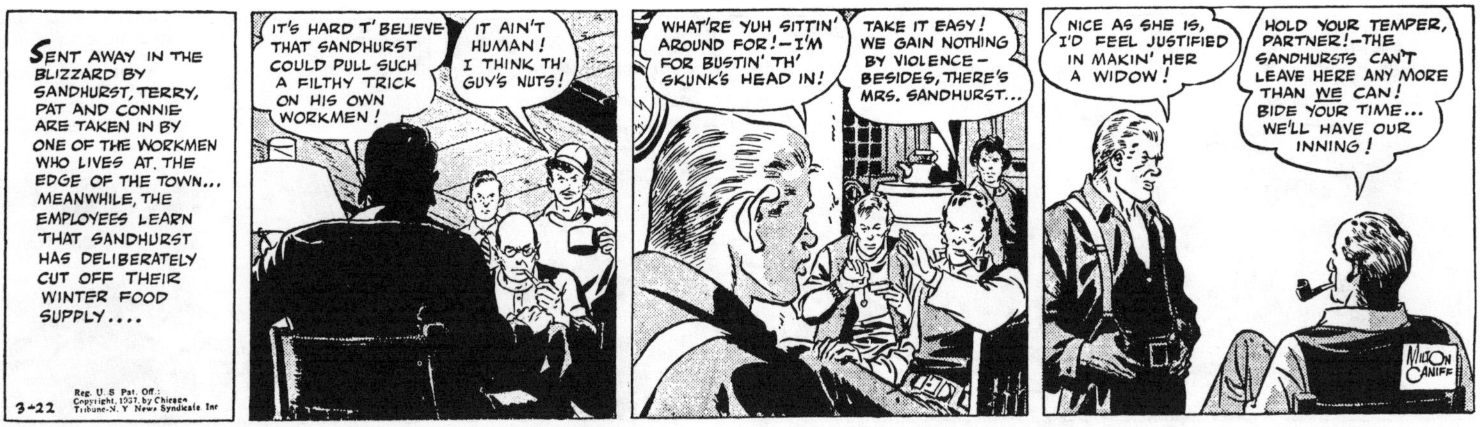
SENT AWAY IN THE BLIZZARD BY SANDHURST, TERRY, PAT AND CONNIE ARE TAKEN IN BY ONE OF THE WORKMEN WHO LIVES AT THE EDGE OF THE TOWN... MEANWHILE, THE EMPLOYEES LEARN THAT SANDHURST HAS DELIBERATELY CUT OFF THEIR WINTER FOOD SUPPLY....
3-22
Reg. U. S. Pat. Off.: Copyright, 1937, by Chicago Tribune-N. Y. News Syndicate Inc
IT'S HARD T' BELIEVE THAT SANDHURST COULD PULL SUCH A FILTHY TRICK ON HIS OWN WORKMEN!
IT AIN'T HUMAN! I THINK TH' GUY'S NUTS!
WHAT'RE YUH SITTIN' AROUND FOR! – I'M FOR BUSTIN' TH' SKUNK'S HEAD IN!
TAKE IT EASY! WE GAIN NOTHING BY VIOLENCE – BESIDES, THERE'S MRS. SANDHURST...
NICE AS SHE IS, I'D FEEL JUSTIFIED IN MAKIN' HER A WIDOW!
HOLD YOUR TEMPER, PARTNER! – THE SANDHURSTS CAN'T LEAVE HERE ANY MORE THAN WE CAN! BIDE YOUR TIME... WE'LL HAVE OUR INNING!
MILTON CANIFF

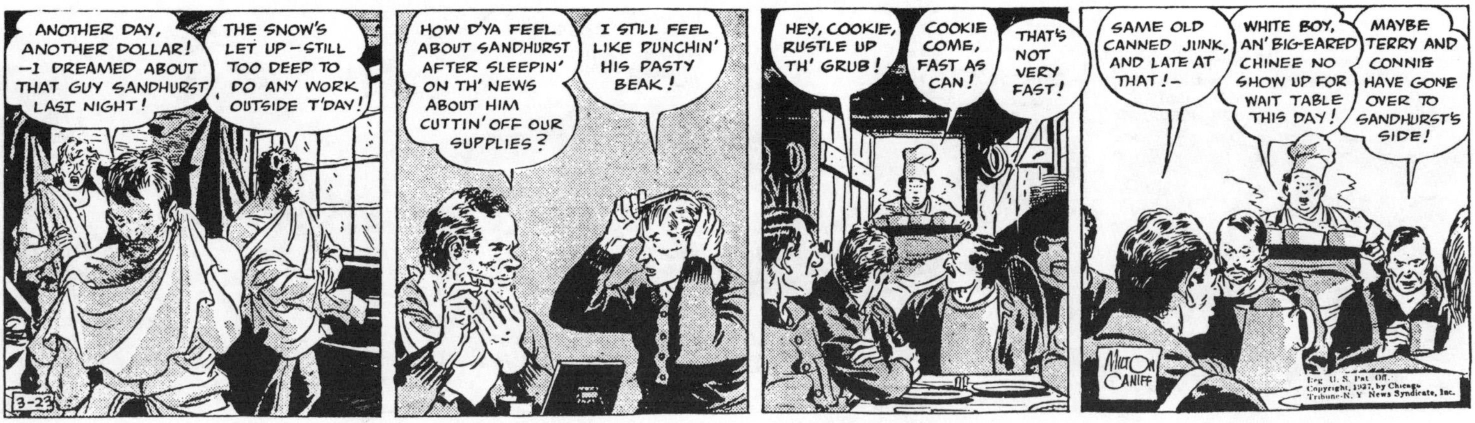
ANOTHER DAY, ANOTHER DOLLAR! – I DREAMED ABOUT THAT GUY SANDHURST LAST NIGHT!
THE SNOW'S LET UP – STILL TOO DEEP TO DO ANY WORK OUTSIDE T'DAY!
3-23
HOW D'YA FEEL ABOUT SANDHURST AFTER SLEEPIN' ON TH' NEWS ABOUT HIM CUTTIN' OFF OUR SUPPLIES?
I STILL FEEL LIKE PUNCHIN' HIS PASTY BEAK!
HEY, COOKIE, RUSTLE UP TH' GRUB!
COOKIE COME, FAST AS CAN!
THAT'S NOT VERY FAST!
MILTON CANIFF
SAME OLD CANNED JUNK, AND LATE AT THAT! –
WHITE BOY, AN' BIG-EARED CHINEE NO SHOW UP FOR WAIT TABLE THIS DAY!
MAYBE TERRY AND CONNIE HAVE GONE OVER TO SANDHURST'S SIDE!
Reg. U. S. Pat. Off.: Copyright, 1937, by Chicago Tribune-N. Y. News Syndicate, Inc.

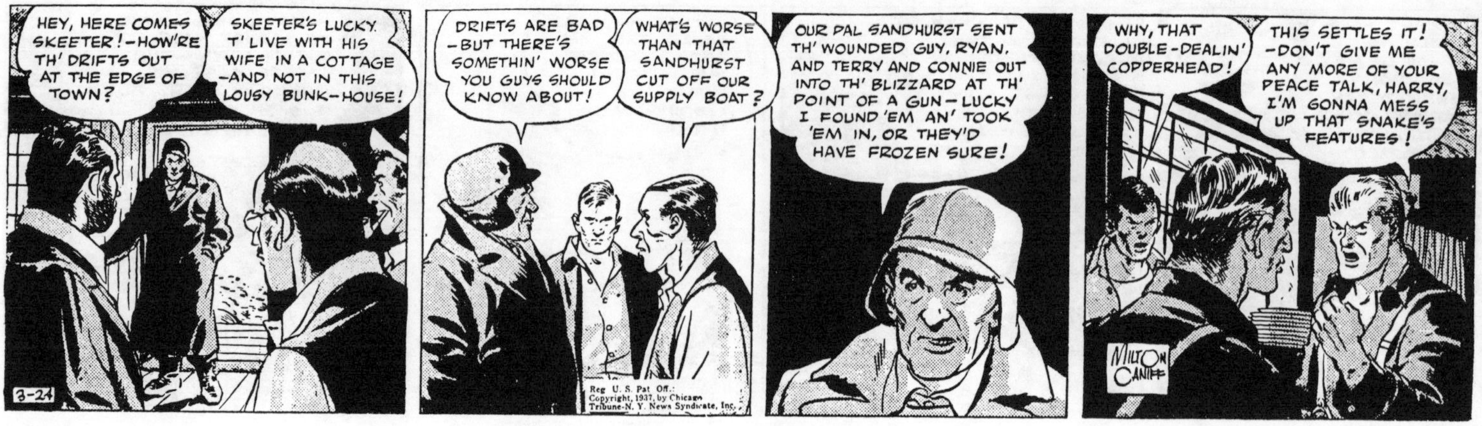
HEY, HERE COMES SKEETER! -HOW'RE TH' DRIFTS OUT AT THE EDGE OF TOWN?
SKEETER'S LUCKY. T' LIVE WITH HIS WIFE IN A COTTAGE -AND NOT IN THIS LOUSY BUNK-HOUSE!
3-24
DRIFTS ARE BAD -BUT THERE'S SOMETHIN' WORSE YOU GUYS SHOULD KNOW ABOUT!
WHAT'S WORSE THAN THAT SANDHURST CUT OFF OUR SUPPLY BOAT?
Reg U. S. Pat. Off.: Copyright, 1937, by Chicago Tribune-N. Y. News Syndicate, Inc.
OUR PAL SANDHURST SENT TH' WOUNDED GUY, RYAN, AND TERRY AND CONNIE OUT INTO TH' BLIZZARD AT TH' POINT OF A GUN - LUCKY I FOUND 'EM AN' TOOK 'EM IN, OR THEY'D HAVE FROZEN SURE!
WHY, THAT DOUBLE-DEALIN' COPPERHEAD!
THIS SETTLES IT! -DON'T GIVE ME ANY MORE OF YOUR PEACE TALK, HARRY, I'M GONNA MESS UP THAT SNAKE'S FEATURES!
MILTON CANIFF

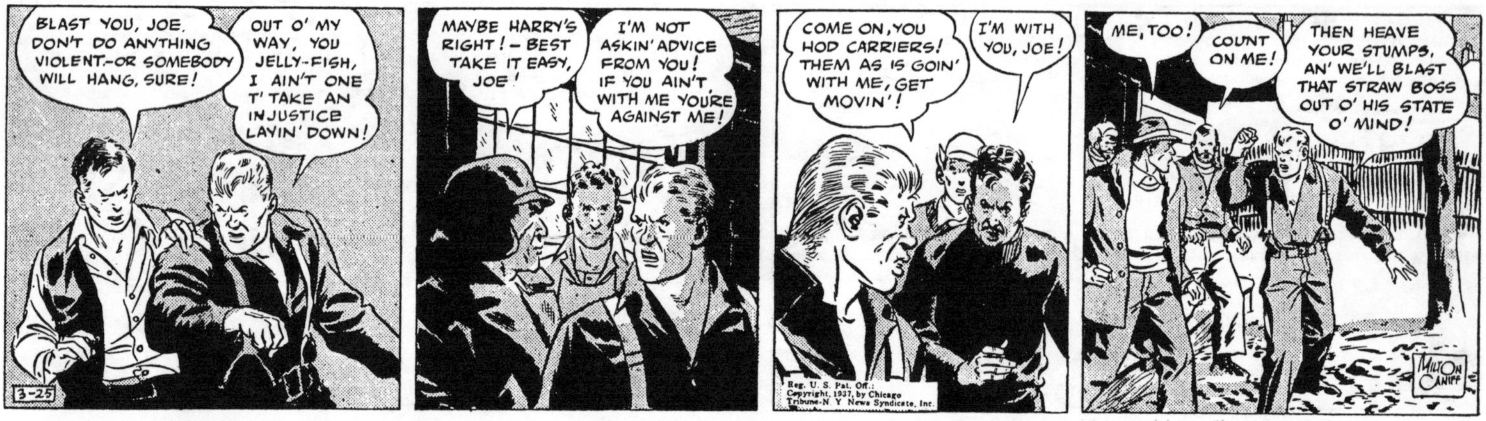
BLAST YOU, JOE. DON'T DO ANYTHING VIOLENT.-OR SOMEBODY WILL HANG, SURE!
OUT O' MY WAY, YOU JELLY-FISH, I AIN'T ONE T' TAKE AN INJUSTICE LAYIN' DOWN!
3-25
MAYBE HARRY'S RIGHT! - BEST TAKE IT EASY, JOE!
I'M NOT ASKIN' ADVICE FROM YOU! IF YOU AIN'T WITH ME YOU'RE AGAINST ME!
COME ON, YOU HOD CARRIERS! THEM AS IS GOIN' WITH ME, GET MOVIN'!
I'M WITH YOU, JOE!
Reg. U. S. Pat. Off.: Copyright, 1937, by Chicago Tribune-N. Y. News Syndicate, Inc.
ME, TOO!
COUNT ON ME!
THEN HEAVE YOUR STUMPS, AN' WE'LL BLAST THAT STRAW BOSS OUT O' HIS STATE O' MIND!
MILTON CANIFF

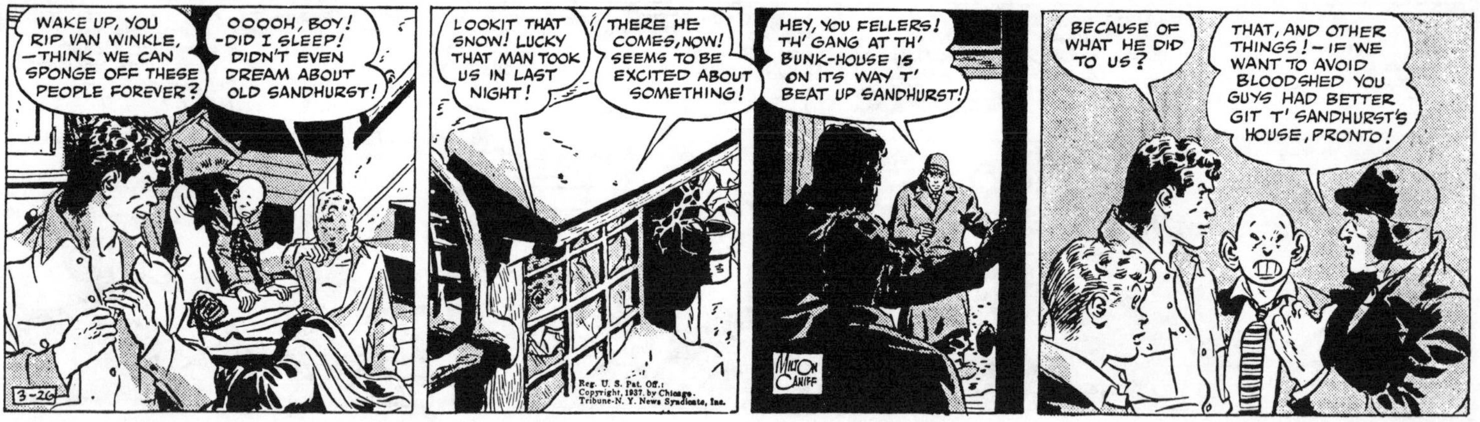
WAKE UP, YOU RIP VAN WINKLE, -THINK WE CAN SPONGE OFF THESE PEOPLE FOREVER?
OOOOH, BOY! -DID I SLEEP! DIDN'T EVEN DREAM ABOUT OLD SANDHURST!
3-26
LOOKIT THAT SNOW! LUCKY THAT MAN TOOK US IN LAST NIGHT!
THERE HE COMES, NOW! SEEMS TO BE EXCITED ABOUT SOMETHING!
Reg. U. S. Pat. Off.: Copyright, 1937, by Chicago Tribune-N. Y. News Syndicate, Inc.
HEY, YOU FELLERS! TH' GANG AT TH' BUNK-HOUSE IS ON ITS WAY T' BEAT UP SANDHURST!
MILTON CANIFF
BECAUSE OF WHAT HE DID TO US?
THAT, AND OTHER THINGS! - IF WE WANT TO AVOID BLOODSHED YOU GUYS HAD BETTER GIT T' SANDHURST'S HOUSE, PRONTO!

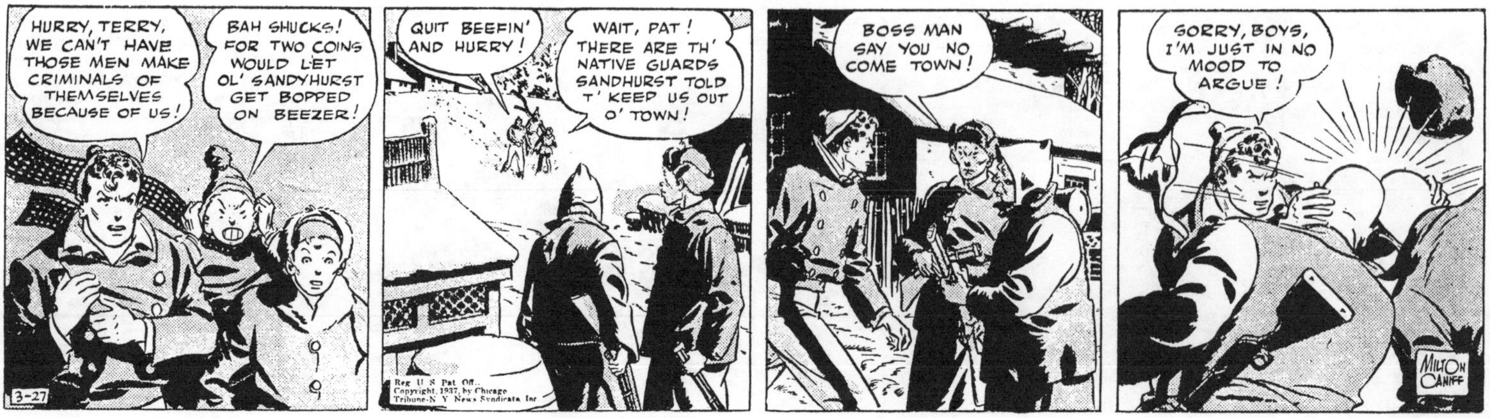
HURRY, TERRY, WE CAN'T HAVE THOSE MEN MAKE CRIMINALS OF THEMSELVES BECAUSE OF US!
BAH SHUCKS! FOR TWO COINS WOULD LET OL' SANDYHURST GET BOPPED ON BEEZER!
3-27
QUIT BEEFIN' AND HURRY!
WAIT, PAT! THERE ARE TH' NATIVE GUARDS SANDHURST TOLD T' KEEP US OUT O' TOWN!
Reg U S Pat Off.: Copyright, 1937, by Chicago Tribune-N Y News Syndicate Inc
BOSS MAN SAY YOU NO COME TOWN!
SORRY, BOYS, I'M JUST IN NO MOOD TO ARGUE!
MILTON CANIFF

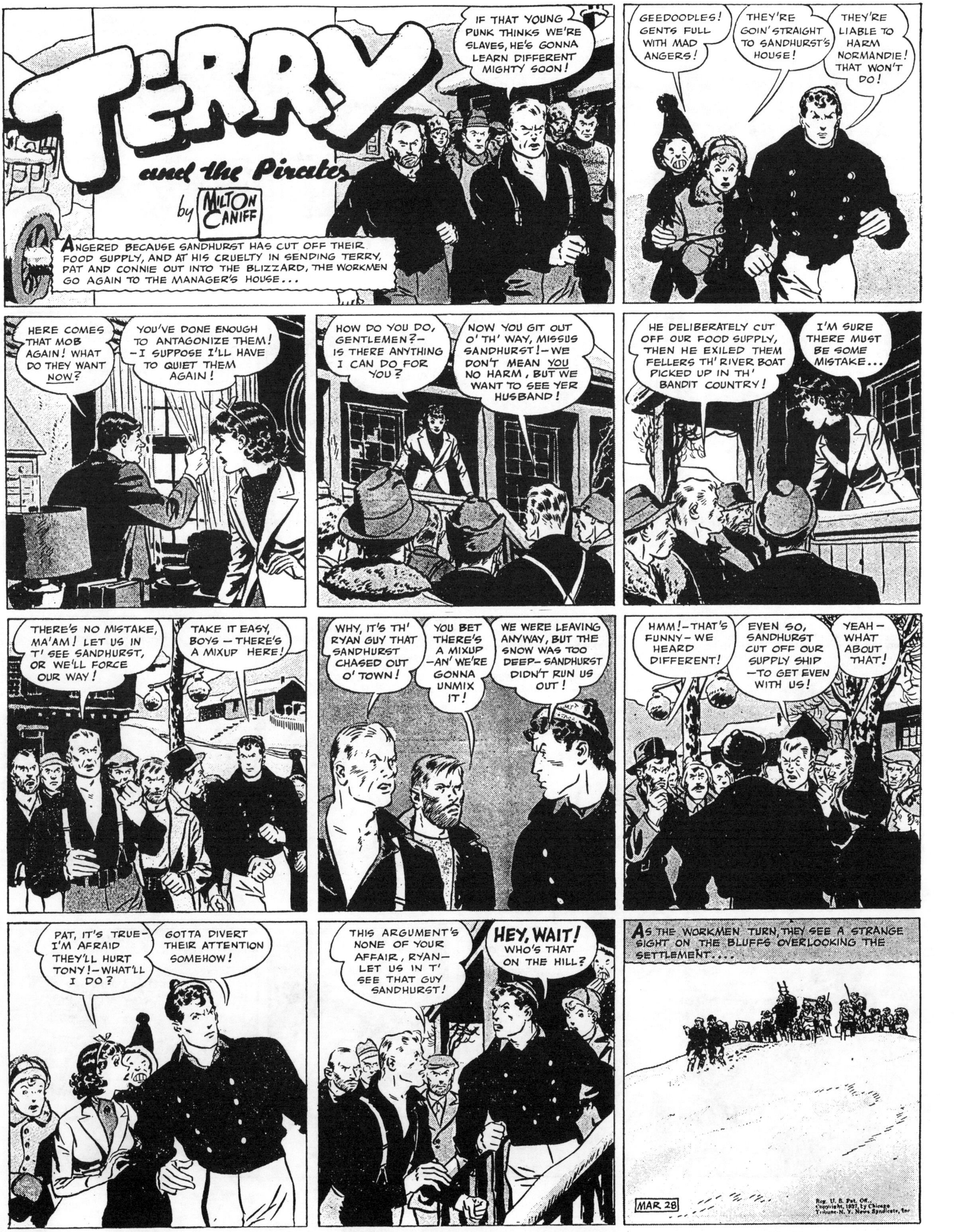
TERRY and the Pirates
by MILTON CANIFF
IF THAT YOUNG PUNK THINKS WE'RE SLAVES, HE'S GONNA LEARN DIFFERENT MIGHTY SOON!
ANGERED BECAUSE SANDHURST HAS CUT OFF THEIR FOOD SUPPLY, AND AT HIS CRUELTY IN SENDING TERRY, PAT AND CONNIE OUT INTO THE BLIZZARD, THE WORKMEN GO AGAIN TO THE MANAGER'S HOUSE...
GEEDOODLES! GENTS FULL WITH MAD ANGERS!
THEY'RE GOIN' STRAIGHT TO SANDHURST'S HOUSE!
THEY'RE LIABLE TO HARM NORMANDIE! THAT WON'T DO!
HERE COMES THAT MOB AGAIN! WHAT DO THEY WANT NOW?
YOU'VE DONE ENOUGH TO ANTAGONIZE THEM! —I SUPPOSE I'LL HAVE TO QUIET THEM AGAIN!
HOW DO YOU DO, GENTLEMEN?— IS THERE ANYTHING I CAN DO FOR YOU?
NOW YOU GIT OUT O' TH' WAY, MISSUS SANDHURST! — WE DON'T MEAN YOU NO HARM, BUT WE WANT TO SEE YER HUSBAND!
HE DELIBERATELY CUT OFF OUR FOOD SUPPLY, THEN HE EXILED THEM FELLERS TH' RIVER BOAT PICKED UP IN TH' BANDIT COUNTRY!
I'M SURE THERE MUST BE SOME MISTAKE...
THERE'S NO MISTAKE, MA'AM! LET US IN T' SEE SANDHURST, OR WE'LL FORCE OUR WAY!
TAKE IT EASY, BOYS — THERE'S A MIXUP HERE!
WHY, IT'S TH' RYAN GUY THAT SANDHURST CHASED OUT O' TOWN!
YOU BET THERE'S A MIXUP —AN' WE'RE GONNA UNMIX IT!
WE WERE LEAVING ANYWAY, BUT THE SNOW WAS TOO DEEP— SANDHURST DIDN'T RUN US OUT!
HMM! — THAT'S FUNNY — WE HEARD DIFFERENT!
EVEN SO, SANDHURST CUT OFF OUR SUPPLY SHIP —TO GET EVEN WITH US!
YEAH — WHAT ABOUT THAT!
PAT, IT'S TRUE — I'M AFRAID THEY'LL HURT TONY! — WHAT'LL I DO?
GOTTA DIVERT THEIR ATTENTION SOMEHOW!
THIS ARGUMENT'S NONE OF YOUR AFFAIR, RYAN— LET US IN T' SEE THAT GUY SANDHURST!
HEY, WAIT! WHO'S THAT ON THE HILL?
AS THE WORKMEN TURN, THEY SEE A STRANGE SIGHT ON THE BLUFFS OVERLOOKING THE SETTLEMENT...
MAR 28
Reg. U. S. Pat. Off., Copyright, 1937, by Chicago Tribune-N. Y. News Syndicate, Inc

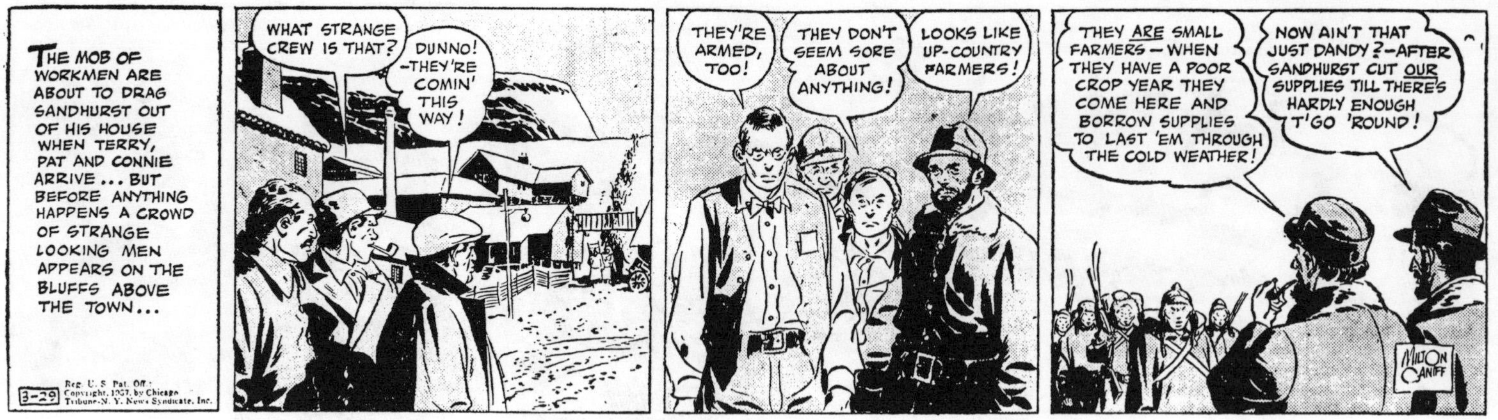
THE MOB OF WORKMEN ARE ABOUT TO DRAG SANDHURST OUT OF HIS HOUSE WHEN TERRY, PAT AND CONNIE ARRIVE ... BUT BEFORE ANYTHING HAPPENS A CROWD OF STRANGE LOOKING MEN APPEARS ON THE BLUFFS ABOVE THE TOWN...
3-29
Reg. U. S. Pat. Off.: Copyright, 1937, by Chicago Tribune-N. Y. News Syndicate, Inc.
WHAT STRANGE CREW IS THAT?
DUNNO! -THEY'RE COMIN' THIS WAY!
THEY'RE ARMED, TOO!
THEY DON'T SEEM SORE ABOUT ANYTHING!
LOOKS LIKE UP-COUNTRY FARMERS!
THEY ARE SMALL FARMERS — WHEN THEY HAVE A POOR CROP YEAR THEY COME HERE AND BORROW SUPPLIES TO LAST 'EM THROUGH THE COLD WEATHER!
NOW AIN'T THAT JUST DANDY? -AFTER SANDHURST CUT OUR SUPPLIES TILL THERE'S HARDLY ENOUGH T'GO 'ROUND!
MILTON CANIFF

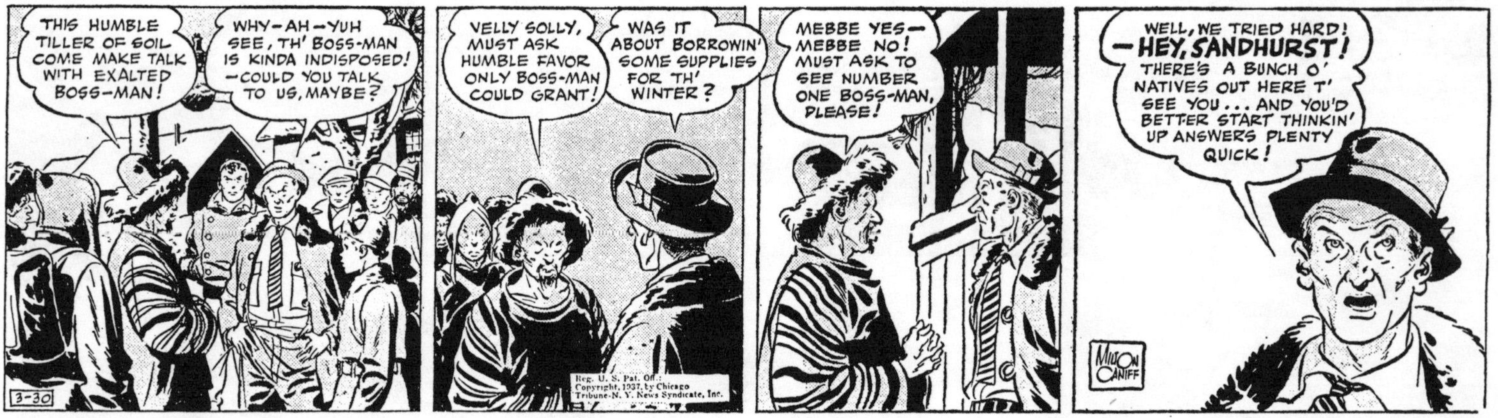
THIS HUMBLE TILLER OF SOIL COME MAKE TALK WITH EXALTED BOSS-MAN!
WHY-AH-YUH SEE, TH' BOSS-MAN IS KINDA INDISPOSED! -COULD YOU TALK TO US, MAYBE?
3-30
VELLY SOLLY, MUST ASK HUMBLE FAVOR ONLY BOSS-MAN COULD GRANT!
WAS IT ABOUT BORROWIN' SOME SUPPLIES FOR TH' WINTER?
Reg. U. S. Pat. Off.: Copyright, 1937, by Chicago Tribune-N. Y. News Syndicate, Inc.
MEBBE YES— MEBBE NO! MUST ASK TO SEE NUMBER ONE BOSS-MAN, PLEASE!
WELL, WE TRIED HARD! —HEY, SANDHURST! THERE'S A BUNCH O' NATIVES OUT HERE T' SEE YOU... AND YOU'D BETTER START THINKIN' UP ANSWERS PLENTY QUICK!
MILTON CANIFF

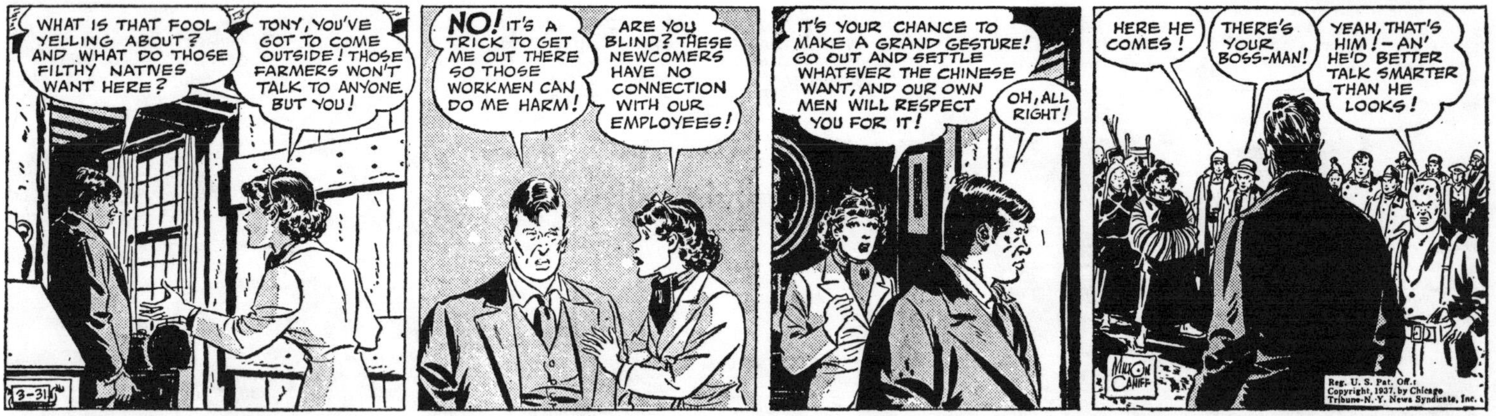
WHAT IS THAT FOOL YELLING ABOUT? AND WHAT DO THOSE FILTHY NATIVES WANT HERE?
TONY, YOU'VE GOT TO COME OUTSIDE! THOSE FARMERS WON'T TALK TO ANYONE BUT YOU!
3-31
NO! IT'S A TRICK TO GET ME OUT THERE SO THOSE WORKMEN CAN DO ME HARM!
ARE YOU BLIND? THESE NEWCOMERS HAVE NO CONNECTION WITH OUR EMPLOYEES!
IT'S YOUR CHANCE TO MAKE A GRAND GESTURE! GO OUT AND SETTLE WHATEVER THE CHINESE WANT, AND OUR OWN MEN WILL RESPECT YOU FOR IT!
OH, ALL RIGHT!
HERE HE COMES!
THERE'S YOUR BOSS-MAN!
YEAH, THAT'S HIM! —AN' HE'D BETTER TALK SMARTER THAN HE LOOKS!
MILTON CANIFF
Reg. U. S. Pat. Off.: Copyright, 1937, by Chicago Tribune-N. Y. News Syndicate, Inc.

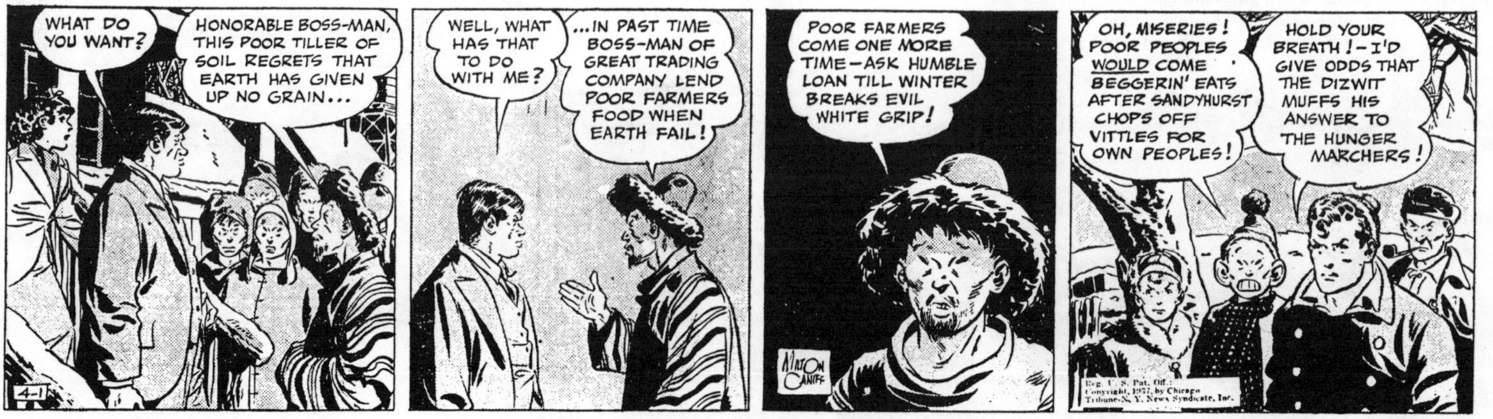
WHAT DO YOU WANT?
HONORABLE BOSS-MAN, THIS POOR TILLER OF SOIL REGRETS THAT EARTH HAS GIVEN UP NO GRAIN...
4-1
WELL, WHAT HAS THAT TO DO WITH ME?
...IN PAST TIME BOSS-MAN OF GREAT TRADING COMPANY LEND POOR FARMERS FOOD WHEN EARTH FAIL!
POOR FARMERS COME ONE MORE TIME—ASK HUMBLE LOAN TILL WINTER BREAKS EVIL WHITE GRIP!
MILTON CANIFF
OH, MISERIES! POOR PEOPLES WOULD COME BEGGERIN' EATS AFTER SANDYHURST CHOPS OFF VITTLES FOR OWN PEOPLES!
HOLD YOUR BREATH! -I'D GIVE ODDS THAT THE DIZWIT MUFFS HIS ANSWER TO THE HUNGER MARCHERS!
Reg. U. S. Pat. Off.: Copyright, 1937, by Chicago Tribune-N. Y. News Syndicate, Inc.

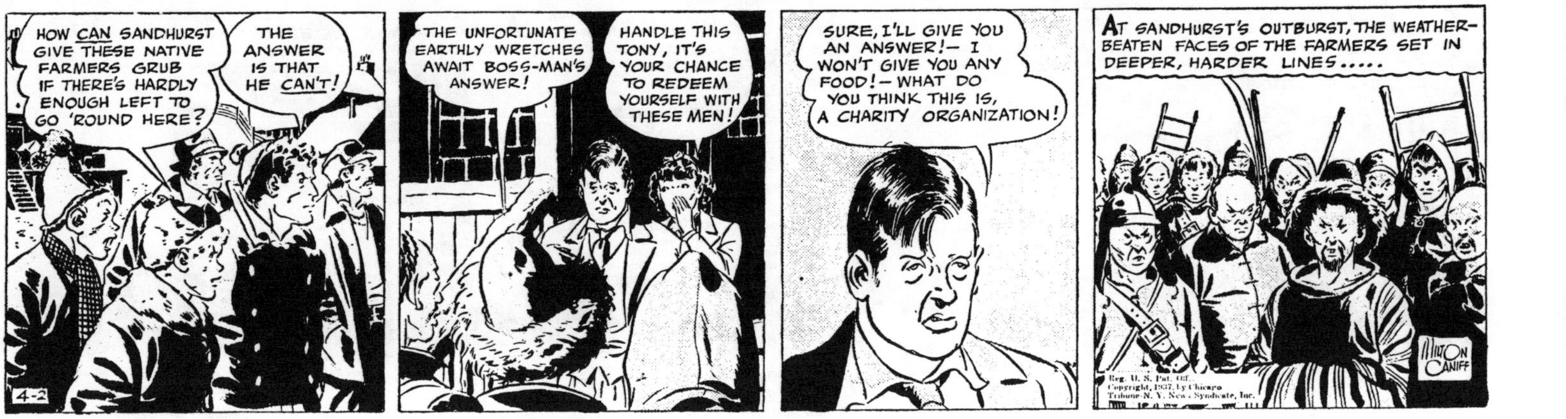

4-2
HOW CAN SANDHURST GIVE THESE NATIVE FARMERS GRUB IF THERE'S HARDLY ENOUGH LEFT TO GO 'ROUND HERE?
THE ANSWER IS THAT HE CAN'T!
THE UNFORTUNATE EARTHLY WRETCHES AWAIT BOSS-MAN'S ANSWER!
HANDLE THIS TONY, IT'S YOUR CHANCE TO REDEEM YOURSELF WITH THESE MEN!
SURE, I'LL GIVE YOU AN ANSWER!— I WON'T GIVE YOU ANY FOOD!— WHAT DO YOU THINK THIS IS, A CHARITY ORGANIZATION!
AT SANDHURST'S OUTBURST, THE WEATHER-BEATEN FACES OF THE FARMERS SET IN DEEPER, HARDER LINES.....
MILTON CANIFF
Reg. U. S. Pat. Off. Copyright, 1937, by Chicago Tribune-N. Y. News Syndicate, Inc.

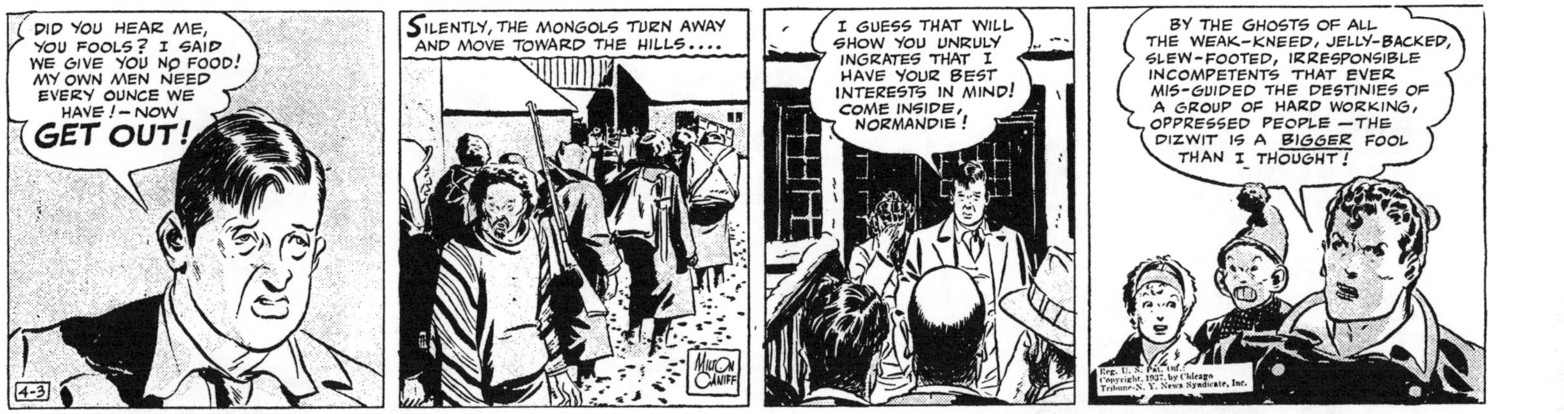

DID YOU HEAR ME, YOU FOOLS? I SAID WE GIVE YOU NO FOOD! MY OWN MEN NEED EVERY OUNCE WE HAVE!— NOW GET OUT!
4-3
SILENTLY, THE MONGOLS TURN AWAY AND MOVE TOWARD THE HILLS....
MILTON CANIFF
I GUESS THAT WILL SHOW YOU UNRULY INGRATES THAT I HAVE YOUR BEST INTERESTS IN MIND! COME INSIDE, NORMANDIE!
BY THE GHOSTS OF ALL THE WEAK-KNEED, JELLY-BACKED, SLEW-FOOTED, IRRESPONSIBLE INCOMPETENTS THAT EVER MIS-GUIDED THE DESTINIES OF A GROUP OF HARD WORKING, OPPRESSED PEOPLE —THE DIZWIT IS A BIGGER FOOL THAN I THOUGHT!
Reg. U. S. Pat. Off. Copyright, 1937, by Chicago Tribune-N. Y. News Syndicate, Inc.

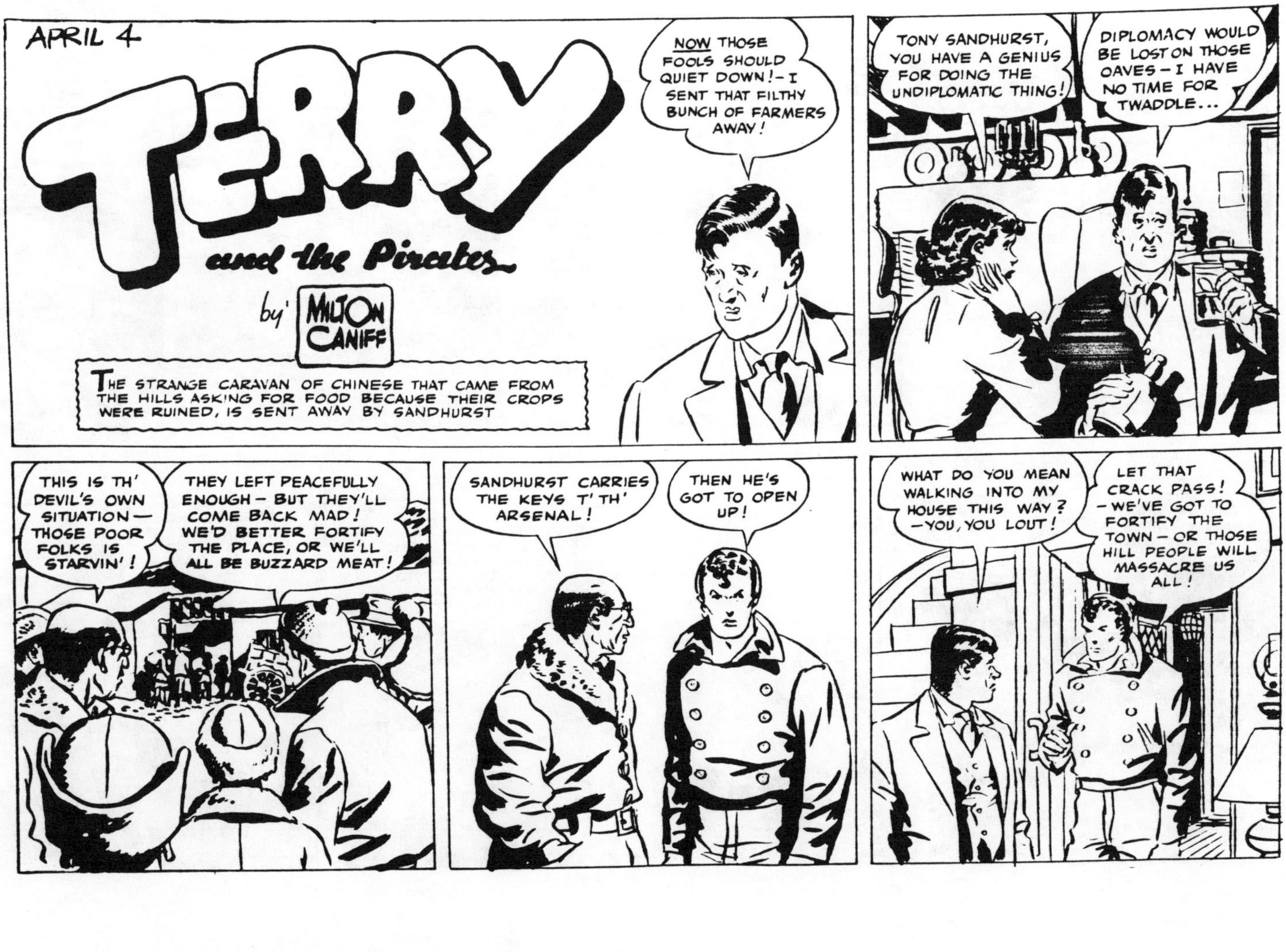

APRIL 4
TERRY and the Pirates
by MILTON CANIFF
THE STRANGE CARAVAN OF CHINESE THAT CAME FROM THE HILLS ASKING FOR FOOD BECAUSE THEIR CROPS WERE RUINED, IS SENT AWAY BY SANDHURST
NOW THOSE FOOLS SHOULD QUIET DOWN!— I SENT THAT FILTHY BUNCH OF FARMERS AWAY!
TONY SANDHURST, YOU HAVE A GENIUS FOR DOING THE UNDIPLOMATIC THING!
DIPLOMACY WOULD BE LOST ON THOSE OAVES — I HAVE NO TIME FOR TWADDLE...
THIS IS TH' DEVIL'S OWN SITUATION — THOSE POOR FOLKS IS STARVIN'!
THEY LEFT PEACEFULLY ENOUGH — BUT THEY'LL COME BACK MAD! WE'D BETTER FORTIFY THE PLACE, OR WE'LL ALL BE BUZZARD MEAT!
SANDHURST CARRIES THE KEYS T' TH' ARSENAL!
THEN HE'S GOT TO OPEN UP!
WHAT DO YOU MEAN WALKING INTO MY HOUSE THIS WAY? —YOU, YOU LOUT!
LET THAT CRACK PASS! — WE'VE GOT TO FORTIFY THE TOWN — OR THOSE HILL PEOPLE WILL MASSACRE US ALL!

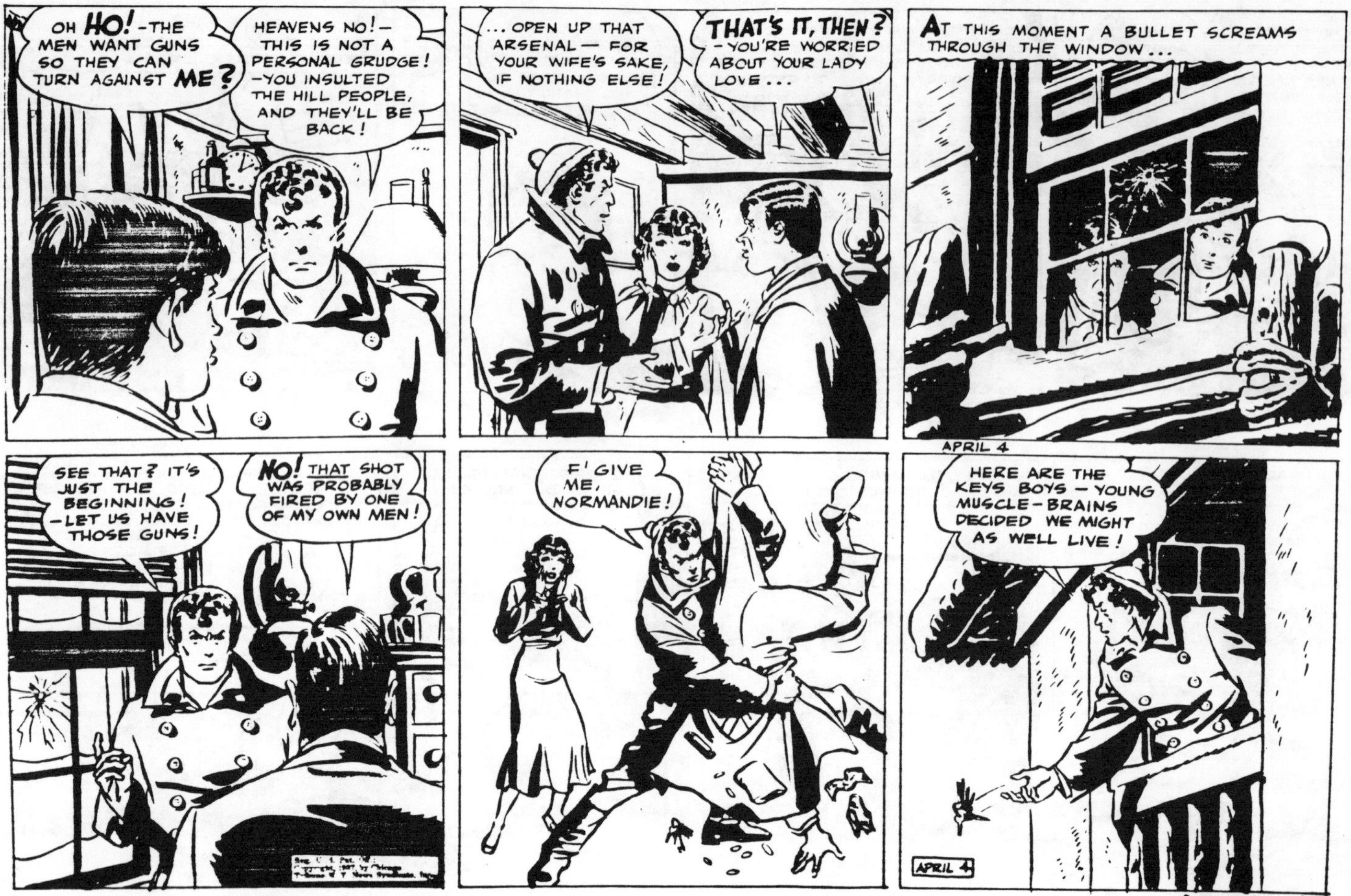

OH HO! -THE MEN WANT GUNS SO THEY CAN TURN AGAINST ME?
HEAVENS NO! - THIS IS NOT A PERSONAL GRUDGE! -YOU INSULTED THE HILL PEOPLE, AND THEY'LL BE BACK!
... OPEN UP THAT ARSENAL — FOR YOUR WIFE'S SAKE, IF NOTHING ELSE!
THAT'S IT, THEN? -YOU'RE WORRIED ABOUT YOUR LADY LOVE...
AT THIS MOMENT A BULLET SCREAMS THROUGH THE WINDOW...
APRIL 4
SEE THAT? IT'S JUST THE BEGINNING! -LET US HAVE THOSE GUNS!
NO! THAT SHOT WAS PROBABLY FIRED BY ONE OF MY OWN MEN!
F' GIVE ME, NORMANDIE!
HERE ARE THE KEYS BOYS - YOUNG MUSCLE-BRAINS DECIDED WE MIGHT AS WELL LIVE!
APRIL 4

APRIL 4

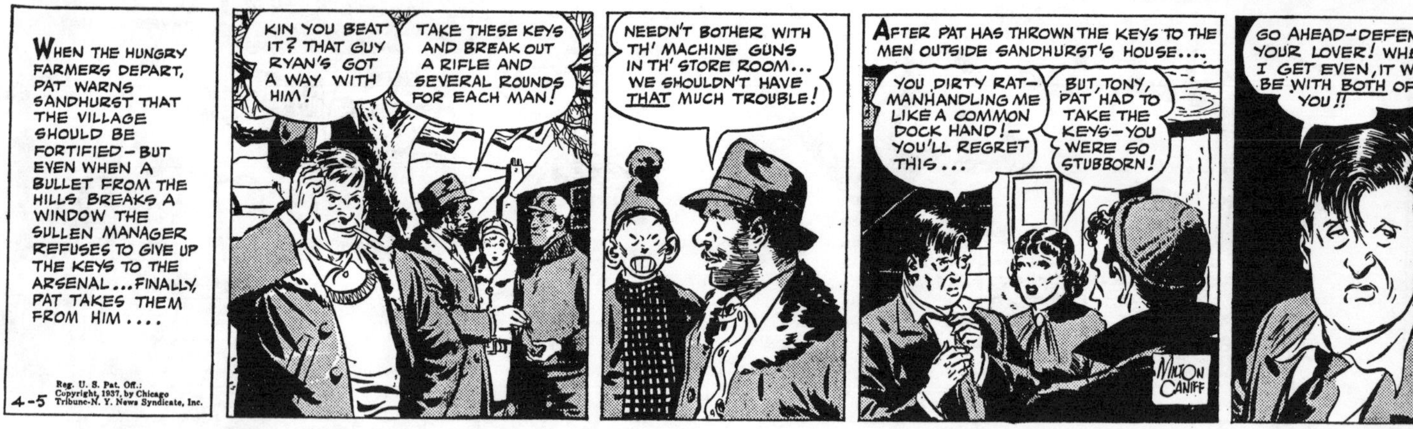

WHEN THE HUNGRY FARMERS DEPART, PAT WARNS SANDHURST THAT THE VILLAGE SHOULD BE FORTIFIED - BUT EVEN WHEN A BULLET FROM THE HILLS BREAKS A WINDOW THE SULLEN MANAGER REFUSES TO GIVE UP THE KEYS TO THE ARSENAL... FINALLY, PAT TAKES THEM FROM HIM....
Reg. U. S. Pat. Off.: Copyright, 1937, by Chicago Tribune-N. Y. News Syndicate, Inc.
4-5
KIN YOU BEAT IT? THAT GUY RYAN'S GOT A WAY WITH HIM!
TAKE THESE KEYS AND BREAK OUT A RIFLE AND SEVERAL ROUNDS FOR EACH MAN!
NEEDN'T BOTHER WITH TH' MACHINE GUNS IN TH' STORE ROOM... WE SHOULDN'T HAVE THAT MUCH TROUBLE!
AFTER PAT HAS THROWN THE KEYS TO THE MEN OUTSIDE SANDHURST'S HOUSE....
YOU DIRTY RAT-MANHANDLING ME LIKE A COMMON DOCK HAND! - YOU'LL REGRET THIS...
BUT, TONY, PAT HAD TO TAKE THE KEYS-YOU WERE SO STUBBORN!
MILTON CANIFF
GO AHEAD-DEFEND YOUR LOVER! WHEN I GET EVEN, IT WILL BE WITH BOTH OF YOU!!

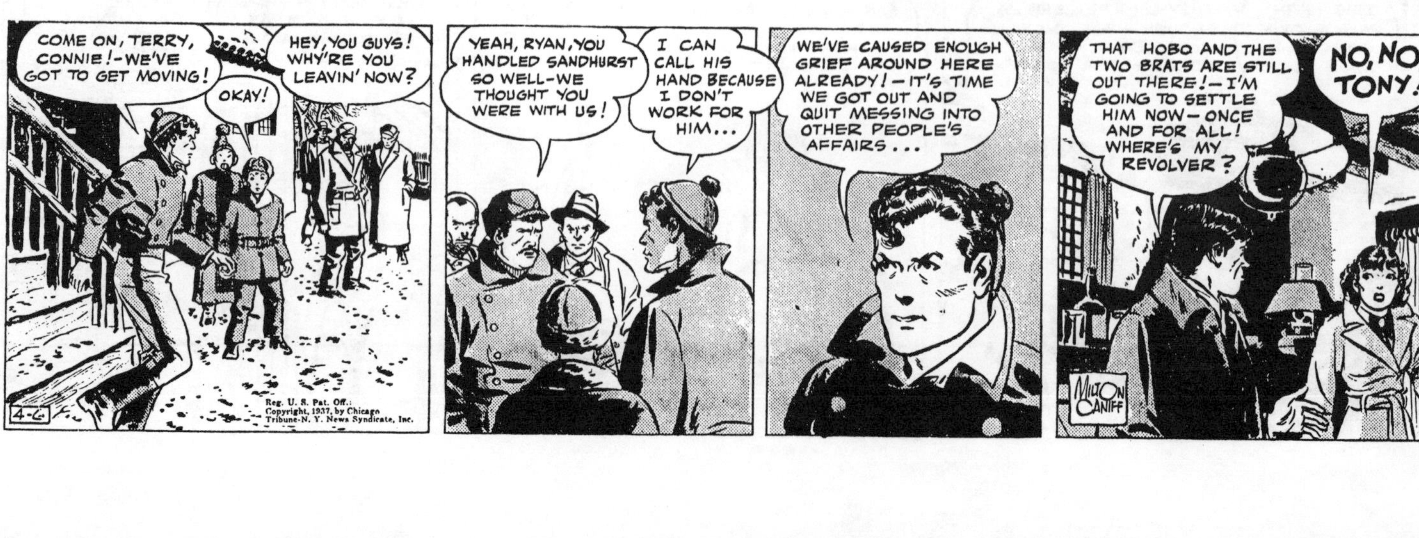

COME ON, TERRY, CONNIE! -WE'VE GOT TO GET MOVING!
OKAY!
HEY, YOU GUYS! WHY'RE YOU LEAVIN' NOW?
4-6
Reg. U. S. Pat. Off.: Copyright, 1937, by Chicago Tribune-N. Y. News Syndicate, Inc.
YEAH, RYAN, YOU HANDLED SANDHURST SO WELL-WE THOUGHT YOU WERE WITH US!
I CAN CALL HIS HAND BECAUSE I DON'T WORK FOR HIM...
WE'VE CAUSED ENOUGH GRIEF AROUND HERE ALREADY! - IT'S TIME WE GOT OUT AND QUIT MESSING INTO OTHER PEOPLE'S AFFAIRS...
THAT HOBO AND THE TWO BRATS ARE STILL OUT THERE! - I'M GOING TO SETTLE HIM NOW - ONCE AND FOR ALL! WHERE'S MY REVOLVER?
NO, NO, TONY!
MILTON CANIFF

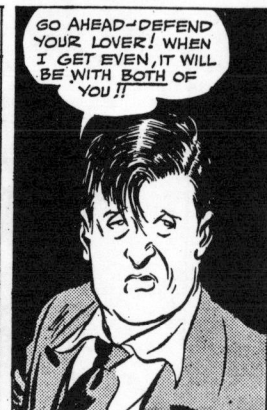

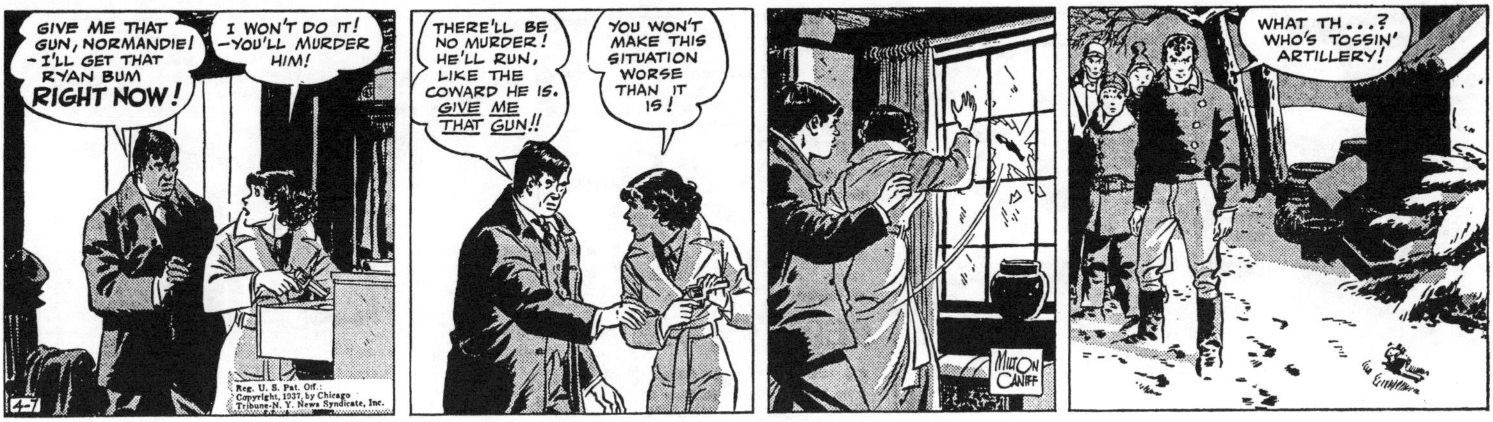
GIVE ME THAT GUN, NORMANDIE! - I'LL GET THAT RYAN BUM RIGHT NOW!
I WON'T DO IT! —YOU'LL MURDER HIM!
Reg. U. S. Pat. Off.: Copyright, 1937, by Chicago Tribune-N. Y. News Syndicate, Inc.
4-7
THERE'LL BE NO MURDER! HE'LL RUN, LIKE THE COWARD HE IS. GIVE ME THAT GUN!!
YOU WON'T MAKE THIS SITUATION WORSE THAN IT IS!
MILTON CANIFF
WHAT TH ...? WHO'S TOSSIN' ARTILLERY!

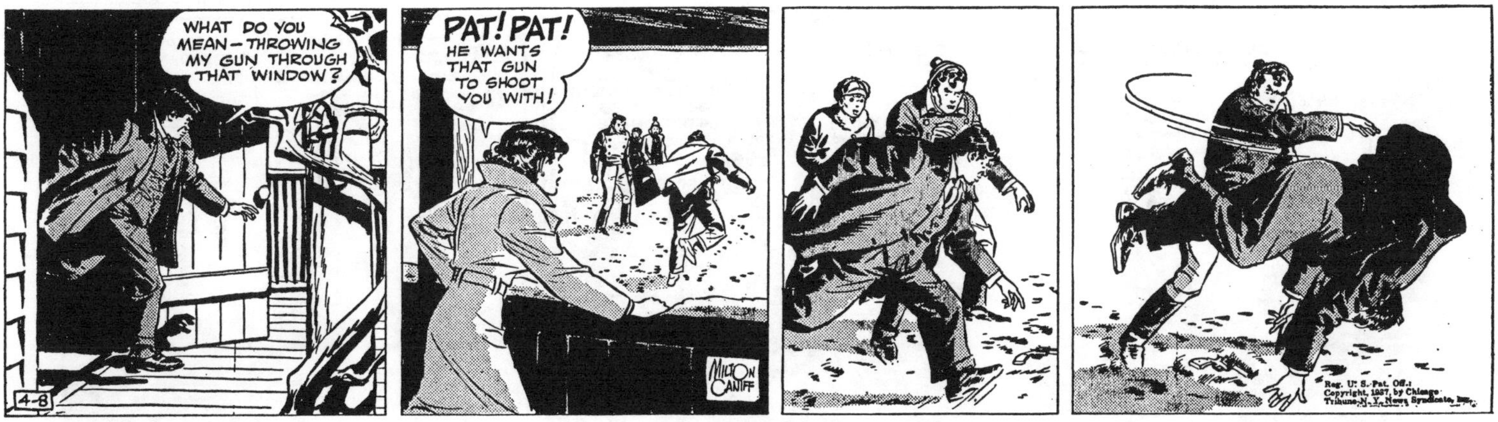
WHAT DO YOU MEAN—THROWING MY GUN THROUGH THAT WINDOW?
4-8
PAT! PAT! HE WANTS THAT GUN TO SHOOT YOU WITH!
MILTON CANIFF
Reg. U. S. Pat. Off.: Copyright, 1937, by Chicago Tribune-N. Y. News Syndicate, Inc.

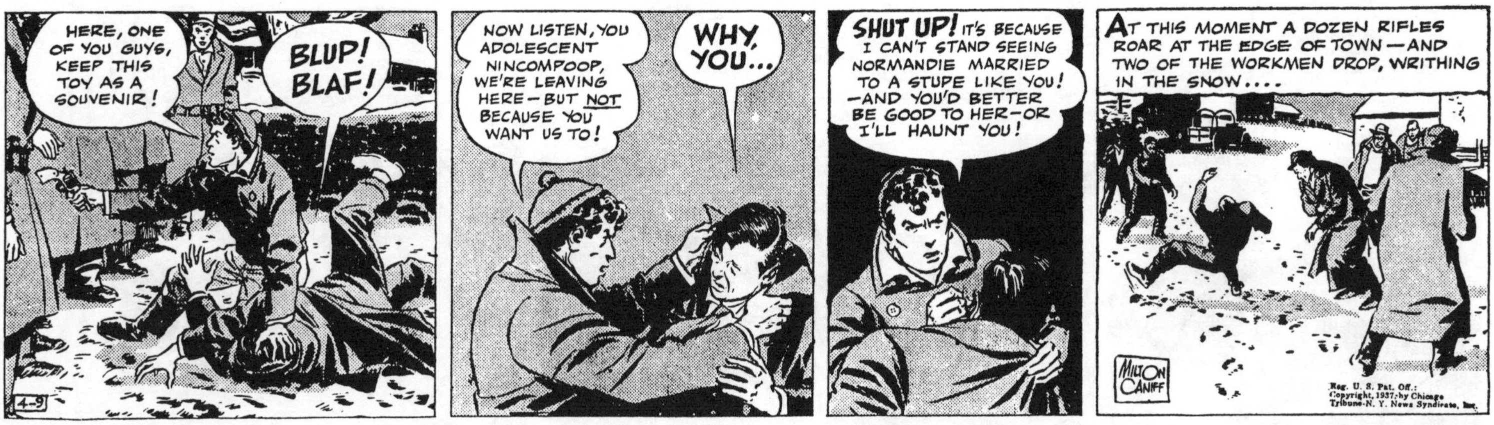
HERE, ONE OF YOU GUYS, KEEP THIS TOY AS A SOUVENIR!
BLUP! BLAF!
4-9
NOW LISTEN, YOU ADOLESCENT NINCOMPOOP, WE'RE LEAVING HERE—BUT NOT BECAUSE YOU WANT US TO!
WHY, YOU...
SHUT UP! IT'S BECAUSE I CAN'T STAND SEEING NORMANDIE MARRIED TO A STUPE LIKE YOU! —AND YOU'D BETTER BE GOOD TO HER—OR I'LL HAUNT YOU!
AT THIS MOMENT A DOZEN RIFLES ROAR AT THE EDGE OF TOWN—AND TWO OF THE WORKMEN DROP, WRITHING IN THE SNOW....
MILTON CANIFF
Reg. U. S. Pat. Off.: Copyright, 1937, by Chicago Tribune-N. Y. News Syndicate, Inc.

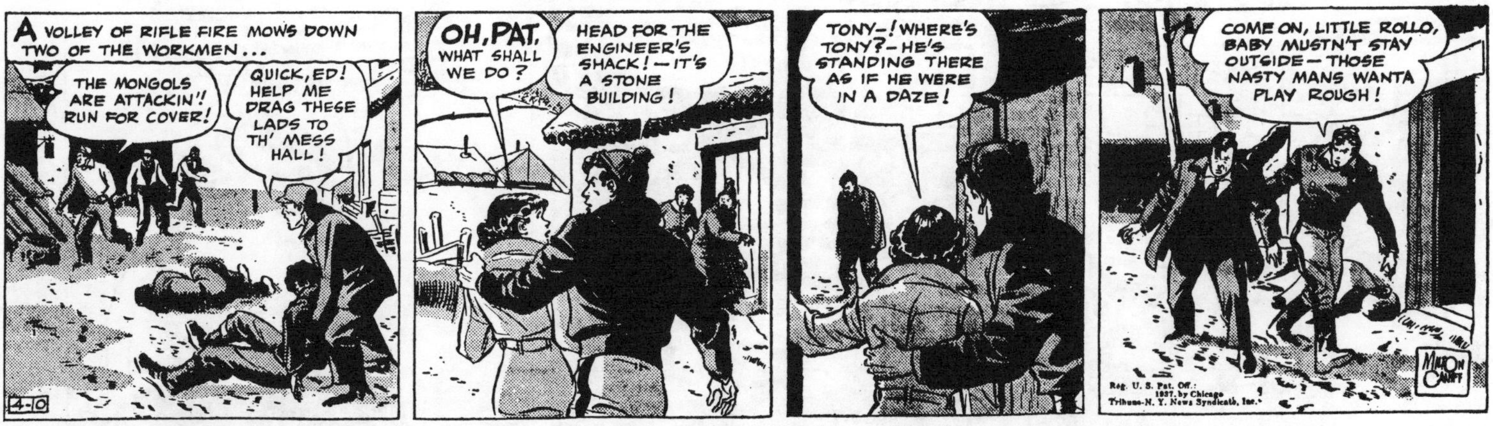
A VOLLEY OF RIFLE FIRE MOWS DOWN TWO OF THE WORKMEN...
THE MONGOLS ARE ATTACKIN'! RUN FOR COVER!
QUICK, ED! HELP ME DRAG THESE LADS TO TH' MESS HALL!
4-10
OH, PAT, WHAT SHALL WE DO?
HEAD FOR THE ENGINEER'S SHACK! —IT'S A STONE BUILDING!
TONY—! WHERE'S TONY?—HE'S STANDING THERE AS IF HE WERE IN A DAZE!
COME ON, LITTLE ROLLO, BABY MUSTN'T STAY OUTSIDE—THOSE NASTY MANS WANTA PLAY ROUGH!
Reg. U. S. Pat. Off.: 1937, by Chicago Tribune-N. Y. News Syndicate, Inc.
MILTON CANIFF

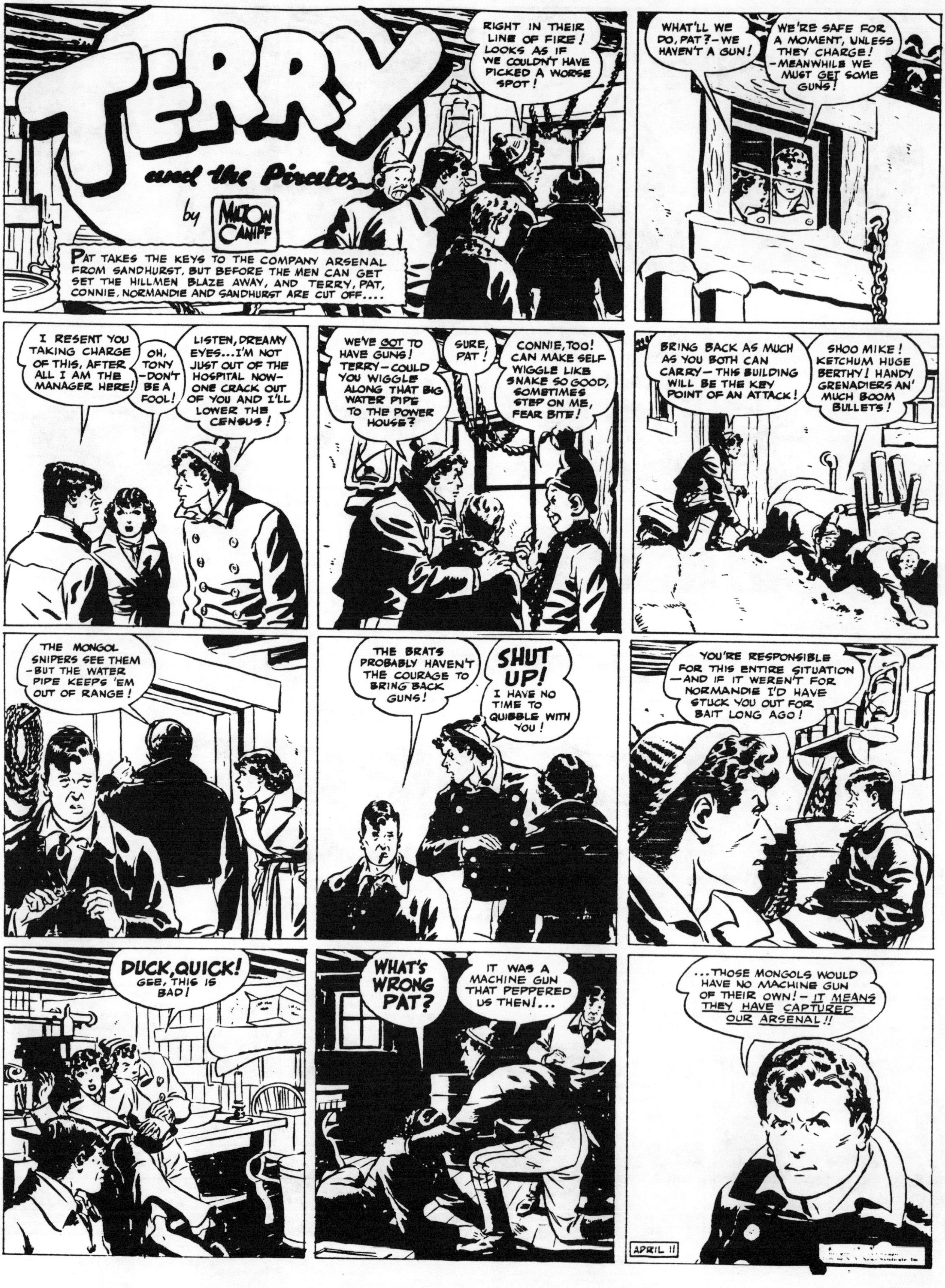

TERRY and the Pirates
by MILTON CANIFF
PAT TAKES THE KEYS TO THE COMPANY ARSENAL FROM SANDHURST, BUT BEFORE THE MEN CAN GET SET THE HILLMEN BLAZE AWAY, AND TERRY, PAT, CONNIE, NORMANDIE AND SANDHURST ARE CUT OFF....
RIGHT IN THEIR LINE OF FIRE! LOOKS AS IF WE COULDN'T HAVE PICKED A WORSE SPOT!
WHAT'LL WE DO, PAT?—WE HAVEN'T A GUN!
WE'RE SAFE FOR A MOMENT, UNLESS THEY CHARGE! —MEANWHILE WE MUST GET SOME GUNS!
I RESENT YOU TAKING CHARGE OF THIS, AFTER ALL I AM THE MANAGER HERE!
OH, TONY —DON'T BE A FOOL!
LISTEN, DREAMY EYES... I'M NOT JUST OUT OF THE HOSPITAL NOW— ONE CRACK OUT OF YOU AND I'LL LOWER THE CENSUS!
WE'VE GOT TO HAVE GUNS! TERRY—COULD YOU WIGGLE ALONG THAT BIG WATER PIPE TO THE POWER HOUSE?
SURE, PAT!
CONNIE, TOO! CAN MAKE SELF WIGGLE LIKE SNAKE SO GOOD, SOMETIMES STEP ON ME, FEAR BITE!
BRING BACK AS MUCH AS YOU BOTH CAN CARRY—THIS BUILDING WILL BE THE KEY POINT OF AN ATTACK!
SHOO MIKE! KETCHUM HUGE BERTHY! HANDY GRENADIERS AN' MUCH BOOM BULLETS!
THE MONGOL SNIPERS SEE THEM —BUT THE WATER PIPE KEEPS 'EM OUT OF RANGE!
THE BRATS PROBABLY HAVEN'T THE COURAGE TO BRING BACK GUNS!
SHUT UP! I HAVE NO TIME TO QUIBBLE WITH YOU!
YOU'RE RESPONSIBLE FOR THIS ENTIRE SITUATION —AND IF IT WEREN'T FOR NORMANDIE I'D HAVE STUCK YOU OUT FOR BAIT LONG AGO!
DUCK, QUICK! GEE, THIS IS BAD!
WHAT'S WRONG PAT?
IT WAS A MACHINE GUN THAT PEPPERED US THEN!...
...THOSE MONGOLS WOULD HAVE NO MACHINE GUN OF THEIR OWN!—IT MEANS THEY HAVE CAPTURED OUR ARSENAL!!
APRIL 11

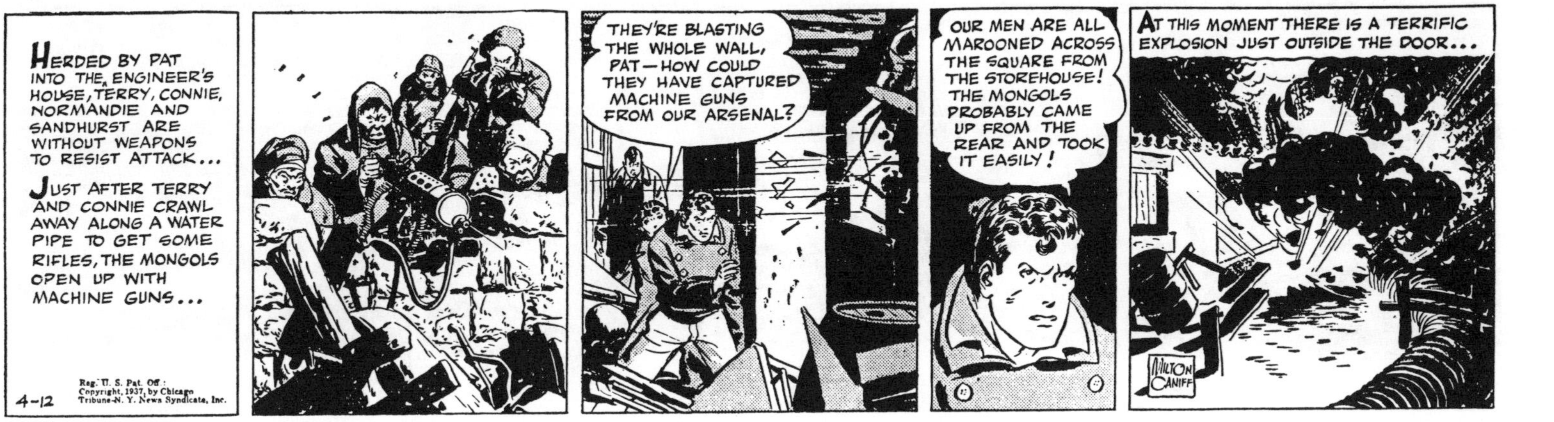

HERDED BY PAT INTO THE ENGINEER'S HOUSE, TERRY, CONNIE, NORMANDIE AND SANDHURST ARE WITHOUT WEAPONS TO RESIST ATTACK...
JUST AFTER TERRY AND CONNIE CRAWL AWAY ALONG A WATER PIPE TO GET SOME RIFLES, THE MONGOLS OPEN UP WITH MACHINE GUNS...
Reg. U. S. Pat. Off.: Copyright, 1937, by Chicago Tribune-N. Y. News Syndicate, Inc.
4-12
THEY'RE BLASTING THE WHOLE WALL, PAT—HOW COULD THEY HAVE CAPTURED MACHINE GUNS FROM OUR ARSENAL?
OUR MEN ARE ALL MAROONED ACROSS THE SQUARE FROM THE STOREHOUSE! THE MONGOLS PROBABLY CAME UP FROM THE REAR AND TOOK IT EASILY!
AT THIS MOMENT THERE IS A TERRIFIC EXPLOSION JUST OUTSIDE THE DOOR...
MILTON CANIFF

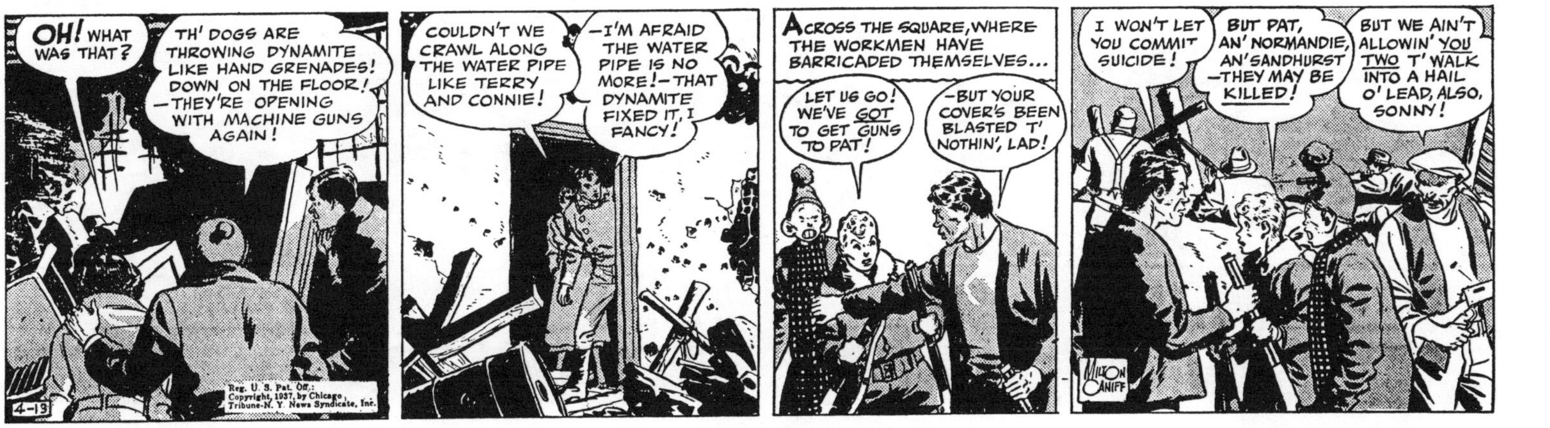

OH! WHAT WAS THAT?
TH' DOGS ARE THROWING DYNAMITE LIKE HAND GRENADES! DOWN ON THE FLOOR! —THEY'RE OPENING WITH MACHINE GUNS AGAIN!
Reg. U. S. Pat. Off.: Copyright, 1937, by Chicago Tribune-N. Y. News Syndicate, Inc.
4-13
COULDN'T WE CRAWL ALONG THE WATER PIPE LIKE TERRY AND CONNIE?
—I'M AFRAID THE WATER PIPE IS NO MORE!—THAT DYNAMITE FIXED IT, I FANCY!
ACROSS THE SQUARE, WHERE THE WORKMEN HAVE BARRICADED THEMSELVES...
LET US GO! WE'VE GOT TO GET GUNS TO PAT!
—BUT YOUR COVER'S BEEN BLASTED T' NOTHIN', LAD!
I WON'T LET YOU COMMIT SUICIDE!
BUT PAT, AN' NORMANDIE, AN' SANDHURST —THEY MAY BE KILLED!
BUT WE AIN'T ALLOWIN' YOU TWO T' WALK INTO A HAIL O' LEAD, ALSO, SONNY!
MILTON CANIFF

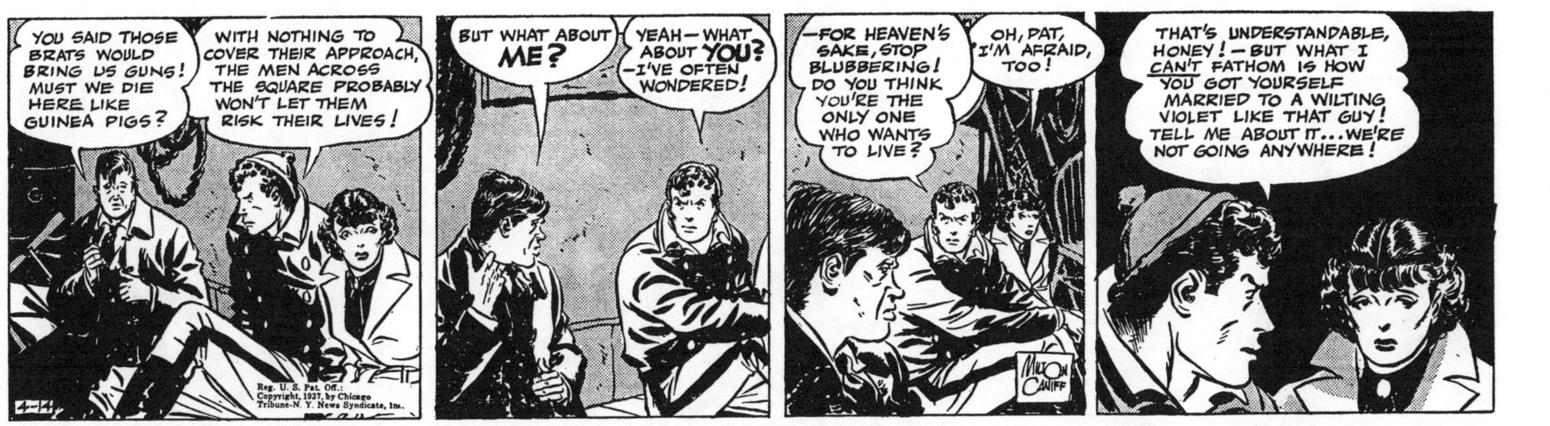

YOU SAID THOSE BRATS WOULD BRING US GUNS! MUST WE DIE HERE LIKE GUINEA PIGS?
WITH NOTHING TO COVER THEIR APPROACH, THE MEN ACROSS THE SQUARE PROBABLY WON'T LET THEM RISK THEIR LIVES!
Reg. U. S. Pat. Off.: Copyright, 1937, by Chicago Tribune-N. Y. News Syndicate, Inc.
4-14
BUT WHAT ABOUT ME?
YEAH—WHAT ABOUT YOU? —I'VE OFTEN WONDERED!
—FOR HEAVEN'S SAKE, STOP BLUBBERING! DO YOU THINK YOU'RE THE ONLY ONE WHO WANTS TO LIVE?
OH, PAT, I'M AFRAID, TOO!
MILTON CANIFF
THAT'S UNDERSTANDABLE, HONEY!—BUT WHAT I CAN'T FATHOM IS HOW YOU GOT YOURSELF MARRIED TO A WILTING VIOLET LIKE THAT GUY! TELL ME ABOUT IT...WE'RE NOT GOING ANYWHERE!

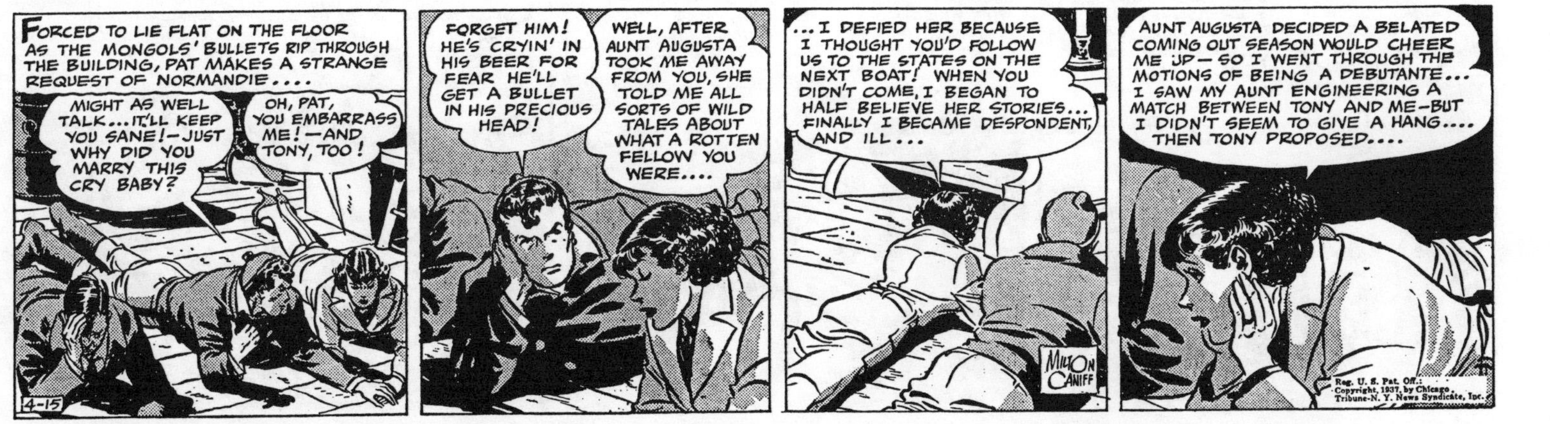

FORCED TO LIE FLAT ON THE FLOOR AS THE MONGOLS' BULLETS RIP THROUGH THE BUILDING, PAT MAKES A STRANGE REQUEST OF NORMANDIE....
MIGHT AS WELL TALK...IT'LL KEEP YOU SANE!—JUST WHY DID YOU MARRY THIS CRY BABY?
OH, PAT, YOU EMBARRASS ME!—AND TONY, TOO!
4-15
FORGET HIM! HE'S CRYIN' IN HIS BEER FOR FEAR HE'LL GET A BULLET IN HIS PRECIOUS HEAD!
WELL, AFTER AUNT AUGUSTA TOOK ME AWAY FROM YOU, SHE TOLD ME ALL SORTS OF WILD TALES ABOUT WHAT A ROTTEN FELLOW YOU WERE....
...I DEFIED HER BECAUSE I THOUGHT YOU'D FOLLOW US TO THE STATES ON THE NEXT BOAT! WHEN YOU DIDN'T COME, I BEGAN TO HALF BELIEVE HER STORIES... FINALLY I BECAME DESPONDENT, AND ILL...
MILTON CANIFF
AUNT AUGUSTA DECIDED A BELATED COMING OUT SEASON WOULD CHEER ME UP—SO I WENT THROUGH THE MOTIONS OF BEING A DEBUTANTE... I SAW MY AUNT ENGINEERING A MATCH BETWEEN TONY AND ME—BUT I DIDN'T SEEM TO GIVE A HANG.... THEN TONY PROPOSED....
Reg. U. S. Pat. Off.: Copyright, 1937, by Chicago Tribune-N. Y. News Syndicate, Inc.

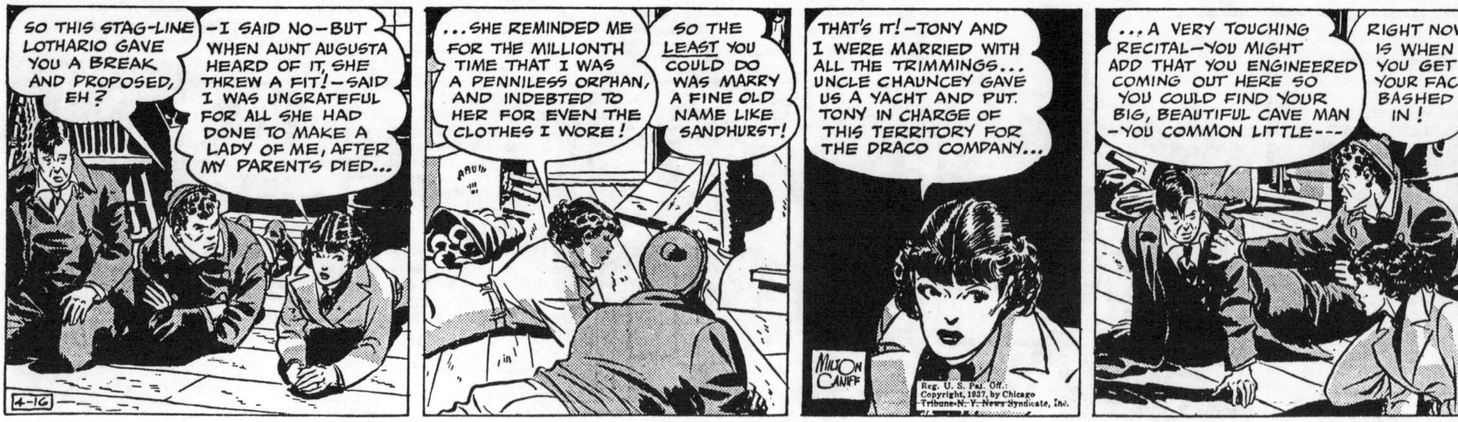

SO THIS STAG-LINE LOTHARIO GAVE YOU A BREAK AND PROPOSED, EH?
-I SAID NO-BUT WHEN AUNT AUGUSTA HEARD OF IT, SHE THREW A FIT!-SAID I WAS UNGRATEFUL FOR ALL SHE HAD DONE TO MAKE A LADY OF ME, AFTER MY PARENTS DIED...
4-16
...SHE REMINDED ME FOR THE MILLIONTH TIME THAT I WAS A PENNILESS ORPHAN, AND INDEBTED TO HER FOR EVEN THE CLOTHES I WORE!
SO THE LEAST YOU COULD DO WAS MARRY A FINE OLD NAME LIKE SANDHURST!
THAT'S IT!-TONY AND I WERE MARRIED WITH ALL THE TRIMMINGS... UNCLE CHAUNCEY GAVE US A YACHT AND PUT TONY IN CHARGE OF THIS TERRITORY FOR THE DRACO COMPANY...
MILTON CANIFF
Reg. U. S. Pat. Off.: Copyright, 1937, by Chicago Tribune-N. Y. News Syndicate, Inc.
...A VERY TOUCHING RECITAL-YOU MIGHT ADD THAT YOU ENGINEERED COMING OUT HERE SO YOU COULD FIND YOUR BIG, BEAUTIFUL CAVE MAN -YOU COMMON LITTLE---
RIGHT NOW IS WHEN YOU GET YOUR FACE BASHED IN!

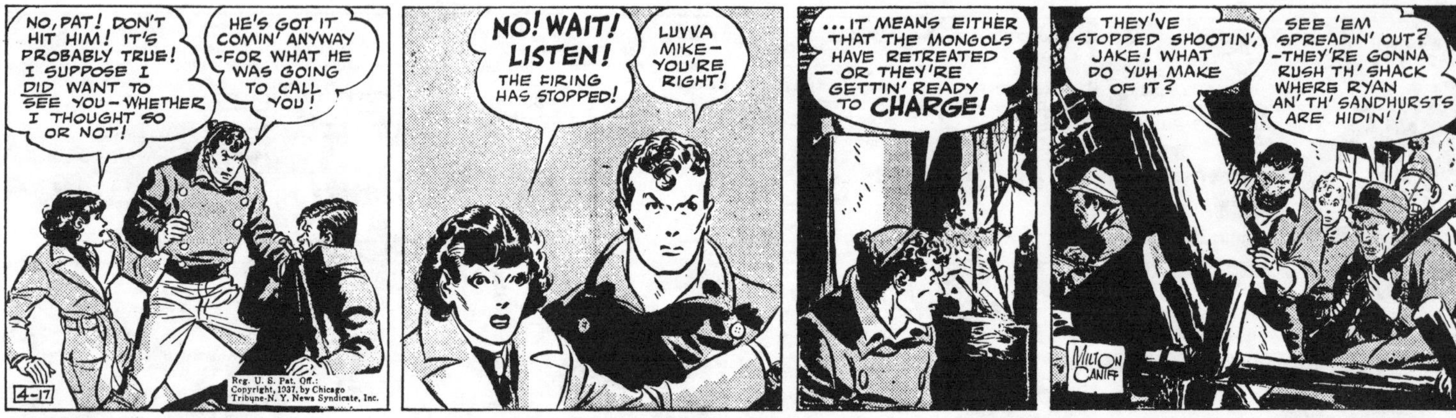

NO, PAT! DON'T HIT HIM! IT'S PROBABLY TRUE! I SUPPOSE I DID WANT TO SEE YOU-WHETHER I THOUGHT SO OR NOT!
HE'S GOT IT COMIN' ANYWAY -FOR WHAT HE WAS GOING TO CALL YOU!
4-17
Reg. U. S. Pat. Off.: Copyright, 1937, by Chicago Tribune-N. Y. News Syndicate, Inc.
NO! WAIT! LISTEN! THE FIRING HAS STOPPED!
LUVVA MIKE-YOU'RE RIGHT!
...IT MEANS EITHER THAT THE MONGOLS HAVE RETREATED -OR THEY'RE GETTIN' READY TO CHARGE!
THEY'VE STOPPED SHOOTIN', JAKE! WHAT DO YUH MAKE OF IT?
SEE 'EM SPREADIN' OUT? -THEY'RE GONNA RUSH TH' SHACK WHERE RYAN AN' TH' SANDHURSTS ARE HIDIN'!
MILTON CANIFF

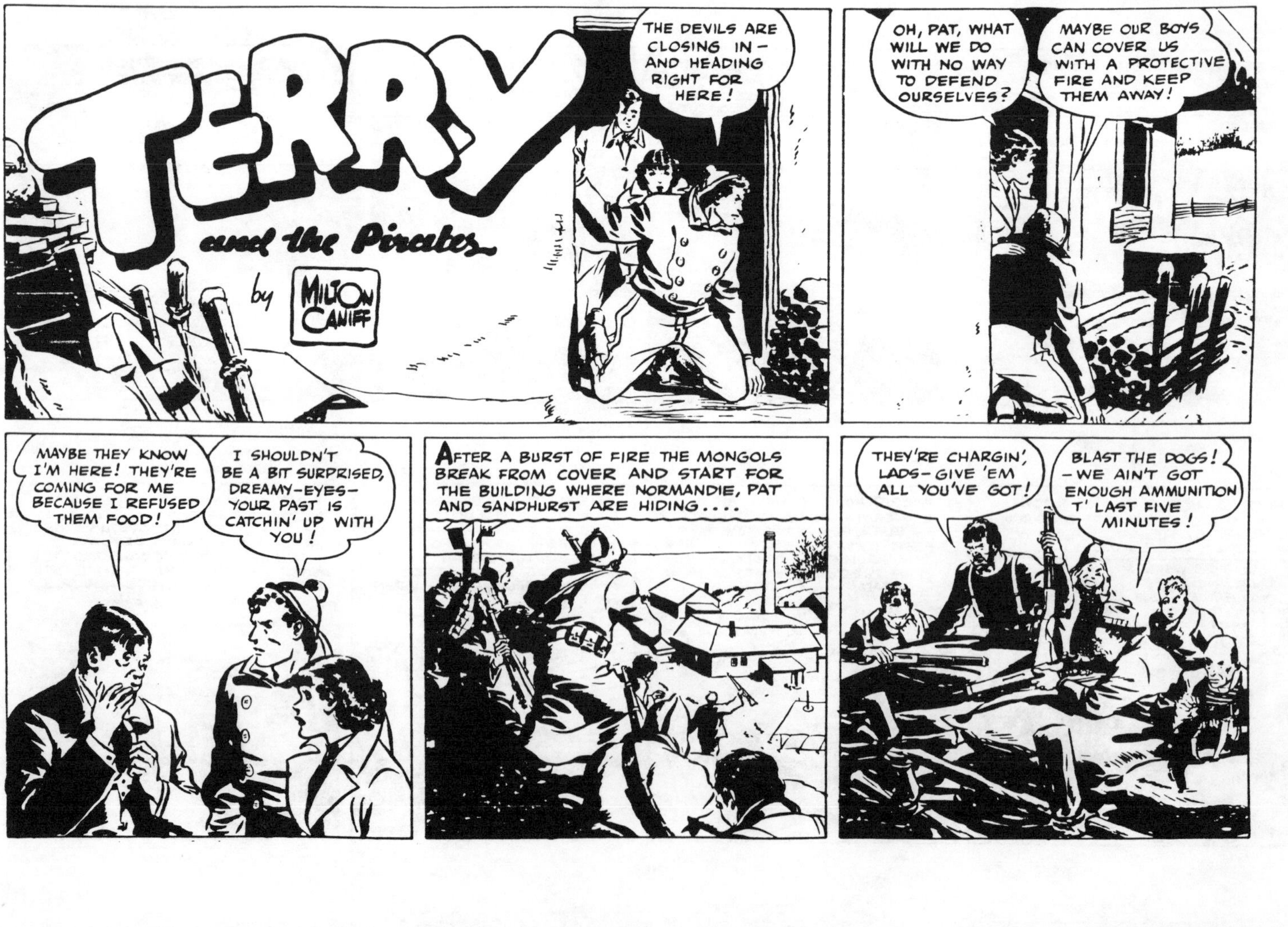

TERRY and the Pirates
by MILTON CANIFF
THE DEVILS ARE CLOSING IN-AND HEADING RIGHT FOR HERE!
OH, PAT, WHAT WILL WE DO WITH NO WAY TO DEFEND OURSELVES?
MAYBE OUR BOYS CAN COVER US WITH A PROTECTIVE FIRE AND KEEP THEM AWAY!
MAYBE THEY KNOW I'M HERE! THEY'RE COMING FOR ME BECAUSE I REFUSED THEM FOOD!
I SHOULDN'T BE A BIT SURPRISED, DREAMY-EYES-YOUR PAST IS CATCHIN' UP WITH YOU!
AFTER A BURST OF FIRE THE MONGOLS BREAK FROM COVER AND START FOR THE BUILDING WHERE NORMANDIE, PAT AND SANDHURST ARE HIDING....
THEY'RE CHARGIN', LADS-GIVE 'EM ALL YOU'VE GOT!
BLAST THE DOGS! -WE AIN'T GOT ENOUGH AMMUNITION T' LAST FIVE MINUTES!

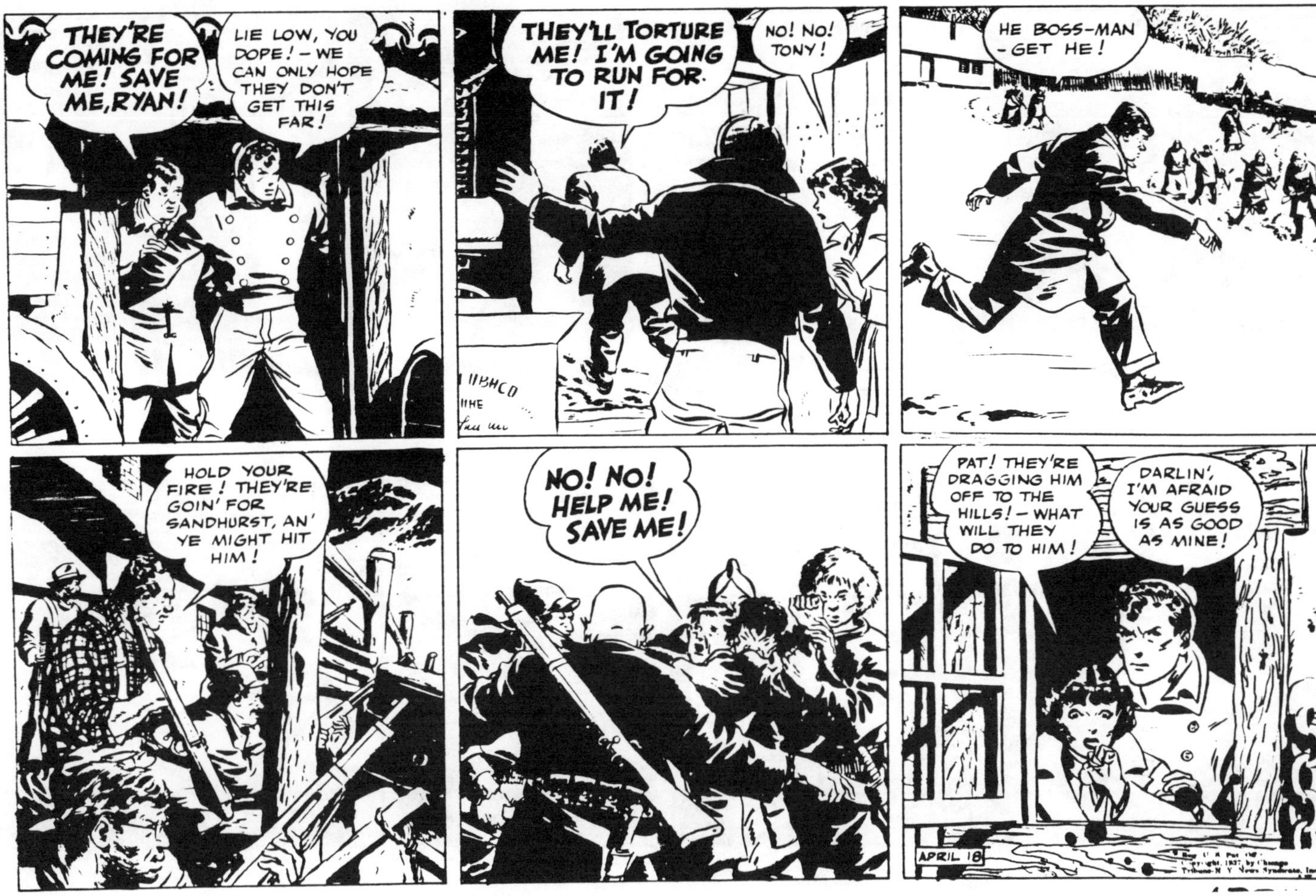
THEY'RE COMING FOR ME! SAVE ME, RYAN!
LIE LOW, YOU DOPE! — WE CAN ONLY HOPE THEY DON'T GET THIS FAR!
THEY'LL TORTURE ME! I'M GOING TO RUN FOR IT!
NO! NO! TONY!
HE BOSS-MAN — GET HE!
HOLD YOUR FIRE! THEY'RE GOIN' FOR SANDHURST, AN' YE MIGHT HIT HIM!
NO! NO! HELP ME! SAVE ME!
PAT! THEY'RE DRAGGING HIM OFF TO THE HILLS! — WHAT WILL THEY DO TO HIM!
DARLIN', I'M AFRAID YOUR GUESS IS AS GOOD AS MINE!
APRIL 18

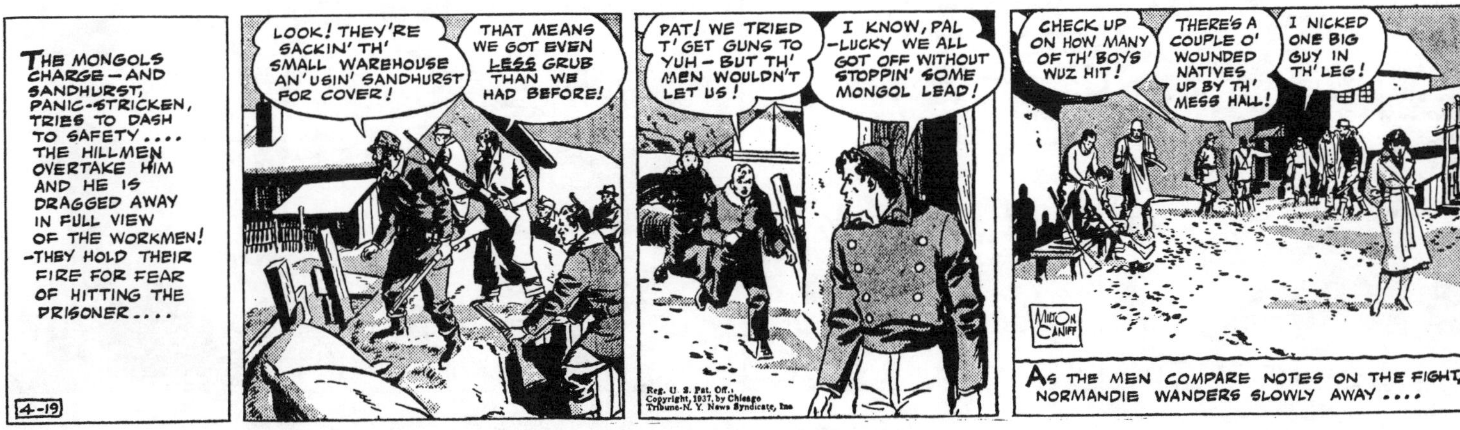
THE MONGOLS CHARGE — AND SANDHURST, PANIC-STRICKEN, TRIES TO DASH TO SAFETY.... THE HILLMEN OVERTAKE HIM AND HE IS DRAGGED AWAY IN FULL VIEW OF THE WORKMEN! — THEY HOLD THEIR FIRE FOR FEAR OF HITTING THE PRISONER....
4-19
LOOK! THEY'RE SACKIN' TH' SMALL WAREHOUSE AN' USIN' SANDHURST FOR COVER!
THAT MEANS WE GOT EVEN LESS GRUB THAN WE HAD BEFORE!
PAT! WE TRIED T' GET GUNS TO YUH — BUT TH' MEN WOULDN'T LET US!
I KNOW, PAL — LUCKY WE ALL GOT OFF WITHOUT STOPPIN' SOME MONGOL LEAD!
Reg. U. S. Pat. Off., Copyright, 1937, by Chicago Tribune-N. Y. News Syndicate, Inc
CHECK UP ON HOW MANY OF TH' BOYS WUZ HIT!
THERE'S A COUPLE O' WOUNDED NATIVES UP BY TH' MESS HALL!
I NICKED ONE BIG GUY IN TH' LEG!
MILTON CANIFF
AS THE MEN COMPARE NOTES ON THE FIGHT, NORMANDIE WANDERS SLOWLY AWAY....

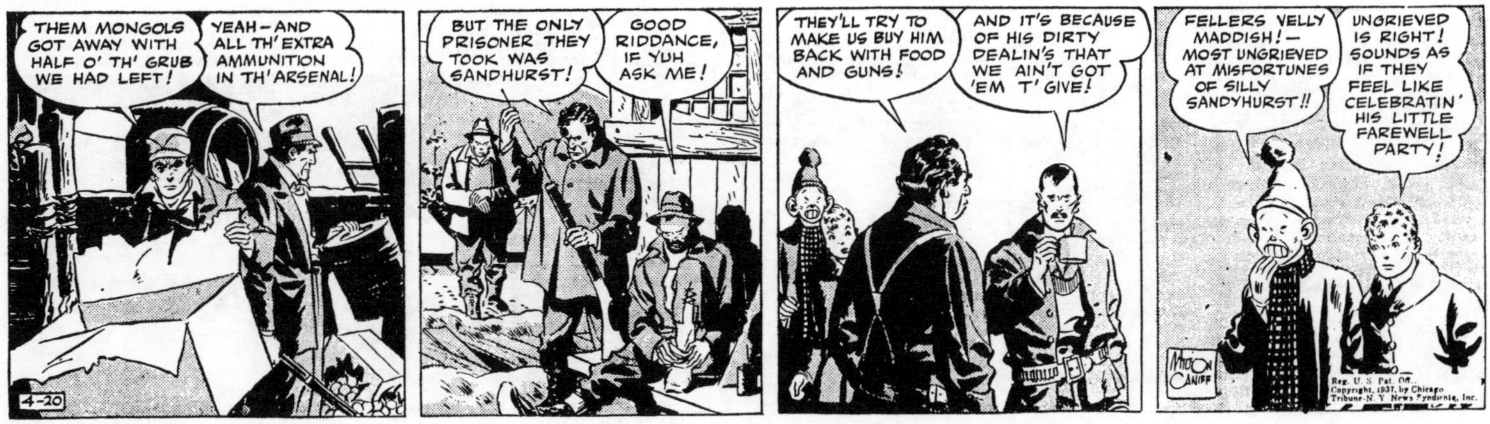
THEM MONGOLS GOT AWAY WITH HALF O' TH' GRUB WE HAD LEFT!
YEAH — AND ALL TH' EXTRA AMMUNITION IN TH' ARSENAL!
4-20
BUT THE ONLY PRISONER THEY TOOK WAS SANDHURST!
GOOD RIDDANCE, IF YUH ASK ME!
THEY'LL TRY TO MAKE US BUY HIM BACK WITH FOOD AND GUNS!
AND IT'S BECAUSE OF HIS DIRTY DEALIN'S THAT WE AIN'T GOT 'EM T' GIVE!
FELLERS VELLY MADDISH! — MOST UNGRIEVED AT MISFORTUNES OF SILLY SANDYHURST!!
UNGRIEVED IS RIGHT! SOUNDS AS IF THEY FEEL LIKE CELEBRATIN' HIS LITTLE FAREWELL PARTY!
MILTON CANIFF
Reg. U. S. Pat. Off., Copyright, 1937, by Chicago Tribune-N. Y. News Syndicate, Inc.

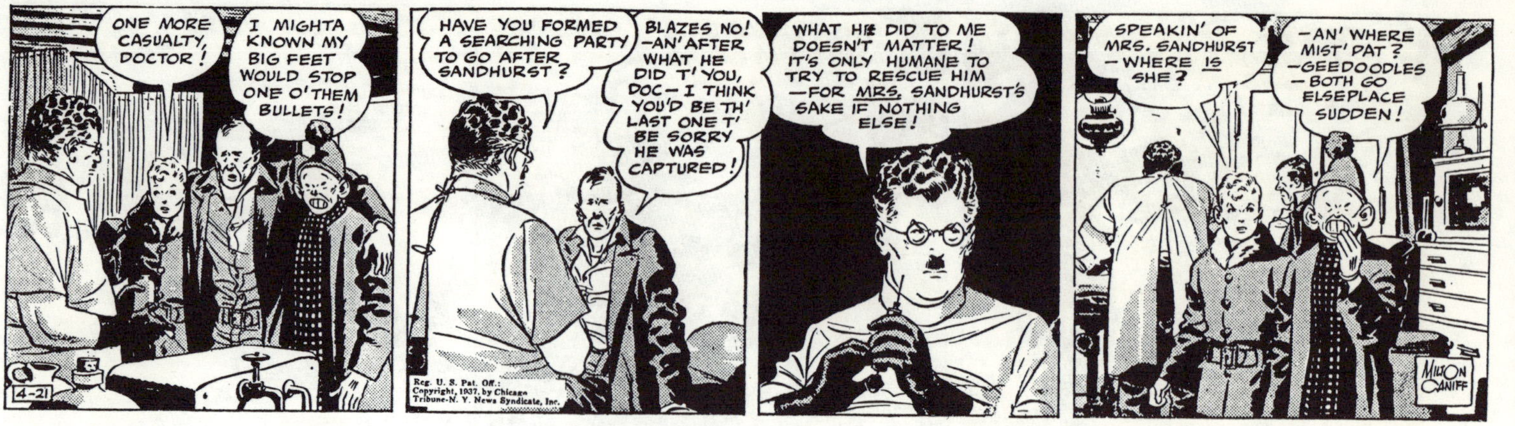
ONE MORE CASUALTY, DOCTOR!
I MIGHTA KNOWN MY BIG FEET WOULD STOP ONE O' THEM BULLETS!
4-21
HAVE YOU FORMED A SEARCHING PARTY TO GO AFTER SANDHURST?
BLAZES NO! —AN' AFTER WHAT HE DID T' YOU, DOC—I THINK YOU'D BE TH' LAST ONE T' BE SORRY HE WAS CAPTURED!
Reg. U. S. Pat. Off.: Copyright, 1937, by Chicago Tribune-N. Y. News Syndicate, Inc.
WHAT HE DID TO ME DOESN'T MATTER! IT'S ONLY HUMANE TO TRY TO RESCUE HIM —FOR MRS. SANDHURST'S SAKE IF NOTHING ELSE!
SPEAKIN' OF MRS. SANDHURST —WHERE IS SHE?
—AN' WHERE MIST' PAT? —GEEDOODLES —BOTH GO ELSEPLACE SUDDEN!
MILTON CANIFF

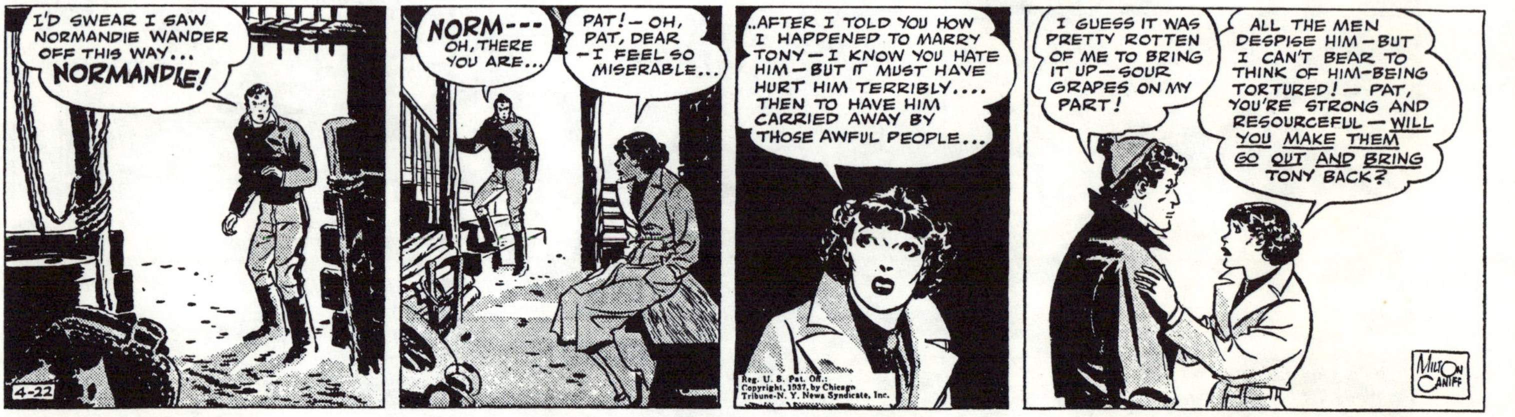
I'D SWEAR I SAW NORMANDIE WANDER OFF THIS WAY... NORMANDIE!
4-22
NORM--- OH, THERE YOU ARE...
PAT!—OH, PAT, DEAR —I FEEL SO MISERABLE...
..AFTER I TOLD YOU HOW I HAPPENED TO MARRY TONY—I KNOW YOU HATE HIM—BUT IT MUST HAVE HURT HIM TERRIBLY.... THEN TO HAVE HIM CARRIED AWAY BY THOSE AWFUL PEOPLE...
Reg. U. S. Pat. Off.: Copyright, 1937, by Chicago Tribune-N. Y. News Syndicate, Inc.
I GUESS IT WAS PRETTY ROTTEN OF ME TO BRING IT UP—SOUR GRAPES ON MY PART!
ALL THE MEN DESPISE HIM—BUT I CAN'T BEAR TO THINK OF HIM-BEING TORTURED!—PAT, YOU'RE STRONG AND RESOURCEFUL—WILL YOU MAKE THEM GO OUT AND BRING TONY BACK?
MILTON CANIFF

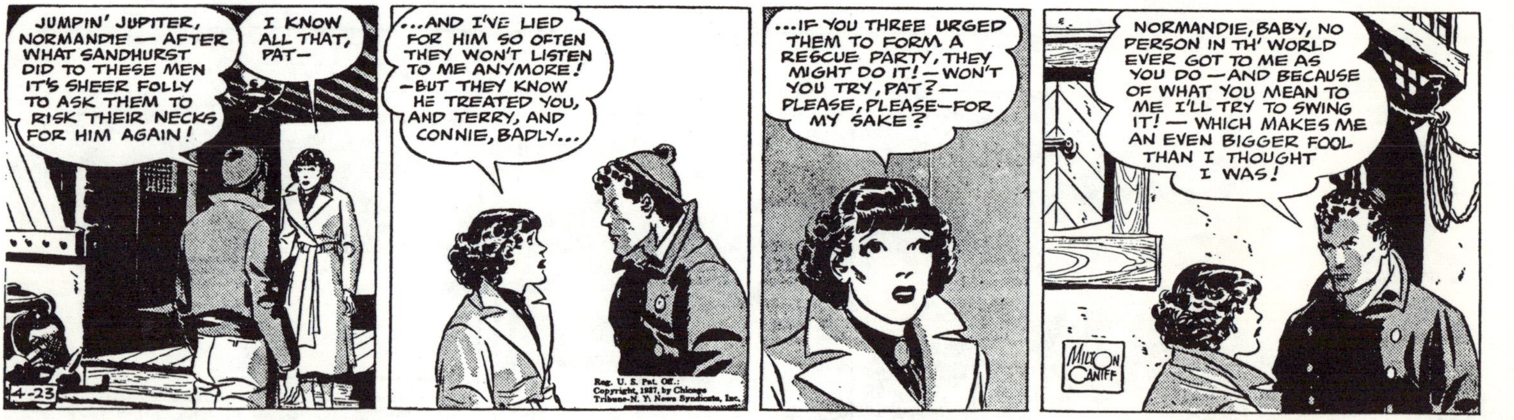
JUMPIN' JUPITER, NORMANDIE—AFTER WHAT SANDHURST DID TO THESE MEN IT'S SHEER FOLLY TO ASK THEM TO RISK THEIR NECKS FOR HIM AGAIN!
I KNOW ALL THAT, PAT—
4-23
...AND I'VE LIED FOR HIM SO OFTEN THEY WON'T LISTEN TO ME ANYMORE! —BUT THEY KNOW HE TREATED YOU, AND TERRY, AND CONNIE, BADLY...
Reg. U. S. Pat. Off.: Copyright, 1937, by Chicago Tribune-N. Y. News Syndicate, Inc.
...IF YOU THREE URGED THEM TO FORM A RESCUE PARTY, THEY MIGHT DO IT!—WON'T YOU TRY, PAT?— PLEASE, PLEASE—FOR MY SAKE?
MILTON CANIFF
NORMANDIE, BABY, NO PERSON IN TH' WORLD EVER GOT TO ME AS YOU DO—AND BECAUSE OF WHAT YOU MEAN TO ME I'LL TRY TO SWING IT!—WHICH MAKES ME AN EVEN BIGGER FOOL THAN I THOUGHT I WAS!

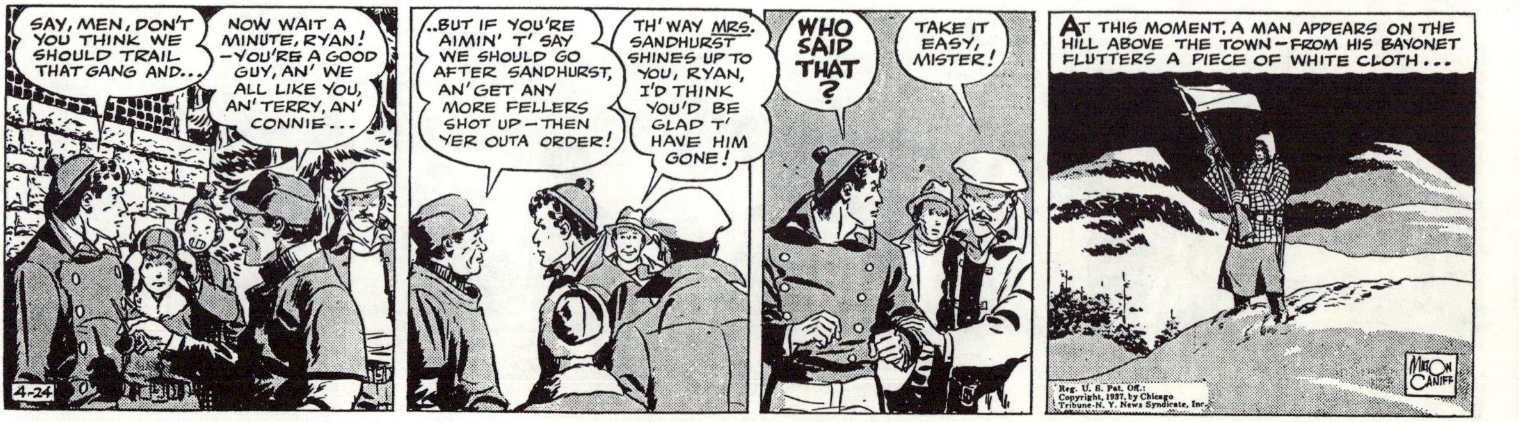
SAY, MEN, DON'T YOU THINK WE SHOULD TRAIL THAT GANG AND...
NOW WAIT A MINUTE, RYAN! —YOU'RE A GOOD GUY, AN' WE ALL LIKE YOU, AN' TERRY, AN' CONNIE...
4-24
..BUT IF YOU'RE AIMIN' T' SAY WE SHOULD GO AFTER SANDHURST, AN' GET ANY MORE FELLERS SHOT UP—THEN YER OUTA ORDER!
TH' WAY MRS. SANDHURST SHINES UP TO YOU, RYAN, I'D THINK YOU'D BE GLAD T' HAVE HIM GONE!
WHO SAID THAT?
TAKE IT EASY, MISTER!
AT THIS MOMENT, A MAN APPEARS ON THE HILL ABOVE THE TOWN—FROM HIS BAYONET FLUTTERS A PIECE OF WHITE CLOTH...
Reg. U. S. Pat. Off.: Copyright, 1937, by Chicago Tribune-N. Y. News Syndicate, Inc.
MILTON CANIFF

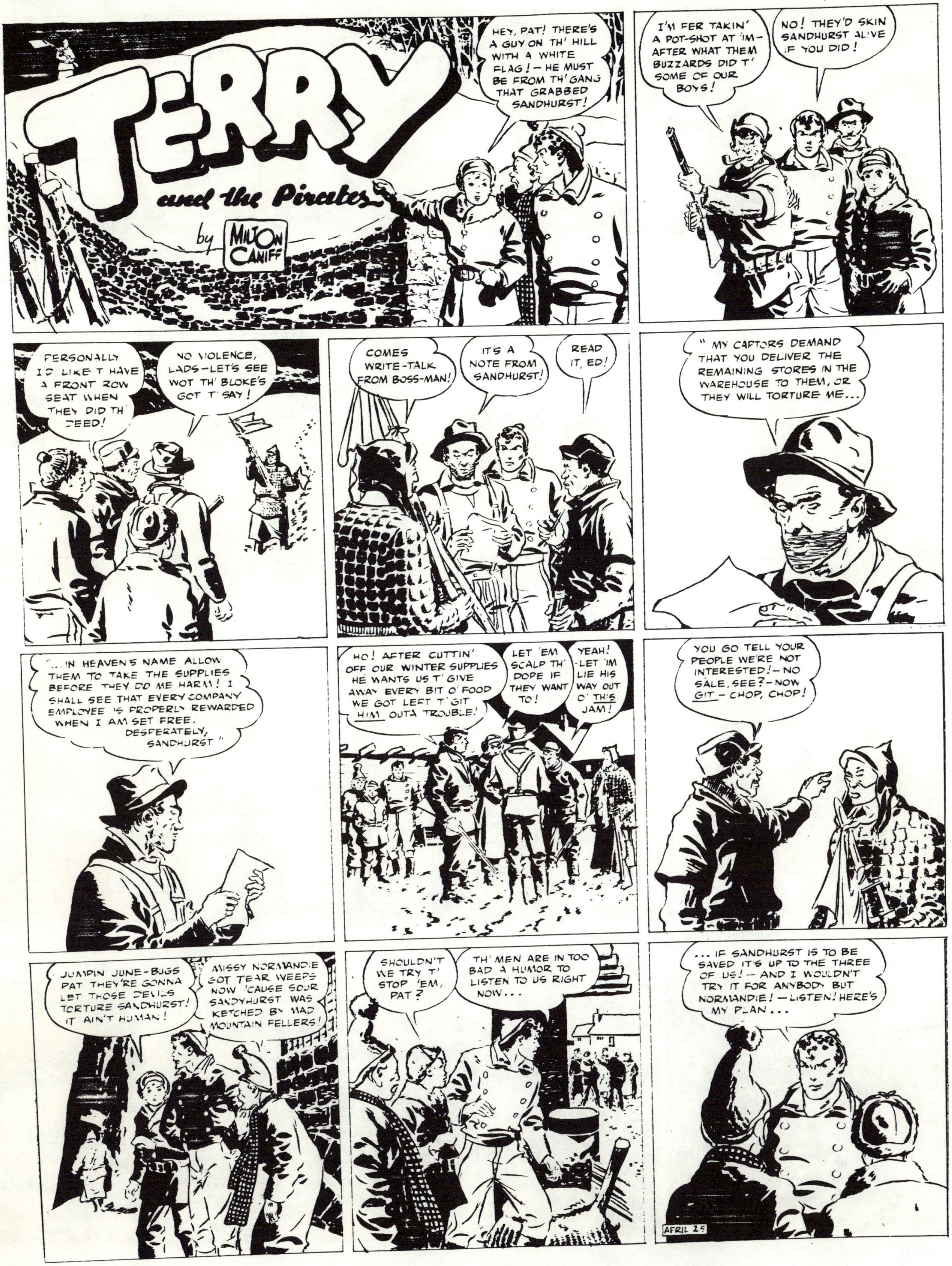
TERRY and the Pirates
by MILTON CANIFF
HEY, PAT! THERE'S A GUY ON TH' HILL WITH A WHITE FLAG! — HE MUST BE FROM TH' GANG THAT GRABBED SANDHURST!
I'M FER TAKIN' A POT-SHOT AT 'IM — AFTER WHAT THEM BUZZARDS DID T' SOME OF OUR BOYS!
NO! THEY'D SKIN SANDHURST ALIVE IF YOU DID!
PERSONALLY I'D LIKE T' HAVE A FRONT ROW SEAT WHEN THEY DID TH' DEED!
NO VIOLENCE, LADS — LET'S SEE WOT TH' BLOKE'S GOT T' SAY!
COMES WRITE-TALK FROM BOSS-MAN!
IT'S A NOTE FROM SANDHURST!
READ IT, ED!
" MY CAPTORS DEMAND THAT YOU DELIVER THE REMAINING STORES IN THE WAREHOUSE TO THEM, OR THEY WILL TORTURE ME...
"...IN HEAVEN'S NAME ALLOW THEM TO TAKE THE SUPPLIES BEFORE THEY DO ME HARM! I SHALL SEE THAT EVERY COMPANY EMPLOYEE IS PROPERLY REWARDED WHEN I AM SET FREE. DESPERATELY, SANDHURST "
HO! AFTER CUTTIN' OFF OUR WINTER SUPPLIES HE WANTS US T' GIVE AWAY EVERY BIT O' FOOD WE GOT LEFT T' GIT HIM OUTA TROUBLE!
LET 'EM SCALP TH' DOPE IF THEY WANT TO!
YEAH! — LET 'IM LIE HIS WAY OUT O' THIS JAM!
YOU GO TELL YOUR PEOPLE WE'RE NOT INTERESTED! — NO SALE, SEE? — NOW GIT — CHOP, CHOP!
JUMPIN JUNE-BUGS PAT THEY'RE GONNA LET THOSE DEVILS TORTURE SANDHURST! IT AIN'T HUMAN!
MISSY NORMANDIE GOT TEAR WEEPS NOW 'CAUSE SOUR SANDYHURST WAS KETCHED BY MAD MOUNTAIN FELLERS!
SHOULDN'T WE TRY T' STOP 'EM, PAT?
TH' MEN ARE IN TOO BAD A HUMOR TO LISTEN TO US RIGHT NOW...
... IF SANDHURST IS TO BE SAVED IT'S UP TO THE THREE OF US! — AND I WOULDN'T TRY IT FOR ANYBODY BUT NORMANDIE! — LISTEN! HERE'S MY PLAN...
APRIL 25

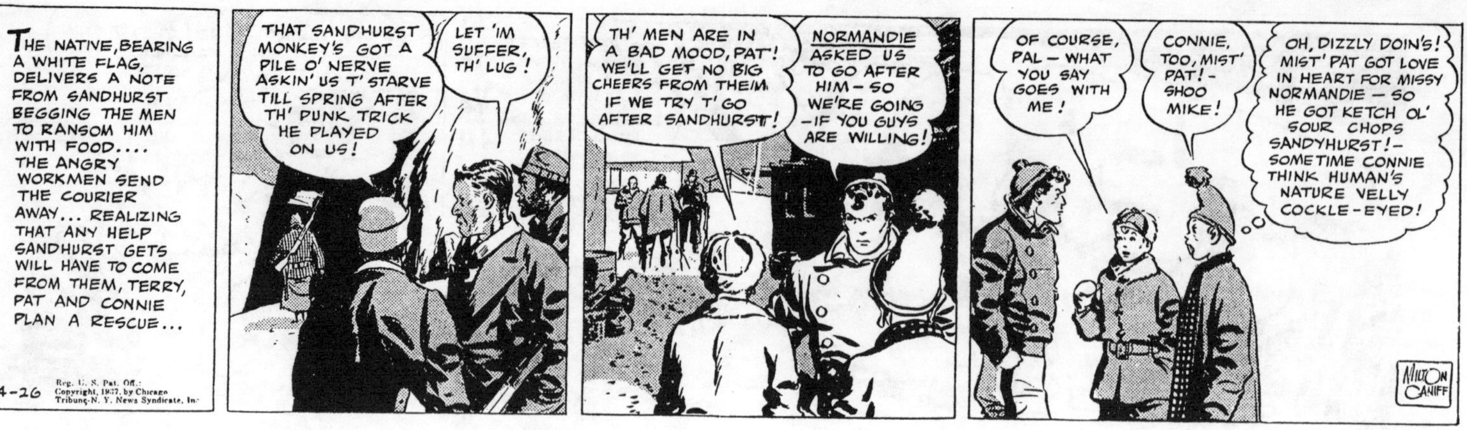

THE NATIVE, BEARING A WHITE FLAG, DELIVERS A NOTE FROM SANDHURST BEGGING THE MEN TO RANSOM HIM WITH FOOD.... THE ANGRY WORKMEN SEND THE COURIER AWAY... REALIZING THAT ANY HELP SANDHURST GETS WILL HAVE TO COME FROM THEM, TERRY, PAT AND CONNIE PLAN A RESCUE...
4-26
Reg. U. S. Pat. Off.: Copyright, 1937, by Chicago Tribune-N. Y. News Syndicate, Inc.
THAT SANDHURST MONKEY'S GOT A PILE O' NERVE ASKIN' US T' STARVE TILL SPRING AFTER TH' PUNK TRICK HE PLAYED ON US!
LET 'IM SUFFER, TH' LUG!
TH' MEN ARE IN A BAD MOOD, PAT! WE'LL GET NO BIG CHEERS FROM THEM IF WE TRY T' GO AFTER SANDHURST!
NORMANDIE ASKED US TO GO AFTER HIM — SO WE'RE GOING — IF YOU GUYS ARE WILLING!
OF COURSE, PAL — WHAT YOU SAY GOES WITH ME!
CONNIE, TOO, MIST' PAT! — SHOO MIKE!
OH, DIZZLY DOIN'S! MIST' PAT GOT LOVE IN HEART FOR MISSY NORMANDIE — SO HE GOT KETCH OL' SOUR CHOPS SANDYHURST! — SOMETIME CONNIE THINK HUMAN'S NATURE VELLY COCKLE-EYED!
MILTON CANIFF

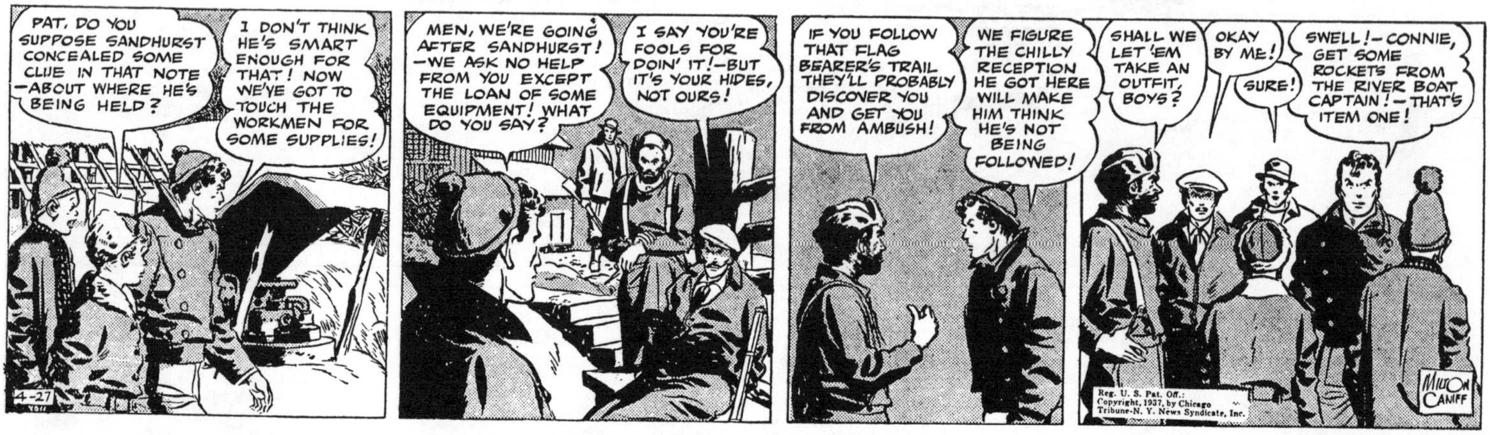

PAT, DO YOU SUPPOSE SANDHURST CONCEALED SOME CLUE IN THAT NOTE — ABOUT WHERE HE'S BEING HELD?
I DON'T THINK HE'S SMART ENOUGH FOR THAT! NOW WE'VE GOT TO TOUCH THE WORKMEN FOR SOME SUPPLIES!
4-27
MEN, WE'RE GOING AFTER SANDHURST! — WE ASK NO HELP FROM YOU EXCEPT THE LOAN OF SOME EQUIPMENT! WHAT DO YOU SAY?
I SAY YOU'RE FOOLS FOR DOIN' IT! — BUT IT'S YOUR HIDES, NOT OURS!
IF YOU FOLLOW THAT FLAG BEARER'S TRAIL THEY'LL PROBABLY DISCOVER YOU AND GET YOU FROM AMBUSH!
WE FIGURE THE CHILLY RECEPTION HE GOT HERE WILL MAKE HIM THINK HE'S NOT BEING FOLLOWED!
SHALL WE LET 'EM TAKE AN OUTFIT, BOYS?
OKAY BY ME!
SURE!
SWELL! — CONNIE, GET SOME ROCKETS FROM THE RIVER BOAT CAPTAIN! — THAT'S ITEM ONE!
Reg. U. S. Pat. Off.: Copyright, 1937, by Chicago Tribune-N. Y. News Syndicate, Inc.
MILTON CANIFF

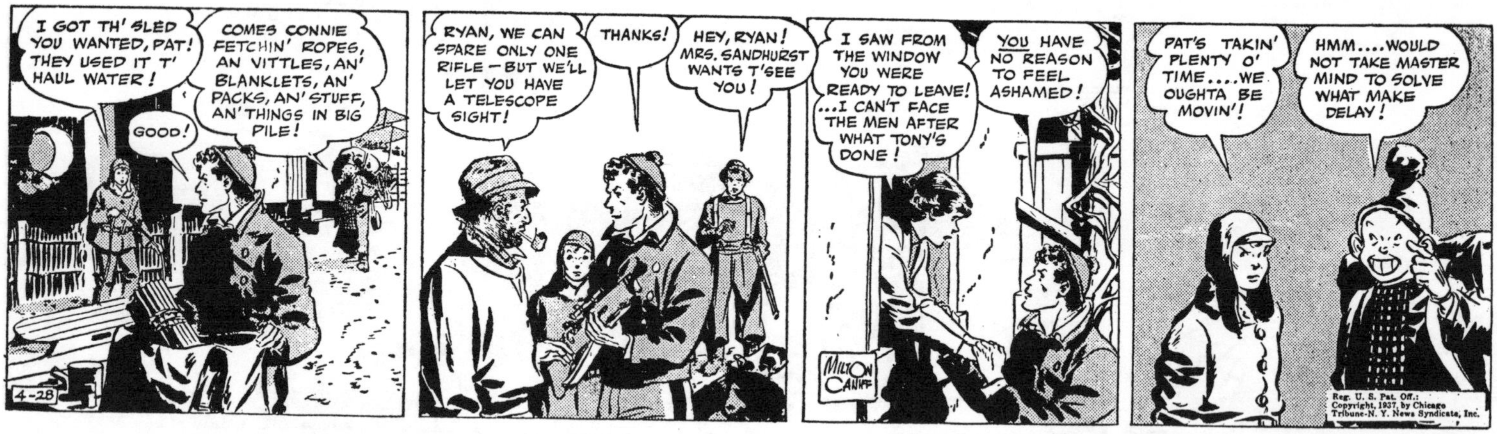

I GOT TH' SLED YOU WANTED, PAT! THEY USED IT T' HAUL WATER!
COMES CONNIE FETCHIN' ROPES, AN VITTLES, AN' BLANKLETS, AN' PACKS, AN' STUFF, AN' THINGS IN BIG PILE!
GOOD!
4-28
RYAN, WE CAN SPARE ONLY ONE RIFLE — BUT WE'LL LET YOU HAVE A TELESCOPE SIGHT!
THANKS!
HEY, RYAN! MRS. SANDHURST WANTS T'SEE YOU!
I SAW FROM THE WINDOW YOU WERE READY TO LEAVE! ...I CAN'T FACE THE MEN AFTER WHAT TONY'S DONE!
YOU HAVE NO REASON TO FEEL ASHAMED!
MILTON CANIFF
PAT'S TAKIN' PLENTY O' TIME.... WE OUGHTA BE MOVIN'!
HMM.... WOULD NOT TAKE MASTER MIND TO SOLVE WHAT MAKE DELAY!
Reg. U. S. Pat. Off.: Copyright, 1937, by Chicago Tribune-N. Y. News Syndicate, Inc.

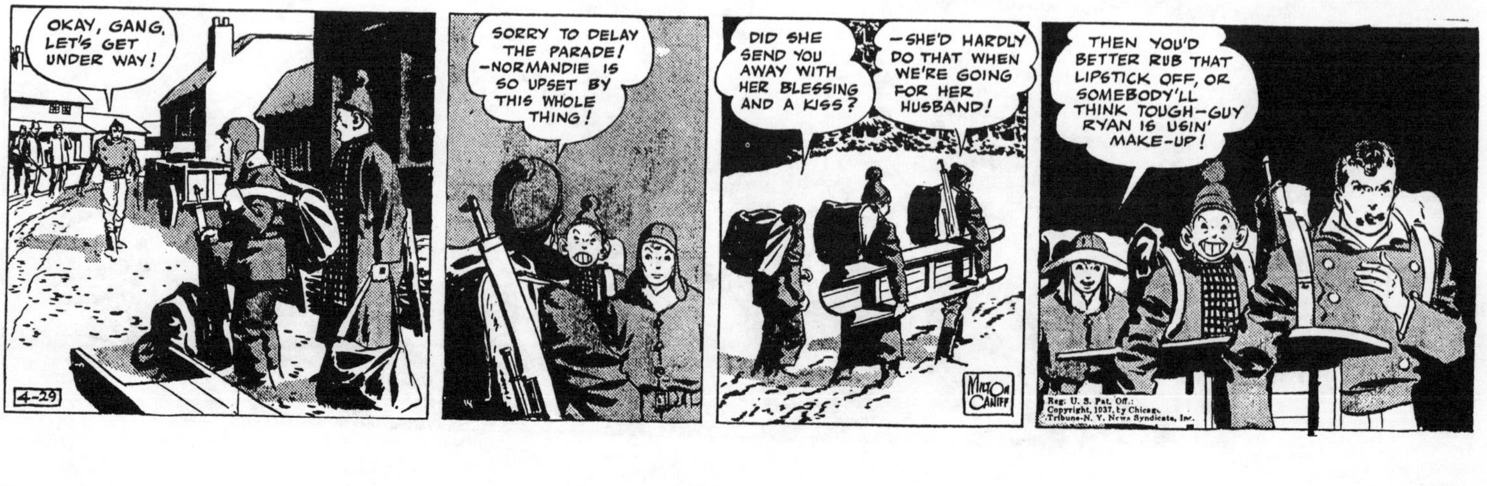

OKAY, GANG, LET'S GET UNDER WAY!
4-29
SORRY TO DELAY THE PARADE! — NORMANDIE IS SO UPSET BY THIS WHOLE THING!
DID SHE SEND YOU AWAY WITH HER BLESSING AND A KISS?
— SHE'D HARDLY DO THAT WHEN WE'RE GOING FOR HER HUSBAND!
MILTON CANIFF
THEN YOU'D BETTER RUB THAT LIPSTICK OFF, OR SOMEBODY'LL THINK TOUGH-GUY RYAN IS USIN' MAKE-UP!
Reg. U. S. Pat. Off.: Copyright, 1937, by Chicago Tribune-N. Y. News Syndicate, Inc.

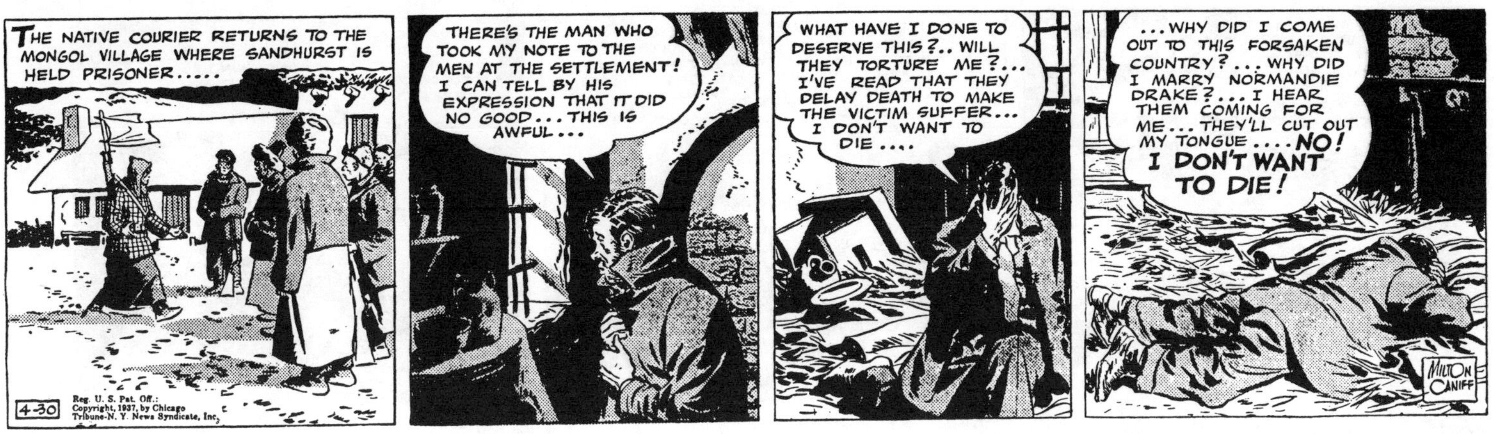

THE NATIVE COURIER RETURNS TO THE MONGOL VILLAGE WHERE SANDHURST IS HELD PRISONER.....
4-30
Reg. U. S. Pat. Off.: Copyright, 1937, by Chicago Tribune-N. Y. News Syndicate, Inc.
THERE'S THE MAN WHO TOOK MY NOTE TO THE MEN AT THE SETTLEMENT! I CAN TELL BY HIS EXPRESSION THAT IT DID NO GOOD... THIS IS AWFUL...
WHAT HAVE I DONE TO DESERVE THIS?.. WILL THEY TORTURE ME?... I'VE READ THAT THEY DELAY DEATH TO MAKE THE VICTIM SUFFER... I DON'T WANT TO DIE....
...WHY DID I COME OUT TO THIS FORSAKEN COUNTRY?...WHY DID I MARRY NORMANDIE DRAKE?... I HEAR THEM COMING FOR ME... THEY'LL CUT OUT MY TONGUE....NO! I DON'T WANT TO DIE!
MILTON CANIFF

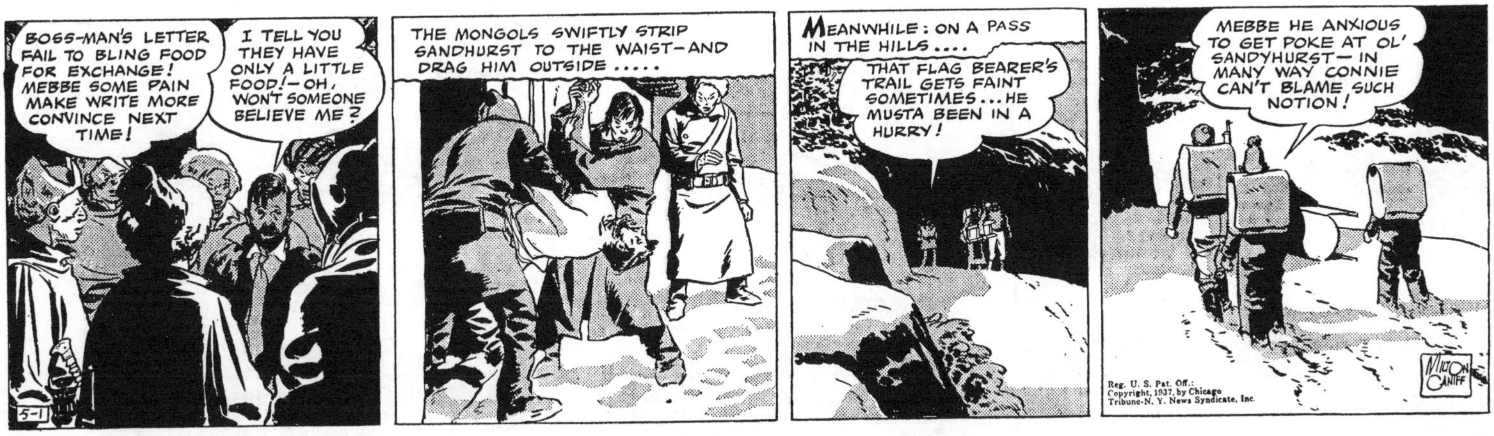

BOSS-MAN'S LETTER FAIL TO BLING FOOD FOR EXCHANGE! MEBBE SOME PAIN MAKE WRITE MORE CONVINCE NEXT TIME!
I TELL YOU THEY HAVE ONLY A LITTLE FOOD!—OH, WON'T SOMEONE BELIEVE ME?
5-1
THE MONGOLS SWIFTLY STRIP SANDHURST TO THE WAIST—AND DRAG HIM OUTSIDE.....
MEANWHILE: ON A PASS IN THE HILLS....
THAT FLAG BEARER'S TRAIL GETS FAINT SOMETIMES... HE MUSTA BEEN IN A HURRY!
MEBBE HE ANXIOUS TO GET POKE AT OL' SANDYHURST— IN MANY WAY CONNIE CAN'T BLAME SUCH NOTION!
Reg. U. S. Pat. Off.: Copyright, 1937, by Chicago Tribune-N. Y. News Syndicate, Inc.
MILTON CANIFF

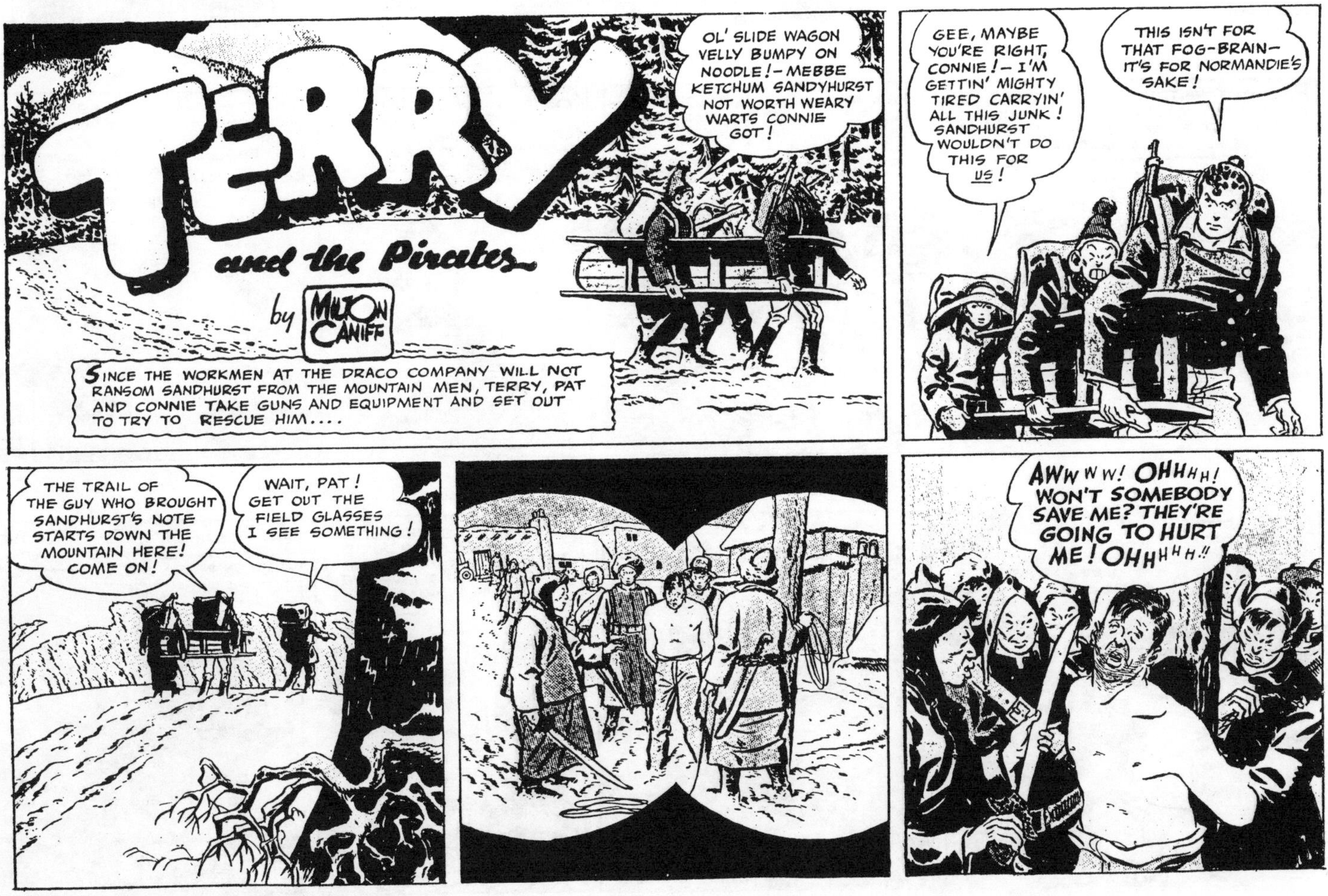

TERRY and the Pirates
by MILTON CANIFF
OL' SLIDE WAGON VELLY BUMPY ON NOODLE!—MEBBE KETCHUM SANDYHURST NOT WORTH WEARY WARTS CONNIE GOT!
SINCE THE WORKMEN AT THE DRACO COMPANY WILL NOT RANSOM SANDHURST FROM THE MOUNTAIN MEN, TERRY, PAT AND CONNIE TAKE GUNS AND EQUIPMENT AND SET OUT TO TRY TO RESCUE HIM....
GEE, MAYBE YOU'RE RIGHT, CONNIE!— I'M GETTIN' MIGHTY TIRED CARRYIN' ALL THIS JUNK! SANDHURST WOULDN'T DO THIS FOR US!
THIS ISN'T FOR THAT FOG-BRAIN— IT'S FOR NORMANDIE'S SAKE!
THE TRAIL OF THE GUY WHO BROUGHT SANDHURST'S NOTE STARTS DOWN THE MOUNTAIN HERE! COME ON!
WAIT, PAT! GET OUT THE FIELD GLASSES I SEE SOMETHING!
AWWWW! OHHHHH! WON'T SOMEBODY SAVE ME? THEY'RE GOING TO HURT ME! OHHHHH!!

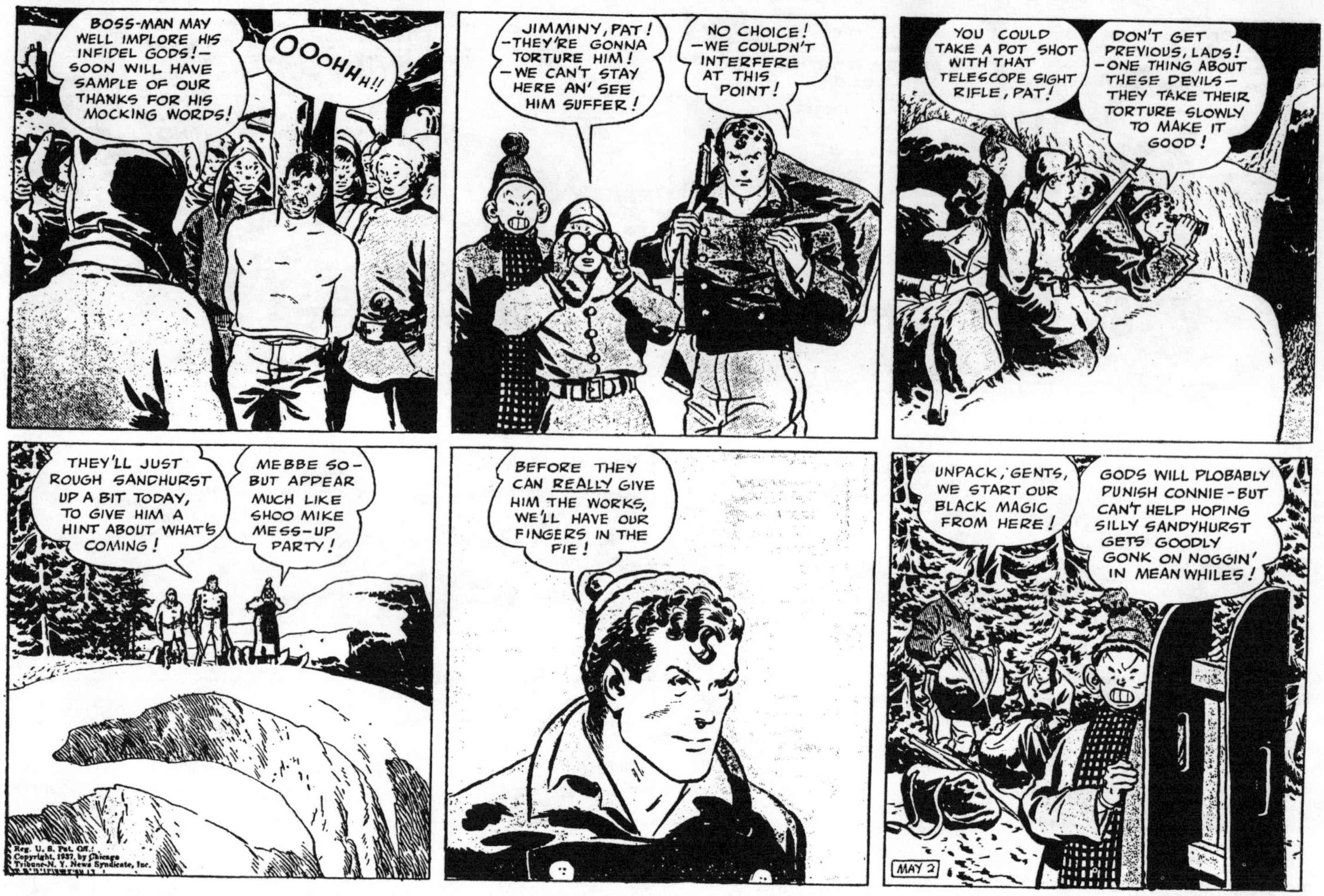
BOSS-MAN MAY WELL IMPLORE HIS INFIDEL GODS! —SOON WILL HAVE SAMPLE OF OUR THANKS FOR HIS MOCKING WORDS!
OOOHHH!!
JIMMINY, PAT! —THEY'RE GONNA TORTURE HIM! —WE CAN'T STAY HERE AN' SEE HIM SUFFER!
NO CHOICE! —WE COULDN'T INTERFERE AT THIS POINT!
YOU COULD TAKE A POT SHOT WITH THAT TELESCOPE SIGHT RIFLE, PAT!
DON'T GET PREVIOUS, LADS! —ONE THING ABOUT THESE DEVILS— THEY TAKE THEIR TORTURE SLOWLY TO MAKE IT GOOD!
THEY'LL JUST ROUGH SANDHURST UP A BIT TODAY, TO GIVE HIM A HINT ABOUT WHAT'S COMING!
MEBBE SO- BUT APPEAR MUCH LIKE SHOO MIKE MESS-UP PARTY!
Reg. U. S. Pat. Off.: Copyright, 1937, by Chicago Tribune-N. Y. News Syndicate, Inc.
BEFORE THEY CAN REALLY GIVE HIM THE WORKS, WE'LL HAVE OUR FINGERS IN THE PIE!
UNPACK, GENTS, WE START OUR BLACK MAGIC FROM HERE!
GODS WILL PLOBABLY PUNISH CONNIE - BUT CAN'T HELP HOPING SILLY SANDYHURST GETS GOODLY GONK ON NOGGIN' IN MEAN WHILES!
MAY 2

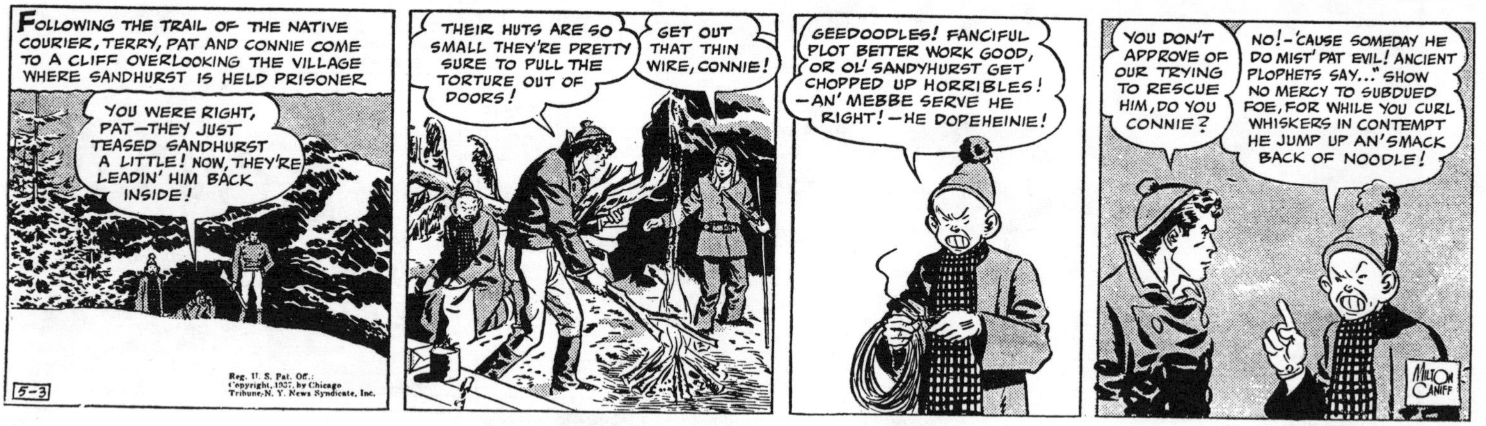
FOLLOWING THE TRAIL OF THE NATIVE COURIER, TERRY, PAT AND CONNIE COME TO A CLIFF OVERLOOKING THE VILLAGE WHERE SANDHURST IS HELD PRISONER
YOU WERE RIGHT, PAT—THEY JUST TEASED SANDHURST A LITTLE! NOW, THEY'RE LEADIN' HIM BACK INSIDE!
Reg. U. S. Pat. Off.: Copyright, 1937, by Chicago Tribune-N. Y. News Syndicate, Inc.
5-3
THEIR HUTS ARE SO SMALL THEY'RE PRETTY SURE TO PULL THE TORTURE OUT OF DOORS!
GET OUT THAT THIN WIRE, CONNIE!
GEEDOODLES! FANCIFUL PLOT BETTER WORK GOOD, OR OL' SANDYHURST GET CHOPPED UP HORRIBLES! —AN' MEBBE SERVE HE RIGHT! —HE DOPEHEINIE!
YOU DON'T APPROVE OF OUR TRYING TO RESCUE HIM, DO YOU CONNIE?
NO! -'CAUSE SOMEDAY HE DO MIST' PAT EVIL! ANCIENT PLOPHETS SAY..." SHOW NO MERCY TO SUBDUED FOE, FOR WHILE YOU CURL WHISKERS IN CONTEMPT HE JUMP UP AN' SMACK BACK OF NOODLE!
MILTON CANIFF

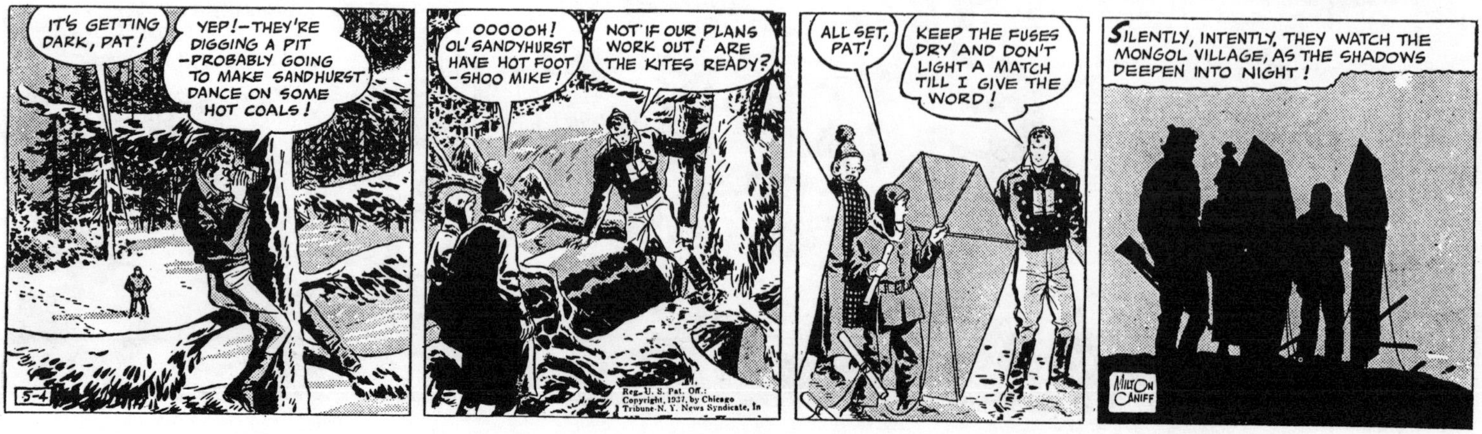
IT'S GETTING DARK, PAT!
YEP! —THEY'RE DIGGING A PIT —PROBABLY GOING TO MAKE SANDHURST DANCE ON SOME HOT COALS!
5-4
OOOOOH! OL' SANDYHURST HAVE HOT FOOT -SHOO MIKE!
NOT IF OUR PLANS WORK OUT! ARE THE KITES READY?
Reg. U. S. Pat. Off.: Copyright, 1937, by Chicago Tribune-N. Y. News Syndicate, In
ALL SET, PAT!
KEEP THE FUSES DRY AND DON'T LIGHT A MATCH TILL I GIVE THE WORD!
SILENTLY, INTENTLY, THEY WATCH THE MONGOL VILLAGE, AS THE SHADOWS DEEPEN INTO NIGHT!
MILTON CANIFF

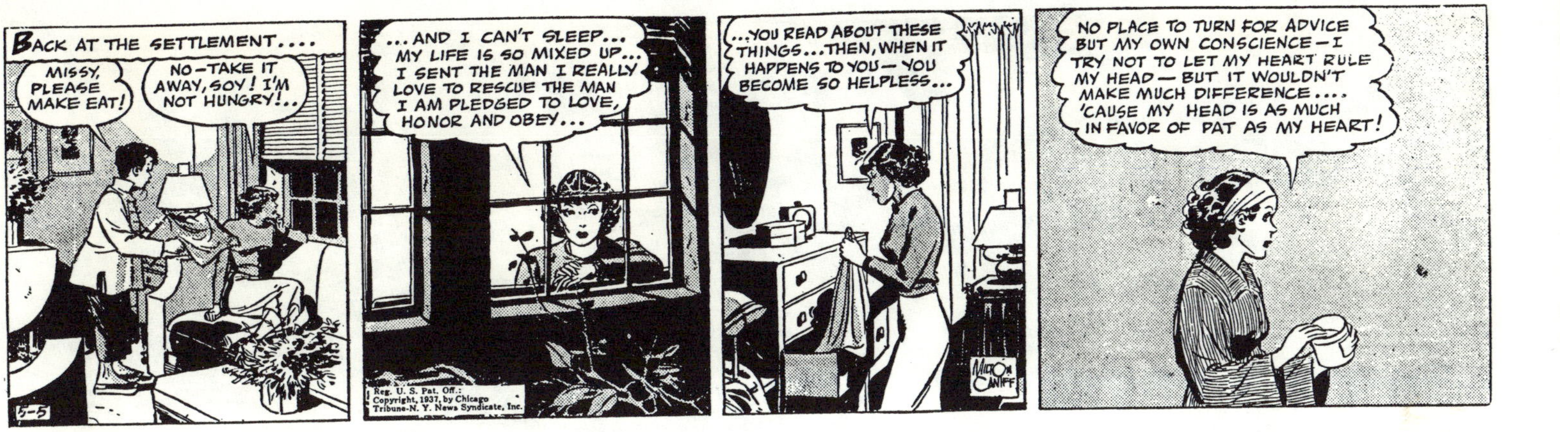
BACK AT THE SETTLEMENT....
MISSY, PLEASE MAKE EAT!
NO–TAKE IT AWAY, SOY! I'M NOT HUNGRY!..
5-5
...AND I CAN'T SLEEP... MY LIFE IS SO MIXED UP... I SENT THE MAN I REALLY LOVE TO RESCUE THE MAN I AM PLEDGED TO LOVE, HONOR AND OBEY...
Reg. U. S. Pat. Off.: Copyright, 1937, by Chicago Tribune-N. Y. News Syndicate, Inc.
...YOU READ ABOUT THESE THINGS...THEN, WHEN IT HAPPENS TO YOU—YOU BECOME SO HELPLESS...
MILTON CANIFF
NO PLACE TO TURN FOR ADVICE BUT MY OWN CONSCIENCE—I TRY NOT TO LET MY HEART RULE MY HEAD—BUT IT WOULDN'T MAKE MUCH DIFFERENCE.... 'CAUSE MY HEAD IS AS MUCH IN FAVOR OF PAT AS MY HEART!

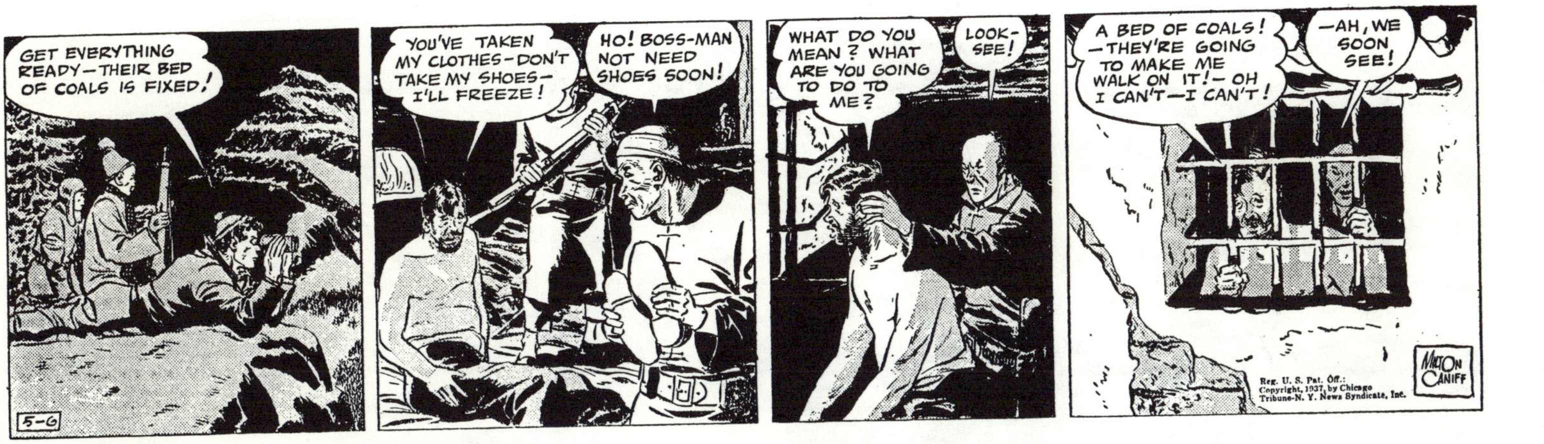
GET EVERYTHING READY—THEIR BED OF COALS IS FIXED!
5-6
YOU'VE TAKEN MY CLOTHES—DON'T TAKE MY SHOES—I'LL FREEZE!
HO! BOSS-MAN NOT NEED SHOES SOON!
WHAT DO YOU MEAN? WHAT ARE YOU GOING TO DO TO ME?
LOOK-SEE!
A BED OF COALS!—THEY'RE GOING TO MAKE ME WALK ON IT!—OH I CAN'T—I CAN'T!
—AH, WE SOON SEE!
Reg. U. S. Pat. Off.: Copyright, 1937, by Chicago Tribune-N. Y. News Syndicate, Inc.
MILTON CANIFF

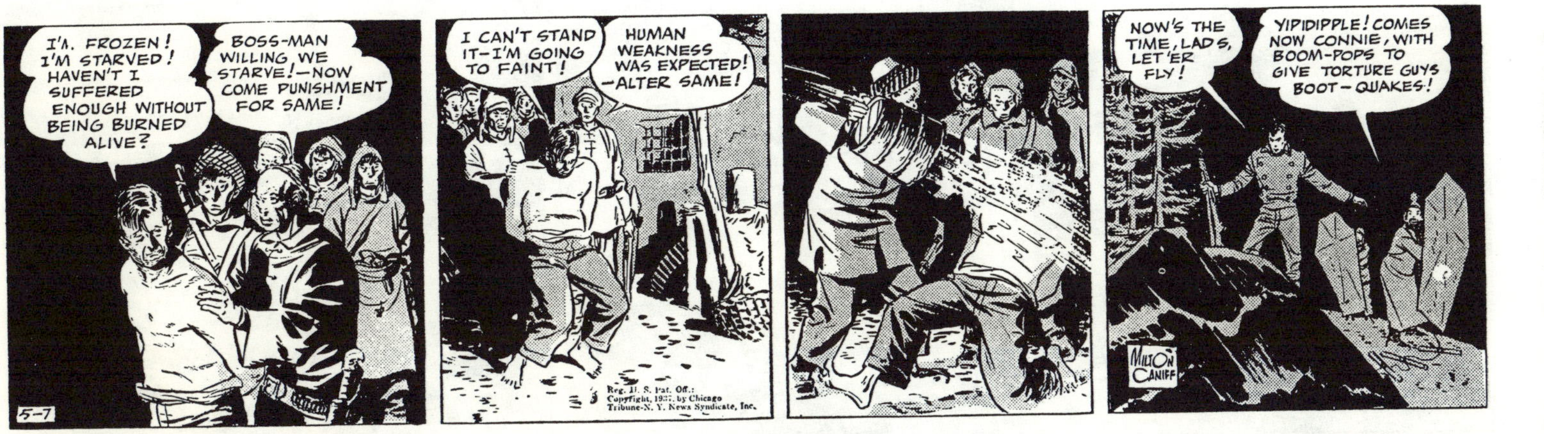
I'M FROZEN! I'M STARVED! HAVEN'T I SUFFERED ENOUGH WITHOUT BEING BURNED ALIVE?
BOSS-MAN WILLING WE STARVE!—NOW COME PUNISHMENT FOR SAME!
5-7
I CAN'T STAND IT—I'M GOING TO FAINT!
HUMAN WEAKNESS WAS EXPECTED!—ALTER SAME!
Reg. U. S. Pat. Off.: Copyright, 1937, by Chicago Tribune-N. Y. News Syndicate, Inc.
NOW'S THE TIME, LADS, LET'ER FLY!
YIPIDIPPLE! COMES NOW CONNIE, WITH BOOM-POPS TO GIVE TORTURE GUYS BOOT-QUAKES!
MILTON CANIFF

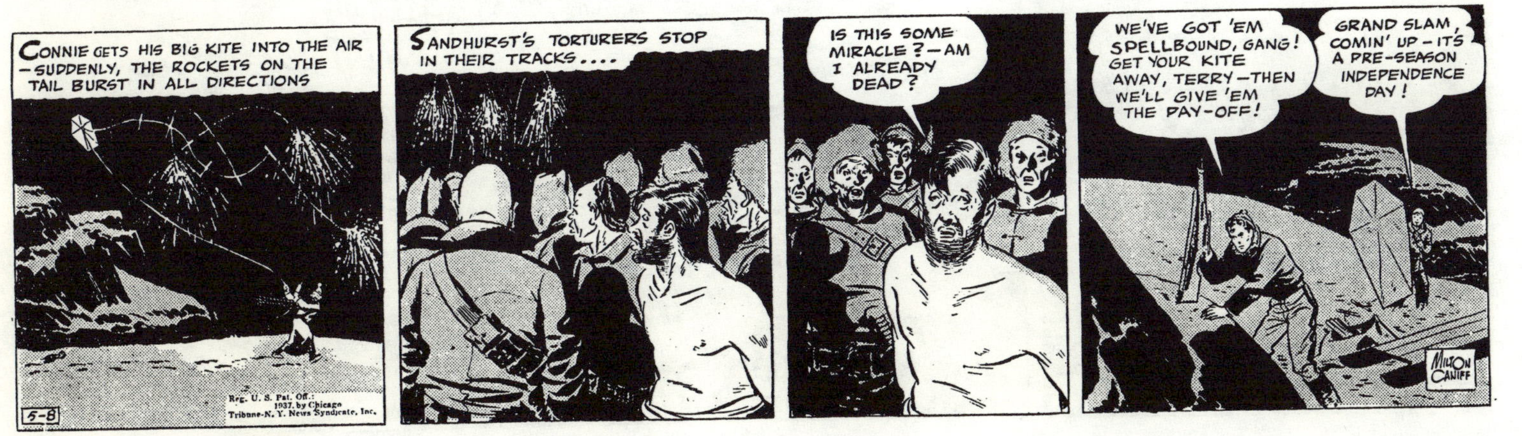
CONNIE GETS HIS BIG KITE INTO THE AIR—SUDDENLY, THE ROCKETS ON THE TAIL BURST IN ALL DIRECTIONS
5-8
Reg. U. S. Pat. Off.: Copyright, 1937, by Chicago Tribune-N. Y. News Syndicate, Inc.
SANDHURST'S TORTURERS STOP IN THEIR TRACKS....
IS THIS SOME MIRACLE?—AM I ALREADY DEAD?
WE'VE GOT 'EM SPELLBOUND, GANG! GET YOUR KITE AWAY, TERRY—THEN WE'LL GIVE 'EM THE PAY-OFF!
GRAND SLAM COMIN' UP—IT'S A PRE-SEASON INDEPENDENCE DAY!
MILTON CANIFF

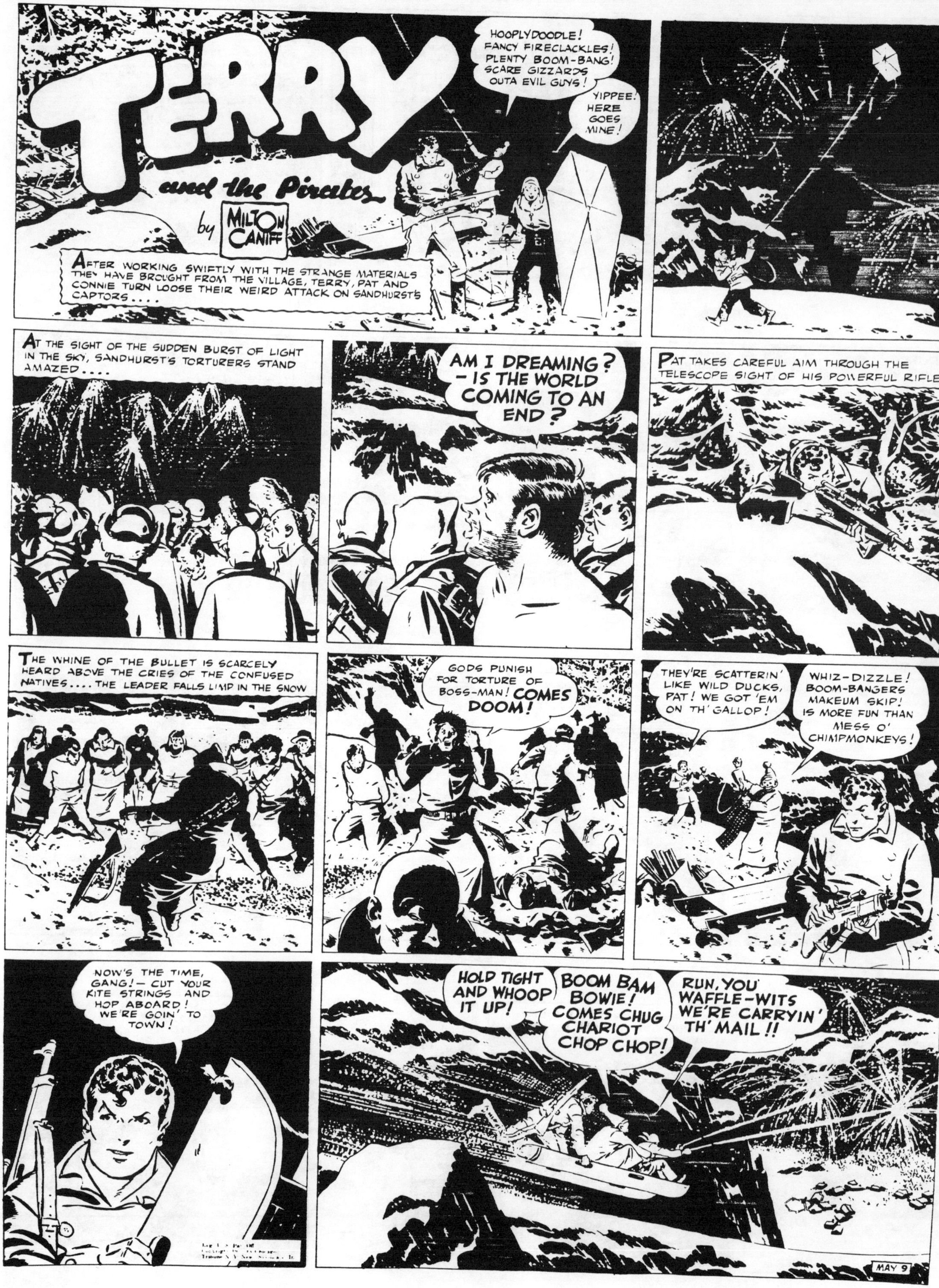
TERRY and the Pirates
by MILTON CANIFF
AFTER WORKING SWIFTLY WITH THE STRANGE MATERIALS THEY HAVE BROUGHT FROM THE VILLAGE, TERRY, PAT AND CONNIE TURN LOOSE THEIR WEIRD ATTACK ON SANDHURST'S CAPTORS....
HOOPLYDOODLE! FANCY FIRECLACKLES! PLENTY BOOM-BANG! SCARE GIZZARDS OUTA EVIL GUYS!
YIPPEE! HERE GOES MINE!
AT THE SIGHT OF THE SUDDEN BURST OF LIGHT IN THE SKY, SANDHURST'S TORTURERS STAND AMAZED....
AM I DREAMING? — IS THE WORLD COMING TO AN END?
PAT TAKES CAREFUL AIM THROUGH THE TELESCOPE SIGHT OF HIS POWERFUL RIFLE
THE WHINE OF THE BULLET IS SCARCELY HEARD ABOVE THE CRIES OF THE CONFUSED NATIVES.... THE LEADER FALLS LIMP IN THE SNOW
GODS PUNISH FOR TORTURE OF BOSS-MAN! COMES DOOM!
THEY'RE SCATTERIN' LIKE WILD DUCKS, PAT! WE GOT 'EM ON TH' GALLOP!
WHIZ-DIZZLE! BOOM-BANGERS MAKEUM SKIP! IS MORE FUN THAN MESS O' CHIMPMONKEYS!
NOW'S THE TIME, GANG! — CUT YOUR KITE STRINGS AND HOP ABOARD! WE'RE GOIN' TO TOWN!
HOLD TIGHT AND WHOOP IT UP!
BOOM BAM BOWIE! COMES CHUG CHARIOT CHOP CHOP!
RUN, YOU WAFFLE-WITS WE'RE CARRYIN' TH' MAIL!!
MAY 9

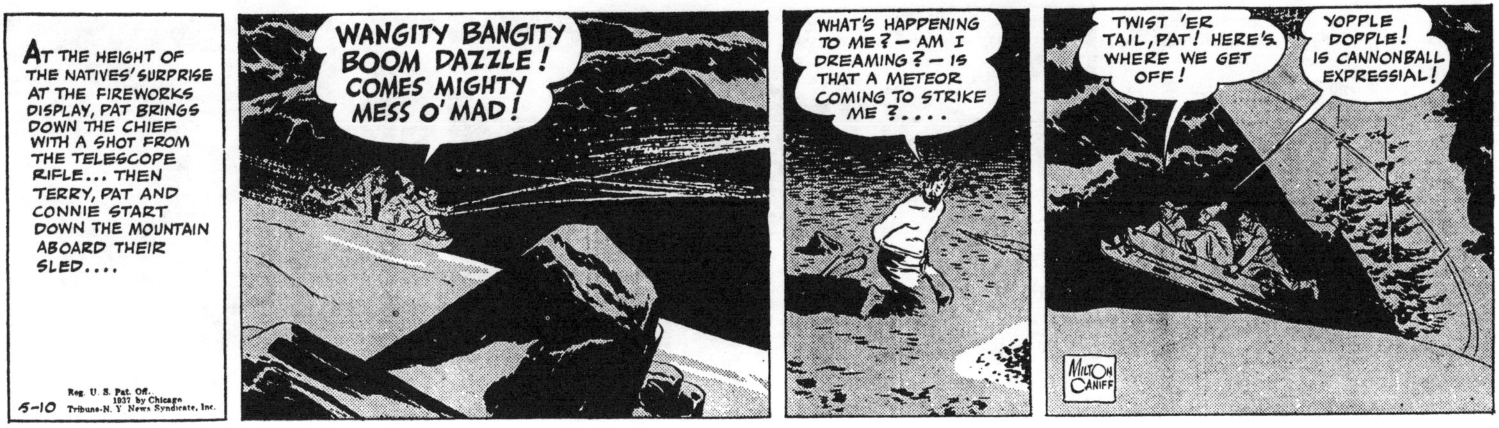
AT THE HEIGHT OF THE NATIVES' SURPRISE AT THE FIREWORKS DISPLAY, PAT BRINGS DOWN THE CHIEF WITH A SHOT FROM THE TELESCOPE RIFLE... THEN TERRY, PAT AND CONNIE START DOWN THE MOUNTAIN ABOARD THEIR SLED....
Reg. U. S. Pat. Off. 1937 by Chicago Tribune-N. Y. News Syndicate, Inc.
5-10
WANGITY BANGITY BOOM DAZZLE! COMES MIGHTY MESS O' MAD!
WHAT'S HAPPENING TO ME? — AM I DREAMING? — IS THAT A METEOR COMING TO STRIKE ME?....
TWIST 'ER TAIL, PAT! HERE'S WHERE WE GET OFF!
YOPPLE DOPPLE! IS CANNONBALL EXPRESSIAL!
MILTON CANIFF

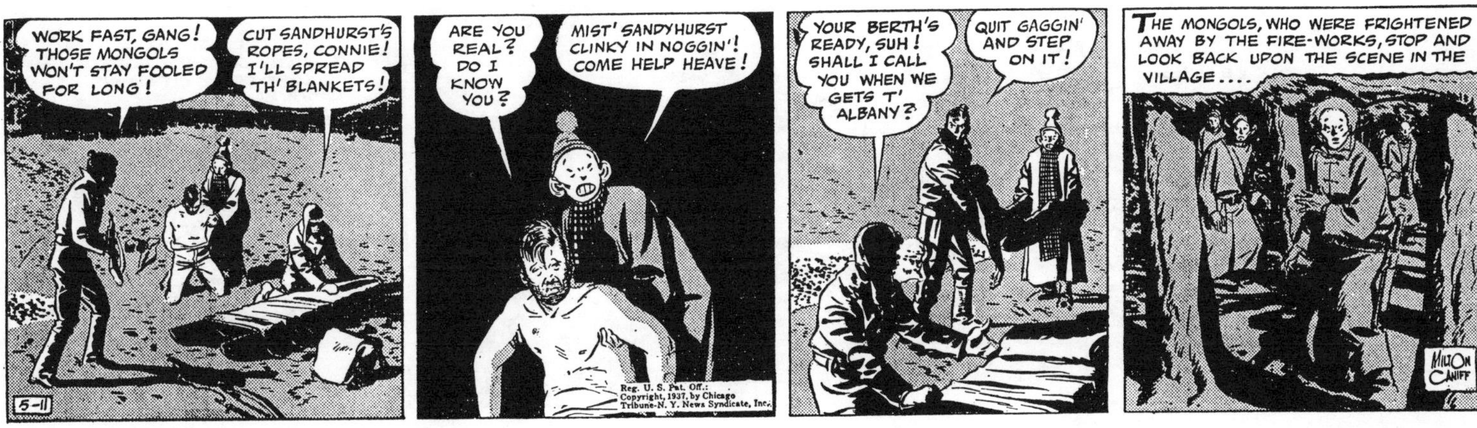
WORK FAST, GANG! THOSE MONGOLS WON'T STAY FOOLED FOR LONG!
CUT SANDHURST'S ROPES, CONNIE! I'LL SPREAD TH' BLANKETS!
5-11
ARE YOU REAL? DO I KNOW YOU?
MIST' SANDYHURST CLINKY IN NOGGIN'! COME HELP HEAVE!
Reg. U. S. Pat. Off.: Copyright, 1937, by Chicago Tribune-N. Y. News Syndicate, Inc.
YOUR BERTH'S READY, SUH! SHALL I CALL YOU WHEN WE GETS T' ALBANY?
QUIT GAGGIN' AND STEP ON IT!
THE MONGOLS, WHO WERE FRIGHTENED AWAY BY THE FIRE-WORKS, STOP AND LOOK BACK UPON THE SCENE IN THE VILLAGE....
MILTON CANIFF

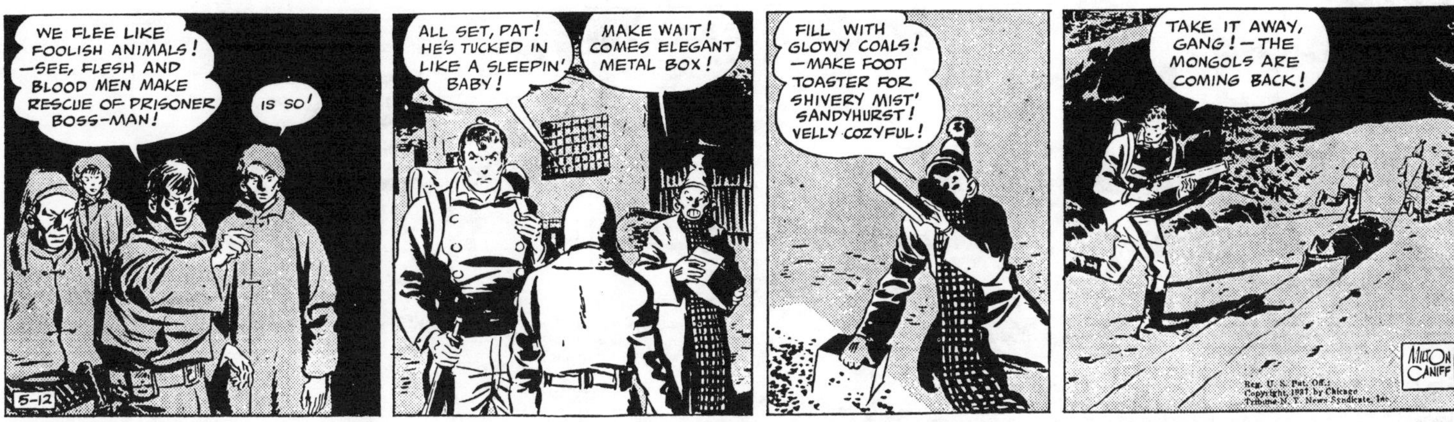
WE FLEE LIKE FOOLISH ANIMALS! —SEE, FLESH AND BLOOD MEN MAKE RESCUE OF PRISONER BOSS-MAN!
IS SO!
5-12
ALL SET, PAT! HE'S TUCKED IN LIKE A SLEEPIN' BABY!
MAKE WAIT! COMES ELEGANT METAL BOX!
FILL WITH GLOWY COALS! —MAKE FOOT TOASTER FOR SHIVERY MIST' SANDYHURST! VELLY COZYFUL!
TAKE IT AWAY, GANG! — THE MONGOLS ARE COMING BACK!
MILTON CANIFF
Reg. U. S. Pat. Off.: Copyright, 1937, by Chicago Tribune-N. Y. News Syndicate, Inc.

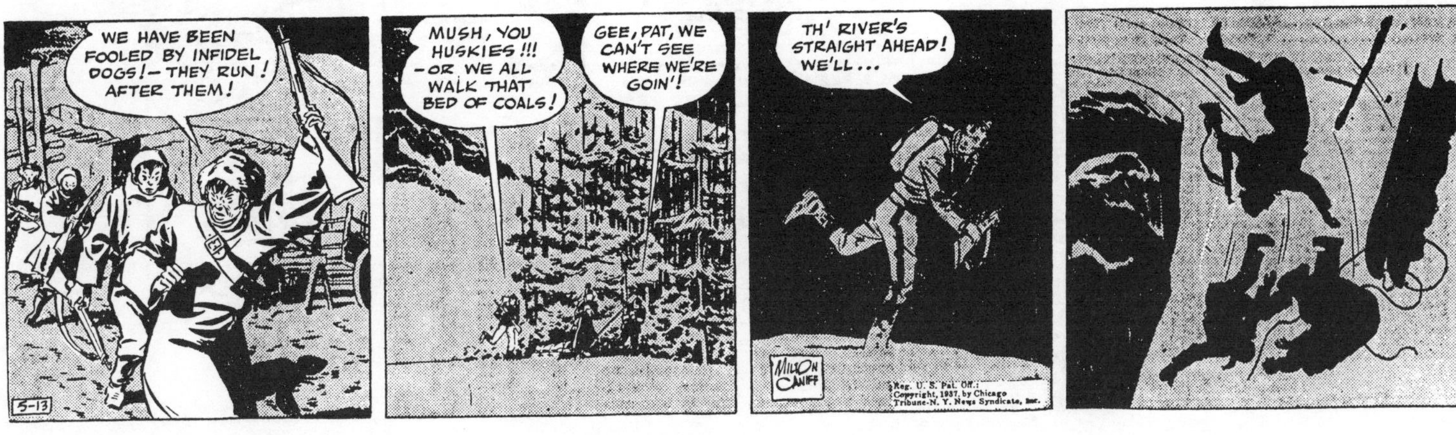
WE HAVE BEEN FOOLED BY INFIDEL DOGS! — THEY RUN! AFTER THEM!
5-13
MUSH, YOU HUSKIES!!! —OR WE ALL WALK THAT BED OF COALS!
GEE, PAT, WE CAN'T SEE WHERE WE'RE GOIN'!
TH' RIVER'S STRAIGHT AHEAD! WE'LL...
MILTON CANIFF
Reg. U. S. Pat. Off.: Copyright, 1937, by Chicago Tribune-N. Y. News Syndicate, Inc.

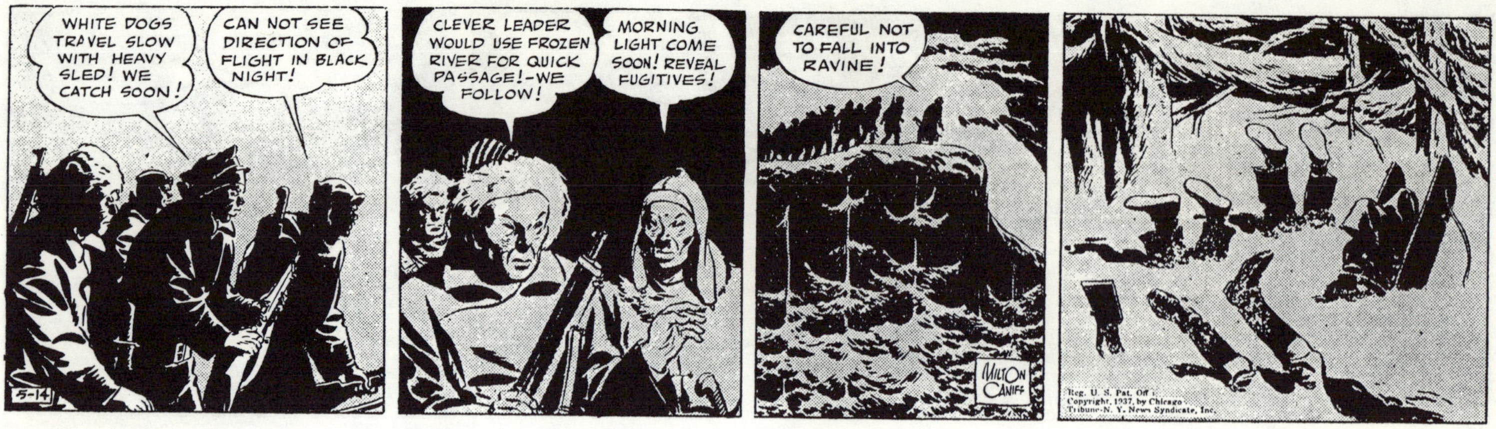
WHITE DOGS TRAVEL SLOW WITH HEAVY SLED! WE CATCH SOON!
CAN NOT SEE DIRECTION OF FLIGHT IN BLACK NIGHT!
5-14
CLEVER LEADER WOULD USE FROZEN RIVER FOR QUICK PASSAGE!—WE FOLLOW!
MORNING LIGHT COME SOON! REVEAL FUGITIVES!
CAREFUL NOT TO FALL INTO RAVINE!
MILTON CANIFF
Reg. U. S. Pat. Off.; Copyright, 1937, by Chicago Tribune-N. Y. News Syndicate, Inc.

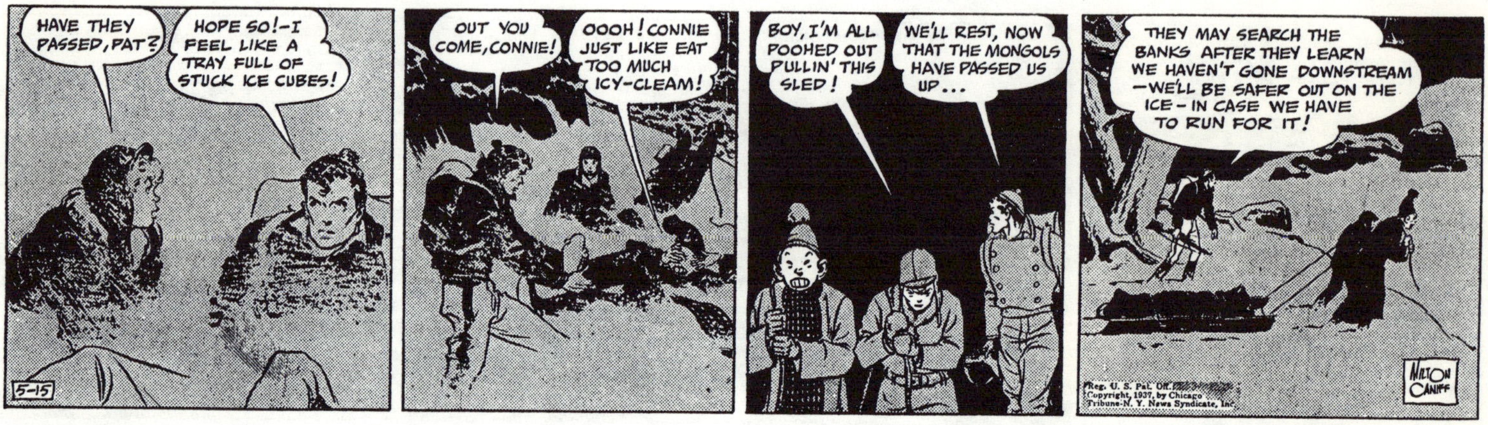
HAVE THEY PASSED, PAT?
HOPE SO!—I FEEL LIKE A TRAY FULL OF STUCK ICE CUBES!
5-15
OUT YOU COME, CONNIE!
OOOH! CONNIE JUST LIKE EAT TOO MUCH ICY-CLEAM!
BOY, I'M ALL POOHED OUT PULLIN' THIS SLED!
WE'LL REST, NOW THAT THE MONGOLS HAVE PASSED US UP...
THEY MAY SEARCH THE BANKS AFTER THEY LEARN WE HAVEN'T GONE DOWNSTREAM —WE'LL BE SAFER OUT ON THE ICE—IN CASE WE HAVE TO RUN FOR IT!
Reg. U. S. Pat. Off.; Copyright, 1937, by Chicago Tribune-N. Y. News Syndicate, Inc.
MILTON CANIFF

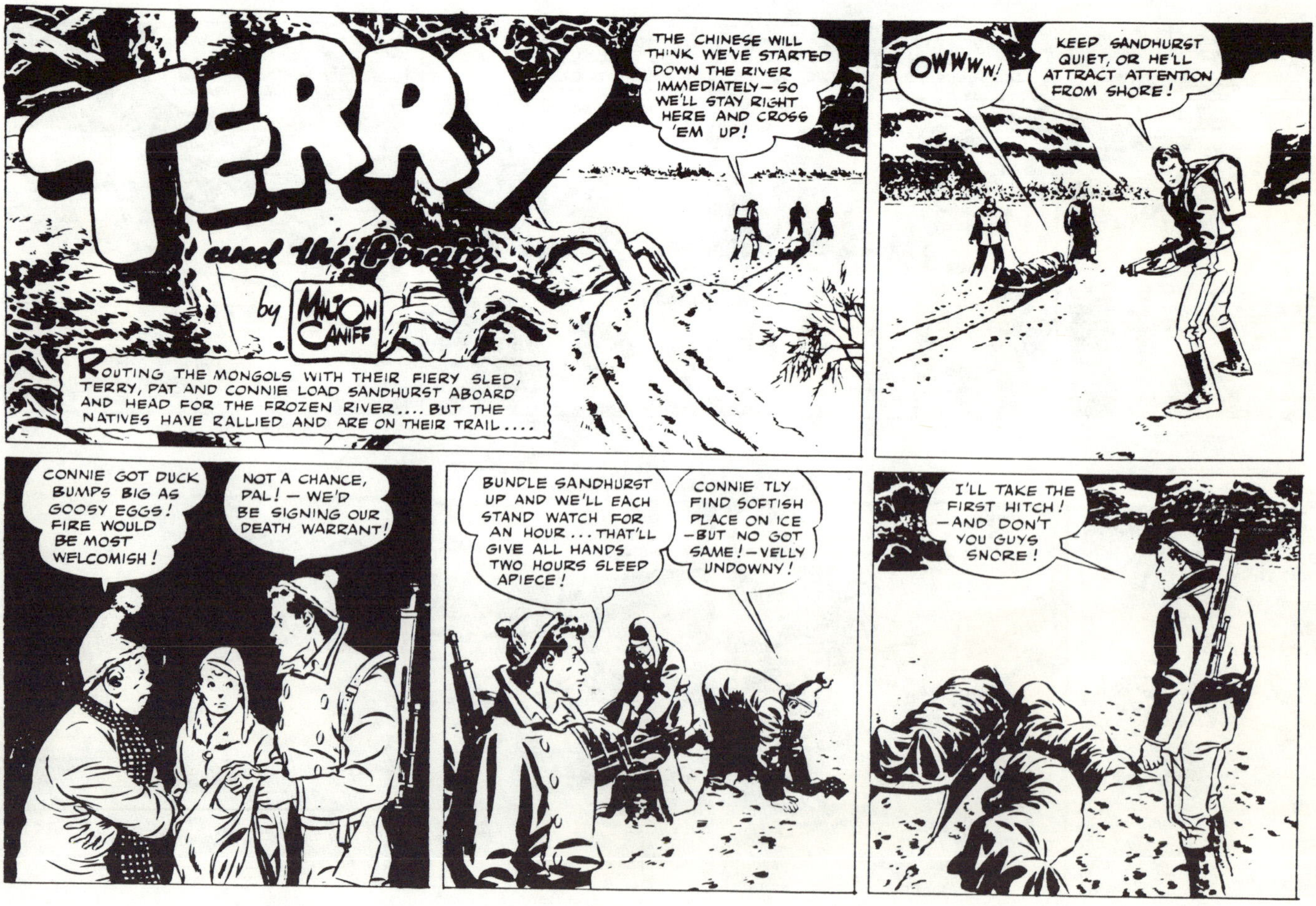
TERRY and the Pirates
by MILTON CANIFF
ROUTING THE MONGOLS WITH THEIR FIERY SLED, TERRY, PAT AND CONNIE LOAD SANDHURST ABOARD AND HEAD FOR THE FROZEN RIVER.... BUT THE NATIVES HAVE RALLIED AND ARE ON THEIR TRAIL....
THE CHINESE WILL THINK WE'VE STARTED DOWN THE RIVER IMMEDIATELY—SO WE'LL STAY RIGHT HERE AND CROSS 'EM UP!
OWWWW!
KEEP SANDHURST QUIET, OR HE'LL ATTRACT ATTENTION FROM SHORE!
CONNIE GOT DUCK BUMPS BIG AS GOOSY EGGS! FIRE WOULD BE MOST WELCOMISH!
NOT A CHANCE, PAL!—WE'D BE SIGNING OUR DEATH WARRANT!
BUNDLE SANDHURST UP AND WE'LL EACH STAND WATCH FOR AN HOUR... THAT'LL GIVE ALL HANDS TWO HOURS SLEEP APIECE!
CONNIE TLY FIND SOFTISH PLACE ON ICE —BUT NO GOT SAME!—VELLY UNDOWNY!
I'LL TAKE THE FIRST HITCH!—AND DON'T YOU GUYS SNORE!

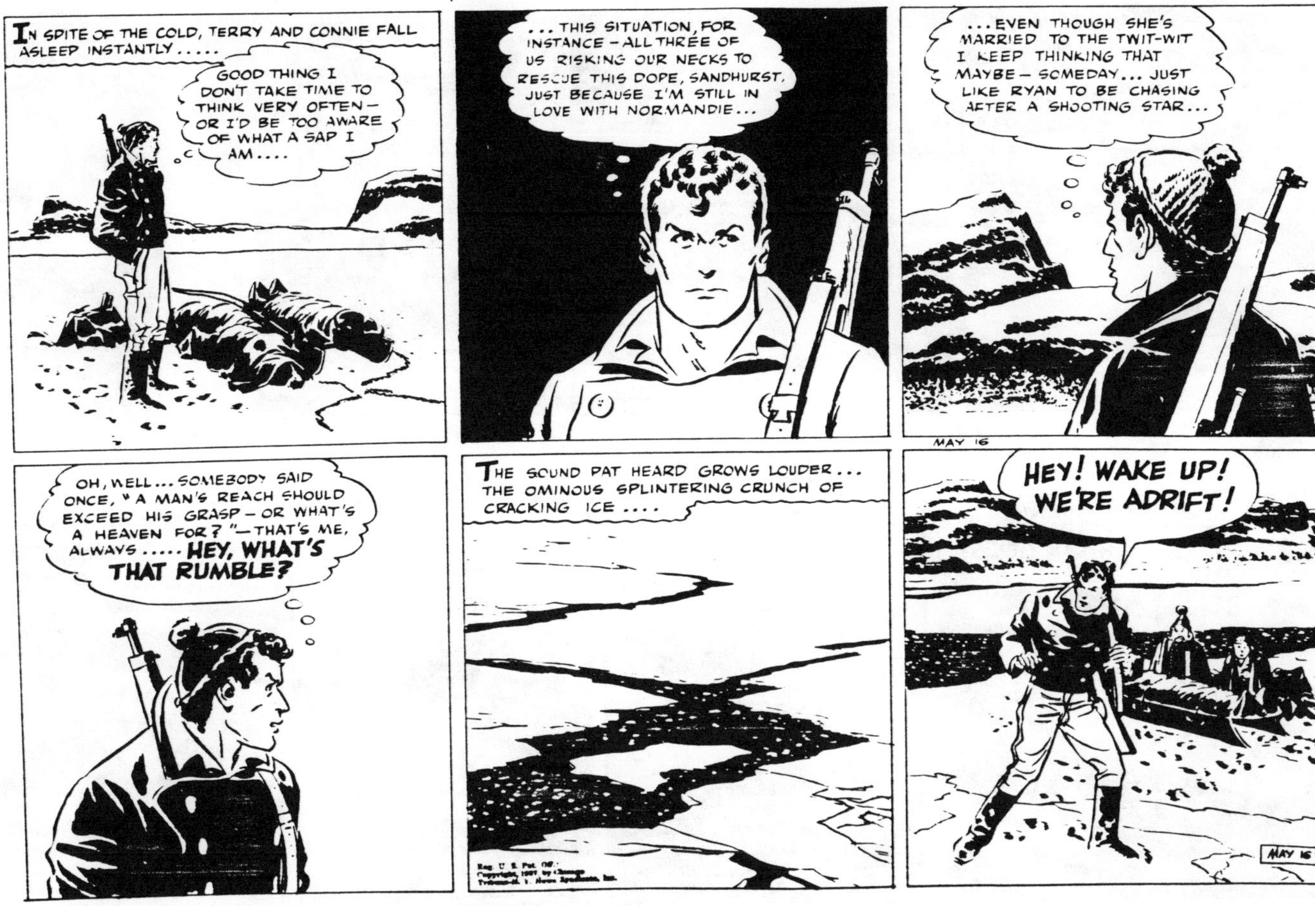
IN SPITE OF THE COLD, TERRY AND CONNIE FALL ASLEEP INSTANTLY.....
GOOD THING I DON'T TAKE TIME TO THINK VERY OFTEN— OR I'D BE TOO AWARE OF WHAT A SAP I AM....
... THIS SITUATION, FOR INSTANCE – ALL THREE OF US RISKING OUR NECKS TO RESCUE THIS DOPE, SANDHURST, JUST BECAUSE I'M STILL IN LOVE WITH NORMANDIE...
... EVEN THOUGH SHE'S MARRIED TO THE TWIT-WIT I KEEP THINKING THAT MAYBE – SOMEDAY... JUST LIKE RYAN TO BE CHASING AFTER A SHOOTING STAR...
MAY 16
OH, WELL... SOMEBODY SAID ONCE, "A MAN'S REACH SHOULD EXCEED HIS GRASP – OR WHAT'S A HEAVEN FOR?"—THAT'S ME, ALWAYS..... HEY, WHAT'S THAT RUMBLE?
THE SOUND PAT HEARD GROWS LOUDER... THE OMINOUS SPLINTERING CRUNCH OF CRACKING ICE....
HEY! WAKE UP! WE'RE ADRIFT!
MAY 16

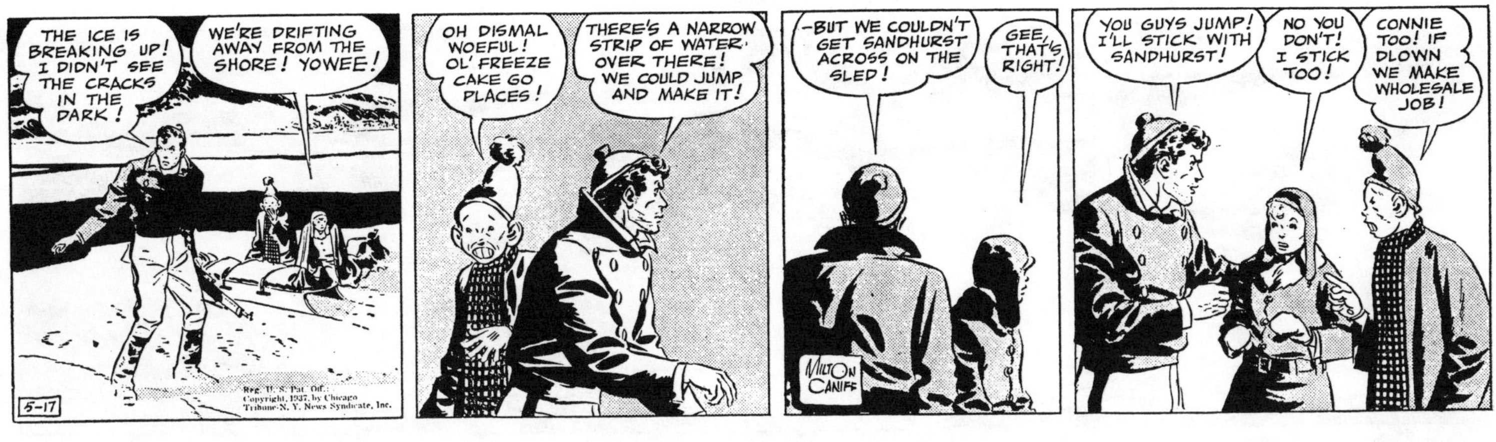
THE ICE IS BREAKING UP! I DIDN'T SEE THE CRACKS IN THE DARK!
WE'RE DRIFTING AWAY FROM THE SHORE! YOWEE!
Reg. U. S. Pat. Off.: Copyright, 1937, by Chicago Tribune-N. Y. News Syndicate, Inc.
5-17
OH DISMAL WOEFUL! OL' FREEZE CAKE GO PLACES!
THERE'S A NARROW STRIP OF WATER OVER THERE! WE COULD JUMP AND MAKE IT!
—BUT WE COULDN'T GET SANDHURST ACROSS ON THE SLED!
GEE, THAT'S RIGHT!
MILTON CANIFF
YOU GUYS JUMP! I'LL STICK WITH SANDHURST!
NO YOU DON'T! I STICK TOO!
CONNIE TOO! IF DLOWN WE MAKE WHOLESALE JOB!

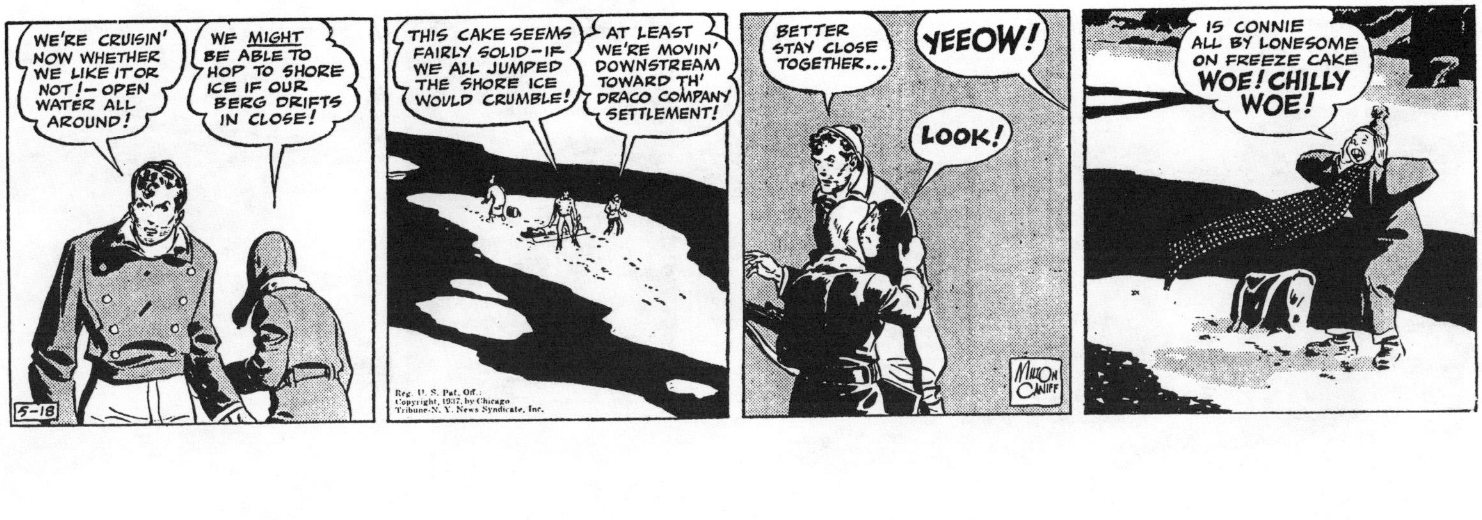
WE'RE CRUISIN' NOW WHETHER WE LIKE IT OR NOT!— OPEN WATER ALL AROUND!
WE MIGHT BE ABLE TO HOP TO SHORE ICE IF OUR BERG DRIFTS IN CLOSE!
5-18
THIS CAKE SEEMS FAIRLY SOLID– IF WE ALL JUMPED THE SHORE ICE WOULD CRUMBLE!
AT LEAST WE'RE MOVIN' DOWNSTREAM TOWARD TH' DRACO COMPANY SETTLEMENT!
Reg. U. S. Pat. Off.: Copyright, 1937, by Chicago Tribune-N. Y. News Syndicate, Inc.
BETTER STAY CLOSE TOGETHER...
YEEOW!
LOOK!
MILTON CANIFF
IS CONNIE ALL BY LONESOME ON FREEZE CAKE
WOE! CHILLY WOE!

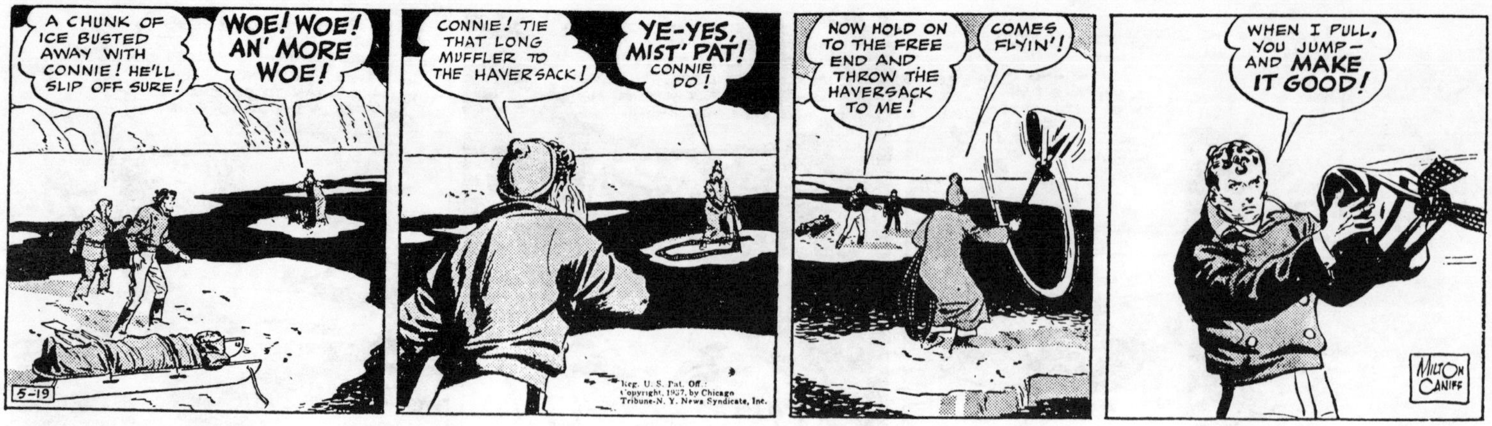
A CHUNK OF ICE BUSTED AWAY WITH CONNIE! HE'LL SLIP OFF SURE!
WOE! WOE! AN' MORE WOE!
5-19
CONNIE! TIE THAT LONG MUFFLER TO THE HAVERSACK!
YE-YES, MIST' PAT! CONNIE DO!
Reg. U. S. Pat. Off.: Copyright, 1937, by Chicago Tribune-N. Y. News Syndicate, Inc.
NOW HOLD ON TO THE FREE END AND THROW THE HAVERSACK TO ME!
COMES FLYIN'!
WHEN I PULL, YOU JUMP— AND MAKE IT GOOD!
MILTON CANIFF

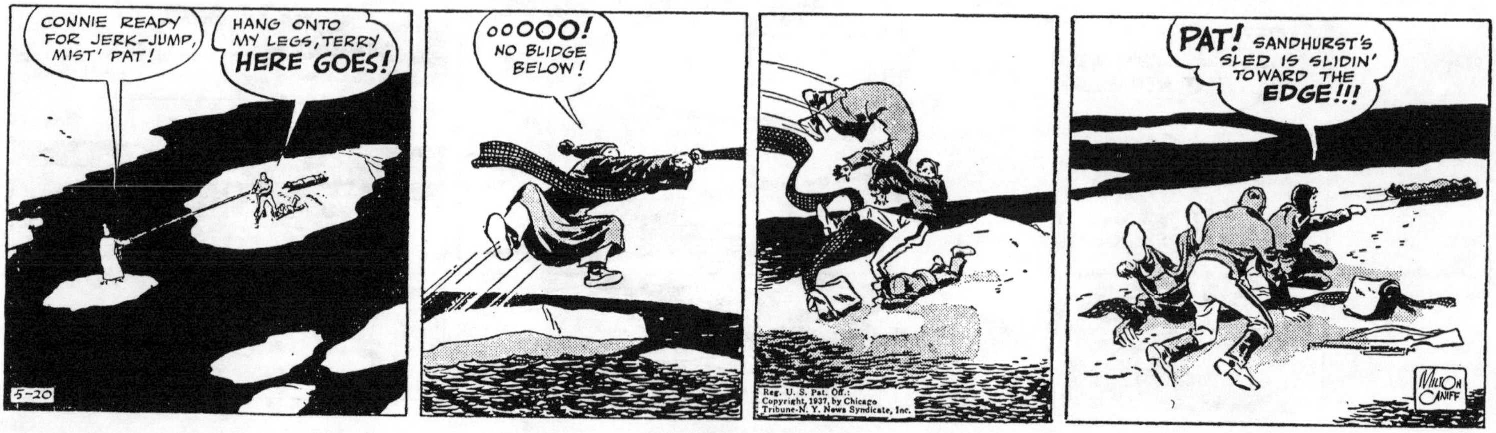
CONNIE READY FOR JERK-JUMP, MIST' PAT!
HANG ONTO MY LEGS, TERRY HERE GOES!
5-20
OOOOO! NO BLIDGE BELOW!
Reg. U. S. Pat. Off.: Copyright, 1937, by Chicago Tribune-N. Y. News Syndicate, Inc.
PAT! SANDHURST'S SLED IS SLIDIN' TOWARD THE EDGE!!!
MILTON CANIFF

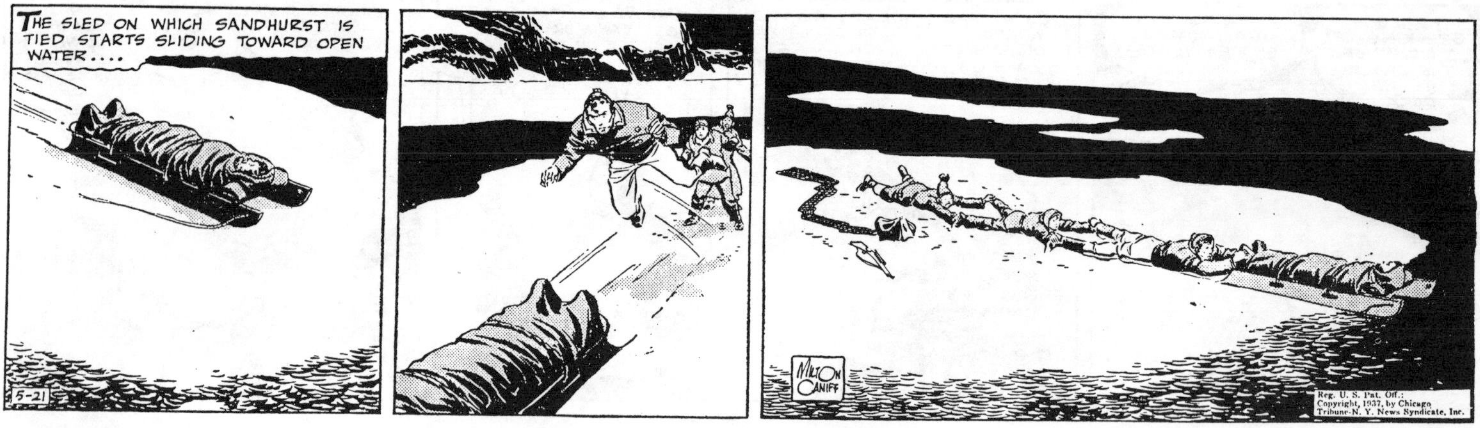
THE SLED ON WHICH SANDHURST IS TIED STARTS SLIDING TOWARD OPEN WATER....
5-21
MILTON CANIFF
Reg. U. S. Pat. Off.: Copyright, 1937, by Chicago Tribune-N. Y. News Syndicate, Inc.

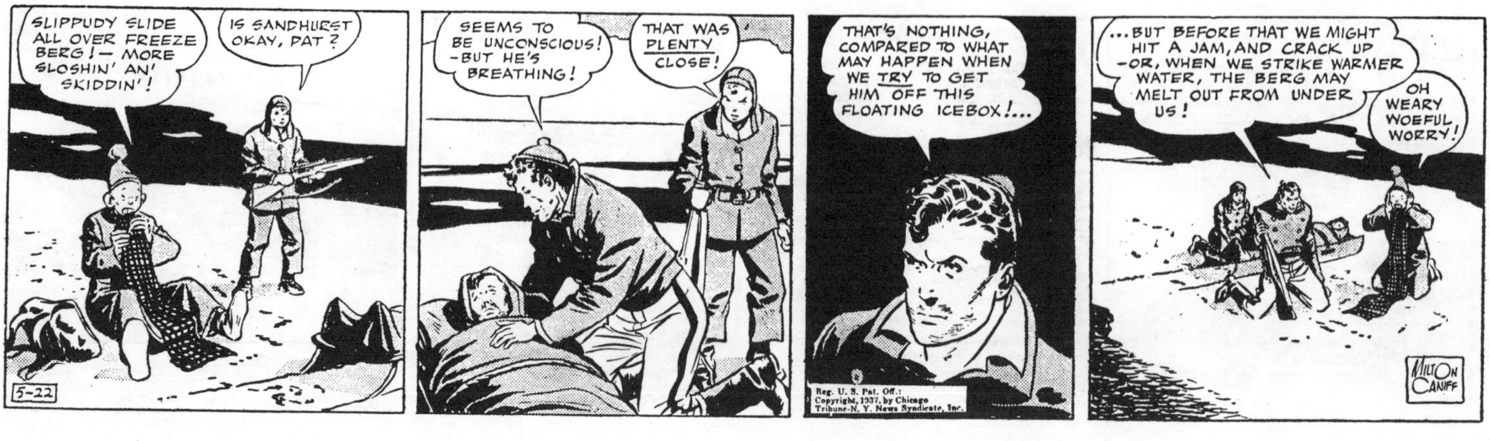
SLIPPUDY SLIDE ALL OVER FREEZE BERG!— MORE SLOSHIN' AN' SKIDDIN'!
IS SANDHURST OKAY, PAT?
5-22
SEEMS TO BE UNCONSCIOUS! -BUT HE'S BREATHING!
THAT WAS PLENTY CLOSE!
THAT'S NOTHING, COMPARED TO WHAT MAY HAPPEN WHEN WE TRY TO GET HIM OFF THIS FLOATING ICEBOX!...
Reg. U. S. Pat. Off.: Copyright, 1937, by Chicago Tribune-N. Y. News Syndicate, Inc.
...BUT BEFORE THAT WE MIGHT HIT A JAM, AND CRACK UP -OR, WHEN WE STRIKE WARMER WATER, THE BERG MAY MELT OUT FROM UNDER US!
OH WEARY WOEFUL WORRY!
MILTON CANIFF

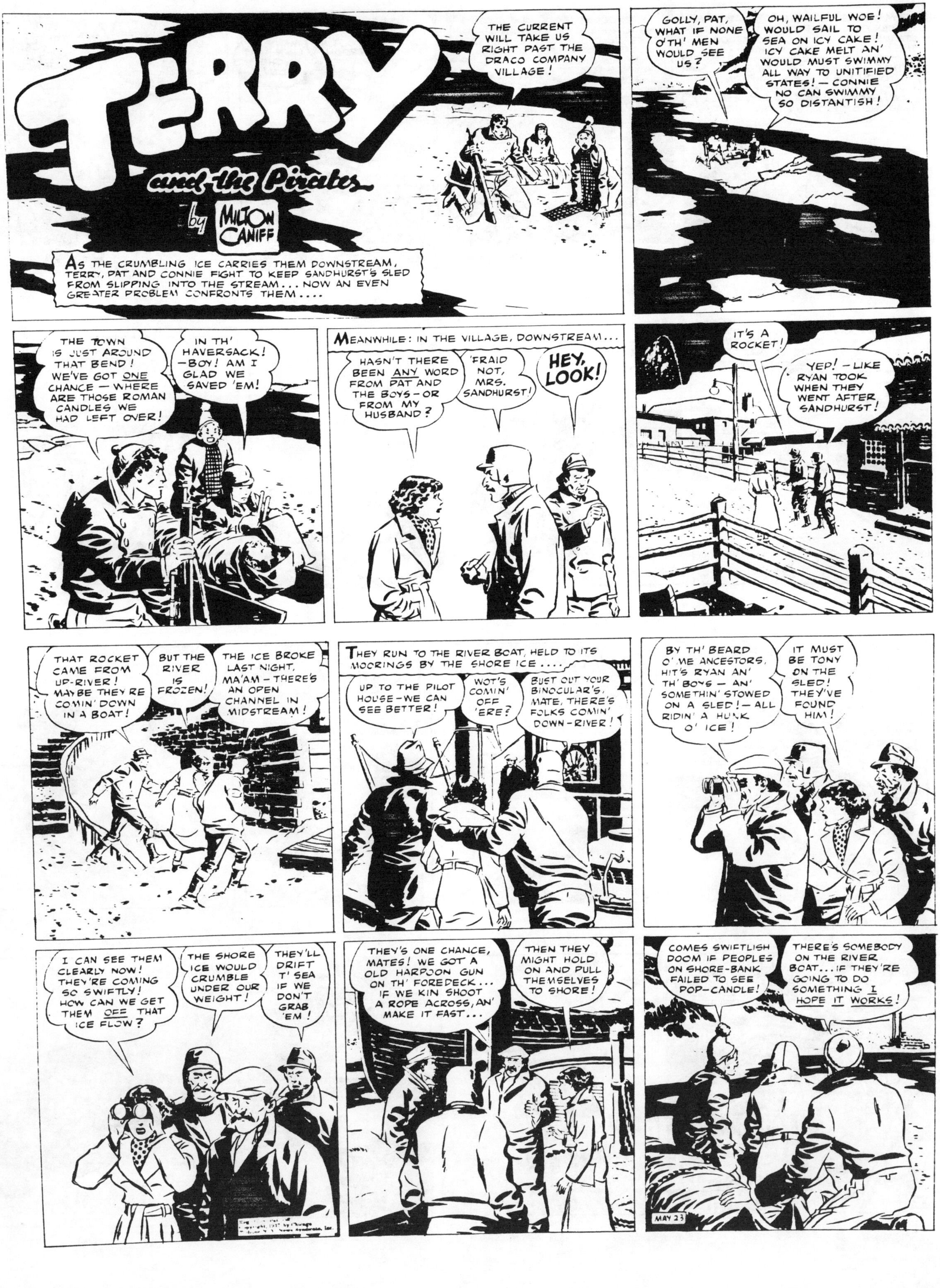
TERRY and the Pirates
by MILTON CANIFF
THE CURRENT WILL TAKE US RIGHT PAST THE DRACO COMPANY VILLAGE!
AS THE CRUMBLING ICE CARRIES THEM DOWNSTREAM, TERRY, PAT AND CONNIE FIGHT TO KEEP SANDHURST'S SLED FROM SLIPPING INTO THE STREAM... NOW AN EVEN GREATER PROBLEM CONFRONTS THEM....
GOLLY, PAT, WHAT IF NONE O'TH' MEN WOULD SEE US?
OH, WAILFUL WOE! WOULD SAIL TO SEA ON ICY CAKE! ICY CAKE MELT AN' WOULD MUST SWIMMY ALL WAY TO UNIFIED STATES! — CONNIE NO CAN SWIMMY SO DISTANTISH!
THE TOWN IS JUST AROUND THAT BEND! WE'VE GOT ONE CHANCE — WHERE ARE THOSE ROMAN CANDLES WE HAD LEFT OVER!
IN TH' HAVERSACK! — BOY! AM I GLAD WE SAVED 'EM!
MEANWHILE: IN THE VILLAGE, DOWNSTREAM...
HASN'T THERE BEEN ANY WORD FROM PAT AND THE BOYS — OR FROM MY HUSBAND?
'FRAID NOT, MRS. SANDHURST!
HEY, LOOK!
IT'S A ROCKET!
YEP! — LIKE RYAN TOOK WHEN THEY WENT AFTER SANDHURST!
THAT ROCKET CAME FROM UP-RIVER! MAYBE THEY'RE COMIN' DOWN IN A BOAT!
BUT THE RIVER IS FROZEN!
THE ICE BROKE LAST NIGHT, MA'AM — THERE'S AN OPEN CHANNEL IN MIDSTREAM!
THEY RUN TO THE RIVER BOAT, HELD TO ITS MOORINGS BY THE SHORE ICE....
UP TO THE PILOT HOUSE — WE CAN SEE BETTER!
WOT'S COMIN' OFF 'ERE?
BUST OUT YOUR BINOCULAR'S, MATE, THERE'S FOLKS COMIN' DOWN-RIVER!
BY TH' BEARD O' ME ANCESTORS, HIT'S RYAN AN' TH' BOYS — AN' SOMETHIN' STOWED ON A SLED! — ALL RIDIN' A HUNK O' ICE!
IT MUST BE TONY ON THE SLED! THEY'VE FOUND HIM!
I CAN SEE THEM CLEARLY NOW! THEY'RE COMING SO SWIFTLY! HOW CAN WE GET THEM OFF THAT ICE FLOW?
THE SHORE ICE WOULD CRUMBLE UNDER OUR WEIGHT!
THEY'LL DRIFT T' SEA IF WE DON'T GRAB 'EM!
THEY'S ONE CHANCE, MATES! WE GOT A OLD HARPOON GUN ON TH' FOREDECK... IF WE KIN SHOOT A ROPE ACROSS, AN' MAKE IT FAST...
THEN THEY MIGHT HOLD ON AND PULL THEMSELVES TO SHORE!
COMES SWIFTLISH DOOM IF PEOPLES ON SHORE-BANK FAILED TO SEE POP-CANDLE!
THERE'S SOMEBODY ON THE RIVER BOAT... IF THEY'RE GOING TO DO SOMETHING I HOPE IT WORKS!
MAY 23

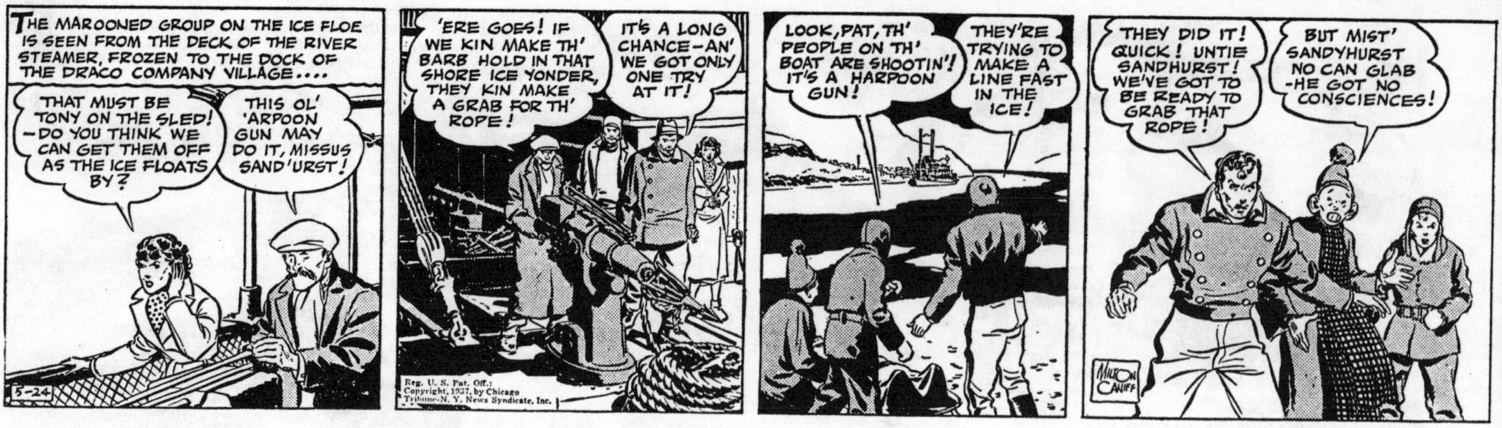
The marooned group on the ice floe is seen from the deck of the river steamer, frozen to the dock of the Draco Company village....
That must be Tony on the sled! -Do you think we can get them off as the ice floats by?
This ol' 'arpoon gun may do it, missus Sand'urst!
5-24
'Ere goes! If we kin make th' barb hold in that shore ice yonder, they kin make a grab for th' rope!
It's a long chance-an' we got only one try at it!
Reg. U. S. Pat. Off.: Copyright, 1937, by Chicago Tribune-N. Y. News Syndicate, Inc.
Look, Pat, th' people on th' boat are shootin'! It's a harpoon gun!
They're trying to make a line fast in the ice!
They did it! Quick! Untie Sandhurst! We've got to be ready to grab that rope!
But mist' Sandyhurst no can glab -he got no consciences!
Milton Caniff

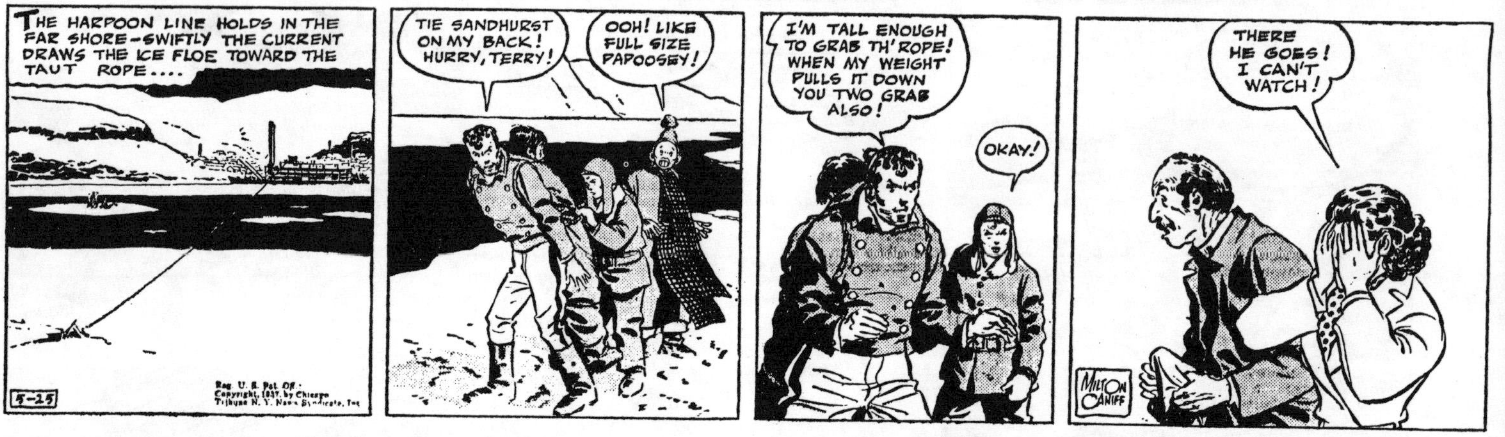
The harpoon line holds in the far shore-swiftly the current draws the ice floe toward the taut rope....
5-25
Reg. U. S. Pat. Off.: Copyright, 1937, by Chicago Tribune-N. Y. News Syndicate, Inc.
Tie Sandhurst on my back! Hurry, Terry!
Ooh! Like full size papoosey!
I'm tall enough to grab th' rope! When my weight pulls it down you two grab also!
Okay!
There he goes! I can't watch!
Milton Caniff

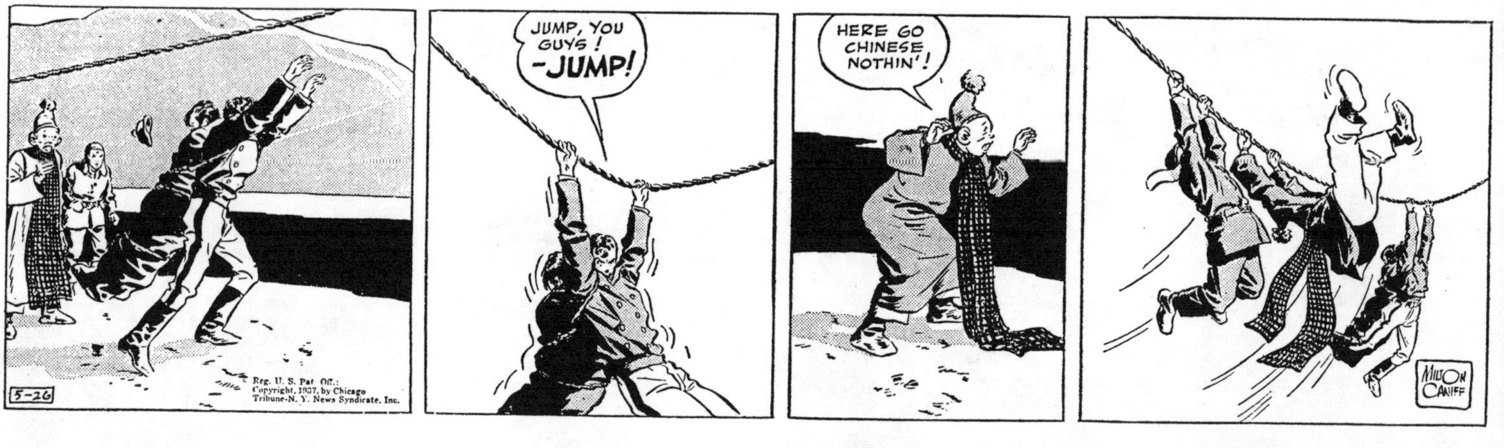
5-26
Reg. U. S. Pat. Off.: Copyright, 1937, by Chicago Tribune-N. Y. News Syndicate, Inc.
Jump, you guys! -Jump!
Here go Chinese nothin'!
Milton Caniff

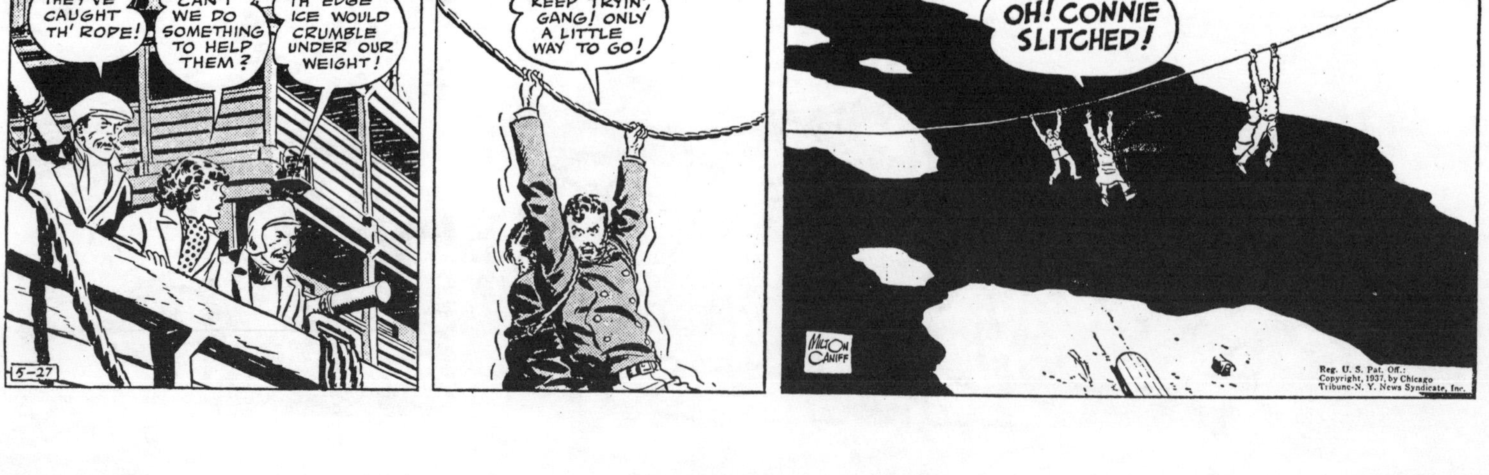
They've caught th' rope!
Can't we do something to help them?
Th' edge ice would crumble under our weight!
5-27
Keep tryin', gang! Only a little way to go!
Oh! Connie slitched!
Milton Caniff
Reg. U. S. Pat. Off.: Copyright, 1937, by Chicago Tribune-N. Y. News Syndicate, Inc.

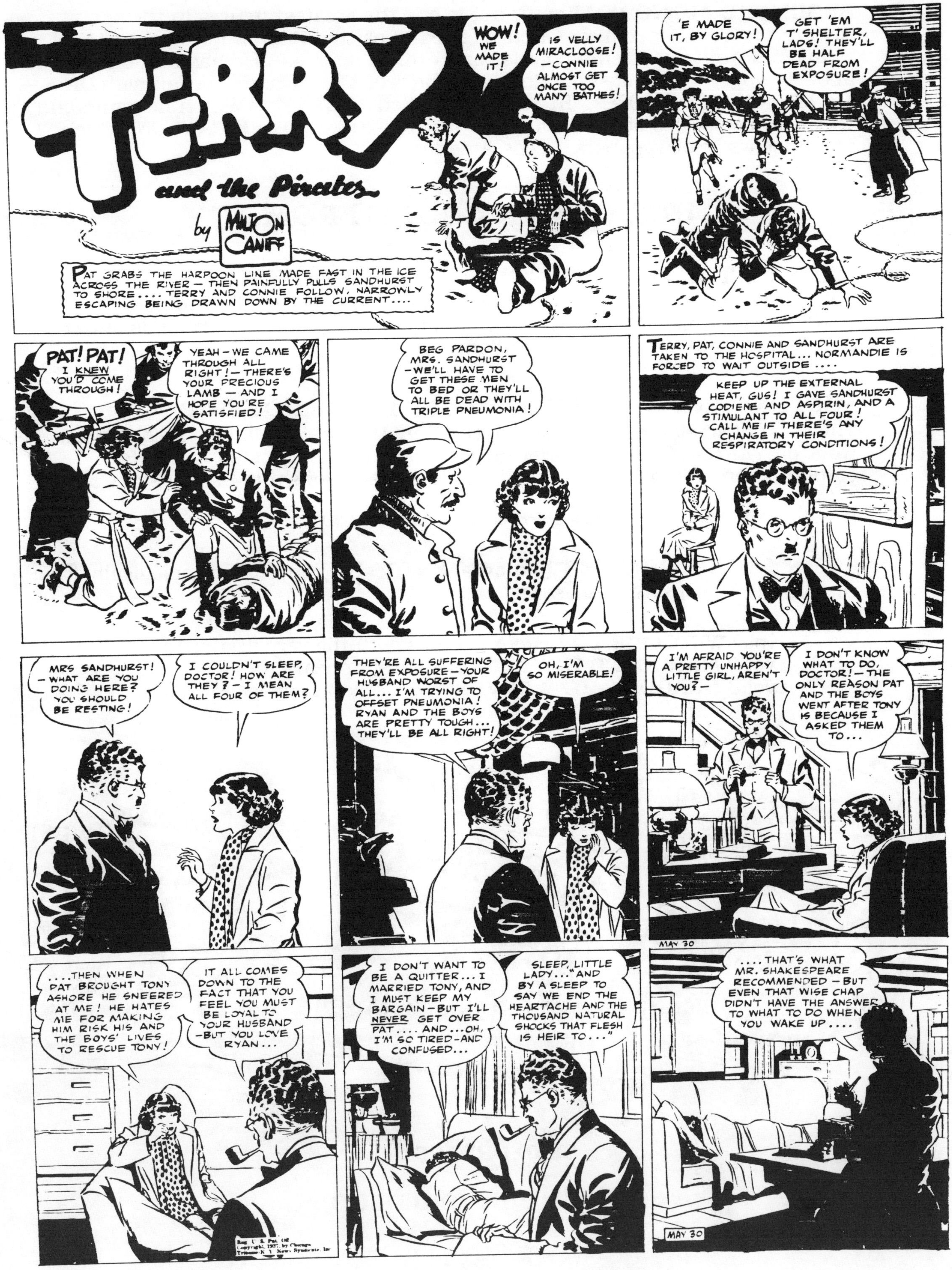
TERRY
and the Pirates
by MILTON CANIFF
WOW! WE MADE IT!
IS VELLY MIRACLOOSE! —CONNIE ALMOST GET ONCE TOO MANY BATHES!
PAT GRABS THE HARPOON LINE MADE FAST IN THE ICE ACROSS THE RIVER — THEN PAINFULLY PULLS SANDHURST TO SHORE.... TERRY AND CONNIE FOLLOW, NARROWLY ESCAPING BEING DRAWN DOWN BY THE CURRENT....
'E MADE IT, BY GLORY!
GET 'EM T' SHELTER, LADS! THEY'LL BE HALF DEAD FROM EXPOSURE!
PAT! PAT! I KNEW YOU'D COME THROUGH!
YEAH — WE CAME THROUGH ALL RIGHT! — THERE'S YOUR PRECIOUS LAMB — AND I HOPE YOU'RE SATISFIED!
BEG PARDON, MRS. SANDHURST — WE'LL HAVE TO GET THESE MEN TO BED OR THEY'LL ALL BE DEAD WITH TRIPLE PNEUMONIA!
TERRY, PAT, CONNIE AND SANDHURST ARE TAKEN TO THE HOSPITAL... NORMANDIE IS FORCED TO WAIT OUTSIDE....
KEEP UP THE EXTERNAL HEAT, GUS! I GAVE SANDHURST CODIENE AND ASPIRIN, AND A STIMULANT TO ALL FOUR! CALL ME IF THERE'S ANY CHANGE IN THEIR RESPIRATORY CONDITIONS!
MRS SANDHURST! — WHAT ARE YOU DOING HERE? YOU SHOULD BE RESTING!
I COULDN'T SLEEP, DOCTOR! HOW ARE THEY? — I MEAN ALL FOUR OF THEM?
THEY'RE ALL SUFFERING FROM EXPOSURE — YOUR HUSBAND WORST OF ALL... I'M TRYING TO OFFSET PNEUMONIA! RYAN AND THE BOYS ARE PRETTY TOUGH... THEY'LL BE ALL RIGHT!
OH, I'M SO MISERABLE!
I'M AFRAID YOU'RE A PRETTY UNHAPPY LITTLE GIRL, AREN'T YOU? —
I DON'T KNOW WHAT TO DO, DOCTOR! — THE ONLY REASON PAT AND THE BOYS WENT AFTER TONY IS BECAUSE I ASKED THEM TO...
MAY 30
....THEN WHEN PAT BROUGHT TONY ASHORE HE SNEERED AT ME! HE HATES ME FOR MAKING HIM RISK HIS AND THE BOYS' LIVES TO RESCUE TONY!
IT ALL COMES DOWN TO THE FACT THAT YOU FEEL YOU MUST BE LOYAL TO YOUR HUSBAND — BUT YOU LOVE RYAN...
I DON'T WANT TO BE A QUITTER... I MARRIED TONY, AND I MUST KEEP MY BARGAIN — BUT I'LL NEVER GET OVER PAT.... AND... OH, I'M SO TIRED — AND CONFUSED...
SLEEP, LITTLE LADY..." AND BY A SLEEP TO SAY WE END THE HEARTACHE AND THE THOUSAND NATURAL SHOCKS THAT FLESH IS HEIR TO..."
....THAT'S WHAT MR. SHAKESPEARE RECOMMENDED — BUT EVEN THAT WISE CHAP DIDN'T HAVE THE ANSWER TO WHAT TO DO WHEN YOU WAKE UP....
MAY 30

ABOUT THE AUTHOR: Milton Caniff is one the greatest figures in the history of American comics. Often referred to as the "Rembrandt of the Comics", Caniff has been a popular and critical success. He has had one strip or another appearing almost continuously for over 50 years. He began with ***DICKIE DARE*** in the early 1930s. In 1934 he created "***TERRY***" Which he wrote and drew until the close of 1946. In 1947 he introduced ***STEVE CANYON*** which still appears in newspapers across America.

OTHER CANIFF BOOKS FROM NBM

TERRY & THE PIRATES "COLLECTORS ' EDITION"

12 288-320 page, hardbound, gold stamped books reprint the complete *TERRY.* Every daily and Sunday strip, many never before reprinted, is shown in full size. Write for more information.

MILTON CANIFF - REMBRANDT OF THE COMIC STRIP

The original version of this book appeared in 1946 as Caniff was finishing his work on *TERRY.* Comic historian Rick Marschall has updated this 1980 edition. There are many rare and beautiful illustrations and blowups of Caniff art.

Paperback - $6.95, Collectors ed. (hardcover/dustjacket) $13.50

TERRY & THE PIRATES (paperback series) reprinting chronologically from the beginning. 64pp, color cover $5.95

vol.1 **WELCOME TO CHINA** - begins with the very first strip
vol.2 **MAROONED WITH BURMA** - first appearance of Burma
vol.3 **DRAGON LADY'S REVENGE** - Dragon Lady vs. Pat Ryan

TERRY
AND THE PIRATES
WELCOME TO CHINA!
SPEAK ENGLISH

MAROONED WITH BURMA
TERRY
AND THE PIRATES
No. 2
MILTON CANIFF
LET 'EM COME - IF IT'S JUDAS, OR THAT MATE, I'LL GET IN ONE GOOD SOCK BEFORE THEY MOW US DOWN!

DRAGON LADY'S REVENGE
TERRY
AND THE PIRATES
No.3
MILTON CANIFF

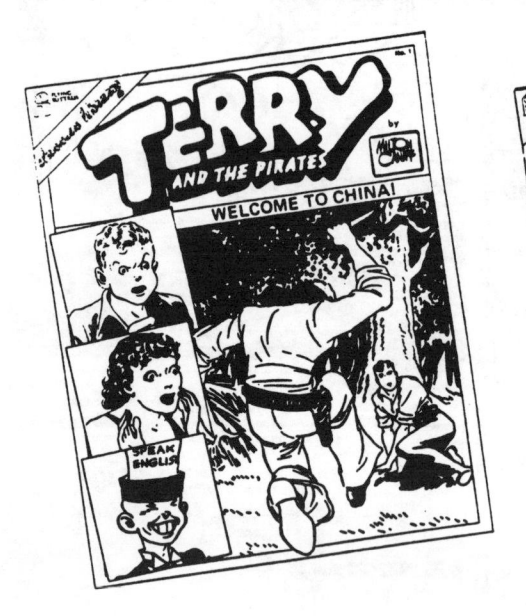

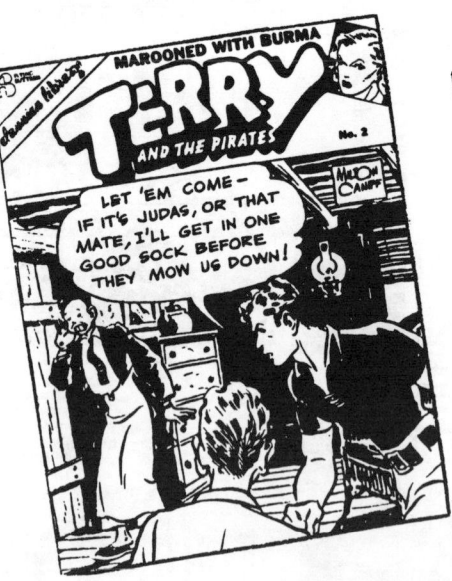

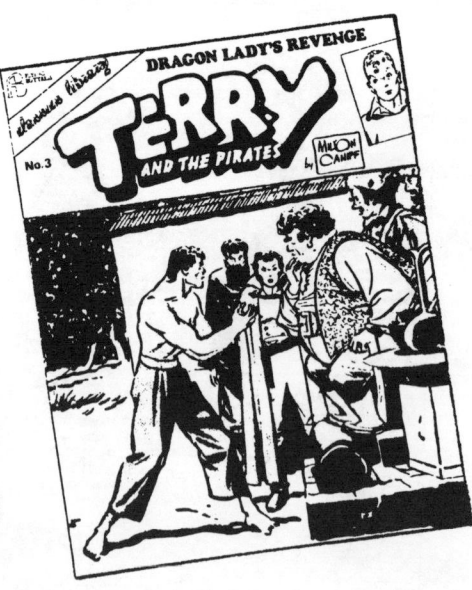

SEND ORDERS TO:

NBM PUBLISHING CO.

35-53 70Th St.
Jackson Heights, N.Y. 11372

add $2.00 P&H for first book, $1 for each additional.
Allow 6-8 weeks for delivery